THE LAST RIDE IN THE BUMBLE BEE JACKET

By Spencer Kope

NORTH WEST CORNER BOOKS

Kenmore, WA

A Northwest Corner Book published by Epicenter press

Epicenter Press
6524 NE 181st St. Suite 2
Kenmore, WA 98028.
www.Epicenterpress.com
www.Coffeetownpress.com
www.Camelpress.com

For more information go to www.epicenterpress.com

The Last Ride in the Bumblebee Jacket
Copyright © 2021 by Spencer Kope

ISBN: 9781945078149 (trade paper)
ISBN: 9781942078159 (ebook)

Printed in the United States of America

Dedication

For my brother, Alexander Ray Darius Kope. Air Force veteran, body man, sprint car racer, and all-around great guy. He died in 2001 racing in the Clay Cup Nationals.

Acknowledgments

To the great folks at Epicenter-Coffeetown-Camel Press, and to my tireless, always amazing agent, Kimberley Cameron. It takes more than a writer to bring a book to life. I'm just fortunate to have wonderful collaborators.

Chapter 1

Roads are a special kind of magic.

They are the arteries and veins that connect and nourish the body of civilization, causing towns and cities to spring up around them as they run here and there like great rivers and small streams, turning every driveway into a tributary, every parking lot into a basin. They lace the landscape in black asphalt and gray dusty gravel, allowing human energy and production to flow about the land, irrigating the world of man and bringing forth greatness from otherwise barren soil.

Roads are life.

Some can be pleasant to look upon, even beautiful, but most lack this quality. They tend toward the ugly and utilitarian, an eyesore of asphalt and stripes—a necessary evil.

Lives are a lot like roads, intersecting other lives, starting in one direction, and then turning off into a *completely* new direction—just like that. Along the way there are potholes to rattle you, reflectors to keep you safe, signs to guide you.

Like roads, all lives come to an end.

It's hard to imagine a world without roads. Certainly, most of the planet's seven billion people would starve without roads to move food and energy across great distances. Technology would grind to a halt without roads. Civilization as we know it would cease . . . without roads. More importantly, the all-American hot rod would have no home without roads.

And that would be a tragedy.

It's the quest for such a hot rod that brings Darius Alexander along an ugly road to the Columbia neighborhood of Bellingham, Washington on an early Wednesday evening in August. The pillared stone at the end of the driveway is etched deep in bold letters that read: *137 Eldridge Avenue.* The blue paint that once filled the etching is all but gone now, faded by wind and time, eaten away by neglect.

This is the agreed-upon time and place.

Darius stares at the house for a long moment before turning his silver Honda Civic onto the small tributary of brick, following the earthen red pavers to a place where they gather and pool in front of the open garage.

The home is an elegant white colonial with two Doric columns standing sentry at the three-panel front door. The columns create a magnificent portico with a half-circle covered balcony on the second floor. Three gabled dormers jut from the roof, and functional black wooden shutters adorn every window. Like bookends on opposite sides of the same shelf, two magnificent chimneys, one at the north end, the other at the south, seem to lock the home in place. To the left side of the house—beyond the chimney and looking so much like an afterthought—is a large, attached garage.

Though Darius can't yet see it, the home is perched on a cliff overlooking Bellingham Bay and enjoys sweeping views of the islands beyond, particularly Portage Island and its big brother, Lummi Island. Below, at the base of the cliff, are the railroad lines and the trains that move freight through town. Beyond the tracks lies the marina with its eclectic gathering of sailboats, pleasure craft, shrimp trawlers, and yachts.

The historic home, while impressive and splendid from the road, takes on a weathered, beaten look as Darius proceeds down the driveway. The white paint is thin—diminished, and the siding is distressed from too many years in the elements.

Easing the Honda to a stop, Darius holds his foot on the brake and casts his eyes toward the yawning mouth of the open garage. He can make out the faintest hint of faded yellow in its murky depths. It's the yellow of dried dandelions resting on a porch swing, or dusty lemons in a neglected fruit bowl. The Craigslist ad didn't give the car's color and was pretty sparse on other details. The key points were that it was a 1951 Plymouth convertible missing the motor and transmission and that it had been in the garage since 1993. Oh, and one final tidbit: the very odd and uniquely precise asking price of seven thousand six hundred and twenty-three dollars and forty-seven cents.

Yes, forty-seven cents.

Firm.

Though the garage is a little out of place juxtaposed with the house, Darius can see that it was built or rebuilt by someone who loved either cars or extra space. Its cluttered but ample interior is large enough for six parking spaces—three across and two deep. A respectable shop by any standard, though now it's filled with the discarded remnants of life. Most prominent is an old twelve-seat wooden table and its accompanying chairs, which are stacked on top, resting against the north wall. Under the table and gathered around it, like ducklings clinging to their mother, are dozens of closed and half-closed boxes of varying sizes.

That's just for starts.

There are at least seven bicycles, all of them are older models from the sixties and seventies, along with a cluster of old bicycle rims, seats, baskets, tire pumps, and related accouterments. Against the south wall are three full-size tool chests, no doubt full of tools, and next to them stands a dusty mid-40s Wurlitzer jukebox—one of the classic round tops with yellow and orange plastic light panels.

As impressive as the Wurlitzer is, Darius' eyes are elsewhere.

The intriguing splash of faded yellow in the right rear corner of the garage has captured his full attention—even though only patches of color escape the busy corner, a splash here, a square there, nothing larger than a yellow sheet of paper or a dandelion plate. The patches are pieces of the whole, and the whole is hidden behind more boxes, a mattress and box spring, and what appears to be the unwanted sum from a now-defunct junk shop.

Slipping the Honda into park and shutting down the engine, Darius steps from the vehicle and shields his eyes. The setting sun rests just above the garage roof, making it more difficult to see into the gloom, but Darius won't be detoured and steps closer for a better look.

He's so absorbed with the garage and the yellow mystery in the back corner that he doesn't see her come around the side of the house, pulling gardening gloves from her frail hands. She pauses and then comes on, watching him as he studies the garage against the glare of the declining day.

He doesn't see her.

He doesn't hear her.

"You the one that called about the car?"

The unexpected voice sends Darius's whole body into a lurching spasm of surprise, arms flailing about as if a swarm of angry bees just zeroed in on him. The shock is momentary; the embarrassment lasts considerably longer.

A smile crosses the old woman's face, but she quickly hides it, pushing it back behind the stoic mask she wears—the mask she's *learned* to wear. There's no emotion on her face when Darius turns to look at her. He grins, pats his chest over his heart, and says, "You scared me."

"I can see that" the woman replies. She's silent for several seconds, either because she's still waiting for an answer or she's letting him settle his nerves. Eventually, she nods. "Well, you're either a burglar here to take advantage of an old woman's garage, or you're here about the car. Since you don't look like a molester of innocent garages, I'm going to venture a guess and say you're here about the car."

"Yes, ma'am."

"Ma'am?" She studies Darius a moment—studies him with her hard, green eyes. "Well, I have to say that I don't hear *that* too often. That's the problem with the country these days; everyone's forgotten their manners." Stuffing the garden gloves into her back pocket, she extends a hand. "My name is Margaret Lipscomb; Maggie, to my friends."

The way she says it is ambiguous and Darius doesn't know if she means he can call her Maggie, or that *only* her friends can call her that, which he clearly isn't. He decides to keep it simple. "Darius Alexander," he says, taking the offered hand. "It's my pleasure."

She smiles, slipping the mask, but then quickly puts it back in place. "Well, Mr. Alexander, let's take a look at her, shall we?"

Leading the way into the garage, Mrs. Lipscomb walks to a door on the north wall that leads into the house and flips a light switch. The garage illuminates, though barely. The dim yellow glow of two incandescent bulbs, spaced fifteen feet apart in the ceiling, seems to struggle against the gloom, wrestlers pushing and pulling against one another, neither gaining advantage.

Darius notices that a dozen four-foot fluorescent light fixtures are spaced evenly across the ceiling, but not a single one holds a bulb, and it looks like they haven't worked in decades.

Blazing a trail through the clutter, Mrs. Lipscomb leads Darius around boxes and furniture and shelves of old books. She leads him deep into the northwest corner of the garage and doesn't stop until a sexy stretch of dusty yellow lays before them.

"This is my old girl," she says quietly. Darius misses the strain in her voice.

To say that he loves the car instantly would be to overestimate the length of an instant. His eyes devour the slow, fat curves, the extensive modifications, and the low-slung glory that only a mid-century lead sled can do right.

The convertible top is up and locked in place, keeping insects and debris from entering the car, but only partially. The white material is cracked and faded from neglect, looking as if one good sneeze would send it tumbling down in a million pieces.

The tires are flat, but the body itself is straight, and though the paint is faded from too many years, no dust has accumulated on the hood, trunk, and tops of the fenders—an impossibility unless someone dusted the old car down at regular intervals. Darius also notes that, despite the empire of boxes and clutter in the garage, not one item has been stacked on the car. Whether it was Margaret or a late husband, someone loved the yellow street rod. Someone looked after it the best they could.

As he walks slowly around the car, Darius can't stop smiling. *This is the one.* He knows it in his mind and his gut. The wait is over; the search complete.

Some dreams start as a small whisper in a quiet room. If the whisper persists it eventually goes to seed, and from one of these, planted and cared for, the dream grows and matures until it's ready to bear fruit. So, it was with Darius' dream. His whisper came during his freshman year of high school. While other kids dreamed of tuned Honda Preludes and Nissan 300Zs, he set his sights on an old-school street rod, the type that came through his uncle's body shop and graced the posters that hung on the office wall.

It was just a dream—a boy's dream.

But the boy turned into a man and, as he grew, so did the dream. Now, at the age of twenty-six, Darius James Alexander is ready to realize that dream.

"I'll take it," he blurts.

Now it's Margaret's turn to be startled. "You haven't even looked at it," she replies in a disapproving, *tsk tsk* tone.

"It's a 1951 Plymouth Cranbrook," Darius shoots back without missing a beat, "though with all the modifications, to simply call it a Cranbrook would be insulting. The trunk has been shorted—considerably. The body's been chopped, sectioned, channeled, and the door handles, and locks have been shaved; that's a nice touch," he adds, waving a finger at the spot where the door handles used to be. "The antenna, headlights, and taillights have been Frenched, and the front of the car has been completely reworked so that the fenders are no longer separate but merged into one piece with a custom grille. The hood doesn't even look like the original."

He bends down and examines the spot where the fender seam should have been. "This is top-notch. Whoever built this knew what they were doing."

"You know your cars, Mr. Alexander," Margaret says.

"I do," Darius replies with a grin. "I can have cash or a money order for you tomorrow."

"Yes, well . . . I'm afraid it's a little more complicated than that."

The grin disappears. "Complicated? How do you mean?"

Margaret clasps her hands together and studies him with kind but firm eyes. "Well, Mr. Alexander, I haven't decided to *sell* you the car yet, have I?"

Darius is confused. "But you listed it on Craigslist . . . for sale . . . and listed a price. Usually, people intend to sell when they—when they post an ad to sell," he finishes rapidly, a touch of irritation in his voice.

"I did and I do," Margaret replies. "I just haven't decided if I'm going to sell it to *you*." When Darius just stares at her—lost—Margaret sighs and forces a smile. "Would you like some tea, Mr. Alexander?"

Chapter 2

From the late 1800s through the early 1900s, Eldridge Avenue, which runs along a bluff overlooking Bellingham Bay, was the hub of economic and political power in Whatcom County. Many of the homes built during that industrious time still stand, monuments to the princes of timber, the lords of banking, the kings of coal, and the men of enterprise who carried Bellingham Bay forward from its founding as a sawmill site in 1853.

Bold beginnings by bold men.

Perhaps the most famous house on Eldridge Avenue is the George Bacon House at 2001 Eldridge, which was designed by George Bacon's cousin, the famous neo-classical architect Henry Bacon, who also designed the Lincoln Memorial. Local legend tells that Henry designed a second home further up the street, at 137 Eldridge Avenue, now the home of Margaret Lipscomb. No documentation exists to support this claim, just the oral history passed down through generations.

Darius follows Margaret across the white-columned portico and into the foyer of the elegant home. She deposits him in the family room and then disappears into the kitchen where a clatter ensues, accompanied by the soft humming of the old woman.

As Darius glances about at his surroundings, he notes with disappointment that the inside of the house is much like the outside: Elegant, but tired.

It's been said that dogs often look like their masters, a purely physical similarity. If this is true, then it must be equally said that homes take on the attributes of their owners. It's not a hard leap: people already refer to solid older homes as having "good bones," and applying fresh paint or trim is called a "makeover."

Ultimately a house is simply a structure, an empty canvas. It's the occupants who pour out their personality and paint the canvas into a home.

Margaret Lipscomb's home is such a place; some of it intentional, some not.

The house reminds Darius in every way of an old woman: the skin is wrinkled and thin, the hair has gone to gray, the jowls sag, the joints ache, and the eyes are tired. Only in this case, the thin and wrinkled skin is the paint and varnish of the old home; the gray hair is the patina that time has placed upon every surface; the aching joints are the rattling and squeaking hinges and doorknobs, which clatter like a bag of bones at every push or turn; the tired eyes are the drafty old windows with their cracked paint and single panes.

Time is a slow eater, it diminishes everyone and everything, yet beneath this slow fade there is eternal beauty: the young girl remains, the new home shines through.

The antique furnishings in the family room defy their surroundings; they are solid, spotless, and beautifully refinished—though not recently. They join an eclectic assortment of art and curios that accent every wall, shelf, and corner. Among this gathering are intricately crafted hand-blown glass bowls, platters, and sculptures. There are three African tribal masks and an accompanying spear, a glass display cabinet with seventeen Lladro figurines of various sizes, a framed map of Bellingham Bay and the surrounding area, circa 1866, a few original oil paintings, and several watercolor paintings, each prominently displayed.

Only one photograph is on display in the room.

It resides in a silver four-by-six frame on the coffee table. The face that stares out at Darius is that of a young Army officer in uniform. His expression is neither stern nor jovial, but rather a restrained combination of the two. Faded as the photo is, you can see the life in his eyes, the humor, the zest. The placement and sole existence of this image suggest the man was either a close family member or friend. Darius is tempted to pick up the frame, to study the image, but he refrains, clasping his hands together in his lap instead.

The clatter from the kitchen subsides and the old woman hurries into the family room carrying a serving tray laden with a fat glass pitcher of iced tea, and two tall glasses. There's also a small plate of sugar cookies.

"When I was younger, I was never much of a tea person," Margaret says, "but now I find myself drinking it all the time. Hot, iced, it doesn't matter." She sets the loaded tray in the center of the coffee table and pours out a tall glass of iced tea from the perspiring pitcher. Placing a coaster on the coffee table in front of Darius, she hands him the glass before pouring a second.

"What got you started?" Darius asks politely.

"Beryl Dawson," Margaret replies with a sad chuckle. "She joined my real estate firm . . . oh—it must be thirty years ago now. She was fresh off the boat, as they say; still had this god-awful British accent. From her first day at the office, Beryl wanted to be friends—I didn't. I *absolutely* didn't. Here was this large, loud Brit with a rasping cockney accent and a pair of overripe watermelons bursting from her blouse; there was *no way* it was going to work, absolutely no way." She sits in the chair opposite Darius and takes her glass of tea to hand. "So, of course, we became best friends — thick as thieves, you might say."

Darius smiles.

"Dear Beryl," Margaret continues with a shake of her head. "Every afternoon she'd heat some water, steep some tea leaves, and drink it with a touch of cream and sugar. She'd always offer up a cup, of course, and I always refused. That went on for a year. Finally, I relented, and we had afternoon tea together on the bench outside the office. That was my fatal error," she says with a wink. "What was *intended* as a one-off event to get her to leave me alone turned into a daily ritual."

Twirling the ice in her drink, Margaret watches it spin a moment and then sets the glass on a coaster. "I still have afternoon tea every day, even though Beryl's been gone seven years."

"I'm so sorry."

"Oh, she's not dead," Margaret quickly adds. "She moved to Florida. We still talk on the phone every Sunday afternoon at three." Her voice grows wistful and quiet. "I do miss her, though." Then, without warning, she slaps her leg with an open palm and says, "Enough of all that. Let's talk about this car and your plans for her." She crosses her arms and some of the friendliness seems to rush from the room. "What, exactly, are your plans?"

Darius swallows a hard mouthful of tea and sets his glass down. "My plan . . . is to restore her; make her right. I'm talking about a full frame-off restoration with everything reworked: new wiring, new suspension, upgraded brakes, any rust removed or repaired, new top, new interior, and new paint everywhere. She'll look like she used to, only better."

"And you have the experience to do this?"

"I do. My Uncle John owns Road Runner Restorations on Iowa Street. Maybe you've heard of it?" He pauses expectantly, and when she doesn't respond he continues undaunted. "I started there in high school and picked it up again after I got out of the Air Force."

"Interesting." The word falls from Margaret's lips with no bias. There's no hint of approval or scorn, though Darius notes that her arms loosen up and her hands fall into her lap, holding one another. "So, you're a veteran?"

"Yes, Ma'am.

She nods. "Did you get mixed up in any of that fighting in Iraq or Afghanistan?"

"What I did doesn't exactly count as fighting," Darius replies with a sheepish grin. "I was a loadmaster; the guy loading and unloading the planes bringing in equipment and supplies. I did one tour in Afghanistan—at Bagram Air Base, north of Kabul. There were a lot of patrols out of Bagram while I was there, and a lot of fighting, but the loadmasters never left the base. Aside from the frequent mortar attacks, what I saw of the war and Afghanistan was as a spectator over the wall and through the wire."

"Don't demean your service," Margaret says firmly. "Logistics is just as important in warfighting as troops on the ground or gunships in the air. Wars have been lost for want of supplies and equipment."

"Yes, Ma'am."

She picks up the plate, selects one of the smaller sugar cookies, and then offers the stacked assortment to Darius. He initially declines, but she insists, so he plucks a single cookie from the plate, and then—again at her urging—a second one.

"So, the work you do at your uncle's shop, do you plan on making a career of it?"

"Well . . . no."

"Why's that?"

Darius shrugs; now a bit uncomfortable with the questions. "I'm starting my fourth year at Western next month. By spring I'll have my bachelor's in computer science, and then it's off to Microsoft, or Google, or one of the other big guys. That's what I want; that's my passion."

Margaret nods. "To hear you speak a few minutes ago, I would have thought cars were your passion. There's no shame in it you know?"

"No shame in what?"

"Learning a trade—getting your hands dirty for a living. Everyone thinks they have to go off to college these days. Granted, it's a good path for some, but too many graduate with nothing to show for it but a mountain of student loan debt and a low-paying job making lattes." She's about to continue, but then a fit of coughing catches her and by the time it subsides she waves the thought away. "What do I know? I'm just a grumpy old woman."

As she finishes, Darius notices that she's slowly turning a simple gold wedding band on her ring finger. The subconscious action is well-practiced, the result of years, even decades of sad repetition. Behind that ring was a man. But where is he now? Why is she alone?

Margaret notices Darius's eyes on her hands and the ring-spinning stops. "One final question then," she says. "Why this car? What makes her so special?"

"Because she *is* special," Darius replies, his face brightening again. "She's everything I've been looking for and more. The chopping, the sectioning, the channeling—that was all stuff I thought I'd be doing from scratch. The amount of craftsmanship that's gone into her," he shakes his head, "well, it's amazing." He's suddenly adamant. "She deserves to be on the road, not stuck in some garage—no offense."

"None taken," Margaret replies. "I couldn't agree more." There's a quiet lull that she lets play out, slowly sipping from her glass as the young veteran and computer science major grows uncomfortable in his seat. "What about the color?" she asks at length. "Any thoughts in that regard?"

"I'd want to keep the same color," Darius replies immediately and unequivocally. "Somehow it seems, well, perfect; I can't imagine another color that would look better."

"Neither can I." Margaret smiles.

They sit quietly in the old family room as the failing day ushers in the shades of night. Sipping their tea, they make small talk about cars and college and times-gone-by. Words and thoughts lead them down familiar and unfamiliar paths and time ceases to have meaning. They soon find themselves talking like old friends, not strangers on opposite sides of the supply and demand equation.

Sadly, the old maxim is true: All good things must end, including conversations. When their meandering exchange is finally picked as clean as the empty plate of cookies sitting on the coffee table before them, Margaret leans forward in her seat, sets her drink down, and says, "Well, it's settled then."

She rises and walks over to a table against the wall and retrieves a manila folder. Turning, she faces Darius and scrutinizes him from top to bottom. "I like you, Mr. Alexander. You have an honest face, an honest disposition. You're intelligent, not afraid of work, and you love cars. That says a lot about a person in my estimation, and I've decided that I'm going to sell you the car."

Darius leaps to his feet and claps his hands together twice.

"The title is here," she adds, waving the manila folder, "and the keys and the paperwork are in a shoebox in my bedroom closet. I'll have it all ready when you come to pick her up."

Darius is grinning broadly. "You won't regret it—" he begins, but then Margaret cuts him off.

"I have two conditions," she insists. Darius instantly quiets and waits expectantly, anxiously. "First, there's a pristine patch of the car's original yellow paint in the trunk; I've cleaned it and waxed it at least once a year and it's been well protected from the elements. I'd like it preserved, even if you decide to change the color. You'll understand when you see it."

"Sure, I get it," Darius says. "It's part of the car's history."

"It is," Margaret replies without elaboration, and though Darius doesn't pick up on it, there's more to the simple two-word response than he can imagine. "My second condition is . . ." Margaret pauses for a long moment as if searching for the words or the emotion to continue, and then a soft smile slowly graces her lips, and her eyes shine with unspent tears. "I want a ride," she blurts, nearly laughing and crying at the same time. "One last ride when she's all put together."

Darius feels a sudden lump in his throat. "You'll have it," he says. "I promise."

Chapter 3

It's not much as far as tow trucks go, but the tan and brown 1983 Ford F350 had served Road Runner Restorations faithfully and with few complaints for the better part of three decades. Rust had long ago chewed small holes along the lower portions of the front fenders, doors, and rockers, and the brown and tan paint job is so faded that the two colors threatened to merge; it's hard to tell where one starts and the other ends.

Still, she runs—and well.

Yes, she coughed and sputtered when first waking, but once she caught her breath and warmed up, she had the grip of a python and the strength of a leviathan. Uncle John once said the old truck could pull the Titanic from her watery grave if the need ever arose.

Darius almost believed it.

Stopping on Eldridge Avenue just past Mrs. Lipscomb's mailbox, he slips the truck into reverse and backs slowly down the driveway. Stopping just short of the garage, he shakes the shifter into neutral and presses the emergency brake pedal to the floor.

A short screwdriver sticks from the steering column at a downward angle, serving as an impromptu key and giving the truck an air of illegitimacy—as if stolen—to anyone curious enough to give the rig a second glance. Twisting the screwdriver counterclockwise, Darius grimaces as the truck sputters, coughs, and goes suddenly quiet. Eldridge Avenue is an upscale neighborhood and the beat-up Ford with its duct-taped passenger window and innumerable flaws is a good twenty years from pretty and five miles out of place.

For a moment, the cab is utterly quiet, and then Darius Alexander turns to his passenger to finish a conversation interrupted. "I'm serious, Spider," he says sternly, "this lady is proper with a capital P. Just say 'Yes, ma'am' and 'No, ma'am' if she asks you anything. Keep it simple and be respectful. And don't use words that no one understands."

"Like what?"

Darius lifts his hands impatiently and begins reciting a list: "Waddup, church, dawg, derp, moss, chirp, styl—do I need to go on?"

"Everyone knows what church means, bro." Spider laughs.

"Not the way you use it . . . bro."

Spider shrugs submissively. "Okay, I got it; simple and respectful." He nods and puts on a big grin. "I can do this."

Darius isn't convinced. "Just pretend you're meeting with the president and act accordingly."

"Yup, yup, that's me, bro; respectful all the way."

"Spider—don't screw this up for me!"

"No, it's cool. I got this."

As fond as Darius is of his longtime friend, the admonition is necessary. Without it, Spider might very well greet Mrs. Lipscomb with a bear hug and a "Yo, my sista!" The irony is that under his slang-slinging exterior lurks a reluctant genius—a true genius, with an IQ exceeding 150.

With his messy red hair, a carefully cultivated nerdy-punk look, a pair of Coke-bottle glasses, fresh gauges stretching out his virgin earlobes, and a tendency to end sentences in odd places, Spider—whose real name is Steve Zalewski—neither looks like nor acts like a genius.

The fact remains.

He and Darius came up together. They met on the playground in kindergarten and by seventh grade it's fair to say that Spider spent more time and slept more nights at the Alexander residence than his own, making him and Darius more like brothers than best friends. And it was a good thing he spent so much time with Darius because his own home was a disaster: alcohol, drugs, domestic violence—all the wrong ingredients for raising a well-balanced kid.

As they step from the truck and bang the hollow doors closed behind them, Margaret Lipscomb exits the front door of the residence, pauses to check her watch, and then moves down the sidewalk to greet them, a glass of chilled iced tea in her hand. She's dressed in a pair of well-used jeans, a simple white t-shirt, and a pair of work gloves that have seen their share of soil and grime.

Darius smiles and waves at her as she approaches, breathing a little easier when she returns the smile. He'd been on edge since parting from her the previous evening, afraid she might change her mind about selling the car—or at least about selling it to him. The smile is reassuring because it's warm and kind.

"Mrs. Lipscomb, this is Spider," Darius says as she draws up in front of them like a queen inspecting a new member of her court. "He's going to be helping me with the restoration."

"I've always wanted to learn how to fix cars," Spider gushes before Darius finishes. He presses forward, extending a hand in greeting.

Margaret ignores the hand and fixes him in a penetrating stare. "Odd name: Spider. Is it your given name?"

"Nah, girl—uh, I mean . . . no . . . Ma'am." He swallows hard and tries to put on a smile. "My given name is Steve, Steve Zalewski. Spider's just a nickname."

"Interesting," Mrs. Lipscomb replies in a tone that suggests anything *but* interest. "And you like this arachnid reference, Stephen, this predatory insinuation?"

"I do . . . Ma'am. It kept me safe on the playground when I was a kid." He grins. "No one messes with a kid named Spider."

"I see," Margaret replies absently, but it's clear that she sees more than just his meaning because her eyes are suddenly transfixed by the jewelry inserted into his earlobes. "And what are those in your ears, Stephen?"

"Um . . . they're called gauges." She stares at him until he adds, "Ma'am."

Moving closer, she studies the metal ringlets a moment before stepping back and announcing, "They're earrings." Her eyes wait for confirmation—squinting tighter if that's possible.

"No, ma'am. Gauges are different from earrings. They're for stretching out your earlobes. I just had them put in," Spider explains, "so this is the smallest size, which means you can't see the stretched-out hole yet."

Darius is shaking his head in micro-movements at Margaret's side, desperately trying to get Spider's attention. It's no use; his friend is enamored with his new gauges and eager to share. "You gotta stretch the lobes slowly," he continues, "or you'll end up with a blowout or scar tissue. As I increase the size of the gauges, I'll eventually be able to stick my finger right through the center." He wiggles his index finger. "A year from now I should have holes an inch wide. Cool, huh?"

Mrs. Lipscomb is quiet for a moment, letting the silence drip slowly until Spider begins to fidget in his shoes and Darius is at risk of rubbing his knuckles raw.

"I was in Kenya in 1981," she eventually says with slow deliberation. "The Maasai people would do something similar, piercing their ears with a knife or even a strong thorn, and then plugging and expanding the hole with a piece of wood or bone or stone." She looks hard at Spider. "You don't look like the Maasai."

"It's the latest thing—" Spider blurts, but Margaret's not having any of it.

"What happens when you're my age and your earlobes are dragging on your shoulders?" She shivers at the thought. "And what do you think your career prospects are with *those* in your ears? Who's going to hire you—unless you're planning on renting yourself out like a plow ox?"

"I'm going into computer engineering," Spider replies in a mousy voice.

Margaret hesitates. "Oh." And just like that her demeanor changes and she forces a smile. "In that case," she says, her voice suddenly casual and airy, "you'll do just fine." She pauses to reflect a moment. "Computer folk are a bit odd . . . aren't they?" Without waiting for an answer, she whirls about and punches her access code into the keypad next to the garage door. The loud hum of an electric motor starts up on the other side. With a catch and a jerk, the garage door begins to slowly lift, as if it were the legendary den of thieves discovered by a poor woodcutter named Ali Baba.

Open Sesame, Darius thinks, smiling at the thought.

He already knows what treasure lies within, and as the opening widens, he spots his yellow jewel in the back-right corner, just where he last saw her. A moment later the motor stops, and the yawning mouth of the garage stands agape. They follow Mrs. Lipscomb into the dim interior.

Finding the light switch, she says, "I moved the boxes away and tried to clear a path, but I couldn't move some of the heavier pieces by myself." The unspoken message was: *You'll have to move the heavy pieces.*

"Whoa, mama!" Spider suddenly purrs, forgetting himself.

Darius shakes his head at the choice of words but forgives his eccentric friend. "I felt the same way when I first saw her," he says. But when he turns around, he sees that Spider isn't even looking at the yellow street rod. His eyes and hands are on the old Wurlitzer jukebox resting against the south wall of the garage. Spider blows dust from the glass face and then rubs his sleeve in a circular motion, quickly bringing the surface to a shine.

"Spider—the car's over here!"

"Yeah, I know, D, but check out the jukebox; it's totally postal."

A frown crosses Mrs. Lipscomb's face. "Postal?" she asks.

Darius sighs. "It means cool or awesome."

"Hmm," Margaret mutters. "It used to mean someone was on a rampage."

"I'm sure it still does, but"—and here he raises his voice and casts it in Spider's direction, "some people seem to find the words *cool* and *awesome* too mainstream and have to make up their own words as they go."

"And why *postal*?" Margaret asks with a smile.

"Well, people order so much stuff online, it seems there's always something cool being delivered, and every package is a little bit like Christmas."

Margaret nods her understanding. "Is this meaning in wide use or is it regional?"

"More like local," Darius replies. "There's only one idiot currently using it."

Margaret laughs and puts a hand to her heart. Her eyes glisten with humor and in a soft voice, so that Spider can't hear, she leans in and says, "I wouldn't judge Stephen too harshly; after all, even cool and awesome were once slang terms."

She straightens and continues in her normal voice. "In my day it was *groovy* and *far out*, and then the 80s gave us *gnarly* and *tubular*, among others. Every generation seems to develop their own vernacular, much of which sounds ridiculous just twenty years later." Her index finger rises into the air. "Dude!" she says with conviction. "Now there's a word that's stood the test of time. Do you know that it dates to the 1800s? The meaning has changed in small degrees, to be sure, but it always referred to a person, usually a man."

"I didn't know that," Darius replies.

Margaret shrugs. "Useless knowledge is my specialty."

It takes several minutes to pry Spider away from the Wurlitzer, and not before he has assurances from Mrs. Lipscomb that, no, the jukebox doesn't work, and yes, if it did work, she would certainly allow him to play one of the records. These assurances satisfy him to some degree, and Darius steers him over to the Plymouth and the still-considerable task of clearing a path to the open garage door.

Just as Mrs. Lipscomb had indicated, the boxes that previously surrounded the car are gone, exposing, and opening up the area around the convertible. Despite this well-begun excavation, there is still a wide swath of garage to clear if they're to have any chance at wrestling the car from its long resting place.

Without wasting time, Darius and Spider throw themselves into the mess, extracting two exercise bikes, two golf bags with clubs, and an electric golf cart they hadn't even seen because of the items stacked on and around it. There's an anvil, eight tires on rims, an antique couch covered over by a blanket, a box spring and mattress, and that's all in the first ten minutes.

They still had the twelve-seat dining room table to contend with.

It rests against the north wall and projects out into the room, as if a permanent part of the old garage. The first time they try moving it, Spider cries, "My arms, my arms, my arms!" and drops his end after shuffling barely three feet across the concrete floor. "I think I crushed a disc," he moans, reaching around and grasping his lower back. "Is there a bulge?" he asks, lifting his shirt and turning his back to Darius.

"No, you're good."

"You didn't even look."

"I looked—there's nothing."

"You're sure?"

"I'm sure."

"Run your finger along my spine; see if there's anything that doesn't feel right."

"I'm not running my finger down your spine."

"You want me to be an invalid?"

"Oh, Stephen, for Heaven's sake," Margaret says. She whips Spider's shirt out of the way and runs her finger along his boney spine.

"Cold, cold, cold!" Spider yammers as he flexes away from her.

"If you can move like that, you're just fine," Mrs. Lipscomb says reassuringly. She gives Darius a wink and holds up the glass of iced tea she used to chill her fingertip. Darius has to cover his mouth to stifle a laugh.

A half-hour later, the heavy hickory table is out of the way, along with the accompanying chairs and miscellaneous clutter that once occupied the northern end of the garage. A clear path now lies before the Plymouth, but still, the old girl isn't ready to move. With a portable tank of compressed air, Darius moves around the car, inflating flaccid tires, and checking for leaks using a spray bottle with soapy water. His biggest concern is that the aged rubber may not survive the several-mile trip to the shop. Despite this, he decides to risk it.

"What's the worst that could happen?" Spider says.

"Don't say that."

"What's the worst that could happen?" Spider repeats. "Seriously?"

"You're jinxing us," Darius replies, only half-kidding.

Hooking the tow truck winch to the front undercarriage, Spider steers as Darius slowly breaks the inertia of the car's long resting place. Foot by foot they draw her out of the garage until she rests in the ready light of a glorious August sun.

The car is magnificent.

Having shed the gloom of the garage, she now stands radiant, despite her faded paint and weathered exterior. Sweeping lines drag Darius's eyes along the length of the body, and for the first time, he realizes just how much work has gone into the car.

"Unbelievable," he mutters, almost unable to speak the word.

Doing a quick walk-around, his excitement grows until it's palpable and contagious. Whether Spider feels the same or is simply drawn in by Darius's reaction, it's hard to say, but Margaret smiles at them as they chatter away excitedly, and then chuckles to herself as Spider jumps up and down like a schoolboy.

It takes a couple of minutes to work out all the tow rigging, and then, with the press of a lever, the front of the old car rises into the air. A minute later it's secure for transport. Margaret, who had disappeared into the house, returns now with an old manila envelope and a set of old, tarnished keys. She digs the title from the envelope and signs it on the trunk as Darius counts out seven thousand six hundred and twenty-three dollars from an envelope in his wallet. He then digs into his front pocket for a quarter, two dimes, and two pennies: forty-seven cents.

Margaret wears a diminutive smile as he places the coins in her hand one by one. When he's done, he gently folds her fingers around them and, with all sincerity, says, "I'll take good care of her, Mrs. Lipscomb. Next time you see her she'll look sixty years younger."

"Can you bottle some of that for me?" Margaret says as she runs her hand gently across the top of the left front fender. Then, unexpectedly, she reaches out and embraces Darius, holding him for a moment and whispering, "Thank you," in his ear before giving one final squeeze and releasing.

Darius nods; he understands.

"What, no sugar for Spider?" Stephen Zalewski purrs, giving Mrs. Lipscomb a coy smile.

She laughs and waves him away—but hugs him still the same.

As they pull gently from the driveway and onto Eldridge Avenue, the inside of the cab is quiet, save for the rumble of the engine. Darius shifts the old truck into second, and then both he and Spider crane their heads around and watch the stoic woman with the ramrod backbone and the hazel eyes as she diminishes behind them.

A shadow of remorse—or perhaps guilt—washes over Darius.

He's too far away to see the single tear rolling down the side of Margaret's nose and onto her chin, and she's gone from their sight completely when her hand comes up to cover her mouth. A muted sob escapes her—and then the tears come in earnest.

Chapter 4

Thursday, August 11

Road Runner Restoration sits on a deep but narrow lot on Iowa Street, a section of town sometimes referred to as Auto Row because of the many auto dealerships cloistered along the road. Founded in 1987, the body shop is named for the metallic green 1970 Plymouth Road Runner that Uncle John Alexander owned in high school. He sold the street rod shortly after graduation, and almost immediately regretted it.

When he tracked down the new owner a month later in the hopes of buying it back, it was already too late: the car had been destroyed in a rollover accident a week after Uncle John sold it. It had proven to be too much car for the new owner, who had upgraded from a Ford Pinto. Fortunately, the only casualty in the mishap was Uncle John's beloved muscle car.

The Plymouth may be gone, but its spirit lives on in Road Runner Restoration.

Customers arriving at the six-thousand-square-foot body shop enter through a glass door at the front left corner of the building, next to a lit sign in the window reading, OPEN. Inside is a modest reception area: close-cropped carpet, a slightly aged counter, an old computer still running Windows XP, a cash drawer, several moderately comfortable and questionably clean chairs for customers, and a soda machine offering fifty-five-cent cans of Coke, Pepsi, Sprite, and a half dozen other beverages. (Though pushing the Coke button will occasionally give you a Pepsi, or the Sprite button might spit out a Mountain Dew.)

The room would be stale—boring—but for the large collection of prints, posters, license plates, hood ornaments, and vehicle badges that completely cover three of the four walls. One could spend hours admiring the collection if time were no concern.

The shop itself is set up to optimize space and workflow.

Vehicles enter and exit the work areas through one of three large roll-up doors along the right side of the building. The first two roll-ups access the large teardown and assembly area at the front of the building, while the third opens into the prep and paint area at the rear. There's also a roll-up door on the inside wall that separates these two main sections. At the back are two enclosed spaces: a fabrication shop in the right corner and a paint booth in the left.

More posters and automotive memorabilia—*automobilia*, as Uncle John calls it—is scattered in a seemingly random pattern on the upper portions of the walls inside the teardown and assembly area. The collection broods over the six men who are the heart of the shop, as if to ensure that each restoration is done correctly and stays true to the spirit of the individual car.

Aside from Uncle John, there's Dallas . . . who's from Portland. His parents wanted to move to Dallas but never got around to it, so naming their son after the city was the next best thing. With twenty-two years on the job, Dallas knows more about restoring cars than all the others combined—excluding Uncle John. He's also a genius with upholstery, particularly leather.

Skinny is next in line by seniority. He joined Road Runner Restoration fifteen years ago, fresh out of Bellingham Technical College. Straining the bathroom scale with his solid two-hundred-and-sixty-pound physique, his nickname seems ironic, like a giant named Tiny, or an obese woman called Peanut. Still, the name isn't meant to mock, and if any irony exists then Skinny is its architect.

In fairness, he had help.

It was about nine years ago when he met Ruby—that's when things started to change. A pleasantly Rubenesque woman with an easy smile and a robust laugh, Ruby's the type that brightens every room and lightens every mood . . . and was an instant hit with everyone at the shop. She also happens to be a masterful chef and a trained saucier. Within three years Skinny packed on a hundred pounds, and his lanky six-foot frame went from heroin-chic to substantial.

Just like that, his name transformed from clear and characteristic to contrary.

Despite the extra baggage, he still moves about like the old Skinny.

Plus, he's an ace mechanic and oversees all the engine, drivetrain, electrical, brake, steering, and suspension work done at the shop.

It's not a car until Skinny says it's a car.

Thirty-five-year-old Armando is the shop's ex-con. He came to Uncle John six years ago looking for a break and a chance to get his life back on course. He hasn't disappointed. Though an excellent body man, his real talent lies in painting. He's not just the paint-the-car-blue type of painter, but the type who wields an airbrush like it's a fine tip pen between his fingers. These days, Road Runner Restoration is known as much for its elaborate paint jobs and airbrushing as it is for its meticulous restorations. That's thanks to Armando.

The newbies at the shop are Jason and Eric.

Jason, the more responsible of the two, has been on the payroll for three years and was with another body shop for five years before that. He's versatile, quiet, and extremely hardworking, but not very outgoing. It's considered a gold-star accomplishment if you can manage to squeeze more than five words out of him at a time. Still, he's an expert body man and the only guy who knows how to use every single piece of equipment in the fabrication shop, no matter how obscure or rarely needed.

If you want conversation, it's best to go elsewhere, but if you need a new floor pan for a 1969 Barracuda, he's the guy who can build you one from scratch.

Finally, there's Eric.

The guys nicknamed him Pig Pen early on, but he didn't take kindly to it, so now it's just Eric. He's a straight-up body man, and though he has less than a year of real shop experience he's skilled when he buckles down and does the job.

If there's dirty work that needs to be done, such as a rusty frame in need of sandblasting, or bearings that need to be packed with grease, it falls to Eric—and his coveralls tell the story of every task he's tackled in the last week. He's been on thin ice with Uncle John lately, mostly because he's twenty-three but acts fifteen. He thinks that every night is a party night, and consistently drags into the shop fifteen or twenty minutes late looking like week-old poached eggs.

Eric is a problem in search of a climax.

If Road Runner Restoration has a 'happy spot' or a 'magic garden' it's not to be found in the teardown and assembly area nor in the paint booth, nor the fabrication shop. It's not even to be found in the colorful front office with its motorcade of automotive memorabilia puttering across the walls.

The magic spot—Darius's favorite spot—is behind the shop in a secretive place hemmed in by a tall chain-link fence with barbed wire strung along the top in three strands. Privacy slats cover the fence along its entire length, frustrating any prying eyes . . . and for good reason: the secure lot is home to a treasure trove of vintage vehicles.

Here you won't find pristine cars with fresh paint and glistening chrome. Instead, the parking lot is haunted by raw barn finds—faded derelicts pulled from a forty-year rest. Here are the field cars, the coupes, convertibles, and trucks that stopped running one day long ago and found themselves pushed into a parking spot behind the house or into a garage where they were simply forgotten. Vehicles that once held little value yet are now priceless with nostalgia.

The well-protected lot was dubbed the Steel Garden in the early years of the business, and for Darius, it was the birthplace of many youthful fantasies. Some of his earliest memories at the shop are of sitting in the old cars and yanking the steering wheel back and forth as he pretended to drive. He would spend hours imagining how *he* would build them, what color *he* would paint them, what the engine *he* built would sound like.

It was the best kind of magic.

Without exception, the Steel Garden contains only the finest classic American street rods and muscle cars. Their names are legend: Camaro, Corvette, Torino, Mustang, Impala, Firebird, Nova, Barracuda, Chevelle, Malibu, Bel Air, Thunderbird, GTO, and, of course, Road Runner.

Uncle John has always been partial to vehicles from the sixties and seventies. They remind him of the cars that filled the parking lot at his high school those many years ago, the cars that performed so well during the annual senior burnout, much to the chagrin of the principal and school administrators.

Darius has heard all the stories.

August heat begins to bear down as Darius turns into the parking lot of Road Runner Restoration. All three roll-up doors along the side of the building stand open and several industrial fans hum loudly as they cycle air through the shop. Easing the tow truck to a stop just past the second roll-up door, Darius kills the engine with a rattle of the screwdriver and then pours from the hot cab in one fluid motion.

He walks briskly down one side of the '51 Plymouth, pauses at the rear, and then walks up the other side, double-checking everything—the tires, the trim, the mirrors, the lights, and the collection of parts stacked on the floor in the back seat. Spider swore up and down that he saw something catapult through the air as they turned off Eldridge Avenue onto Broadway.

Despite his insistence, everything seems to be in one piece, or at least in one place, so Darius manipulates the levers on the hoist and lowers the front of the lead sled to the ground. He quickly unencumbers the vehicle from the cradle straps and tow hitch.

"So that's it, huh?" a voice calls from the open roll-up door behind them.

A man in his early- to mid-fifties is wiping his hands on a rag as his eyes slowly walk over the Plymouth, taking in every detail. His coveralls are dirty with dust and rust and grease, but despite the smudge on his right cheek and another across his forehead, his full head of salt-and-pepper hair is perfectly in place, seemingly unscathed by the rigorous demands of the body shop.

Darius smiles at the deep, growly voice and the simple words. Without turning, he asks, "What do you think?"

Uncle John leaves the shade of the shop and walks over, peering into the convertible. His eyes dissect the interior in an instant, and then he moves along the side, taking in every detail, poking at the rocker panel with the toe of his left shoe in search of areas weakened by rust, and then continues around the back, up the other side, and finally to the front, where he pauses and gives a low whistle.

"Someone sure did a lot of work," he says, admiring the customized grill, hood, and fenders. He suddenly leans in close and picks at some loose paint. Peeling a small piece free, he says, "Hmm," and leans in still closer. "Looks like all the original lead work is still in place." He shakes his head. "I bet this car hasn't been touched in over fifty years, not even a fresh coat of paint."

"That's good, though—right?"

Spider watches them from the rear of the tow truck, his glasses pulled halfway down his nose and his head motionless as his eyes dart back and forth between the two.

Uncle John doesn't exactly nod a yes, nor does he shake a no. Instead, his head sways to the left and then to the right in perfect time, like his neck is mounted to a metronome. Darius waits for some words of wisdom to go along with the motion, and then realizes that the head bobble is the extent of Uncle John's acumen for the day.

"What's that supposed to mean?" he says with a laugh, wobbling his head back and forth in exaggerated imitation.

Uncle John laughs at Darius's impression. Stuffing the rag into his back pocket, he turns and strolls toward the shop. "Guess we'll see soon enough," he says before disappearing inside.

Darius looks at Spider and shakes his head. "There's no getting a straight answer out of him. I swear it's like he has some kind of genetic mutation that prevents his mouth from forming the words yes and no."

Spider chuckles. "He was diggin' the car, though."

"Yeah, he was."

After adding more air to one of the tires, they recruit Dallas and Skinny to help push the heavy Plymouth into the shop and over to its new home in the rear corner of the teardown and assembly area. To be more precise, Dallas, Skinny, and Darius push, Spider steers. It's not even the type of steering you do as you run alongside the car *pretending* to push. No. Spider plants himself in the driver's seat and then makes honking noises as they push him through the shop.

Dallas and Skinny think it's funny.

Darius—well, not so much.

With the car safely parked, and with chocks placed on both sides of the right rear wheel to keep it from rolling—on account of the complete lack of brakes—Spider rubs his hands together and then throws an arm across Darius's shoulders, saying, "What's first, boss?"

If Darius hears the words, they're lost on him, his mind is that absorbed by the car and the daunting task in front of him. He stands silently, appraising the vehicle, disassembling it piece by piece in his mind, admiring it. His eyes—his very pores—consume the car by inches, as if it were a radiant burst of sunlight after a blustery winter night.

Spider's question remains unanswered, but he smiles. The look on Darius's face tells him everything he needs to know, so he sets the question aside and lets it simmer, choosing instead to make a quiet memory with this, his best friend and brother.

Time stops.

For a moment—for millennia—the universe condenses in a way that few have the privilege of experiencing or understanding. Time and space pull together and combine until all light, all existence, and all knowledge is embodied in the silhouette of two men standing before a pleasant patch of yellow. There is nothing else—nothing so important, nothing so eternal.

As quickly as the moment comes it passes.

Time never tarries for long.

An air ratchet barks to life on the other side of the teardown and assembly area, jerking Darius and Spider back to the present, back to the monumental task before them.

"Let's clear all this stuff out," Darius says, stepping forward and leaning into the car. "Then we can start removing seats, door panels, carpet—all of it."

It takes three hours to gut the interior of the car.

The heavily rusted bolts that hold the seats down create a considerable amount of grief and burn up precious time, but they make up for it on the door panels, which come off with ease, even considering the problems inherent in removing old window cranks and latch handles. In the glove box, they find a vintage tube of red lipstick that still seems viable. (Spider tries a dab on his upper lip before quickly wiping it off.) There's also some faded paperwork dating back to the car's original purchase, and some receipts for parts, such as spark plugs and oil filters.

Removing the convertible top proves a nightmare.

The unwieldy mass of crumbling, cracking, dry-rotted canvas presents a puzzle: how to remove it from the metal framework without destroying either it or the framework in the process. Just trying to figure out how to detach the fabric from the header bow, the part that latches down to the windshield and secures the top in the closed position, is an enigma beyond comprehension. Then there's the back bow, the middle bows, the various side rails, and a whole host of fasteners, glues, and attachments to overcome.

Darius is tempted to just cut the top off—it's garbage anyway. But Uncle John warned him that they might not be able to buy a replacement. If you're restoring a vintage Mustang, Camaro, Thunderbird, or even a Corvair, there are plenty of aftermarket parts readily available. But this is a 1951 Plymouth Cranbrook convertible; even the least ambitious list of collectible cars will likely overlook it.

As tattered and torn as the old convertible top is, it may still be the only template they have to craft a replacement from scratch . . . and the more intact it is when they hand it over to Dallas, the less grumpy he'll be.

It takes the better part of two hours, but they finally lay the deboned convertible top out on the concrete floor and fold it into a two-foot by two-foot square. The rest of the interior is easy by comparison.

"What's next?" Spider soon asks, staring at the collection of seats, door panels, carpet fragments, and trim pieces stacked on the floor beside them.

"Time for the exterior," Darius replies. "Let's start with the badges, hood ornament, lights, and such, and then we'll move on to the doors, the hood, and the trunk lid. There may be more clutter in the trunk. Why don't you check it out while I pop the hood and take a look at the engine compartment?"

"You got it, boss."

Walking to the rear of the car, Spider finds a hole in the trunk lid where the handle used to be. "Yo, D! There's no . . . you know . . . handle thingy." Right as he's finishing, a high-pitched metallic groan rakes through the shop, emanating from the front of the car as Darius lifts the hood against the shrill protests of the stiff hinges.

Looking around the side of the car, Darius says, "What?"

"The thingy." Spider makes a twisting motion with his hand. "It's not here. How do I get the trunk open?"

"The thingy? You mean the handle thingy?"

"Yeah."

"Use a flathead screwdriver."

"What, and pry the lid open with it? Wouldn't a crowbar be better?"

"I'm going to pretend you were joking," Darius says flatly. "Stick the end of the screwdriver into the hole where the handle used to be and move it around a little until you find where the end slips into the latch mechanism. Then just turn—probably counterclockwise. The trunk should pop open."

Darius next has to explain what a flathead screwdriver is and where to find one. Spider mutters, "*Regular* screwdriver. All you had to say was *regular* screwdriver," as he wanders over to Darius's toolbox and starts pulling out one drawer after another, not noticing that the third drawer down is marked SCREWDRIVERS.

In the meantime, Darius starts photographing the engine compartment, paying particular attention to what's missing—which is most everything. He takes pictures of the remaining wiring, the steering assembly, the brake fluid reservoir, the suspension, and what remains of the throttle assembly.

A harsh grating sound tells Darius that his aspiring apprentice has finally figured out how to get the trunk open. Then Spider calls out again.

"Um . . . Darius?"

"Hmm."

"Uh . . . have you *looked* in the trunk?"

"You know I haven't."

"Yeah, well I think maybe you should."

It's not so much the words he says, but the way Spider says them that gives Darius pause. He looks up from the engine compartment, then sets the camera down and walks to the rear of the Plymouth. Stepping in front of the open trunk, his head suddenly shakes—as if from a chill—and he stands motionless, just staring. For a moment he's speechless—stunned to silence.

"What does it mean?" Spider asks.

Darius shakes his head. "Mrs. Lipscomb said something about a patch of yellow," he mutters. "She didn't say anything about . . . this."

Chapter 5

Over three decades, a lot of cars have passed through Road Runner Restoration. Some came in as stripped-down hulks barely worth rebuilding; others were intact but diminished from too many years sitting in a field, a barn, or a storage locker. Some—though few—were daily drivers in need of nothing more complicated than cosmetic work, a valve job, or a tune-up.

All of them had a story.

Some had secrets.

Many trunks had been opened in the shop's history, revealing a long list of interesting finds. There was the collection of three hundred and forty-seven early sixties science fiction paperback books, which would have been worth a tidy sum if the mice, bugs, mildew, and dampness hadn't gotten to them. There was also the nearly intact skeleton of a dog and a wood and leather prosthetic right leg with JOE C. carved into the side.

Most mysterious was the rusty sawed-off double-barrel shotgun stuck down in the gap behind the left wheel well of a 1966 Mustang; everyone in the shop was convinced it was used in some heinous crime. When they tracked down the original owner of the car and asked him about the derelict double-barrel, he just laughed and said, "So, that's where it went."

Of all the unusual finds, perhaps most interesting were the twelve intact bottles of bootleg whiskey packed in straw inside one of several hidden compartments they discovered in a 1931 Ford coupe. The bottles hadn't seen daylight since sometime before prohibition ended in 1933. Uncle John kept one of the bottles and added it to his collection in the front office, where it sits on a high shelf, well out of reach. The other eleven vintage whiskey bottles were kept with the Ford when it went to auction, no doubt adding to the bid price of the now-storied coupe.

They'd seen collectible books, guns, whiskey, and more . . . but nothing like this.

"The Bumblebee Jacket," Uncle John says, screwing his mouth up. "Must be the name of the car, though most of the time I'd expect to find it painted on a fender, or a hood, or even on the *outside* of the trunk. Don't recall ever seeing a car name painted on the *inside* of a trunk."

"And the E.E. Atwood part," Spider says; "what's that supposed to mean?"

"Well, obviously it's the name of the builder."

"Obviously," Spider says with a shrug of his shoulders.

Darius is taken by the beauty of the inscription, with its flowing letters spelling out THE BUMBLEBEE JACKET. The characters are essentially black, but with varying shades making up the intricate workings and bevels of the individual letters so that each is a work of art unto itself. Interspersed throughout are dollops of yellows, matching the brilliant yellow canvas that the letters are painted upon—in this case, an inner fender wall.

The depiction has been well tended and waxed with regularity so that this small one foot by two-foot section of the car looks as it did the day it was finished. Here, also, Darius and Spider see the true nature of the yellow paint that once graced the car, before oxidation, rain, time, sun, and dust wore away its deep glow.

"That's a pretty piece of yellow," Darius says at length.

"Yeah," Uncle John replies, "best see if you can protect it during the rebuild. That's a piece of history right there. You don't want to lose that." He reaches in and rubs a clean finger along the edge of the section. "When it's time to spray the trunk, we might be able to feather the paint and blend it into the original yellow."

"You think that'll work?"

Uncle John shrugs. "Either it'll work or . . . it won't." He gives Darius a wink, and then turns and starts back toward the front office.

"Really?" Darius calls after him. They hear Uncle John chuckle, but he doesn't look back.

Spider chuckles along with Uncle John, but it's a lackluster laugh and he seems distracted. His right elbow is planted like a flag in his cupped left hand, and his chin rests in his right palm as he stares at the collection of letters making up "the trunk words," as he dubbed them shortly after discovery.

"So, who's E. E. Atwood?" he says after a moment, dropping his arm. Darius shrugs, which Spider immediately copies.

"Aren't you curious? If it was *my* car, I'd be curious—just saying."

"Just saying," Darius apes.

"Serious, D! This Atwood dude built your car—all that chopping and channeling stuff you were so excited about. He could live right down the street from here and you don't even know it."

"Right now, I'm more curious about what I'm going to find on the undercarriage when I get her up in the air. Knowing who built her isn't going to help with the restoration."

"You're killing me."

"If it troubles you so much," Darius says, showing some exasperation, "you know where the computer is."

"You don't mind?" Spider presses. "You don't need me here?"

"I'll scrape by."

The front office is deserted when Spider plants himself behind the counter and launches the web browser. He starts by running a Google search for Bumblebee Jacket, thinking the name unusual enough that if the old Plymouth was ever featured in a hot rod magazine or referenced at a car show it would immediately jump out. What he gets is 416,000 unrelated search results, mostly of children's bumblebee-themed clothing.

Next, he types in 'E.E. Atwood' and 'car.' The first link that pops up leads to an oil painting of a hundred-year-old car parked under a spectacular oak tree in the full of autumn. Spider thinks it's a Model A or a Model T but doesn't know the difference. The convertible top is down and a picnic for two is laid out on the ground next to the car. In the distance, a young couple can be seen running hand in hand toward a small lake. Whether they mean to dive in fully clothed or just stop at the lake's edge and admire the view is unclear.

It doesn't matter.

A cursory glance tells Spider that all the search results link to various paintings and images; granted, all of them feature old cars of one sort or another, but if he wanted to buy a 1974 poster of an even older painting, he would have started his search on eBay. Frustrated, but not to be outfoxed by a search engine, he crafts a Boolean search using the phrase 'E.E.

Atwood' and the words 'Bellingham' and 'bumblebee." He also adds a NOT operator to exclude the terms 'children' and 'clothes.'

Again, the search spits out more images of old cars.

Spider's just about to delete the search and start from scratch when the title to one of the links catches his eye: THE LEGACY OF EVAN ELMORE ATWOOD.

"Evan Elmore," he mutters to himself. "E.E. Atwood?" He clicks on the link.

More paintings of old cars.

"What is it with all the old—" his words fall away as the obvious truth settles upon him. "Crap!" he exclaims. "Didn't see that coming." Then he begins to read.

Links lead to more links and he devours every word, resisting the urge to run into the shop yelling at the top of his lungs. He wants to know *everything* before telling Darius—or at least as much of everything as there is to know. Most of what he reads is lacking detail: the Wikipedia article is barely five paragraphs long and essentially restates the information from *The Legacy of Evan Elmore Atwood*. Spider suspects that it was submitted by the same author.

The next forty-five minutes flit by and Spider finds it increasingly difficult to contain himself. The emotions coursing through him unfold like layers of an onion: joy, fear, amazement, bewilderment, trepidation, and absolute exhilaration. Clicking back to the original article, he pushes away from the computer with such sudden force that he nearly topples over in the office chair. Collecting himself, he walks briskly into the shop.

"Darius," Spider calls out when he finds the '51 Plymouth unattended with its doors stripped off and its ragged guts—that's to say, its interior— still spilled out on the concrete floor.

"I'm here," a voice calls out from somewhere underneath the car.

It's only then that Spider notices the passenger side of the car is slightly higher than the driver's side. Crouching, he looks under the low-slung carriage and spots Darius on the other side. A pair of jack stands and one of the shop's five-ton floor jacks hold the car in the air just enough for someone to slide under the car on a creeper—which is essentially a flat piece of wood with a head cushion and six wheels that allows you to roll around on your back without dragging yourself across the filthy floor.

"What are you doing?"

"Unbolting the body from the frame."

"Why?"

"So, we can lift the body off."

"You can do that?"

"Of course, Spider. Cars don't just pop out of some giant mold at the factory ready for an engine." With his wrench, he taps a crusty-looking square-tube steel rail next to his head. "This is one of the frame rails. There's another on your side," he points with the wrench, "and they run from the front of the car to the rear," again, pointing, "with cross supports along the way. The frame holds the car body, but it also supports the engine, the transmission, the axles, suspension, even the bumpers. It's like the skeletal system of the car—or at least the spine."

"Cool—oh, D!" he suddenly blurts. "You gotta come out from under there. I've got something I need to show you. This is gonna trip your head right off your shoulders."

"I'm kind of in the middle of something. Can it wait?"

"No, D! This is big, like Jumbo-the-elephant big. I think it's something really good, but I'm afraid it could turn out to be something bad at the same time, at least for you. It's just . . . well, I've got to show you, otherwise, you won't understand."

Darius sighs, clearly not buying into Spider's sense of urgency—and he has reason to be skeptical. Among Spider's numerous eccentricities is a penchant for making unscalable mountains out of diminutive molehills.

When they were twelve, he was convinced that the oddly triangular stone in the backfield at Darius's house was the tip of an ancient Atlantean temple. He even named it the Temple of Xena after the heroine of *Xena: Warrior Princess*, forgetting, perhaps, that Xena was an Amazon warrior princess, and had nothing to do with Atlantis. After convincing Darius to help him uncover the supposed lost temple, mostly with promises of untold wealth buried within, they spent the next week digging and digging, only to create a muddy mess and, ultimately, discover that the large stone was just that: a large stone.

Spider is often the victim of his overly active imagination.

Sliding out from under the car, Darius stands and wipes his hands off on a clean rag from his back pocket, looking for a moment like his uncle. "All right, show me," he says, and then follows Spider into the front office.

Standing next to the computer, he reads the headline and first few paragraphs of *The Legacy of Evan Elmore Atwood* before Spider grows impatient and starts clicking through to other web pages. "Whoa, whoa," Darius says. "Go back; I wasn't finished."

"There's more, though," Spider insists. "You need to see this."

"How about you let me understand what I'm looking at first," Darius says, a bit irritated. "It's obvious you think this Evan Elmore Atwood is our E.E. Atwood—I get that. So, either explain why or let me finish reading."

"Well, first, he was from Bellingham—"

"That doesn't mean anything. The car could have been built in California or Florida for all we know."

"Yeah, but he worked at a body shop here in Bellingham starting in the late forties and on through the fifties and sixties." When Darius doesn't stop him, Spider plunges on. "And more than that, the dude painted cars."

"That kind of goes with the whole body man thing," Darius says, still unconvinced. "First you fix the car, then you paint it."

"No, I mean he *painted* cars."

"Spider, you're giving me a headache."

"On canvas, D!—you know, with a brush, and maybe one of those funny French hats on your head."

Finally understanding, Darius leans into the computer and peruses some of the images as Spider scrolls down. He soon commandeers the mouse and begins clicking on the pictures, enlarging, and examining the paintings one by one. "These are good," he says after a few moments. "Kind of reminds me of Norman Rockwell, but with cars."

"Yeah, his Wikipedia page says that every painting he ever did was focused on cars in one way or another, and not just any car, but American cars, going right back to Henry Ford's Model T, and some Duryea car built in Massachusetts in 1893. There are pictures of some totally tight cars I've never seen before."

"Geez, look at this '57 Studebaker Golden Hawk," Darius says, as if oblivious to Spider. "That's gorgeous—almost looks like a photograph rather than a painting." He shakes his head, both in admiration of the art and in skepticism of Spider's conclusions. "How do we know if this Evan Elmore Atwood is the same E. E. Atwood who built the Plymouth?" he says. "Granted, it looks encouraging, but just having some initials match up isn't enough to prove anything."

Spider doesn't answer. Instead, he takes the mouse back from Darius, scrolls to the top of the page, and clicks on a small image to the right. Instantly, a large signature pops up."

"E.E. Atwood," Darius reads.

"It's nearly identical to the signature in the trunk," Spider says, pointing out the concave back of each capital E, the dangling second leg on the A in Atwood, and the way the crossbar in the A extends out to cross the T. It's all there.

Darius is silent, taking it in, looking for flaws in the logic but finding none. "Wow," he says at length, followed by a resigned, "Huh," and a shake of his head.

"Wow, yeah!" Spider says excitedly. "Try wow rare! There are only eighty-seven Atwood paintings that have ever been documented, and of those, only fifty-three are known to still exist." Thumbing toward the shop, he adds, "Fifty-four if you count the Plymouth. This Dr. J. Morgan seems to be the expert on Atwood," he continues, tapping the byline at the top of the article.

"Seattle Art Museum," Darius says, reading the tag behind the byline. "Maybe we should give him a call. He's gotta know if Atwood ever built any street rods, right? I mean, he's the expert."

"He knows," Spider says assuredly, rubbing his hands together gleefully. Then, abruptly, he slaps both of his cheeks simultaneously and holds his face. "I bet he tells you this car is worth like a hundred grand."

"Even if that's true, it's not for sale," Darius replies.

"Yeah, of course," Spider says, waving the thought away.

A quick query brings up the number for the Seattle Art Museum and Darius punches it into the shop's landline. Pushing back from the computer he takes a deep breath. "How in the world do I start *this* conversation?" he mutters to the wall.

The phone begins to ring.

Chapter 6

Thursday, August 11

Stu Yates pauses just outside the office.

The sign on the door reads, DR. MORGAN, ASSISTANT COLLECTIONS COORDINATOR, and the figure at the desk looks the part, all hunched over, eyes intent on a draft document, a pen in hand ready to strike out any offending or ambiguous words.

Stu does a quick check of his clothes: He brushes a small bit of dandruff from his right shoulder, tucks his tailored shirt in so that it's perfectly placed front and rear, and then checks his hair in the faint reflection of the office window. Satisfied, even pleased at his appearance, he casts himself dramatically in the doorway of Dr. Morgan's office, leaning against the metal frame like an action hero on a Hollywood set. Any nervousness or trepidation he might feel is quickly quashed by his overwhelming sense of majesty.

Everyone loves Stu—just ask him.

When seconds pass and no adoration or even acknowledgment issues from the room, he shifts on his leaning post and clears his throat. "Soooo, *Dr. Morgan*," he says with a satisfied grin, "any big plans for the weekend?"

"Research," the figure at the desk replies.

Stu nods knowingly. "Still working on that book of yours, I suppose. What was it called again, *Legacy of Steel*, or something like that?"

"*Steel on Canvas: The Legacy of Evan Elmore Atwood*," Dr. Morgan replies.

"Kind of a spin-off on that article you wrote last year, right?"

"Was there something you wanted, Stu?"

He smiles broadly, misinterpreting the cues. "Some of us are thinking of catching a movie tonight. I thought it might do you some good to relax;

you know, socialize with friends, that sort of thing." He shifts position against the frame and sticks his left hand halfway into his pants pocket, striking a James Dean pose. "If you'd like, I could pick you up at six and we could grab something to eat before the show. I know this Thai place near the Needle with pineapple chicken that'll curl your toes."

Dr. Jenny Morgan sets her pen down. The movement is slow, but with such purpose and weight in its significance that you can almost hear the thud. Despite the obviousness of the act, Stu remains oblivious, grinning at her from the doorway as she looks up and makes eye contact.

He's not an unhandsome man; in fact, most women would consider him quite fetching. Any physical appeal, however, is washed away by his arrogance and the long list of single-minded conquests he'd accumulated over his three-year tenure at the museum. Impressionable interns and starry-eyed volunteers are his specialties.

In Jenny Morgan's vernacular, he's a low-quality abstract.

Several responses pop into her head immediately as she stares at him, but she dismisses them just as quickly. She's been around this racetrack one too many times with Stu; it's time to put an end to his pursuit once and for all.

"The smooth pickup lines didn't work when I was an intern, Stu," she begins, "what makes you think they're going to work now?" The sentiment is delivered with her usual good temper and sweetness, and she intends to leave it at that and let Stu slink off to harass someone else. As the last word falls from her lips, something else pushes forward, something unsummoned but wickedly welcome.

"You run around this place, Stu, like some kind of inbred Neanderthal." Her voice is calm and measured, but a hint of venom laces her words. "You chase anything that'll give you a second look, like some thirteen-year-old boy incapable of controlling his impulses. Why on earth would I waste—"

She stops abruptly, not because she's having second thoughts about her diatribe, but because her assistant, Chelsea, appears behind Stu and waves a hand in the air to get her attention.

"Yes, Chelsea, what is it?"

"There's a guy on the phone I think you need to talk to. He says he found Atwood's signature in the trunk of some old car."

"His signature?"

"That's what he said."

"On a painting, a piece of paper, what?"

Chelsea blushes. "I didn't ask."

Seeing the color in her cheeks, Jenny waves the concern away. "I guess we'll find out in a minute, won't we?"

"I *did* ask how he knew it was Atwood's signature," Chelsea offers up. "He said he Googled it and found your article. I was going to transfer the call to your phone, but I figured it was too important and I didn't want to lose it."

Jenny smiles at her assistant. Though a brilliant art historian and an amazing researcher, Chelsea is lousy when it comes to technology. Her primary nemesis seems to be the museum's interconnected phone system. She has the bad habit of pushing the wrong button during a call transfer and either disconnecting the call altogether or sending it to some unknown region in the outer ether.

"It's holding at my desk," Chelsea says sheepishly.

Jenny rises quickly—eagerly— from her desk and is halfway across the room when she remembers Stu, who's blocking the door looking a bit shell shocked. When he doesn't move out of the way, she shuffles past him, intentionally brushing up against him as if to say, this is what you'll never have.

She's almost through the door and into the hall when she pauses and places her left hand gently on his chest; it lingers there a moment. "Give it up, Stu," she says sweetly, "I'm gay." And then, before he can respond, she's gone, making her way down the hall.

Chelsea races to catch up, hissing, "Since when are you gay?"

"I'm not."

"Well, he's certainly going to *tell* everyone you are."

"Won't *he* look stupid?"

The conversation lasts less than five minutes, but you'd think it was an hour by the pained expression on Spider's face. Hearing just half the conversation proves too much for him and he keeps pressing his head up to Darius's ear. Each time he pushes close, Darius shoves a forearm into his chest until he backs off: push, shove, repeat.

It's like a herky-jerky dance-off without prizes.

When Darius finally disconnects the call, Spider is absolutely beside himself. Sucking in every ounce of air in the room, he says, "Wellll?" in one long exasperated push.

Darius is unfazed. "She's coming up after work tomorrow to take a look."

"She?"

"Yes, Spider, *she*."

Spider bulks at the tone. "I just thought that Dr. Morgan was a dude."

"Why?"

"Well, because he's totally into cars—like he's obsessed with them."

"She."

"Huh?"

"You said *he* twice."

"I did?" Spider's shoulders slump. "Sorry, man. I got this image of a dude in my head. If she shows up looking all androgynous, I'm going to have problems. What's her name?"

"Jenny."

Spider sighs and gives a big grin. "Thank god."

"Why?" Darius says with a chuckle.

"I was afraid it was going to be Pat, or Kris, or something like that. I can work with Jenny; can't be too many dudes named Jenny, right?"

"I don't know," Darius replies. "You ever hear that song about a boy named Sue?" He pauses a moment, enjoying the look of bewilderment on Spider's face, and then, without another word, he turns and makes his way into the shop.

The door is still swinging closed when Spider yells after him. "You know that's the same crap your uncle pulls? D? You know that, right?"

There's no response.

Chapter 7

At 5:47 p.m. on Friday, a deep rumble pulls Darius and Spider out from under the '51 Plymouth and over to the open roll-up doors. Though the shop closed at five, the large doors into the teardown room remain open out of necessity, providing some much-needed ventilation in the otherwise stuffy interior. It's August in Bellingham, which pretty much guarantees blistering heat and little-to-no rain.

The rumble is not unique.

Indeed, it's a fairly regular occurrence at a body shop that specializes in restoring sixties- and seventies-era muscle cars. So, it's mostly curiosity that draws Darius and Spider from their work; that, and the fact that the shop has been closed to the public for the better part of an hour. The only person they're expecting has a Ph.D. in art history—not exactly the hot rod type.

As the source of the low rumble creeps into view, Spider lets out a whistle and says, "That is one nice ride." Looking over at Darius, he quickly adds, "Not vintage, but still nice."

The late-model charcoal gray Camaro does a slow roll until it's parallel to them and then comes to a stop. Every bit of it shines, the glass, the paint, the chrome, even the beefy black tires. A moment later the driver kills the engine and a wall of quiet rushes over them. Behind the heavily tinted windows, nothing is visible, not even the silhouette of the sole occupant.

Still expecting a customer, Darius wipes his hands clean with the rag in his back pocket and steps forward to break the bad news that the shop's closed and won't open again until Monday morning.

He's almost to the car when the door opens and a pair of long legs steps out, followed by a stunning blonde in a charcoal pantsuit that perfectly matches the shade of paint on the Camaro. It's either an uncanny coincidence or this is a woman who's passionate about her car.

It's instantly seductive.

Her blouse is royal blue, and she wears a necklace and earrings to match. There's little makeup on her face because none is necessary, and the simplicity of the look adds to her striking allure.

"Is one of you Darius Alexander?" she asks, tipping her sunglasses up onto her head to reveal a pair of piercing blue eyes—a blue that's almost unnatural in its intensity and depth.

"Darius Alexander . . . I am," Darius blathers, sounding a bit like Yoda. He quickly corrects himself. "*I'm* Darius."

"Jenny Morgan. Seattle Art Museum," she says pleasantly, extending a hand. "We talked on the phone yesterday?"

"Of course," Darius replies. He extends a hand in return but then jerks it back quickly when he sees how filthy it is—despite his earlier efforts with the rag. Holding both hands up for inspection, he says, "Sorry, we're in the middle of a teardown. It gets pretty messy."

"I'm not allergic to grime," she replies with a smile.

"Okay," Darius says reluctantly and takes her hand.

"Nice shop you have here," Jenny says, glancing around.

"Yeah, it's my uncle's. Feels like a second home, though. I was playing in cars around here as far back as I can remember, long before I was old enough to work on them. I guess it's in the blood. What about you?" He nods toward the Camaro. "That's a pretty nice ride for an art geek—no offense."

"None taken," Jenny says with a grin. "I guess you could say it's a graduation present. I promised myself I'd buy my dream car when I finished my doctorate. As it turns out, I couldn't afford my dream car, so this was my second choice."

"Not a bad second choice. What year is it?"

"It's a 2012 ZL1," she replies in a matter-of-fact tone, glancing back at the gray beauty. "Just the most powerful production Camaro ever built. It's got a supercharged 6.2-liter engine cranking out five hundred and eighty horses, and more than five hundred pounds of torque." She shrugs. "It'll curb stomp just about anything on the road."

Darius stares at her mesmerized, a look of delight on his face.

"You go, girl!" Spider blurts enthusiastically, his eyes appreciating every inch of the car. The outburst breaks Darius's trance.

"Dr. Morgan—" he begins.

"Jenny. Please. I'm not stuck on titles."

"Jenny . . . this is Spider." He steps aside so they can do a proper handshake, but as Spider glides forward it's clear he has other intentions. Before Darius can stop him, he takes Jenny's delicate hand, turns it clockwise a quarter turn, bows ever so slightly, and kisses her on the knuckles.

"Enchanté," he says.

"Delighted to meet you," Jenny replies with a smile, unfazed by the gesture.

"Sorry," Darius mutters, shaking his head. "He was born that way."

Jenny laughs. "No, it's very sweet."

Spider smiles and tips his head in acknowledgment. He's about to add to his introduction when Jenny suddenly holds a finger up, saying, "Almost forgot," and turns back to the gray Camaro. Opening the door and leaning in, she fumbles about for a moment and then emerges with a large black folder in her hand. She doesn't offer an explanation, just tucks it under her arm, closes the door, and says, "So, this signature you found . . . ?

"Right," Darius replies. "Follow me."

He leads Jenny through the open overhead door and across the large shop floor as Spider trails behind. The Plymouth still rests on its frame in the corner, but it's been stripped down to a shell—even the windshield is gone. Likewise, the front fenders, hood, bumper, and grille have been removed, leaving nothing forward of the cowl but the frame where the engine would have sat, and the front axle.

Weaving their way through a parade of automotive debris, Darius, Jenny, and Spider stop at the rear of the convertible. The trunk lid has already been removed and the opening offers an unobstructed view of the lettering and signature within. As Jenny's eyes sweep across the preserved piece of yellow, she utters an involuntary gasp, and her hand covers her mouth.

Shaking her head, she points. "That . . ." she begins, but she can't seem to finish the thought, letting the solitary word fall discarded on the shop floor. Moving closer, and then still closer, she practically crawls into the trunk to get a better look at the collection of letters and the fine brushstrokes that made them. She's silent for a full three minutes, and when she finally extricates herself from the trunk, her first words sound a bit . . . odd.

"We need to find the lion," she blurts.

Darius and Spider exchange a puzzled look.

"We need to find . . . the lion?" Spider repeats flatly—but then, a moment later, his face suddenly brightens. "You can be the tinman," he says, turning to Darius, "I'll be the scarecrow, and Dorothy is obviously"— his words are cut off as Darius puts a hand over his mouth.

Jenny laughs, regaining some of her composure. "What makes you think I'm not the wicked witch?" she says with an evil grin.

"Oh, I've known some witches," Spider says, fighting out from behind Darius's hand. "If you're a witch, I'm a flying monkey."

"Well, maybe not *flying*. . . ." Darius mutters, releasing his friend.

Jenny laughs again, which only encourages Spider to do a monkey dance around the car parts scattered on the floor. When he finally settles down, she explains her odd lion comment. "A lot of artists have recurring images or themes within their work," she says. "Salvador Dali, for example, included ants, snails, elephants, bread, and many other images in his paintings. With Atwood, it was a lion's head—a golden lion's head— and it makes an appearance in every one of his paintings, or at least in those we know about."

Jenny sets her notebook on the rear quarter panel and flips the cover open. Thumbing past the first three pages, she says, "Here," and steps to the side, holding the notebook in place so they can move closer and have a look. There are seven images on the page, each of a golden lion with a mane of large curls that comes to some semblance of a point at the bottom, much like a goatee.

"These are close-ups I took, each from a different painting." She draws her finger across the vertical lines that partially obscure the face of the lion in the upper right-hand corner. "He hides them well, but not so well that you can't find them quickly enough. This one," she starts flipping through the book, "is right"—more flipping—"here."

The painting she presents is that of an early production car, back when they were still referred to as horseless carriages because that's exactly what they were. In this case, it's a 1901 Winton motor carriage, which has suffered a small mishap and is lodged nose-first over a two-foot embankment with its front end resting in a shallow pond. The driver, obviously pitched from the vehicle, sits in the water four feet away staring back at the empty driver's seat in bewilderment.

"It's called *Unhorsed*," Jenny adds.

The painting is ripe with irony and humor: two Holstein cows stand at the water's edge with bits of grass hanging from their mouths as they look on casually, unperturbed. On the other side of the pond is an amused horse that looks as if it could break into laughter at any moment. A mother duck and five ducklings paddle by the driver as if he were nothing more than a waterlogged stump.

"Do you see it?"

Darius is so taken by the image that he's already forgotten about the lion. Scanning the image for a full minute he finally gives up. In fairness, the eight-by-ten print in Jenny's notebook is minuscule compared to the original, so it's not surprising he misses it.

"Right . . . here," Jenny says, circling a spot along the overgrown embankment near the road. Sure enough, hidden among the reeds and cattails, and peeking out from behind their stalks, Darius spies a hint of gold that is the lion's head.

"It's easier to find on the original," Jenny says consolingly, "though, even there it's not much bigger in diameter than a pencil eraser." She starts turning the notebook pages slowly, one Atwood painting after another, each as striking as the one before. "It's like that with all of them; always small, always hidden."

"Whoa!" Darius suddenly cries. "Go back."

Jenny flips back one page as both Darius and Spider lean in for a better look—Darius because he saw something, Spider because he can't help himself.

"That's—" Spider begins.

"Yep," Darius replies.

Stepping away from the car, he motions for Jenny to follow, leading her across the shop floor and through the door into the front office. His finger finds the light switch and he bathes the room in a fluorescent glow as he steps out from behind the counter. His eyes quickly scan the wall, and he points to an aged poster in a cheap Plexiglas frame that hangs near the ceiling and is almost lost in the clutter of the wall.

Jenny gasps.

The poster, printed in 1972, shows three field hands gathered around the banged-up and dusty front end of an olive green 1937 Ford pickup. Their half-eaten lunches are scattered across the hood and along the passenger fender, forgotten for the moment as they study the playing cards before them.

One of the workers is at the front of the truck facing away at an angle, a cowboy boot resting on the bumper. The five cards in his hands show a full house: three nines and two jacks. The other two players have already revealed their cards and wait eagerly to see who takes the pot. Off to the side, the remains of the deck sit patiently, waiting for the next deal. Printed dead center on the back of each card is a barely discernable golden lion.

"That's one of the McNaughton posters," Jenny says.

Spider gives her a look. "I thought it was an Atwood?"

"No—I mean, yes. McNaughton was a publishing company in the sixties and seventies that specialized in posters. They went out of business in 1979, but not before printing millions of posters." She tilts her head to the poorly framed print. "This one is called *Full House*. It's one of three Atwoods that McNaughton printed. From what I've been able to learn, they only printed a thousand of each, and though that seems like a small print run, it was the biggest break in Atwood's career . . . at least his artistic career. The posters sold out quickly and it was very promising, but for some reason, the company never printed more."

"And no one knows why?" Darius asks.

"There's speculation. Even in the early '70s, the company was on shaky financial ground. Half the posters they printed never paid off."

"Velvet Elvis," Spider says with a knowing nod.

Jenny smiles at him, still not sure what to make of him. "In the end," she continues, "Atwood's big break turned into nothing. He died a year later."

"So, this is one of a thousand," Darius says, gesturing toward the print.

"And one of about thirty that are known to still exist."

"So, it's rare?"

Jenny nods. "The last one sold at auction for thirty-five hundred dollars."

Spider lets loose a low whistle. "Dude, you should tell your uncle to lock that up someplace."

Darius stares up at the poster for a long moment. "No," he finally says in a low voice. "I like it right where it is." He looks at Jenny. "What good is it if no one can see it?"

She smiles and the room grows warm.

After some additional discussion about Atwood, his paintings, and his life, they return to the disassembled 1951 Plymouth inside the shop. Somehow, it looks different to Darius. It was already a special car—the car he'd been searching for, the one that fit all his requirements and desires. Now it seems almost . . . hallowed.

Jenny glances over the scattered pieces of the car, her eyes bouncing from the tainted seats to the awkward front end to the crumpled mass of material that was once the convertible top, and finally to the disembodied hood, trunk, and doors. "It has to be here," she says firmly. Opening her notebook back to the page with the images of the various lion heads, she places it open on the hood of the 1965 Chevelle SS coupe occupying the space next to the now-disheveled Plymouth.

Looking at Darius, then at Spider, her hands rise and rest on her hips. "This may not be his usual canvas," she explains, "but he did sign it—just like he would one of his paintings. That means the lion's head has to be somewhere on the car."

"I've been all over this car," Darius replies patiently. "Something like that would have stood out." He shakes his head. "I'm telling you, it's not here."

"Wh-what would that mean?" Spider asks. "You know . . . if it's not here?"

"It's the proof we need," Jenny says unequivocally. "It's everything."

"I don't get that." His words are frustrated. "What about the signature?"

"The signature means little without the lion's head."

"But it's *his* signature."

Jenny sighs and walks over to look Spider square in the eye as Darius looks on. "Any automotive or art enthusiast could have forged Atwood's signature in that trunk," she says matter-of-factly. "It's not hard to do and his signature is easy to find online. The recurring presence of the lion's head, however, was only recently discovered—a discovery that's still a bit of a secret, even in the art world."

"So . . . how do you know about it, then?" Darius asks.

"She's the expert," Spider chimes in.

"I discovered it." Jenny retorts, holding Spider's gaze for a moment before turning away. Absently, as if suddenly lost in some mental exercise, she muses, "It *has* to be here . . . probably someplace that's not overly obvious, someplace hidden."

Spider watches her, a curious expression on his face. "What's it mean, then?" he finally asks. "Can you tell us that?"

"Hmm?"

"The lion's head," Spider clarifies. "What does it mean?"

"No one knows."

"It must mean something if he put it in every painting."

"I'm sure it does, but there's little known about Atwood—either as a man or as a painter. That's what makes him so difficult, so challenging. It wasn't until well after his death that his work started to gain attention."

Jenny casts her gaze at Darius, letting her eyes linger momentarily before stepping back to the hood of the Chevelle and pointing at the open page of the binder. "You're sure you haven't seen anything like that?" she presses. "Think hard. With age and corrosion, it may not even look like a lion's head anymore."

Darius shakes his head. "I think I'd remember it."

Jenny picks the notebook up, closes it, and tucks it under her arm. Refusing to accept defeat, she grows quiet again as her eyes devour the car and her mind digests it. She moves ideas around in her head, recalling everything she knows about Atwood, regarding the car and the missing lion's head as some grand puzzle awaiting solution.

As the seconds tick into minutes, Jenny walks a very slow circle around and through the car and its debris field. Low utterances come from her slightly moving mouth, but the sounds are too low to carry meaning— they are simply a side effect of her mental gymnastics, a habit she's had since she was a girl.

The wait is killing Darius, who grows increasingly fidgety in the silence of the shop. Spider, too, is uncomfortable, crossing and uncrossing his arms, shifting his posture, and generally maintaining a constant state of movement.

When he can't take it anymore, Darius says, "I suppose we can look again."

Just like that, Jenny's trancelike mummer's dance ends. She looks at Darius with eager eyes. "You don't mind?" It's more of a statement than a question. Without waiting for a response, she looks down at her clothes and asks, "Do you have a pair of coveralls I can borrow?"

"Spider and I can handle it. You don't need to—"

"I won't have you two doing my work for me," Jenny interrupts in a patient tone, "much as I appreciate the offer." She strips off her charcoal gray jacket and lays it on the hood of the 1965 Chevelle. Rolling up her blouse sleeves past her elbows, she turns to find Darius and Spider staring at her in bewildered. "What," she says, raising her hands in supplication, "a girl can't get dirty?"

"Oh, sure, absolutely," Darius sputters as he heads off to search for a pair of coveralls. Ten feet away, he pauses. "This old car is a filthy mess . . ." It's a statement, a warning, and a final plea, all rolled into one.

"Uh-huh?" Jenny says . . . and that pretty much settles it.

Recognizing defeat when it stands before him, Darius shrugs resignedly and makes his way to the supply room adjacent to the front office. He disappears inside for a full minute before emerging with a clean pair of blue coveralls cradled in his arm. "They're the smallest I could find," he says as he hands them over. "You might have to roll up the sleeves and cuffs a bit."

Jenny unfolds them and holds them to her body, checking for fit.

"The bathroom's right over there," Darius says, pointing across the large teardown room to a door midway along the north wall. Her eyes ignore the gesture; in fact, they don't move at all, but hold Darius in a steady gaze, unblinking, as she kicks off her shoes where she stands, and then quickly slips into the coveralls. Her clothes bunch up as the material pulls over them, and she does a little shimmy to get the fabric to settle properly before pulling the zipper up to the center of her chest.

"Ready," she announces brightly.

There's no pattern to the search that ensues, no grand design to their quest, no method to the hunt. They just start where they stand, grabbing the nearest piece of the old Plymouth, inspecting it for the elusive lion's head, and then moving on to the next piece, and the next, and the next.

A fruitless hour slips by.

They inspect the inside of the fenders, the backside of door handles, the frames of the seats, the brackets of the visors. Every conceivable part of the old car is inspected, from the undercarriage to the weathered convertible top. Their earlier enthusiasm is beginning to wane when Darius starts reciting a checklist of parts and locations, pausing after each for the inevitable yes from Jenny or Spider. In a few cases he has to explain what a particular part looks like before getting the yes but the yes always comes.

Yes, yes, yes . . . until one question draws silence.

"Did anyone check the glove box?" Darius repeats.

There's silence for a moment, and then Spider says, "I was busy . . . you know . . . with the other thing." He doesn't know what *other thing* he was busy with, but it sounds like a good excuse, so he goes with it. "Besides, D, we already looked in there. Remember the red lipstick and the paperwork?"

Darius isn't convinced. "We were looking at the *contents* of the glove box," he says as he moves to the passenger side, "not the glove box itself." The door to the small compartment is one of the few detachable pieces still affixed to the body, and it opens easily when Darius pushes the button. Spider and Jenny watch as his eyes scan the underside of the box and the inner walls in one quick, fluid motion. A second later his gaze falls upon the backside of the glove box door . . . and stops.

"I . . . I found it."

Jenny practically leaves her shoes behind as she springs forward. She crowds up next to Darius, so close her scented hair brushes his face and their cheeks almost touch. She's so absorbed by the discovery that she doesn't notice the strawberry blush that momentarily paints Darius's cheeks.

On the inside of the glove box door, dead center both vertically and horizontally, the lion's head stares up at them. There are no other marks to distinguish it, just the golden lion's head resting chameleon-like against the car's distinct yellow hue; if you looked from the wrong angle you might miss it entirely. The yellow paint is well preserved; not as well preserved as the patch in the trunk, but still in remarkable condition for the presumed age of the paint job.

Jenny is beyond words.

She stares at the symbol with the intense joy of one who has birthed a theory or a movement and watched it grow to righteous maturity.

"You know what this means," she eventually utters in a low voice. "The lion's head *is* part of his signature; this removes all doubt. It's no longer just a notion—my own wild-eyed interpretation." She pushes herself back from the glove box and finds her feet.

"This car is going to be legendary in the art world; it's irreplaceable—a treasure." She turns to Darius, grasping him by the shoulders. "You need to consult an art conservationist before you continue, someone who can offer guidance and assistance." She seems almost in a daze. "There are elements that must be preserved."

"We've got it covered," Darius assures her. "This is one of the best rebuild shops on the west—"

Jenny puts a slender finger to his lips, and the mere touch stops him cold.

"You don't understand," she says. "This car is going to ignite the art world. Those who didn't know about E.E. Atwood before will be drawn to him as word of this gets out. I've seen it before. This is a Holy Grail moment, the type of event that will send the value of Atwood paintings through the"—she suddenly covers her mouth as a thought rampages through her reeling mind. "We have to keep this a secret," she whispers in realization. Her eyes find Darius.

"Secret?"

She moves in close and her hands clutch his shoulders, not in a controlling manner, but with the kind of firmness meant to impart the seriousness of the situation. "You don't understand," she says. "If word gets out . . . well, you don't have the security here to protect it."

"This place locks down pretty tight," Darius argues, still not understanding her concern.

"Trust me," Jenny insists. "If the car's going to stay here, no one can know about its history—its link to Atwood—until it's restored and ready to be moved to a more secure location." She looks at the old Plymouth in its many parts, then at Darius, and slowly shakes her head. "This car is worth millions; maybe tens of millions."

Chapter 8

Friday, August 12

It's just after nine when Darius, Jenny, and Spider settle into a booth at the Red Robin adjacent to Bellis Fair Mall for a late dinner. The conversation they started on the drive from Road Runner Restoration is put on hold momentarily as they order an onion ring tower and three glasses of lemon water from Amber, their abundantly cheerful waitress.

"I'll give you a few minutes to look at the menu," Amber says, and just as soon as she turns and walks away, Spider leans across the table.

"Moral issue!" he hisses. "What moral issue?"

"Come on, Spider," Darius insists, "I'm not going to take advantage of an old woman." He looks briefly at Jenny who's on the seat next to Spider, but when she offers no immediate support he turns back to his frustrated friend.

"*Caveat venditor*: Let the *seller* beware," Spider proclaims before Darius can speak. "It may not be as well-known as its more popular cousin, *caveat emptor*, but it's just as valid." His voice grows firm. "It's not *your* responsibility to notify someone if they sell you something on the cheap and don't bother to learn its value first. There *is* no moral jeopardy here. Period."

"She's an old lady—"

"Old ladies are cunning!" Spider shoots back. "Don't let them fool you!" The words come out as an exaggerated growl and his left eye settles theatrically into a Popeye squint, causing Jenny to snicker.

Darius smiles. "You're an idiot," he says, shaking his head.

Spider grins broadly.

Undaunted, Darius continues. "You may find it old-fashioned or silly, and you may disagree and think I'm the world's biggest fool, but I have to do what I think is right, regardless of the consequences." He looks hard at

Spider, who's now leaning back in the booth with his arms crossed over his chest, a soft smile on his lips. "You of all people should know this."

"I do, brother—God help me."

The debate continues until Amber returns with the onion rings and they pause the conversation long enough to look over the menu. Darius settles on the Arctic cod fish and chips, while Jenny opts for the much healthier avo-cobb-o salad. Spider decides to live large and try the sautéed mushroom burger, even though he doesn't like mushrooms. Amber takes their order with joyful enthusiasm and then floats off to the kitchen to inform the chef, leaving them once more standing at the edge of that sluggish mire between right and wrong, moral, and immoral, ethical and unethical.

No one wants to be the first to speak.

The silence grows sharper as the seconds tick by, and it soon begins to cut at the edge of every conversation around them until Spider can stand it no longer. "Tell us about Atwood," he says to Jenny, hoping to steer the conversation away from the controversial.

"What do you want to know?"

"I don't know—everything, I guess."

She chuckles and places her notebook on the table. "Well, *everything* can be summed up in about fifteen minutes—sadly."

"Yeah, about that," Spider presses, "how is it that Atwood is this famous artist, yet no one knows anything about him? I mean, we have the dude's car with his signature in the trunk, and the only stuff we could find was all written by you. Mrs. Lipscomb didn't know who Atwood was, otherwise, she wouldn't have sold the car so cheaply."

Darius nods as Spider speaks. "My thoughts exactly."

Jenny tilts her head to the side, and she hesitates a moment—not because it's a difficult question, but because it's embarrassingly simple. Drawing a deep breath, she begins.

"Well, frankly, it's because he hasn't been studied much until just recently. The fact that I'm a year and a half out of grad school and I'm the art world's expert on Atwood pretty much says it all." The corner of her mouth curls up and she shrugs.

"So . . . no one knows much about him," Spider presses, trying to understand, "but he's famous, and his paintings are worth a lot of money, right?"

"*Blue Belle* sold at auction last year for three hundred and twenty-five thousand dollars," Jenny says.

Spider lets out a low whistle.

"Not chump-change," Jenny quickly agrees, "but there are plenty of artists whose paintings draw those kinds of prices, and I guarantee you that ninety-nine percent of the country has never heard of them, either . . . and that's a conservative estimate."

"Whoa, so go back—what's *Blue Belle?*" Spider asks.

Jenny flips open her thick notebook and fans through several pages near the middle before stopping and sliding the book in front of Spider. "This one here," she says, pointing at the picture of a bright blue early thirties' sedan rolling down what could be Main Street in any small town in America between the world wars.

Darius leans across the table for a better look, albeit upside down. "Is that a Duesenberg?"

"It is," Jenny confirms. "A 1930 Model J, from what I can determine."

Between the amazing photo-quality detail of the painting and the elegant beauty of the Duesenberg, Darius can't seem to take his eyes from the picture. "Look at the suicide doors," he says, running his finger along the picture where the doors meet. "Beautiful."

Jenny smiles and nods. "Funny thing is, there's a good chance Atwood never even saw that car—not in person, anyway. There were only about a hundred built in 1930, making it exceptionally rare."

"Okay—and what's with that?" Spider suddenly says, swiping his hand toward her as if appraising her clothing and accessories.

"What?"

"The car stuff. I get it when it comes from D—he's a total motorhead, but you're this art doctor."

"Ph.D. in art history," Jenny corrects.

"Yeah, yeah—you know what I mean. You're supposed to be into paintings and sculptures, abstracts and cubism, that type of thing, but you drive this beastly pavement pounder, and you know stuff like how many of a certain type of Duesenberg were built in a given year."

Jenny smiles. "What, a girl can't talk shop?"

"No, don't get me wrong, it's awesome, it just doesn't make sense."

Jenny laughs—which comes out more like a huff—and says, "Trust me, I started as a doll-and-Easy-Bake-Oven kind of girl. That all changed when I met Mr. Atwood . . . figuratively speaking," she quickly adds, seeing the confused looks on their faces.

Jenny spends the next ten minutes providing the abbreviated version of her rise from four-year-old aspiring finger-paint artist to sideline art observer to amateur collector, and on through her Ph.D. in art history.

"I was in high school when I saw my first Atwood in a Seattle art gallery," she says, bringing the topic back to the little-known artist. "They were asking eighty-five hundred for it—way beyond my budget. Nonetheless, I stood there for the longest time just staring at it. I remember being struck by his use of light and shadow, as if they were his first consideration in the painting rather than his last."

A small smile finds its way to her lips as she recalls that first chance meeting. "When I got home, I started scouring the internet for everything I could find on Atwood." She shrugs. "As you know, there isn't much, so I made it my mission to find out more, which included researching the cars he painted. I guess I had it in my head that if I could figure out what drove him to choose those particular vehicles, I might have a better understanding of the man."

"Did it work?" Darius asks.

"Not really. Some of the cars are rare, some are common. Some look new, while others are old and beat up, like the old Ford truck in the poster on the wall of your uncle's shop. In the end, the only thing I discovered is that Atwood painted the world as he saw it, both the good and the bad. Seems as if he had an almost piercing comprehension of everything around him. Where that came from and why it bled into his art—what experiences led him to it—remains a mystery." She takes a drink of water and then, almost as an afterthought, says, "Oh, and along the way, I fell in love with cars."

Darius chuckles.

"What?"

"Nothing," he says quickly. "I like it."

She wipes the tips of her fingers on a napkin, soaking up the small droplets of moisture deposited by her perspiring drinking glass. Then, setting the napkin in her lap, she says, "Well, what's your story?"

"How do you mean?"

"The two of you," she points her chin at each of them in turn. "You don't exactly strike me as your average body shop workers—no offense."

"None taken."

"He's the body shop guy," Spider quickly clarifies. "I'm the misunderstood genius."

"Okay, Mr. Genius," Jenny replies with a laugh.

"Yeah . . . he's not kidding," Darius says in a gloomy tone. "IQ of a hundred and fifty-three. Don't get him started."

Jenny gives Darius a scoffing look and then realizes he's serious. Turning nearly sideways in her seat, she looks at Spider next to her, who gives her an exaggerated grin and takes a healthy, goofy, gulping drink from his glass . . . some of which spills out the corner of his still-grinning mouth and dribbles down his shirt.

Darius just shakes his head. "After we graduated high school—"

"Wait, you went to school together?"

"Since kindergarten, if you can believe it."

"That's nice," Jenny says with a nod. "So . . . after graduating?"

"Yeah, I went into the Air Force and he went to college."

"Stanford," Spider says with a wink, "full scholarship."

Darius shrugs. "Air Force wouldn't take him."

"Too smart," Spider shoots back.

Jenny grins.

"Anyway, by the time I finished my enlistment he had his bachelor's in applied physics, but for some dumb reason, he decided to enroll at Western with me and get a second degree in computer science. Now he's finishing his masters."

"We graduate next spring," Spider says.

"And what then?"

He shrugs.

Jenny looks across the table at Darius, who also shrugs.

"You must have something in mind?" she presses.

"Maybe Microsoft or Google," he says without much enthusiasm. "Then again, maybe we'll start our own little venture. In either case, I can't exactly unleash Spider on an unsuspecting world, so whatever we do, it'll be a package deal."

Spider grins broadly and leans forward in his seat, resting his chin on the back of his hand in a horribly wrong rendition of Rodin's *The Thinker*. "I've contemplated a career as a nude model," he says in a pious voice.

"Idiot," Darius says, shaking his head.

Their food arrives and either because of the late hour, the company, or the evening's work that's now behind them, it tastes exceptionally good. They devour it to the accompaniment of light and enjoyable conversation.

After finishing off the last of his fish, Darius suddenly waves a pudgy steak fry in the air and says, "Going back to your love of art for a minute, what took you from aspiring artist to art history major? How come you're not doing your own paintings, or working as a commercial artist, something like that?"

Jenny doesn't answer right away but picks at the remains of her salad. "Okay, if we're telling truths here—" She hesitates again, searching for the right words, the right phrase, the best possible way to make such an admission based on all her years of education. In short, how to describe the enigma that was her nascent career as a painter.

"I suck as an artist," she finally says.

Darius busts into laughter. "Isn't art supposed to be subjective?" he says a moment later.

Jenny nods. "Yeah, subjectively speaking, I *suck* as an artist."

"So, art history was the next best thing?"

"Those who can, do," Jenny says resignedly. "Those who can't . . . well, apparently they work at a museum."

With plates empty and bellies full, the conversation eventually finds its way back full circle to the more serious ethical question presented by the *Bumblebee Jacket*, that exceedingly rare car they now call by name.

"There's no moral obligation to return it," Jenny states unequivocally after the debate goes back and forth repeatedly and without resolution. "It's an admirable sentiment, Darius, but Spider is right—seller beware. She sold you the car. It's a done deal."

Darius is shaking his head. "You buy something at the store and hand the clerk a ten. He thinks you gave him a twenty and gives you change based on that assumption. What do you do?"

"That's different," Spider argues. "That's a simple mistake."

"What do you do?"

"You return the change, I suppose—but it's an unfair comparison. Both the buyer and the seller knew the value of the items and agreed on the price. Because the clerk errs in counting the change doesn't relieve you from the responsibility to do the right thing. That's completely different from what we're talking about."

"Okay, different question," Darius continues. "Say you find a wallet stuffed full of cash, and I mean thousands of dollars, but you also find the driver's license of the owner. What do you do?"

"Pocket the cash and toss the wallet," Spider says without hesitation.

Jenny, who's in the middle of several large gulps of water, has to cover her mouth to keep from spraying.

"Yeah, yeah, I know," Spider says, laughing. "Return the wallet *and* the money."

"Oh, Spider," Darius says with a resigned sigh, shaking his head as if his friend were a petulant two-year-old who just dumped a bowl of Cheerios down the heater vent.

"You realize you both sound like fossils from the 1940s or something," Jenny finally chimes in, still wiping water from her chin. "Those ideas are from a different time, different people. I'm not saying I don't agree with you, but let's be realistic, no one thinks like that anymore."

"I do," Darius says, leaning back and slumping against the seat. "Maybe that makes me odd or naïve. Maybe it *is* old-fashioned like you say." He glances at Jenny. "I look around at the way we live, the way people act, this rude, self-centered, self-indulgent *me-me-me* attitude that's infected the country over the last fifty years and I worry about our future. There's no such thing as personal responsibility anymore, and no one cares about doing the right thing—especially if it costs them time or money or, god forbid, inconvenience."

Spider gives a big nod. "Church, that."

"What?" Jenny says, giving him an odd look.

"Church," Spider repeats with a lift of his shoulders.

"He means he agrees," Darius clarifies.

"Okay."

"Yeah, and *I'm* the odd one," he mutters, thumbing at Spider. "All I'm saying is that mass shootings were almost unheard of in the fifties, sixties, and seventies. And it wasn't because there weren't any guns. My grandpa still talks about how he and his friends took their guns with them to school. They'd just lean them in the corner inside the door and retrieve them after school so they could go shooting." He shakes his head. "We can't even imagine such a thing today. If a third grader even draws a picture of a gun it's grounds for expulsion in some schools. Still, the problem grows."

"So, what's changed since the fifties?" Jenny asks.

"Technology, affluence, culture—"

"Drugs," Spider interjects.

They look at him and he shrugs. "Can you imagine Ozzie and Harriet shooting heroin in the bathroom, or Beaver lighting a bowl?"

"The Munsters on meth," Jenny offers.

"Exactly," Spider says, clapping his hands together dramatically. "It doesn't fit, right? Eddie Munster huffing on a meth pipe. That's some *Breaking Bad* shizzle. And meth is just one of the nasties out there that'll cook your brain from the in—side—out. No wonder people are going psycho."

Darius is shaking his head. "It's not like drugs are a new invention; just look at the opium dens that sprang up in the eighteen hundreds. Even then you had men and women strung out all the time, abandoning their families, their jobs, everything. Even the original formula for Coca-Cola included cocaine, that's where it got its name—and let's not forget Sherlock Holmes's famous, or infamous, use of both cocaine and morphine."

"So . . . what are you saying?" Jenny presses. "The war on drugs was a good idea?"

"Good, bad, I'm not sure. But, for the record, whoever called it a war was an idiot. It's like declaring war on poverty—another stupid idea. *War* implies something that can be defeated, never to rise again. Drugs, crime, poverty, deceit, lies, injustice; they've all been with us since the beginning, anyone who thinks they can eradicate them is either delusional or they're selling something. I'm just saying that we, as a people, have to find our moral compass."

"So, you've never used drugs?"

"No, never," Darius says. Pointing a finger across the table at Spider, he adds, "I learned from his mistakes."

"Mushrooms," Spider explains, crinkling his nose and shaking his head. "Bad stuff. Purely experimental."

Jenny smiles. "Yeah, that's what they all say."

They stare back and forth at each other for a moment until Jenny says, "Mushrooms, meth, and cocaine . . . how did we get on this topic?"

"Moral decay and the decline of western civilization," Spider pontificates in an artificially deep voice, causing Jenny to giggle and even pulling a grin from Darius's stubborn face.

"Joke if you want," he says, tossing a French fry across the table where it lands limply on Spider's shoulder. "I just think there must be a better way."

"A better way for what?" Jenny asks.

"Living." Darius smiles and looks down. "It doesn't matter. Much as I've enjoyed our philosophical discussion, I'm taking the car back tomorrow morning."

"No," Spider groans, and drops his head onto the table.

"I have to do what I think is right," Darius insists. "The car meant something to Mrs. Lipscomb, otherwise she wouldn't have put me through the ringer before selling it to me. I think I owe her the truth. Besides . . . I like her."

"I like the car," Spider retorts.

"You don't think I do? It's everything I've been looking for. It's everything I dreamed about and saved for. Don't think for a moment that this is easy—it's not. It's just . . . right."

The table is quiet for the better part of a minute, which is an eternity if you've ever sat and counted seconds out one by one.

"So . . . there's no talking you out of this?" Jenny eventually asks.

"No."

"Then I'm going with you."

"Wha—No! Why?"

Jenny shrugs. "I want to meet the lady who, for so many years, had the art world's rarest vehicle parked in her garage." She smiles, a hopeful gleam in her eye. "Who knows, maybe she *met* Atwood."

Chapter 9

The coughing spell comes in the early morning hours when the world outside is dark and her room is steeped in shadow. After a few minutes of persistent hacking, Margaret rises from bed and makes her way to the kitchen for a glass of water, something to quell the itch.

She'd always been susceptible to summer colds, but this one has proven more persistent than most. Perhaps it's a reflection of her own stubbornness, she muses as she takes a glass from the cupboard and turns on the faucet, waiting for the water to chill.

Finding a cough drop, she takes her glass and moves to the family room, where she sits in a vintage high back chair and looks at the paintings gathered about. In the unlit gloom, they are just angles and shadow, but she knows every inch of them by heart. In her mind, she sees every brushstroke.

Melancholy finds her, and she moves her head to the rhythm of unheard music from a time long passed. She begins to hum along until the corners of her eyes grow moist, and then she shakes it off. "Remember the hourglass," she tells herself in the darkness.

At two-thirty, she returns to her room and places a collection of pillows against the headboard; better to sleep propped up, she reasons, than risk another coughing fit. As she drifts off to sleep, the music comes to her once more, ripe with memories both beautiful and sad.

They paint her dreams.

By ten o'clock on Saturday morning, the temperature is already eighty and rising.

Still exhausted from her interrupted sleep, Margaret retrieves her coffee-stained mug and pours herself a second cup, sweetening it with sugar and cream. The faded logo of Windermere Real Estate is still visible on the side of the mug, a relic from her years as a local realtor.

She loved selling houses.

She hated selling houses.

She did both with all her heart.

Stepping out onto the back patio, she sips gingerly as she walks slowly about the yard, checking her small garden, running her fingers through the leaves of a honeysuckle bush, and eventually finding herself at the western edge of the lot looking out over the marina and the Puget Sound beyond.

The view is breathtaking, and the sight soothes her, more so even than the coffee or the warm morning air. She begins to hum a tune—a different one from the night before. Those her age would likely recognize the notes and the intonations, but to most, it would be little more than a pleasing tune of no particular significance.

When the song is complete, she turns her back to the harbor and the ponderous water beyond, and looks to the eastern horizon, letting the new sun wash her face in light and radiant heat. As the air around her continues to warm, it carries the aromas of summer, particularly lavender and honeysuckle mixed with a hint of sweetness drifting in from the nearby apple tree. Finding a lounge chair next to the standing outdoor fireplace, Margaret settles in, breathing deeply of the air and remembering bygone days when life was simpler and oh-so-exciting.

Sleep finds her there at last, blessed sleep.

And the birds sing in the trees . . . a pleasing song of no particular significance.

Before parting the previous evening, Darius, Jenny, and Spider—the unlikely trio—agreed to several things as they stood in the parking lot outside the Red Robin. First, and perhaps the only thing they all agreed on entirely, was that they'd meet at Jenny's hotel the next morning at eleven. This was followed by a much more robust debate regarding the manner and method by which they would return the car.

Darius finally conceded that it couldn't be towed, and it was in too many pieces at the moment to be placed on a trailer or flatbed. More importantly, at least to Darius, was the fact that he had purchased the car in one piece and felt obligated to return it in a similar state.

Jenny finally convinced him that instead of simply carting the old

Plymouth back, whether in one piece or many, he needed to talk to Mrs. Lipscomb first. "You're handing back a car that's worth millions," she argued convincingly. "You've decided that this lady has some kind of claim on the car—though she doesn't, and that's fine. So be it. I'm just saying that if you're going to proceed under the assumption that she *does* have a claim, you need to talk to her first, get her thoughts on the matter."

So, it was settled.

Eleven o'clock. Talk to Mrs. Lipscomb. Return the car.

As the Hampton Inn emerges ahead and to the left, Darius glances at the dash clock and realizes that he and Spider are running eight minutes early—which is fine by him. Always early, never late; it was almost a code with him. If Spider was driving, they'd still be backing out of the driveway, which would be even more annoying since the only vehicle Spider owns is a black 2009 Vespa scooter.

Darius refuses to ride on it.

He did once when Spider first bought the contraption three years ago. The near-death experience that followed convinced him that Spider's days were numbered, and for the next year whenever his friend came into the house totting his helmet, Darius would call out, "Dead man walking!"

In fairness, Spider's riding skills have improved considerably since.

"Right there," Spider says, pointing to the parking lot on the east side of the hotel.

The gray 2012 Camaro ZL1 is an imposing presence, its low-slung nose facing out from the parking spot where Jenny backed in the night before. Though it sits motionless, it has the appearance of a dark beast, crouched and ready to pounce. There are few cars around it; probably why Jenny chose this part of the parking lot.

Swinging into a parking space nose first, Darius intentionally leaves a space between his worn Honda and the flawless muscle car. Spider digs the phone from his pocket, saying, "I'll give her a call." Unfolding a crumpled white fragment of paper, he punches the number in, but before he can hit send the familiar figure of Dr. Jenny Morgan rounds the front corner of the hotel and she starts across the parking lot toward them. Her movements are seamless and graceful, almost cat-like, another characteristic she seems to share with her car.

Their eyes follow her, unable to look away.

No business attire today, Darius notes. Instead, she sports something more casual: tight jeans, knee-high boots, and a sleeveless royal blue V-neck top. Combined, the ensemble creates a sophisticated, stunning look, and Dr. Morgan wears it well. More than that, she *knows* she wears it well, which only adds to the appeal.

As she saunters across the parking lot in their direction, Spider mutters, "Mamma Mia," and Darius just nods his agreement.

Leaning down at the open driver's window, Jenny dangles a set of keys, saying, "Why don't we take mine," and then tosses them in Darius's lap. "You can drive."

"Wh—No!" Darius says, pouring from the old Honda with the keys extended in his hand. "I'm not insured for"—he waves his hands at the Camaro—"this. If something happened, I couldn't . . . well, I just couldn't live with myself."

"Wow! You are one tightly-wrapped guy."

"Church," Spider says with an exaggerated nod, fist-bumping Jenny.

"No—honest, I'm not."

"Please," Spider says with a laugh. "You're like one of those stretchy gauze bandages wrapped around a fat guy's leg. It doesn't get any more tightly wound than that."

"I don't like driving other people's cars," Darius growls. "Accidents happen."

Spider snickers and throws a thumb in Darius's direction. "He rolled his mom's new Cadillac the day he got his learner's permit." Jenny turns a pair of big eyes on Darius. "And not a regular roll, either" Spider continues, "D decided to go end over end—totaled the car." He demonstrates with a dramatic hand gesture. "I've got the bent hood ornament on my dresser at home." When she gives him a quizzical look, he shrugs, "You know— souvenir."

Without a word, Darius extends his hand, the keys to the Camaro dangling from his fingertips.

"Seriously," Jenny says, refusing to take them, "my insurance covers anyone driving—even Cadillac killers." She grins. "You've got nothing to worry about. Besides, if you do end up going, you know, end over end, it just means I get the fun of shopping for a new car." She pats Darius on the arm. "You'll do fine."

They leave him standing there, Spider and Jenny, as they climb into the waiting muscle car. After a moment, and left with no choice, Darius slides into the driver's seat. Adjusting the seat and then the mirrors, he says, "What did you say the horsepower was on this thing?"

"Five hundred and eighty horse," Jenny purrs, "all of them thoroughbreds." Unable to restrain herself, she asks, "Is that more than you're used to?"

"Nah, it's good. The Honda's kicking out a hundred and ten."

"Like, you could get four more Hondas," Spider says, "and link them all together and you'd *still* be forty horses short." He seems to find the thought amusing.

"All kidding aside," Jenny says, "I saw five or six cars yesterday at the shop that probably have more horsepower than my little ol' Camaro. Doesn't your uncle let you drive any of them?"

"No," Darius says, flatly. "Not really."

There's an awkward silence, and then Spider whispers, "The Cadillac incident."

Jenny doesn't ask any more questions.

Destiny, it seems, is proceeded by a rumble.

Mrs. Lipscomb pays little mind to the noise, assuming it's a particularly loud train moving on the tracks below the bluff, or perhaps one of the vintage aircraft from the Heritage Flight Museum at the Bellingham International Airport. Their P-51 Mustang "Val-Halla" has a particularly throaty growl and it's not that uncommon to hear it overhead.

Then comes the doorbell—most unexpected.

She can count on one hand the number of visitors she's had in the last two months. She credits the NO SOLICITATION signs at the road, but the truth is that Mrs. Lipscomb has become something akin to a hermit in the years since her retirement. Her yard and gardens occupy her in the spring and summer, while various hobbies, to include needlepoint and pottery, fill her hours in the fall and winter. Her favorite TV shows are reserved for evening hours.

Downton Abbey is her current favorite, but there are others.

All things considered, Margaret's doorbell is the least exercised element of her home, and she can't imagine who would be on her doorstep on a Saturday morning in August. Despite her short nap, she's still weary from her restless night, so it's with little patience that she jerks the door open and glares at the trespassers.

Her face immediately softens.

"Mr. Alexander," she says, and the surprise on her face borders on delight. Her eyes quickly shift from Darius to Spider, and she immediately assesses him, saying, "My word, Stephen, what is that you're wearing?" But before Spider can process the question, let alone spit out an answer, she spots Jenny and says, "Well, good morning, my dear. Are you part of this motley crew?"

Jenny likes her immediately.

"Yes, ma'am. I suppose so."

Mrs. Lipscomb glances past them at the Camaro in the driveway. "I expect that's the reason my teacups were rattling on the shelf. For a moment, I thought it was the big one. Earthquake," she clarifies, directing the word at Spider and speaking it slowly as if he were thick in the head. "What brings you back to my door so quickly?" she asks, this time addressing Darius. "Is there a problem with the car?"

"Yeah, about the car . . ." Darius fidgets, searching for the words. "I don't suppose we can sit down for a minute, have a talk?"

She studies him a moment, and in a soft, contemplative voice, as if speaking to herself, says, "So serious." Opening the door wide, she steps aside, saying, "Please, come in."

Instead of leading them into the family room off to the right, Margaret continues past the kitchen and out onto the back patio. "No sense in languishing inside on such a day," she says, pulling several of the patio chairs into a circle. Urging them to sit, she offers coffee, tea, and lemonade, and refuses to take no for an answer. Spider and Darius agree to coffee, and Jenny says yes please to some lemonade.

"As it happens, I have some raspberry coffee cake," Margaret adds and then whisks off to the kitchen.

"I love old ladies," Spider says, leaning into Darius. "They always have food."

Rising from her seat, Jenny takes a dozen steps toward the back of the lot, staring off to the west.

"What's up?" Darius asks, and then stands and moves up beside her.

"The water," she replies. "I have a pretty good view of the sound from my apartment in Seattle, but this is different. Less cluttered, I suppose. What's that island there?" she asks, pointing.

"The big one is Lummi Island, the smaller, lower one in front of it is Portage."

"Have you been there?"

"Just Lummi—when I was a kid."

She has more questions about other islands, the bay, and Bellingham in general, but is disappointed to learn that Darius has fewer answers than she has questions. "I suppose it's that way with everyone," she concedes, as they make their way back to their seats. "No one seems to appreciate where they live until they leave it behind. Me—I've spent a good chunk of my life in Seattle and I've never been to the top of the Space Needle."

"Really?"

"Horrible, right?"

"Are you afraid of heights or something?"

"No, it's just . . . the Needle is always there. There's no urgency; it's not like I'm visiting and only going to be in town a few days. That's the way it is. We always think we'll get around to stuff like that but never take the time to make it happen." She gives Darius a look. "Have you? Been up the Needle, I mean?"

"Well, yeah; twice. Once when I was ten, and again with Spider in high school—we skipped class our senior year and went to the Pacific Science Center."

"Oooh!" Jenny says dramatically, "the science center; such delinquents."

"They had a robotics display," Darius says with a shrug. "It was a temporary exhibit."

Mrs. Lipscomb soon returns bearing a tray heavily laden with drinks, the coffee cake she mentioned, and a small plate of lemon squares sprinkled with confectioner's sugar.

"Mmm, breakfast of champions," Spider says, his hand moving for the lemon squares even before the tray comes to rest on the patio table.

They drink and eat and make small talk in a tight circle around the patio table for several minutes until Margaret masterfully brings the conversation full circle and to its original intent as if placing all unnecessary talk into a small box and setting it on a shelf, something to be played with later.

"So, Darius, you had something dreadful to tell me about the car?"

"Uh . . . yeah." He fiddles with his fingers a moment, choosing the words, failing, and then deciding to just blurt it out. "I've got to return the car, Mrs. Lipscomb. There are some things you need to know about it. It's not bad," he quickly adds. "It's amazing and exciting, but it would be wrong to keep the car with what I've learned."

With a considerable amount of help from Jenny, they tell the story of Evan Elmore Atwood and his amazing paintings. Jenny opens her notebook and points out the various iterations of the golden lion's head as Darius describes the one found on the back of the glove box door. For fifteen minutes they talk as Mrs. Lipscomb listens attentively without interrupting. Her only reaction during the entire recitation is a small smile that graces her lips momentarily when Darius compares the works of E. E. Atwood to prints by Currier & Ives, and the masterful works of Norman Rockwell.

When they finally stop, out of words and out of breath, Margaret takes a sip from her glass, sets it gingerly on the table, stands, and says, "Follow me."

Her demeanor is casual, as if completely unfazed by all that she's just seen and heard. They may as well have told her it was dollar taco night at the local Mexican restaurant for all the wonder and awe it inspired. Obediently, though somewhat puzzled, they follow, casting questioning looks at one another along the way.

Mrs. Lipscomb sets a brisk pace as she leads the threesome into the house, down the hall to the very front of the house, and then to the right, into the living room. With a flourish, she presents a painting to them. It's on the wall separating the living room from the hall, nestled in a dark walnut frame perhaps three feet wide by four feet tall. The frame's patina hints at its age, but this is quickly forgotten when Darius's eyes fall upon the bright watercolor within, and for a moment he stands transfixed.

"It's called *A Girl and Her Car*," Margaret says in something close to a whisper.

The painting glows with the colors of summer as if someone placed a bulb behind it and backlit the image. Every stroke on the canvas seems to come with a purpose, rendering a flawless and brilliant watercolor. It's not the perfection of the piece, however, that gives Darius pause.

Stepping back, he takes in the canvas.

The canary-yellow Plymouth convertible is almost three dimensional as it stretches out like a cat in the midday sun. It's parked on a verdant blanket of lawn with trees and mountains rising in the background. Overhead, a blue sky reigns, with just a trace of white clouds. Standing on the front bumper, a young lady in a yellow and tan sundress lies facedown upon the hood, arms outstretched as if hugging the car. Whether or not she's old enough to drive is unanswered by the painting, but her love for the car is beyond doubt—it's painted in her face, her arms, her embrace.

Jenny gasps at the sight, and Spider says, "Is that—"

"Yes, the Bumblebee Jacket," Mrs. Lipscomb says with a smile, "and you're right, Mr. Alexander, it's no ordinary car. It was built by E.E. Atwood for his daughter and presented to her on her sixteenth birthday, June 1st, 1960. When she got behind the wheel for the first time, her father said it looked like she was wearing a giant bumblebee jacket."

"Are you talking about Grace Atwood?" Jenny asks in a startled tone.

"You've done your homework," Mrs. Lipscomb replies.

Jenny shakes her head. "The only thing I ever found was her name and a couple of pictures in the Bellingham High School yearbooks between 1959 and 1962. She seems to have up and disappeared after that. I assumed she moved out of the area." She studies Mrs. Lipscomb a moment. "You knew her, didn't you?"

"I know her still."

Jenny is beyond excited at the revelation. With hands pressed together in a steeple of prayer, she spews an entire sentence that rushes out of her mouth in the space of a single word: "Oh please tell me she's still alive?"

"Well, I certainly hope so," Mrs. Lipscomb replies with a chuckle and a humorous glint in her eyes. Patting her chest, she says, "She's me. Grace Margaret Atwood. Lipscomb is my married name." After a moment of stunned silence, the coy old matriarch shrugs her frail shoulders and says, "Grace is a lovely name, of course, but I always preferred Maggie."

Chapter 10

Turning points are funny things.

We rarely recognize them when they happen, and it's only through retrospection, often many years later, that we perceive where our path suddenly branched to the left or the right. That choice we made, wittingly or unwittingly, for better or for worse, will be significant enough to change the course of our life, though we have no way of knowing so at the time.

Sometimes the turning point—the fork in the road—is one we neither wish for nor desire, but one foisted upon us, nonetheless. Such turning points take many shapes, such as a pink slip at work, a divorce, a death in the family.

Other times, the fork in the road may be something as simple as following one's moral compass, even when one's heart and head want the opposite. When faced with such a turning point, it would be easy to continue along the same direction, ignoring the cautions of logic and conscience, for such a path is well established. It has momentum.

Darius Alexander is not one to follow a path simply because it lies at his feet.

He is among the fortunate few who have learned that he alone dictates the course of his life. With such knowledge comes an acceptance that the path will not always be easy, but its rewards will more than balance the scale.

Such is the machinery of life.

Several minutes pass before voices finally lower and the riotous conversation returns to a somewhat normal tempo and volume. Jenny has a thousand questions, and in her excited state, she continues to rattle them off one after another, though at a slower pace. Mrs. Lipscomb answers the simplest of them, often with just a yes or no, but soon grows weary of the interrogation and waves away any further questioning.

Darius is slumped deep into a vintage chair in the living room, silent, his head hanging low, his mind churning at Mrs. Lipscomb's revelation. The truth of her admission is almost tangible: an aftertaste in the mouth, a lingering smell, the rise of goosebumps on the arm. It doesn't change anything, though, or so he tells himself. Margaret may be the daughter of the famed painter, and fully aware of his work, but perhaps she doesn't know the car's value. *How could she?* Darius suddenly thinks. *It's been sitting in her garage for decades, unknown to the world.*

Mrs. Lipscomb never told a soul.

If she had, the art community would have cast an ever-present shadow on her front door. Conservators would beg her to store the car in a temperature-controlled environment, acquisition specialists would try to acquire it, and researchers would . . . well, do what researchers do best, which is ask endless questions and then re-ask the same questions with slightly different words.

The din in the living room continues, and between Jenny and Spider—who keeps repeating how dope this is—there are few breaks in the river of words. Darius waits patiently, his mind firmly set, and when at last silence blossoms, he plucks it from the air and makes his thoughts unequivocally clear.

"This change nothing," he says from his chair. When no one reacts, he says it a second time in a louder and firmer voice. "This change nothing."

The room is now utterly still.

"Meaning what, Mr. Alexander?" Margaret's words are soft but pointed.

Looking directly at her, Darius says, "I'm bringing the car back." He stands and begins to pace the room slowly, his mind a whirling vortex. "It's in pieces right now . . . it'll take a day or so to put it back the way it was, but then I'm towing it back."

"Hmm. You say that as if I have no choice in the matter."

"You don't." The words come out sharper than he wants, and he sighs. When he speaks again, he sounds tired, almost sad. "Mrs. Lipscomb, with all due respect, that car is worth a fortune—maybe millions." Glancing at Jenny, he says, "Tell her."

"It's true," she says with a nod. "Seven figures at least, maybe eight. Hard to tell what would happen at an auction, but the story of its discovery and the hype it will generate once the art world hears of it will drive the price up substantially, maybe astronomically."

"Oh, I don't doubt that" Mrs. Lipscomb says, unimpressed. "However, I already sold you the car, and you already paid for it. In my world that's a completed transaction. Barring any deception or harmful misrepresentation on my part, a new transaction is required if you want to return the car, and that's provided I'm willing to entertain such an option."

Darius's head begins to hurt. "But you have to!"

Margaret laughs. "I'm an old woman; I don't have to do much of anything if I don't want. One of the benefits of age is that you've had years and years to learn and practice such things as kindness, wisdom, patience, and . . . oh, yes . . . stubbornness."

Jenny snickers, but quickly stifles it when Darius turns her way.

"I'm very open-minded, though," Margaret replies quickly, "so of course, I'll consider a new transaction if that's what you want." She does some quick calculations in her head, eyes turned to the ceiling, and then says, "How's one million dollars sound?"

"One mill—you want to pay me one million dollars for something I just bought from you for a few thousand?" Darius sits dumbfounded for a moment, trying to figure out the old woman, trying to guess her game, but no logical explanation comes. "I'm not going to steal your money— because that's what it would be. Just give me back the money I gave you, and we'll call it even."

"You misunderstand me, Darius," Mrs. Lipscomb replies sweetly. "If you want to return the car, it'll cost *you* a million dollars. I'm not running a wrecking yard here, so that's my price, take it or leave it."

It takes a moment for her meaning to register, not just with Darius, but with Jenny and Spider as well. "That's—that's absurd. I'm offering to return a car that could be worth tens of millions, and you want me to pay you to take it back."

"Is that a no?"

"Yes—I mean no! No! Even if I *had* a million dollars it would be no."

"Well, then," Margaret says. "I suppose that settles it."

Darius stands in the middle of the room, speechless. His mind replays the last minute of conversation, sure that he missed a word or misheard a sentence. At length, defeated, he slumps into the same old chair and utters a single word: "Why?"

Taking a seat on the sofa opposite him, Mrs. Lipscomb folds her hands on her lap and watches Darius, studying his face. "Young man," she eventually says, a smile tickling the corner of her mouth, "I'm perfectly aware of the car's value. I'm not some senile old dolt—not yet anyway." She leans toward him, and in a quieter voice, says, "I knew what I was doing when I sold you the car, and I chose you carefully, just as I did the price."

She lets that sink in a moment and then continues. "I wanted someone who would love the car as I did, someone who would care for it, restore it, and make it what it was—what it should be." Warmth emanates from her generous smile, and her kind and glowing eyes wear Darius down by ounces and pounds until he can't help but smile back.

"Of all the scoundrels that showed up at my door," she says, "you were the one I trusted."

The joy on her face seems to transform her, and for a moment she looks like a schoolgirl once more; she looks like the young woman in the picture, still loving her car.

When the grandfather clock in the hall chimes one o'clock, Mrs. Lipscomb insists that they have some lunch and refuses to answer any more questions until they do. Fifteen minutes later they find themselves once more on the back patio, this time eating shrimp salad sandwiches and split-pea soup.

Glasses of iced tea rest at every elbow and Margaret makes sure they're always topped off. As they eat, she talks about her garden and the hummingbird that nests at the back of the property. She points out the grand old tree on the north edge of the property that once held a rope swing. She confesses to using it on more than one occasion in years gone by.

"What did you mean about the price of the car?" Darius asks as he pushes his empty bowl away and settles into the lawn chair, hands draped over his happy belly.

Margaret gives him a quizzical look.

"Earlier," Darius clarifies, "when you said you chose me carefully, just like you chose the price of the car: seven thousand six hundred and twenty-three dollars and forty-seven cents. That's a pretty odd number, and I thought, well—"

"You thought I was eccentric, maybe a little off my rocker?"

"I think the word he used was *medicated*," Spider interjects.

Jenny laughs and then quickly covers her mouth.

"Thank you, Spider," Darius replies stiffly.

Spider winks and nods, as if having rendered a great service.

"Medicated," Margaret says, mulling over the word. "I suppose that's generous, considering some of the alternatives." She sighs. "The simple truth is I need to put a new roof on the house before winter sets in. I should have replaced it years ago, but it's always the expensive repairs we seem to put off until we can't." Taking a drink of tea, she sets the glass to the side and wipes her moist fingers on her pants.

"I noticed a large leak during a rainstorm in May, the kind of leak you put a bucket under. We've had rain since, of course, and it hasn't returned, but I know it will with the coming of fall. It's in one of the upstairs bedrooms, which I use for . . . storage." She casts her eyes tellingly up toward the second floor of the old house.

"I'm worried about the damage such a leak might cause over the winter." She shrugs. "In the last month, I've had four roofing companies out to give me an estimate, only two of which were remotely trustworthy. Naturally, I chose the more expensive quote, which came to—"

"Seven thousand six hundred and twenty-three dollars and forty-seven cents," Darius finishes.

"Precisely and to the penny." She gives him a warm smile. "It sounded like a good number."

"It *is* a good number," Darius agrees, "especially the forty-seven cents. Who's going to argue over loose change? I had to go through all my coat pockets and dig under the couch cushions just so I had it right."

"I kicked in a dime," Spider reminds him.

"Yes, you did," Darius replies, patting his friend on the shoulder. Turning to Mrs. Lipscomb, he says, "Spider kicked in a dime."

He opens his mouth to continue—but then his face suddenly freezes, mid-thought. "That's it," he whispers. Slowly, the eureka moment creeps into his features, coming from all directions as it works its way across his cheeks, down his forehead, and up his chin before merging in his eyes, which now glisten with a special kind of delight. "That's it," he says again, more firmly this time.

He turns to Mrs. Lipscomb. "Don't you see? That's it! *I* can reroof your house! Spider and I both have experience—well, he has a lot more than I do, but—but the point is we can do it. That way I can pay more for the car and you can save that money for something else."

Margaret is already shaking her head skeptically.

"No. Seriously," Darius continues. "It's the least I can do, and the only thing that's going to make me feel good about not returning the car." He puts his hands together. "Please."

"One doesn't replace a roof by sheer will," Mrs. Lipscomb says gently, trying to ease Darius down. "If you don't know what you're doing, you simply end up with another bad roof and more leaks. I've been in the real estate game long enough to know that money spent poorly is money spent twice."

Before Darius can reply, Spider rises to his feet, saying, "Chill, D. I got this." Fishing in his back pocket, he wrestles a worn black wallet free and flips it open. Scanning the contents, he quickly finds a stained business card, which he plucks free and hands to Mrs. Lipscomb.

"Seven Gables Roofing." she reads aloud.

Spider shrugs. "My cousin has his own roofing company—his wife chose the name. Bottom line: I paid for half my tuition laying shingles with my cuz during summer breaks. I know everything there is to know about roofing. And Darius, well, he worked at least a dozen jobs with us, so he's no slouch."

"Well, maybe just a bit of a slouch," Darius mutters.

"What I'm saying, Ma'am, is that we got you covered—no pun intended."

Silence follows.

Mrs. Lipscomb studies the card, and then the three faces before her, and then the card again. She huffs to herself as she works it out, and a quirky smile appears at the corner of her mouth, only to disappear just as quickly.

After an unbearable pause, she sighs and says, "Well, if you're going to fix my roof, I suppose you best start calling me Maggie."

The patio explodes with excitement, cheers, and words of thanks. Spider tries leaning over and hugging Maggie, but only half succeeds. As Jenny, Darius, and Spider talk excitedly, Maggie leans back in her chair and watches them, enjoying their energy and enthusiasm with a quiet smile.

Why she agrees to let them roof her house is a mystery, but in the years to come, they will imagine that, even then, she was growing fond of them, much in the way that they were growing fond of her. Ultimately, the reason doesn't matter.

A bargain is struck.

A second transaction is begun.

A turning point is reached . . . one that will make all the difference.

Chapter II

By two o'clock, the full heat of August is upon them.

While Maggie and Jenny take cover in the shade of a giant patio umbrella, Darius and Spider dig an old aluminum ladder out of the garage and dauntlessly make their way up to the roof. Heat rises in waves off the black composite shingles as if Hell itself had settled upon the house. Darius and Spider shrug it off. It's not their first summer roofing job, and right now they just want to get a first-hand look at their new project.

"Do be careful," Maggie calls out to them from below.

Spider looks out over the edge and waves. Teetering on one foot, he pretends to lose his balance for a moment before grinning broadly and disappearing in pursuit of Darius.

"Boys!" Maggie huffs dismissively. "They never change." She pushes back in her chair and closes her eyes. Moments slip by, and she feels Jenny staring at her. "I'm not sleeping," she assures her, eyes still closed. "I'm taking a moment to meditate. It's a practice I fell into some years ago."

"Does it work?"

"Sometimes, but my version is more like speed mediation, which, I suppose, defeats the whole purpose. Still," she continues in a listless voice, "there's something calming about closing your eyes, even if it's only for the briefest of moments." As the last word slips out, her eyelids flutter and open. Turning, she studies Jenny.

"You want to ask about my father, don't you?"

"I do," Jenny replies, the words coming out in a rush, like a great sigh finally released. "You've been so gracious, and I don't want to seem ungrateful it's just that your father's work is so important, yet so little is known about him, about his paintings, his inspirations. There are eighty-seven canvases we know of, and only fifty-three are known to still exist. We don't know if there are hundreds more, thousands, or if that's it."

Maggie nods her understanding.

"I know my father's history is important," she says, "and I know it's a story that needs telling, it's just that"—her voice wavers ever so slightly—"it's still hard for me, even now."

Jenny takes her hand. "We can do it a little at a time," she offers in a soft voice. Then, smiling, she adds, "As long as you don't mind me coming up once or twice a week to pester you?"

"You're hardly a pest, my dear," Maggie replies. As she says this, the most peculiar idea comes to her. "Does anyone still say a *penny for your thoughts*?"

"Everyone knows it, but I don't think anyone uses it—at least not from my generation."

"Shame. Though I suppose it is a bit dated. The original phrase dates to the 1500s, if I remember correctly, back when the British penny was still worth a tidy sum. I can't even imagine what it would be today, after inflation. In any case, it was still a penny for your thoughts when I was your age, so let's tack on a modest increase and call it a nickel." Satisfied, she continues. "I'll answer twenty of your questions for a dollar, that's a nickel each, and a bargain if you ask me."

"You want me to pay you a dollar to answer twenty questions?"

"I do."

Jenny twists her mouth into a half-smile. "Am I missing something?"

Maggie chuckles. "Yes, I know it seems odd, but indulge me. I believe, as my father did, that everything either has value or it doesn't. If you give something away, especially if you do it repeatedly over time, people tend to take it for granted or treat it like the trash it is. After all, if you don't value it, why should they."

Sitting forward in her chair, she rests her hands in her lap.

"My father's legacy is important to me, and the nickel is . . . well, I suppose it's a token, from you to me, acknowledging its worth. Besides," she says in a warm voice, "I have no intention of spending them, so when I pull them out and look at them it'll be a reminder of our time together."

Jenny feels a sudden warmth for this odd and wonderful woman. "Then I'm happy to pay. For the information *and* the company." Digging around in her purse, she pulls a worn dollar bill free and is about to hand it over when Maggie stops her.

"Oh, pay as you go, dear—one nickel per question, one question per sitting. You do have a nickel, don't you?"

Jenny returns the dollar to her purse and fishes around in her change pocket, which is mostly pennies and dimes, but one nickel stands out and she quickly plucks it up. "A nickel for your thoughts," she says as she hands it over.

Maggie doesn't say a word, she just stands and disappears into the house. When she returns a moment later, she has her purse in hand and begins digging through it as she reclaims her seat. "There it is," she says. "I knew it was in here somewhere."

She extracts a vintage coin purse fashioned from brown mohair with a clasp at the top. Her practiced thumb snaps the purse open and she upends the contents onto the small table next to her. An old padlock key, three pennies, two bobby pins, a quarter, and some lint fall out. Satisfied that the purse is empty, she places the nickel inside and snaps the bag closed.

"Well, a bargain has been struck," Maggie says in a business-like tone. "So then, let's cut to the chase, shall we? What's the one question that's most important to you? The one answer you simply must have?"

Jenny laughs. "I might be able to narrow it down to the twenty most important, but one? I don't think it's possible."

"There must be one that stands out?" Maggie presses.

Jenny lets out a breath that flutters her lips, making her sound for a moment like an exasperated schoolgirl. "Um . . ." she begins, but the word travels no further.

"Try this," Maggie offers: "Close your eyes and imagine a wall of empty shelves before you. Then, one by one, place your questions upon those shelves. Fill them up and then step back and take a look. See if one question stands out more than the others."

Feeling a bit silly, Jenny closes her eyes and tries to visualize the shelves. She casts her head from side to side, placing imaginary boxes on imaginary shelves. Eventually, the movement stops, and her closed eyes fix on one spot.

"I've got it," she says, her voice betraying a hint of surprise. "What does the lion mean?" she asks as her eyelids flutter open.

A satisfied smile fixes itself on Maggie's lips. "A good question," she says, "but before I can answer, I need to get something from the house, something that may explain it better than I." Without another word, she rises and disappears inside, moving like a woman half her age.

When she returns, she has an 8x10 picture frame in her left hand—turned away so that Jenny can only see the back. In her right hand are two pens and a yellow notepad. "I'm sure you're going to want to take some notes," she says, as she hands the pad and pens over.

Jenny takes them but sets them to her side and begins to dig through her purse. "If you don't mind," she says, "I prefer using a recorder. I don't want to miss anything." From the depths of the bag, she produces a small Sony digital recorder, which she holds out for inspection.

Maggie hesitates. "I already sound older than I feel. I'm not sure that's something I want to preserve and share."

"It's not your voice they'll be listening to," Jenny says, "it's your words. Oral histories are more powerful than anything one could write. They're the thoughts, words, and memories of a person directly from their own mouth. Textbooks have a way of being edited and interpreted, but this," she holds out the recorder, "this is all you."

Silence follows, and Jenny lets it simmer.

Maggie's face is an unflinching mask, yet behind her steady eyes is a machine honed by decades in the business world. Right now, that machine is analyzing the request, testing its logic, and visualizing a dozen possible outcomes. Maggie does little that isn't first calculated.

"You're right, of course," she replies at length. "You have my permission."

Setting the picture frame facedown at her side, Maggie crosses her legs and lays back in the chair. "Did you know my father was in the Second World War?" she asks Jenny.

"No. I knew he was the right age, but my records search came up empty."

"That's because he enlisted under the name Holcomb."

Jenny raises an eyebrow, but before she can ask the obvious question, Maggie continues. "He moved to Bellingham after the war to be near his aunt and uncle, Paul and Doris Atwood, his only remaining relatives. My father was never fond of the name Holcomb, mostly because it came from *his* father—so he changed it shortly after arriving here.

"Now, if you go back and search military records for the name Evan Elmore Holcomb, you'll see that my father was with the 106th Infantry Division—same division as the novelist Kurt Vonnegut." She raises an index finger as if about to make a point. "Vonnegut said that his experience as a POW inspired him to write *Slaughterhouse Five*. Did you know that?" She shrugs. "I never read it.

"The 106th arrived near the German-Belgian border in December 1944, at a place called Schnee Eifel. Turns out they were just in time for one of the biggest disasters of the war. Bad luck, some would call it, but I think when it comes to war, it's more about timing than luck. In any case, their divisional headquarters was in a town called St. Vith, and when a major German offensive began on December 16th, so began the Battle of St. Vith. The problem was that St. Vith was at the heart of a much larger campaign we now call the Battle of the Bulge."

"I've heard of it," Jenny says, "but I'm afraid I don't know much about it. History was never one of my strong points. Why was it called the Battle of the Bulge?"

"Because that's what it was, my dear. The Nazis pushed across the German border into Belgium and France, creating a so-called bulge of occupied territory into those two countries. I don't mind using the word *hemorrhoid* when it comes to Nazis, so I'll equate it to that. The German border developed a sudden case of hemorrhoids filled with Nazis, and they bulged out toward Belgium and France."

"That's one way of describing it that I'm sure to remember," Jenny says with a crooked smile.

"Oh, honey, I'm just getting started," Maggie says, patting Jenny on the knee. Compulsively, she picks up the picture frame and stares at it momentarily before setting it back in its place, still unrevealed, still mysterious.

"The battle raged for days," she continues. "The 106th Infantry Division was comprised of three regiments, two of which were encircled and cut off by the Germans. My father was with the 422nd Regiment. The other one was the 423rd Regiment. Though they regrouped and continued to fight, it was a lost cause. On December 19th, they surrendered, just some of the seventy-five thousand soldiers who were captured during the Battle of the Bulge." She sighs. "Then began a tougher battle."

Maggie grows quiet as she worries her hands in her lap, rubbing at them ceaselessly as if they'd never been clean nor would be. Her eyes take on the vacant stare of one looking back through time and across continents as if she were able to see the snow, feel its sting, and experience the painful pull of hunger in the bellies of the soldiers.

"I don't know how many days or weeks it took, but they were marched across Germany to a place near the eastern border and about thirty miles north of Dresden. Sometimes they were loaded onto boxcars like cattle and transported a short distance before being offloaded again. Mostly they marched. My father talked about the biting cold, the hunger, and about being strafed by allied fighters while they were locked helplessly in the boxcars. In the end, he found himself at Stalag IV-B, the largest German POW camp of the war.

"Now, throughout all this, my father had one friend who'd been with him from the beginning. I use the word *friend*, but in truth, they were more like brothers. His name was Jimmy Boggs, and he arrived for training at Fort Jackson, South Carolina on the same train as my father."

"Jimmy Boggs," Jenny says to herself as if to imprint the name upon her memory.

"Yes, Jimmy Boggs," Maggie echoes wistfully. "I never met the man, but I knew him in my bones. My father said his people were from Delaware. I didn't think anyone was from Delaware, but there you have it. All of them were decent folk, according to my father, all but one. Family lore had it that Jimmy's Aunt Goldie had run a house of ill repute during the Great Depression." Maggie shrugs. "I wouldn't presume to judge her for it. People did what they had to, times being what they were."

"Still," Jenny says with a hint of mischief, "you have to wonder how *that* piece of dirty laundry came up in conversation."

"Oh, I imagine if you spend enough time in a foxhole with someone, those types of things just work their way to the surface."

"I'm sure they do."

"In any case," Maggie continues, "they were in Stalag IV-B from December 1944 until April 1945. That may not seem long in retrospect, but it came at the worst time of the year, and at the end of a war that left Germany stripped of resources. They didn't have enough food for their own people, let alone prisoners. Starvation was a constant companion, and death a daily visitor to the camp.

"In early March, Jimmy came down with a nasty cold or flu. It was bad enough to leave him bedridden, and my father was there at his side through most of it. They played cards and shared stories, and at some point, he sketched a portrait of Jimmy."

Retrieving the picture frame from her side, Maggie gazes upon it for a long moment. "This was my father's most prized possession," she says in a hushed voice. "Jimmy died a week after he drew it, and I think a part of my father died with him. The injustice of it, at least in the eyes of my father, was that the camp was finally liberated just three weeks later." She taps the picture gently with her finger. "The fate of Jimmy Boggs was sealed because he had the misfortune of falling ill three weeks too early."

Slowly, she extends the frame to Jenny, the picture still facing down. "The answer to your question," she says simply.

Taking it, Jenny doesn't immediately turn it over but instead runs her hand reverently along the edge of the frame. Inhaling, she lets the breath out slowly and then flips the picture over. Her reaction is immediate and raw. Her hand trembles slightly as a gasp bursts from her mouth. Her eyes hint at unbidden tears but she composes herself and ushers them away.

The image before her is of a young man, perhaps twenty years old, with a glowing face pushed wide by a contagious smile. The pencil etching is on a piece of plain white paper that had at one point been folded into quarters, the fold marks still plainly evident. Taking up the lower right corner of the paper is a lion's head, perhaps two inches tall, and below that is the signature *E.E. Atwood.*

"He'd been sketching for years," Maggie explains, "but that was the first time he ever used the lion's head. It was also the first time he used the signature E. E. Atwood. You see, he had already decided to take his uncle's name, even then. I think it was the POW camp that set that idea in his head. I imagine you start looking at your life differently when you go through something like that."

Jenny's eyes haven't left the etching. "What does it mean?" she whispers.

Maggie reaches over and rests her hand on Jenny's. "The lion's head is the symbol of the 106th Infantry Division, which was nicknamed The Golden Lion." She lets the words settle a moment before continuing. "When my father began painting in earnest a few years after the war, he included the lion's head on each piece. He did it to remember Jimmy Boggs and all the others who didn't make it home. He never forgot them, not for a single day."

Maggie stares off into the distance, or perhaps into the past.

"He had a single golden lion patch that he'd saved from his uniforms," she continues. "Just the one. I'd sometimes catch him sitting in the chair in his studio, Jimmy's picture in one hand and the patch in the other as if they were two halves of a whole. I don't know if he was grieving or just remembering, and I never disturbed him to find out." She sighs. "War is a great, deep scar, I suppose, and Jimmy Boggs was just another cut my father had to bear."

"What came of the patch?" Jenny asks.

"It's gone—regrettably. I didn't realize it was missing until years after his death."

She takes the picture of Jimmy Boggs into her hands and in a contemplative voice says, "The lion looks out at me from every one of his paintings, and yet what I would do to have the original, the one that inspired it all."

"What about a replacement?" Jenny suggests.

Maggie smiles. "It wouldn't be the same." Rising, she holds up the framed drawing. "I best put Jimmy back before he gets lost too."

Chapter 12

Sunday, August 14

It's precisely 9 A.M. the next morning when Darius coasts into the driveway at 137 Eldridge Avenue. Maggie is on the front porch by the time he shuts the car off, so he joins her, politely refuses a cup of tea, and explains his goals for the day, which, when condensed, is really only one goal: strip the old shingles from the roof.

They chat for a few minutes and then Maggie goes inside while Darius returns to his car and begins unloading. This is no small task because after leaving Maggie's the previous evening, he and Spider paid a visit to cousin Posey and borrowed a portable air compressor, two nail guns, some demo shovels, a chalk line, hammers, pry bars, a roof anchor, two safety harnesses, buckets, a garbage can, and tons of old tarps.

As Darius begins to unpuzzle the clutter from his car, a black Vespa zips down the driveway and sputters to a stop near the garage. Spider dismounts like an outlaw biker after a hard ride. Shedding his helmet and leather jacket, he says, "Sorry I'm late," and hurries over.

Together, they remove the contents of the Honda and stack the various implements in a pile nearby. Within minutes the car stands empty, but the mound of construction equipment and material occupying the driveway is considerable. Neither of them seems to want to make the next move and they find themselves just standing there staring at the house.

"Ready for this?" Spider asks at length.

"Nope."

"Yeah, me neither."

The summer morning hums with industry as the raking sound of shovels dragged over shingles fills the air and the rattle of loose nails stands juxtaposed against the huffing and grunting of lungs feeding muscles. Aside from the murmur of distant traffic, these are the only sounds on the roof.

Twenty minutes into the job, Spider pauses to catch his breath. Leaning on his shovel, he says, "You know what we need up here?"

"More help?"

"No, D. We need some tunes. I'm tired of hearing myself suck breath."

"I could back the car up and turn on the radio?"

"I was thinking about that Wurlitzer in the garage; the cool box with the fat socks. You know what I'm talking about? If we could get it working, we'd have music all day long, and probably stuff we've never heard before."

"I'm sure you're right, Spider, but that thing hasn't spun a record in decades. If it had, Maggie would have it in the house, not sitting in a musty garage. Even if you *did* manage to power it up, it's just as likely to catch fire as play . . . and since when do you know anything about old jukeboxes—in all deference to your geniushood?"

"I looked it up," Spider says briskly. "Last night."

"I don't mean to burst your bubble, but it's probably going to take a lot more than some internet research to get it going."

"I don't know, bro. Based on the serial number, that's a 1946 Wurlitzer model 1015, and from what I read, they're designed to take a beating. I found repair manuals online and a bunch of YouTube videos that walk you through the troubleshooting process. I'm telling you; we can do this."

"That may be," Darius replies slowly, measuring his words, "but in case you haven't noticed, we kind of have a full plate at the moment."

"Yeah, yeah, I know," Spider says resignedly. Then, clenching his fist, he says, "But just imagine." He holds the thought a moment and then, as if releasing it, opens his fist and lets his hand fall to his side. Grasping his shovel, he says, "Just imagine," once again, this time in a low voice that borders on a whisper.

Hefting his shovel, he plunges the blade under the next row of shingles and quickly loses himself in his work. Darius watches him, and because he knows his friend so very well, he also knows that the jukebox issue is far from settled.

Once Spider gets an idea in his head, it's hard to dislodge.

At ten-thirty Maggie emerges from the house and, ignoring the walkway, steps out onto the lawn to avoid any falling debris. She needn't have worried, for the tarps around the house are still unblemished, and if a single nail or the smallest corner of a broken shingle *had* fallen from the roof, there was no evidence of it.

Standing on the grass, she watches them work for a moment, silently impressed by the progress they've already made and the tidiness of the work area. Spider sees her first and gives a low whistle.

"Now *that* is a very pretty dress, Mrs. L," he says. "Where are you off to looking so grand? It's a little early in the day for a hot date."

"It's a secret," Maggie replies with a playful glint in her eyes.

"Ooh! That's even better. I like secrets, and I rarely tell."

"Well, that's very reassuring, Stephen. I'll keep that in mind. Meanwhile, if you get hungry or thirsty, there's iced tea and lemonade in the fridge, and some cookies on a covered plate on the counter."

She shoulders her purse, looking ever so proper. "And help yourselves to anything else in the kitchen, but don't fill up too much. I'll make us some lunch when I get back. Mind you, I'm not much of a cook, but no one heats a can of soup like me."

Darius chuckles. "That would be great."

"I'll swing by and pick up some cold cuts on the way home," Maggie adds. "Nothing goes with soup like a ham and turkey sandwich."

"Now you're talking," Spider says with a big grin on his face.

Maggie smiles in return and then starts toward her car.

"You know," Darius calls down to her, "it may not be the wisest thing to leave two perfect strangers alone in your house while you're out and about. I mean, you don't even know us. What if we rob you blind while you're away?"

Maggie clasps her hands together in front of her and looks up at Darius with the most serious of expressions on her face. "Wise words, I suppose," she muses. "But then, I imagine if you meant to take advantage of an old woman you wouldn't have tried to return a million-dollar car, now would you?"

"She's got you there," Spider mutters.

"Besides," Maggie continues, "Jenny is going to be here in an hour or two." She nods knowingly at Darius. "I imagine that bit of news will keep you from running off."

Pivoting on her heels without waiting for a response, she makes her way to a deep blue Acura TL parked next to the garage, fires up the engine, and zips out of the driveway.

Darius turns to Spider. "What was that supposed to mean?"

"I think she's under the impression that you like Jenny"

"That's ridiculous. Where'd she get that idea?"

"I haven't the faintest idea," Spider replies, though his tone suggests he knows *exactly* where Maggie got that idea and probably agrees with her.

"Sometimes, I can't tell if she's toying with me, or just plain odd," Darius continues.

"Odd," Spider says flatly. "But the good kind of odd," he adds quickly; "like crazy old Uncle Marvin riding a unicycle in his underwear."

"You don't have an Uncle Marvin."

"Yeah, but if I *did*, I'd want him to be crazy—like jumping in the ocean in December crazy, or shaving off half his beard and going to the mall crazy."

"I don't picture Maggie doing anything even close to that," Darius says, "but there's a lot more going on in that head of hers than you or I can imagine. She's a puzzle; I just can't figure out if she's missing any pieces."

"A riddle, wrapped in a mystery, inside an enigma," Spider quotes. When Darius turns and looks at him, he shrugs. "That's what Winston Churchill said about the Soviet Union. I was just thinking that Maggie's a bit like that—you know, all mysterious . . . and stuff . . ."

When Darius continues to stare at him, Spider begins to fidget.

"What? I have a thing for quotes!"

Darius laughs and holds up a hand of surrender. "Sorry, you just surprise me sometimes. For someone who claims he doesn't have a photographic memory, you seem to remember every obscure thing you've ever read. It's freaky." He pauses and gives Spider an up and down look. "You have your own bit of odd-Maggie going on, but I think we both already know that."

"I'll take that as a compliment," Spider replies, lifting his chin.

"Yeah, I know," Darius replies, turning his eyes to the end of the empty driveway.

Chapter 13

Sunday, August 14

Jenny's arrival is hard to miss.

The low rumble of the Camaro ZL1 announces her coming like thunder before the rain, the rich exhaust growing louder with each passing moment. Darius notes with an odd sense of satisfaction that she's heavy on the gas pedal as she turns off Broadway onto Eldridge, only to slow immediately for the turn into Maggie's driveway.

Parking next to Darius's Honda, Jenny revs the engine until the air throbs and then shuts the car down. The silence in the wake of the Camaro is so deep that it's almost disorienting, and Jenny plays it for all it's worth as she steps out in sneakers, old jeans, and a form-fitting t-shirt.

"Morning," she calls up.

Darius is speechless, so Spider says, "Morning," with a bit of drawl tucked in.

"How are things going?"

"Good," Darius replies, finding his voice. "We should have it stripped by the end of the day, which means we'll be able to start laying paper and shingles tomorrow."

"That's the easy part, right?"

"Compared to stripping old shingles it's a piece of cake. We should be able to finish in a couple of days."

"Can I help?" Jenny asks. "I wore my grubbies."

"Those are your grubbies?"

She looks down at her clothes. "Why? What's wrong with them?"

"Nothing," Darius replies quickly.

Jenny still has a concerned look on her face, so Spider thumbs at his friend, saying, "Don't worry about him. Your grubbies are twice as nice as just about everything in his closet." He taps a finger in Darius's direction.

"You know that thing where people say you're a spring or an autumn, or that green is your color? Well, Darius is a sort of calico. His work clothes are so used that his stains have stains."

"They're not stains, they're just spots of primer and paint."

"Yeah, well there's enough of both to paint a Buick."

"Spider"—Darius begins, but then realizes that he's already lost this exchange. Changing tack in mid-sentence, he looks down at Jenny. "How do you feel about picking up nails and shingles?"

"If that's what you need."

"It would be a big help."

Spider opens his mouth and Darius shuts him down with a look.

Maggie returns at 12:20 and after exchanging some pleasantries with Darius, Spider, and Jenny she heads off to make lunch. "You have fifteen minutes," she warns before closing the front door behind her.

Spider, who can always be counted on when food is involved, enthusiastically calls out "Lunch" when the requisite time has passed. He's also the first down the ladder. In the hall bathroom, they take turns cleaning up and then gather around the table on the back patio. Before each of them is a porcelain plate containing a turkey and ham sandwich and a small pile of ordinary, old-fashioned potato chips. Next to each plate is a giant mug filled to the brim with chicken noodle soup.

In the center of the table, of course, is a pitcher of iced tea.

"Stephen, would you pass me a napkin," Maggie says a few minutes into the meal, gesturing toward the diner-style napkin holder off to the side.

"Sure," he replies, handing the entire holder over to her, "but if I'm going to call you Maggie, shouldn't you start calling me Spider?"

"No," Maggie replies cheerfully and without elaboration. Pulling two napkins from the holder, she hands it back, smiles, and then wipes the corner of her mouth gently.

"But nobody calls me Stephen," Spider argues desperately. "Every time you say it, I think you're talking to someone else, and then I'm like 'hey, she's talking to me.' It's a bit confusing."

"*Spider* makes you sound like some sort of criminal," Maggie replies gently.

"No, see, it's totally legit. I *earned* that name."

"You earned that name? Let me guess: You kill people for the mob? No, no, I've got it: You're an international assassin disguised as a college student."

"He's telling the truth," Darius says, shrugging his right shoulder and trying not to laugh.

"Oh, do tell," Maggie says, turning on Darius.

Glancing at the potato chip in his hand, he sets it back on his plate.

"Well, being the highly intelligent idiot that he is, Spider used to make quite a spectacle of himself in middle school. See, he had this Spiderman costume and he'd put it on under his clothes before leaving for school. Then, during lunch, he'd shed his clothes, don his mask, and race through the cafeteria, sometimes running on top of the tables. When the teachers got wise to him, he avoided the cafeteria and started showing up in the hallways, the clinic, the library—even the principal's office.

"They tried to catch him, but he was just too fast. The other kids were no help, and cheered him on, even blocking the way behind him several times to slow the teachers. After the first week, the kids started calling the masked troublemaker 'Spider' and it was a big game among them trying to figure out who it was. I knew, of course, but I didn't say a word to anyone, and Spider managed to keep his mouth shut, so there's no way anyone would have ever figured it out if it wasn't for a bit of bad luck."

"Dumb luck," Spider chimes in.

"Well, it was some kind of luck," Darius concedes. "The teachers knew he was changing his clothes somewhere and figured out that it wasn't in any of the bathrooms or the locker room."

"They posted teachers in the bathrooms for the entire lunch period," Spider says with a snicker. "Remember Mr. Jacobs? He'd be in there leaning against the sink trying to eat his tuna sandwich as boys came and went, and every time a toilet flushed, he winced and covered his sandwich like it was going to get contaminated."

"You're so bad," Jenny says, shaking her head.

To which Spider gives a small bow.

"Two weeks into his little experiment in social unrest," Darius continues, "a teacher's aide sees a kid in a Spiderman costume emerge from behind a storage shed near the playground. The aide goes to investigate and finds a pair of pants and a shirt neatly folded and resting on top of a wood crate.

"Well, this was just a disaster," Darius says. "The aide takes the clothes to the principal's office and they wait for the bell that ends lunch recess to see which kid shows up to class in a Spiderman costume."

Jenny's on the edge of her seat with her hand over her mouth, while Maggie, being Maggie, hosts the smallest of smiles on her face, a dash of mirth in her eyes.

"Now, Spider had an extra pair of pants and a shirt in his locker, just in case, but he was so freaked out after finding his clothes missing that he couldn't remember the combination."

"Yeah," Spider says, "like that dream people have where they're at school in their underwear, or they can't remember their locker combination, only this was real."

"After the final bell rings, Spider knows he's finished," Darius continues, "so he marches into the front office and plants his feet at shoulder width with his hands on his hips." He looks at his friend. "And what did you say?"

"Can I have my pants?" Spider replies with an exaggerated shrug.

Jenny can no longer contain herself, and even Maggie lets out a laugh that comes all the way up from her gut. "Oh, Stephen," she says, with a *tsk-tsk* shake of her head.

"What else was I going to say?" Spider asks, raising his hands.

"Did you get in much trouble?" Jenny asks, still laughing.

"Ehh, they suspended me for two days. No biggie."

Darius is watching Spider, a sober look on his face. "The school was easy on you; not so much with your parents."

Spider just nods, but Jenny catches the undertone of the words.

"Are they strict?" she asks.

"No," Spider replies slowly. "I pretty much did what I wanted. Let's just say that they don't like extra attention, whether it comes from the school system, child protective services, or law enforcement."

"Oh."

"They beat him silly," Darius says. "That's when he finally moved in with me for good."

Spider doesn't say a word but extends a closed fist to his friend, who bumps knuckles with him.

Silence settles around them. Not the uncomfortable silence of new acquaintances, but the quiet that comes with reflection and introspection.

"I guess you did earn your nickname," Maggie replies softly. The mirth in her eyes is gone, replaced by a glistening sheen, the harbinger of tears.

Picking up the pitcher, she says, "Would you like some more tea . . . Spider?"

Stephen Zalewski grins and takes his glass in hand. Holding it out to her, he says, "Thank you," and the words mean so much more than *thank you for the iced tea* or *thank you for calling me Spider*. In that briefest of moments, Stephen is once more the young boy in the Spiderman costume.

He can almost hear the kids cheering.

Chapter 14

Sunday, August 14

The hot afternoon is measured not in minutes and hours but by the number of iced tea refills and short breaks taken in the shade. Darius and Spider continue working the demo shovels, but with Jenny coming behind them pulling stray nails and gathering debris, their job moves along more quickly.

Shortly after three, a touch of bad luck sets them back on their heels. By this time, the front of the roof is completely stripped, and they're a third of the way down the backside.

Several times already, Spider has voiced his concern about the deteriorating condition of the plywood at the north end of the house. The further down from the peak of the roof, the worse it gets, until every footstep causes the crumbling wood to sag and sigh, and they're forced to keep to the rafters for fear of falling through.

"All this wood is sus," Spider grunts in frustration.

"Suspicious?" Darius clarifies.

"Yeah, D, sus to the truss. Can't exactly lay shingles over it if it won't even hold a nail. We've got like three hundred square feet of bad plywood held together by rot and inertia."

"Maggie said the roof was leaking," Darius replies. "I'll bet it was right here."

"Probably means the wood underneath has some savage damage, as well. We need to get this up—all of it—and see what we're dealing with."

As they speak, Jenny scrounges about the roof looking for the pry bars. Finding one of them in the gutter and the other inside one of the five-gallon buckets, she carries them back and hands them to Darius and Spider.

"What are we waiting for?" she asks, just as curious as they are to see what lies beneath.

It's not good.

Pushing his pry bar loosely into a two by six, Spider mutters, "Dry-rot," as he twists the bar counterclockwise and breaks off a large chunk of crumbling wood.

"Can we brace it?" Darius asks.

"Not if you want to do it right. We're going to have to replace this one and any others like it. That means stripping off the plywood up to the peak."

"That's a lot of plywood."

Spider does some quick counting. "Sixteen sheets," he says, "but we were already replacing eleven, so it's only another five. If we don't damage the ones near the peak, we should be able to reuse them, so that'll save Maggie some money."

"*I'm* paying for the plywood."

Spider balks. "That's like three or four hundred dollars, D."

"Million-dollar car," Darius reminds him.

They borrow a truck from Uncle John—a flatbed this time, and make their run to the hardware store, Jenny jostling around on the bench seat between them. Every time they hit a pothole or a rough patch in the road, they bounce up and down on the old springs. Sometimes this bouncing causes Jenny to brush up against Darius, and she lets it happen—perhaps on purpose. Darius, meanwhile, does his best to keep his eyes on the road, despite the warm sensation that explodes and emanates from each wondrous touch.

It takes an hour, two lumber carts, and four tie-down straps before they head back to Maggie's with sixteen new sheets of plywood and twelve reasonably straight two by sixes.

Darius's wallet is four hundred and eighty-seven dollars lighter, but the unexpected expense doesn't seem to trouble him. He seems almost pleased by it, prompting Spider to ask if he's *Opus Dei.*

"*Opus Dei?*" Darius replies. "What are you talking about?"

"Flagellation?" Spider hints.

"You lost me."

"Didn't you see *The DaVinci Code?*"

"Yeah, I did—years ago."

Spider huffs and waves his arms about. "The albino dude who whipped himself. He was a member of *Opus Dei*. They thought pain brought them closer to God or washed away sins or something like that."

"You know that was just a movie, right?"

"A movie based on fact, brother—the Holy Grail is *real*."

"But the movie—is a work—of fiction," Darius replies firmly.

"You're trying to dodge the question."

"Seriously, you're asking if I like to whip myself?"

"Four hundred and eighty-seven dollars," Spider says with a shake of his head. "That's quite a beating, D. Just saying."

Darius doesn't answer right away, but when he does it's with deliberation. "Million—dollar—car," he says, enunciating the words one at a time and hoping he doesn't have to repeat it. He throws in a stern finger-pointing for good measure.

The remainder of the ride is on the quiet side. Spider randomly mouths a parade of silent sentences, but the only words to escape are two mutterings of *Holy Grail* and one *Opus Dei*.

Back at the house, they unload the new lumber and pack it straight up to the roof, using the ladder as an impromptu slide to bring up the plywood. The two-by-sixes are considerably easier. When this is done, Jenny excuses herself and goes inside to spend time with Maggie.

This is a fortuitous parting, for when they're called to dinner an hour later, they find a smorgasbord laid out on the back patio. There's baked salmon, crescent rolls, twice-baked mashed potatoes, oven-cooked broccoli drizzled with olive oil and spices, a pickle-and-olive platter, even a unique macaroni dish that hints at cream of mushroom.

Filling their plates hungrily, they dive into the heavenly meal.

Almost immediately, Spider begins to moan in ecstasy, his eyes rolling with delight at every other bite. When he begins to heap praise on Maggie, she stops him cold.

"I was just a student in this venture," she says, motioning toward Jenny. "The master is sitting across from you."

Jenny's face takes on the reddish hue of freshly cut roses and her eyes dip to her lap.

"This is magnificent," Spider raves, casting his gaze across the table. "Where'd you learn to cook like this?"

She lifts her face, cheeks still flush. "My dad."

"You're kidding?"

"No. He's a chef in Seattle—has been since before I was born."

Spider takes another bite, and his eyes roll back in his head as if he were a shark feasting on fattened seals. He moans, chewing slowly as he savors every morsel. "How do you *teach* this," he cries. "It's a gift. It's genius."

"It's just cooking," Jenny says with a laugh. "Dad always made meals at home, and he loved it when I joined him. He'd talk nonstop, explaining everything, even if he'd explained it a dozen times before. I never stopped him—at least not till I was fifteen and suddenly thought I knew everything."

Spider points to his left with a loaded fork. "Darius knew everything when he was fourteen."

She chuckles. "And you?"

"Oh, I didn't know everything till I was sixteen. Then, when I was twenty-two, I realized I knew all the wrong stuff."

Jenny smiles.

"Now," Spider continues, "I'm learning everything all over again. With luck, I'll be finished by the time my kids know everything. Then I can tell them they're wrong, and they can ignore me."

Maggie slumps back in her chair. "My god, he *is* a genius."

With dinner finished and the promise of dessert in the air, Darius explains to Maggie the extent of the water damage to the roof: the sagging plywood, the crumbling rafters, the black mold. "I'm guessing your leak was in the northwest corner," he finishes.

"It was, indeed. Fortunately, the worst of it didn't come until the end of spring, and by that time I had a regular bucket brigade standing guard on the second floor. Every once in a while, a new drip would appear in a new place, but I kept on top of it. I had to, otherwise . . . disaster." She utters the last word with conviction, as if ruin would fall upon her if such happened, and not just the calamity of wet carpet and dripping walls, but something far worse. Seeing the puzzlement in Darius's eyes, she suddenly cocks her head. "How much was the wood?"

He's caught off guard. "Oh—don't worry about it."

"Nonsense. You must have a receipt. Let's see it."

"It's an electronic receipt," he lies. "I had them send it to my home email account."

"Surely you remember the cost. Or at least some close approximation?"

Darius shrugs.

"Come now, Mr. Alexander," Maggie replies patiently. "I've earned every penny, dime, and dollar I've ever spent, and if you think that's going to change now, you're gravely mistaken. Now, tell me how much the wood cost or . . . or there'll be no dessert for you—either of you." Her eyes drift slowly to Spider and she holds him in her gaze.

"How'd I get dragged"—Spider begins to protest but Darius cuts him off.

"Million . . . dollar . . . car," he says firmly, using the same argument he used earlier. But Maggie's having none of it. With the speed of a tortoise and the firmness of a granite boulder, she holds her index finger erect and wags it from side to side.

"Million-dollar car," Darius repeats, the words now rammed together and desperate.

Turning her gaze, Maggie says, "Spider, how much did the wood cost?"

"Four hundred and eighty-seven dollars, ma'am."

Darius shoots him a pinched scowl and Spider shrugs helplessly.

"Thank you," Maggie replies serenely.

Turning back to Darius, she's all business. "I'll give you a check before you leave tonight, and I expect it to be deposited tomorrow. I'll know if you don't."

Darius has no choice. "Yes, ma'am."

Before they leave for the night, Maggie has one more thing up her sleeve. Leading them back into the house, she opens the door to the master bedroom—her room—and ushers them inside. She doesn't say anything, just stands in the middle of the room and waits for them to find it.

Jenny's the first.

Tucked away in an alcove in the southeast corner of the room is an easel, upon which rests a thirty- by forty-inch canvas. Gathering around it, they take in the colors, the shapes, the seemingly random symmetry.

"Cadillac?" Darius guesses.

"Indeed," Maggie replies softly, "a 1939 series 61, to be precise."

The burgundy two-door convertible occupies the lower-left corner of the painting. It's parked on a beach, the driver's door flung wide, yet there's no one in sight. The only hint of humanity lies in the footsteps leading first to the water, and then along the water's edge, disappearing to the right. Oddly, Darius notes that only the driver's footsteps trail away from the car, but as he walks along the beach he's joined by others, fellow pilgrims to an unknown destination. It could be a bonfire. It could be a beach party. The picture gives no clue, just an empty car and empty footprints.

"It's beautiful," Jenny manages.

"My father called it *End of the Road*—at least in the beginning. Over time, he found a better name."

All eyes are on her, expectant.

"*Stepping Out*," she finally says, her lips pinched together as if to keep something inside. "He called it *Stepping Out*". She gives a shake of her head as if to clear the cobwebs. "Something happened to my father in the war, I think, something that shook his soul. He once confessed that he lost his religion in Stalag IV-B, and at the same time gained his faith. I never really understood what that meant until much later. Maybe that's how it is: Life has to beat you up a little before you understand the deep things, the important things.

"This painting," she continues, "it's more than just a car on the beach, it was my father's life philosophy. He always said that cars are useless without a driver, just as the body is pointless without a soul. Car and driver; body and soul—the metaphors write themselves." Her voice grows quiet. "When a car breaks, you get out and walk. It's the same with the body."

She sighs, and Jenny wraps her in her arms.

"It was that simple to him," Maggie says quietly. "Life and death and the great beyond. It was simple and beautiful, and I loved him for it."

Long they stand, and not a word spoken.

Chapter 15

Monday, August 15

Sometimes the biggest part of any project is simply breaking inertia—finding someplace to start and just, well, starting. For Darius and Spider, the starting place is clear. Having already loosened one sheet of plywood during the previous day's exploratory surgery, it only makes sense to begin there.

Attacking the partially lifted sheet of plywood with leverage and brute force, they pry it from the last of its nails and fold it over onto the roof, downside up. Spider insists on pulling all the nails as they go, so while he works on those buried in the rafters, Darius hammers, pulls, and pries at those still attached to the plywood.

Jenny's absence makes the work less tolerable.

As the blistering afternoon trundles on, the repair work falls into a boring cycle of repetition: pop the sheet, pull the nails . . . pop the sheet, pull the nails . . . pop the sheet, pull the nails. Apart from the occasional iced tea and bathroom break, the only deviation from this homely routine is when Spider visits the Wurlitzer in the garage for the umpteenth time and decides that he *must* hear the old jukebox play—most assuredly and without reservation.

He pushes buttons to no effect, polishes the glass to a sparkle using the bottom of his sweaty shirt, and even figures out how to open the large front panel so he can inspect the mechanical guts inside.

"I can fix this," he says with confidence.

"Don't mess with it," Darius cautions as Spider begins moving parts and spinning rods.

"I'm not going to break it."

"You know you have a habit of saying that *right* before you break something."

Spider shoots him a scowl.

When he continues to fiddle with the guts of the machine, Darius insists. "Come on, Spider, leave it alone before you do something, we both regret."

"It can't be that complicated."

"Yeah, well, I get the feeling that it's somehow special to Maggie, so complicated or not, leave it be." He grabs Spider by the upper arm and pulls him back, while at the same time closing the panel.

"Hold on!" Spider says an instant later, his voice slightly off.

"You've had your look"—Darius begins, but then Spider cuts him off sharply.

"Serious, D!"

It's not a tone he's used to, so he pauses and watches as Spider reaches for the bottom inside lip of the panel. And then he sees it, dusty and overturned, as if it had lain in the same place since the jukebox rolled out of the factory.

Picking it up, Spider blows the dust from the back and then the front. Holding it flat in his palm, he asks, "Is this what I think it is?"

Darius just stares.

"We have to show it to Maggie," Spider insists a moment later.

"She'll know you were messing around with her jukebox," Darius warns. When Spider doesn't respond, he says, "Fine, but put everything back the way you found it first."

They call out for Maggie in one voice as they come through the front door and she answers from above, from somewhere on the second floor. A moment later she appears at the top of the stairs looking a bit windswept.

They start toward her, but she waves them back down, saying, "I need some tea." Gliding down the steps, she drifts past them and turns into the hall.

Darius pauses on the staircase, glancing toward the landing above with its wide hall and high ceiling. Little else is visible from the base of the stairs, but Darius is curious, nonetheless. The previous afternoon, after discovering the roof rot, he'd asked Maggie if he and Spider could check for water damage upstairs, but she'd have none of it, assuring him all was well.

He persisted, but so did she.

Now, as she bustles past, attempting to draw them down the hall and into the kitchen, her words and actions seem almost furtive, as if some great secret lay hidden above.

Or is it his imagination?

He's not so sure.

They wait for Maggie to take a seat at the kitchen table, a sweating glass of iced tea at her side, and then Spider stretches out his hand and lays the dusty find on the tablecloth before her.

She gasps and tears puddle in her eyes, unbidden.

"I thought it lost," she says after a long moment, the words rough in her throat as if drawn from the earth itself. With a trembling hand, she reaches out and gently lifts the patch from the table. "Where in the world did you find it?"

Darius looks at Spider.

"So . . . so, I was walking by the jukebox in the garage," Spider explains, "and I found it on the front panel, just lying there."

Maggie's brow presses together. "Well, I've moved that jukebox a dozen times over the years. I don't see how I could have missed it if it was just *lying* there."

"Well, it was kind of on the *inside* of the panel," Spider confesses sheepishly. Maggie looks up at him and he swallows hard. "I'm a bit of a snoop. Sorry."

Twisting her mouth, Maggie points at the jewelry in Spider's earlobes, the primal instruments meant to stretch holes in his skin. "I suspected as much when I saw those in your ears," she says, only half-kidding, and then turns her attention back to the patch. "Where exactly was it?"

"The bottom of the door; it was lying upside down and looked like it had been there a while."

"All this time." The words come softly, slowly, measured.

"Yes, ma'am," Spider replies.

"It's the golden lion, isn't it?" Darius asks.

Maggie sets the embroidered patch on the table before her and lays her hands on either side, palms down, with thumbs outstretched, as if framing the patch for a camera shot.

"It's the only thing my father kept of his Army gear," she explains.

"Uniforms, hats, duffle bag, even his combat boots, all of it he either threw in the trash or gave away." She looks down. "All but this."

Silence lingers in the room.

Clearing his throat, Spider asks, "How'd it end up inside the jukebox?"

"Good question." Maggie shrugs and shakes her head. "There are a thousand mysterious and beautiful ways it could have landed where you found it." She lifts her chin. "He may have placed it there himself for all I know. My father had an ancient sense of honor"—her eyes find Darius—"even when others mocked him for it. He never forgot those he fought beside. Guys like Jimmy Boggs."

She sighs deeply, once more staring at the patch.

"While some joined veterans' groups or marched in parades, my father painted lions into his pictures and visited the hometowns of those who had been closest to him in the war. Sometimes he'd visit friends who made it home, other times it would be next of kin. Though he never drank, he would walk into a bar every April 13th, the day they were liberated from Stalag IV-B, and he'd order a single shot of whiskey for Jimmy Boggs and a beer for the rest of the boys. He'd just leave them on the counter next to each other with a note of explanation. Sometimes those drinks would sit there for days in front of an empty barstool, even when it was standing room only."

She looks at Spider. "In answer to your question, I imagine my father placed it on the glass of the Wurlitzer, perhaps—in his mind—so that Jimmy and the others could share in each song. That was how he did things. I always thought he had a mystical air about him. You could feel it when he walked into a room, an excited shiver of anticipation, as if an invisible wave washed through the crowd, announcing his arrival. Such was the momentum of his presence."

"They loved him," Darius whispers.

Maggie smiles and pats his arm. "He was easy to love."

Jenny ducks out of work early and flagrantly violates the speed limit for most of the ninety miles between Seattle and Bellingham, arriving just before six. She waves up at the roof and shoots Darius a smile but continues toward the front porch. As the door closes behind her, Darius and Spider disagree over the smiles intended recipient.

"She was looking at me," Spider insists.

Darius scoffs. "In your dreams. She was looking at me."

"Dude, she was looking *past* you." He reaches out and pinches Darius's bicep between his thumb and index finger. "It's not the meat in your arm, you know. It's the heat in your charm."

"Well, that rules you out on both counts, Romeo."

"Oh, charm is my middle name."

This back-and-forth fades to a steady drone as the sound of hammers and prybars once again fills the sky. Joining this chorus, perhaps even intruding upon it, a slow-moving train rattles and groans at the base of the bluff, the worn tracks protesting the passing weight.

Jenny hears none of this.

A question has been tugging at her all day, a persistent itch begging to be scratched. It's not one of Maggie's nickel questions, a dive into the history of E. E. Atwood. Rather, it's a request. One that Jenny fears Maggie will shy away from. She's been mulling it over for the better part of the day, practicing the asking in her head, trying different variants, looking for something that might work. With each iteration, her anxiety grows, yet she feels that if she doesn't get the question out soon, she'll simply burst in half.

Despite this, it was hard walking past Darius with nothing but a wave.

The roof is sweltering and smelly and the last place she'd want to be on an August afternoon—except now it's the *only* place she wants to be. Mostly she wants to be on the roof because Darius Alexander is on the roof. It's a curious yet simple truth that she admitted to herself around eleven o'clock that morning as she squirmed in her chair and wondered why she couldn't concentrate.

There's something about him.

She hates the admission, hates that someone could affect her so.

It feels weak, compulsive, even adolescent, but there's something quietly honorable about the Air Force vet, the college student, the craftsman. He's quite apart from the men she'd met in her time at the Seattle Art Museum, or in the art world as a whole. Guys like Stu Yates, huffing about as if they were the bull of the herd. Or Lenny Johnson, a nice enough guy she dated a few times in college, but who'd never worked a hard day in his life—though you wouldn't know it from listening to him.

No. Darius Alexander was decidedly different, a curiosity, a distraction.

Maggie's at the kitchen table sorting mail when Jenny enters from the hall. She lays a gentle hand on the woman's shoulder in greeting and then inhales deeply. A wonderful smell fills the room and the timer on the stove shows ten minutes on its countdown.

"Cooking without me?" she teases.

"Lasagna," Maggie says flatly. "If they're brave enough to eat it, I'm brave enough to cook it." She pats the seat next to her and Jenny obliges, pulling out the chair and hooking her purse over the back before sitting.

Slicing an envelope seam with her letter opener, Maggie extracts a credit card offer and stacks it neatly in the shred pile to her left. She pauses before picking up the next piece of junk mail. "They lied; you know?"

"Who lied?"

"The internet people."

"How so?"

"They said that email would kill the post office, that it would get rid of junk mail. They called it snail mail like it was somehow an atrocity that you had to wait three days for a bill to arrive." She shakes her head. "All it did was give me twice as much junk mail—half in my mailbox, half in my inbox." Looking at Jenny with all seriousness, she adds, "What kind of jackass advertises Viagra to an old woman?"

"Maybe they think you have a boyfriend," Jenny suggests with a mischievous grin.

Maggie snorts and then laughs.

They make small talk until the timer on the oven shows five minutes remaining, and then Jenny can no longer contain herself.

"I have something I need to ask," she says.

Her hesitance and tone cause Maggie to pause in mid-rip. Looking up and seeing the turmoil in Jenny's eyes, she sets the letter opener on the table and clasps her hands together before her. "And you're worried I won't like the question?"

"A little."

She nods. "In my experience, when asking a tough question, the best thing to do is just ask. The outcome is likely to be the same, but you save a lot of fuss along the way. Besides, who's to say that your version of tough is the same as mine? It may well be the easiest thing I've answered all week."

"Or it may be an insurmountable obstacle."

"Or that," Maggie agrees. She leans forward and takes Jenny's hand in her own, giving it a gentle squeeze. "Ask your question, dear."

There's a moment of hesitation . . . a deep intake of breath . . . an exhaled string of words: "I was hoping you'd let me bring a photographer up. I want to get some professional photos of *A Girl and Her Car* and *Stepping Out* . . . and the Jimmy Boggs etching."

She pauses for a heartbeat and then presses the point. "These paintings are unknown to the art world. More importantly, they were important to Atwood—I mean your father."

She wants to keep going, extolling the value of such photos if the paintings were to be lost or destroyed, or the excitement the images would stir up once word of the new Atwoods spread to the art community, but she doesn't. Instead, she falls silent and lets the words fall as they may. The look on Maggie's face is a mixed-bag, impossible to decipher, so she does the only thing she can: she waits.

Standing, Maggie moves to the fridge and tops off her iced tea. She raises the pitcher to Jenny, who shakes her head.

Instead of returning to her seat, Maggie leans with her back against the counter, the chilled glass held in both hands at chest height. "I'm a private person," she eventually says, the words subdued. "Pictures mean articles, and articles mean people flocking to my door"—she whirls her hand in a flourish—"to see the new Atwoods."

Jenny shakes her head. "It doesn't—" she begins, but Maggie stops her.

"I'm not saying no, dear, I'm just . . . concerned."

Jenny rises and walks the few steps to the counter. Turning, she puts her back against it, side by side with Maggie, resting her hands together at her waist. "I wouldn't include your name or the location of the paintings in any articles, and the photographer is one we use often, someone we trust. He knows how to keep his mouth shut. At some point, though, people will learn about you."

"Preferably after I'm dead," Maggie remarks.

"That's not funny," Jenny chides her. "I just met you; I expect you to be around for a long time, a few decades at the least."

Maggie shakes her head slowly. "I make no promises," she says with a soft smile. "Of all the things mankind can predict, the future is the least reliable. The only thing we know with absolute certainty is that tomorrow will become yesterday . . . and yesterdays have a way of accumulating."

"That may be so, but I expect a lot of yesterdays before you go."

"I'll do my best."

Maggie puts her arm around the young woman, and they stand in silence for a long moment, as if they'd known each other for years rather than days. Eventually, she brings them back to the sticky question of confidentiality.

"I can keep your identity hidden for a while," Jenny says, "but I don't know for how long. Even if the paintings don't out you, people will demand answers when the Bumblebee Jacket is finished, when its true origin is learned." She straightens and turns to face Maggie. "I'd never say anything, nor would Spider or Darius, but there are others who already know. My boss, for one; and who knows who she's told—could be half the museum by now."

"It's inevitable, then: word will get out?"

"I'm afraid so."

Maggie turns the thought in her head and eventually shrugs. "In truth, I expected it when I sold the car, though I thought it would take a bit longer to come around." She smirks. "Darius and Spider are a lot smarter than I took them for."

She shifts uncomfortably against the counter. "Buy me some time, if you can," she tells Jenny. "I'm dealing with some . . . well, some personal issues, I suppose, and don't relish the thought of a bunch of art people poking around asking questions." She pats Jenny's arm. "Present company excluded."

"Thank you."

"As for your photographer, how about next Saturday?"

"Perfect," Jenny replies—and then gives Maggie a tremendous hug.

Chapter 16

Much as he wants to work on Maggie's roof straight through until it's finished, there are obligations on Darius's plate, things he can't ignore. The most pressing of which is to Uncle John and the crew at Road Runner Restoration. After taking Monday off to strip plywood and shore up rafters, he returned to the shop Tuesday morning and spent the next four days working twelve-hour shifts to get caught up.

As the weekend arrives, it brings with it a sense of accomplishment, a sense that somehow, against the odds, he'd balanced his wants against his needs. He even managed to put in some hours on the Bumblebee Jacket. Not a bad week, all-in-all.

It's with a certain measure of delight that he finds himself once more on Maggie's roof. A fresh weekend is stretched out before him, and the sun is warm on his face. The forecast calls for nothing but blue skies—perfect roofing weather.

Pulling the tarp from the exposed rafters, he and Spider set themselves to the task of finishing the structural work on the roof. By ten o'clock the first of the new plywood goes down, the sheets falling in place like pieces of a puzzle, speeding the work along.

They hear Jenny long before they see her.

Walking to the peak of the roof, they watch as she pulls her gray grumbling beast into the driveway and coasts to a stop next to Darius's silver Honda. She shuts the car down and they hear *Shake it Off* pouring from the speakers.

"Taylor Swift," Spider grumbles.

"What's wrong with Taylor Swift," Darius replies.

"Nothing, I just figured her for a Def Leppard or Nirvana type of girl."

When the song ends the door opens and Jenny peels herself from the driver's seat, her legs leading the way. Once out, she reaches back in to retrieve something from the driver's seat.

Spider lets out a long sigh and just stares at her. He turns to say something to Darius, but then his face sours and he begins to hurriedly brush filth from his friend's shoulders and hair, like a valet preparing his employer for an important meeting.

Darius pushes his hand away. "What are you doing?"

"You're a mess, man."

Looking down, Darius sees that it's true.

Every ounce of water and tea they'd consumed that morning had somehow found its way to his shirt, his pants, even his socks—all of it pushed from his body in the form of cooling perspiration as his body struggled to ventilate against the heat rising from the roof. Spider begins to briskly iron the wrinkles from Darius's shirt using the flat of his hand, but Darius again pushes the hand away.

"Dude!" he exclaims in a crisp tone. "We're close, but not *that* close."

"Just trying to help, bro."

By this time, Jenny's almost to the sidewalk.

"Making any progress?" she calls up.

"We're almost finished putting the plywood down," Spider replies as he greets her with a smile. Unbidden, as if having a mind of its own, his hand reaches out and brushes another crumb of rotted wood from Darius's shoulder. "Another twenty minutes or so and we'll be rolling out the tar paper."

"Does that mean you'll finish this weekend?"

"Yep. Maggie should have a new roof sometime tomorrow."

"Oh." She sounds disappointed.

"What about you?" Spider continues. "Aren't you supposed to be taking pictures today?"

"The photographer just texted. He'll be here in an hour." Hefting two plastic bags into the air, she says, "I brought lunch if you're hungry?"

"What is it?"

"Chinese."

"Mandarin or Cantonese?"

Jenny hesitates a heartbeat and simply replies, "Yes." Then, without waiting for a follow-on question, she makes her way to the front door and greets Maggie with a hug.

After they hear the front door close, Darius turns to Spider and thumps him in the chest. "Mandarin or Cantonese? Really? Since when would you know the difference?"

"Sure, pick on the smart guy," Spider shoots back. "There *is* a difference, you know, a very distinct difference. If someone said, 'hey, I got us some European for lunch,' and I asked if he meant Italian or French, you'd think it was a logical question, but ask if it's Cantonese or Mandarin and I'm suddenly splitting hairs."

"Sorry," Darius says unapologetically. "I didn't know you were an expert on China."

"I'm not, nor am I an expert on Europe, but everyone knows that pizza comes from Italy and French fries come from France."

Darius stares at him.

"I'm kidding," Spider says with a roll of his eyes. "And *I'm* the one who's socially awkward?" he mutters, stepping past Darius and descending the ladder two rungs at a time.

The lunchtime conversation is boisterous and fun, one of those gatherings that you know must end but still pray that it doesn't. As always, Spider proves to be the king of stories, both as the teller and the subject, and Darius takes delight in describing his friend's first car—a 1978 AMC Pacer—and the circumstances that led it to its final resting place at the bottom of Wiser Lake.

"Cars are supposed to sit there until you push the gas pedal," Spider argues in his defense.

"That may be the case with your mother's thirty-year-old Lincoln," Darius replies, "but a Pacer weighs a lot less. Besides, since when do you get out of a car while it's still in gear?"

"I only stepped out for a minute."

The laughter is contagious, and the stories carry on until the food is well-settled in their stomachs and the unfinished work on the roof beckons. Before they push away from the table, though, Darius has a question of his own.

"Go ahead," Maggie coaxes, "speak your mind; I'm not easily offended."

"No, I suppose not," Darius replies with a smile, "but this might be a little too personal. I don't want to open old wounds."

"Nonsense," Maggie says, waving the concern away. "But I need my nickel."

"Nickel?"

It takes a minute to explain the nickel-for-your-thoughts bargain previously struck between her and Jenny, and Darius accepts the odd arrangement without question. When he finds his pockets empty of change, Jenny offers up a nickel, but Maggie refuses. "It's Darius's question, it has to be his nickel."

It takes another four minutes for Darius to go to his car, search the glove box, the door pockets, and the change holder before finally resorting to pulling the bottom cushion up from the backseat, where he finds a small horde of nickels, pennies, and dimes, plus a pair of quarters.

They're sticky—as car change often is—so he stops in the bathroom on the way back to the kitchen and scrubs them down with soap and hot water.

"One nickel," he says as he places the pristine coin in Maggie's palm.

"Thank you, my boy," she says with a sly smile, and quickly drops the token into her brown coin purse. "Now, what was your question?"

"Okay," Darius says with a nod, "here it is, and no offense if it's too personal. When you were talking about moving out here with your dad, it just made me wonder about your mom. You *do* have one—unless certain universal laws have been upended. I'm just wondering what part she had in all this?"

"None," Maggie says immediately and with conviction.

As the word settles and fades, her left hand begins to toy absently with her fork.

"My mother was never a part of my life, short of giving birth to me—universal laws and all that." She casts a soft smile at Darius and then continues. "Sad to say, I've never missed her, except in the silly way that one misses something they've never had. I wish her no ill, and on a few occasions, I've even prayed for her, but how could I miss her?"

"What was her name?" Jenny asks as she digs through her purse for a pen.

"Ruth Portman," Maggie replies. "She and my father met in August 1943, while he was stationed at Fort Jackson, South Carolina." She sets the fork aside and draws herself up in the chair.

"You have to understand the times," she continues. "The whole world was on fire. All of Europe had fallen to the fascists and communists. No one knew how it was going to end, only that it would take blood and sacrifice." Her voice rises and falls as she recalls events she never witnessed.

"The country had enemies on all sides, and my father said it was as if the future nested upon a single egg. No one knew what would hatch from such an egg, or when, and most didn't want to know, because it was just as likely to be something bad as good."

Maggie suddenly turns away and coughs into her cupped hand. "Excuse me," she says, and then coughs again, and again, each cough growing stronger and more persistent.

Spider picks up her glass of iced tea and holds it out to her. She coughs again and then takes the tea and drinks down a third of the glass before stopping for air. It seems to quell the itch. "Summer cold," she says by way of apology. "I get them every year, but this one just won't go away. Every time I think I've beat it; it comes back around." Taking another drink, she sets the glass down. "Where were we?"

"The world was on fire," Spider says.

"Yes, of course. I was going to say that those who experience such times tend to live life in the moment; day by day, hour by hour, nothing set and everything uncertain. No one was much surprised when my father married Ruth on the first Saturday in September, just weeks after they met. I was born nine months later, on June 1, 1944—five days before D-Day, as it turned out.

"By that time, my father had transferred with his division to Tennessee while my mother stayed behind in South Carolina. He never said why she stayed behind, but everyone knew the Army was getting ready to invade Europe. I think—at the time—he told himself that she just couldn't bear the thought of something happening to him, and so kept her distance to avoid the pain."

Maggie's lips pinch together, and then she continues. "We tell ourselves stuff like that, don't we? The most convincing lies, after all, are those we tell ourselves." The words hang ominously before them, harbingers of approaching truth. "We're always so eager to believe what we want to believe. As if the truth were malleable and facts subjective." She shakes her head in disappointment. "Especially, it seems, when it comes to love and politics."

She takes another drink from her glass and contemplates the swirling tea within.

"I was a year old when he saw me for the first time. By then the war was over and the boy who left for Europe was a hardened veteran, a different man. He once told me that that moment, when I looked up at him, he didn't know that a person's heart could swell with such joy and break with sorrow all at the same time. I think I was ten years old when he said that, and I didn't really understand it at the time, but I do now."

"Why sorrow?" Jenny asks.

Maggie's eyes drop to the floor. She'd convinced herself long ago that the question of her mother didn't bother her, that the mistakes of others were just that, mistakes, and not worth dwelling upon. It worked—most of the time. Every once in a while, a touch of melancholy would overcome her and sweep her off to places rarely visited.

"It was the beginning of October 1945 when my father returned from Europe. As was the experience of most returning soldiers, his ship docked in New York, where it was greeted by throngs of people. My mother was not among them. The next day, his unit was deactivated, and he made his way back to Columbia, South Carolina by bus and train, back to the small one-bedroom house he and Ruth so briefly called home."

Maggie pauses, picturing her father.

"He said he stood on the doorstep for the longest time, unsure whether he should knock or just walk in. Eventually, he chose to knock, which was a fortunate thing because my mother no longer lived there. Imagine his surprise."

Finding the fork again, she takes to rubbing slow circles into the tablecloth with the handle, as if doodling but without result. When she continues a moment later, her voice has a stiff edge to it.

"Ruth's mother—my grandmother—was an unpleasant woman named Bethany, who was partial to whiskey and cigars and didn't care who knew. Father met her once shortly after he and Ruth were married. It was an uncomfortable meeting, by all accounts, but father remembered where she lived, and so set off in search of his wife and daughter."

"Whiskey and cigars," Jenny says. "That must have been scandalous."

"A minor offense among many," Maggie says. "Bethany was loud and vulgar and in desperate need of a bra, a wardrobe deficiency that she never hesitated to highlight."

"Oh."

Maggie chuckles. "Yes, the whiskey and cigars were easily overlooked through the fog of inappropriateness that was my grandmother." She shakes her head. "Father would never tell me what words were exchanged between him and Bethany during their second meeting, but I know they weren't pleasant. The result, however, was an arranged meeting the next day on the sidewalk in front of the old JB White department store in downtown Columbia.

"Ruth showed up with me in her arms and a bag of cloth diapers slung over her shoulder. Few words were exchanged between them, and those that were, my father never shared. She simply placed me in his arms, handed over the bag, and then turned and left, as if she'd just dropped off the weekly laundry."

Maggie sighs, not from regret but from the finality and truth of her words. "Just that quick she was gone from our lives . . . and good riddance. I only ever saw her twice after that, years later.

"The next day, father and I caught a train west, and a week later we were here in Bellingham. For my father's part, he closed out an old chapter in his life and began a new one, a better one. Father helped his Uncle Paul on the farm for about a year, but he'd realized after the first month that farming wasn't for him. In the fall of 1946, he got work at a local body shop, and so began a love affair with the American auto that lasted the rest of his life. In 1949, he painted his first canvas, and, ever mindful of Jimmy Boggs, he hid a small lion in the picture. So, it began."

Maggie leans back, glancing from face to face. "And that's that," she says.

Chapter 17

At exactly one o'clock, a noise carries up to Darius and Spider on the roof. Their heads pop up over the ridge of the roof, their bodies stretching up for a look. To anyone watching from the lawn, they might have looked like a pair of curious meerkats checking out the new arrival.

A tan Hyundai putters into the driveway and pauses near the road, as if unsure of its destination. After some undiscernible movement behind the wheel, perhaps to doublecheck the address, the driver motors slowly forward and parks where the walkway meets the driveway.

"Photographer," Darius mutters.

Spider just nods. "Probably one of those rugged-looking National Geographic types." He eyes his friend. "Bet he's sweet on Jenny, too, always offering up his services, that sort of thing. Just watch; he's going to be tall and tan with wavy brown hair down to his shoulders . . . probably has an accent. Like Fabio, but on the other side of the camera."

Darius gives his friend a dubious look. "I guess it's a good thing Jenny's not superficial."

"I guess so," Spider parrots. "Okay, what's your prediction?"

Darius glances at the Hyundai a moment. "Female in her forties, professionally dressed, hair pulled back into a ponytail, with an extensive portfolio and some magazine covers to her credit."

"Laundry or dishes?"

"Laundry," Darius replies. "For a week." They shake to seal the bet.

The shadow of the driver flits about through the tinted glass, giving no clue to his or her identity. A second later, the engine goes quiet, and their anticipation spikes. The figure behind the wheel shuffles around inside, unbuckling and then messing with some unseen collection of items on the passenger seat—equipment, papers, lunch, it's anyone's guess.

A moment later, the door opens and out steps . . . well . . .

"Danny frickin' DeVito," Spider mutters.

"That's a draw, right? That's gotta be a draw."

The short, huffing man extracts himself from the car in a series of exhausting steps as if the driver's seat had a good grip on him and refused to let go; a carnivorous seat with a fat bug in its clutches.

The resemblance to the actor is passing at best.

Mostly it's his hair . . . and maybe his body type. He wrestles a large waterproof camera case from the trunk, followed by two tripods, and a cardboard box of lights and reflectors from the trunk, all of which he sets on the ground at the side of the car. Wiping the heat from his brow, he slams the trunk lid and picks up the camera case, leaving the other items where they rest, at least for the moment. As the photographer turns toward the house and makes for the walkway, Darius and Spider quickly duck their heads down below the ridge.

Meerkats are shy that way.

The front doorbell rings and they listen as Jenny greets the older man, calling him Kermit.

"Like Kermit the Frog?"

"I'll get the rest of your gear," they hear Jenny say. As the sound of her footsteps pauses near the car, Darius risks a glance and sees Jenny picking up the cardboard box. As she turns, she spots his head poking over the roofline, and, for a moment, they make eye contact. What she does next Darius can't say: He drops like a gravity-infused apple.

He swears he hears her laugh, though.

"She's laughing at you," Spider points out, confirming the suspicion.

"Shut up."

Forty-five minutes later, Danny DeVito says his good-byes and rolls out of the driveway, photos of *A Girl and Her Car*, *Stepping Out*, and *Jimmy Boggs* captured on his memory card and already backed up to the cloud.

Another ten minutes pass and they hear light footsteps making their way up the ladder. Jenny's head emerges above the gutter line and Darius hurries over to help her onto the roof. "Thought you might want an extra set of hands," she offers.

"If you're finished with Kermit," Darius replies.

Spider lets out a "*Ribbit!*" and then chuckles at himself.

"You realize it was a name *before* the Muppets, right?"

"I'm sure it was."

Jenny crosses her arm and studies Spider. "Did you know that Teddy Roosevelt's second-oldest son was named Kermit? There's a long list of distinguished Kermits, including Kermit Kenny."

"Who?"

"Kermit Kenny," she replies and then tips her head symbolically toward the empty driveway. "The photographer."

"You mean Danny DeVito?"

Reaching out and covering his friend's mouth before he can do more damage, Darius says, "Looks like you missed the fun part. We just put down the last piece of plywood."

Jenny continues to smirk at Spider for a moment, the way an older sister might a pesky younger brother. At last, she unfolds her arms. "Plywood? That's the fun part?"

"Oh, yeah!" Spider says, peeling the hand from his mouth. "Who doesn't want to wrestle with a four-by-eight sheet of plywood on a hot, slick roof? That's some next-level *American Gladiator* awesome, that's all."

"I'd hate to see what your idea of a bad time is, Spider."

He just grins.

"So, what's next?"

"Paper," Darius answers quickly before Spider can assify himself further.

"Is that something I can help with?"

Darius cocks his head to the side. "If you don't mind getting . . . sweaty."

"Oh, I don't mind," Jenny says, her eyes teasing.

Early evening finds them on the back patio with supper settling in their bellies and the sun easing down the western slope of the endless sky. Content, they settle back into their chairs and enjoy the peace and beauty of Maggie's lush backyard. For Darius, Spider, and Jenny, exhausted from their labors, the setting is tranquil, almost sleep-inducing. Though their muscles ache and their bones are weary, they shake it off like so much ash from a spent fire.

The resilience of youth, Maggie calls it.

By degrees, the brightness of day slips into the quiet pale of evening, bringing with it a soft melancholy that wraps around them like a woolen blanket, both sad and welcome at the same time. Maggie turns on the outdoor speakers and *Nights in White Satin* begins to play, only adding to the mood. For a moment, they all close their eyes and just listen, enchanted by the song, perhaps Maggie most of all.

"That was one of my father's favorites," she says as the music fades. "It affects me in different ways every time I hear it. It's songs and smells and powerful emotions that stir us to remembering I suppose. Not just remembering the bad things, but the good things, the quirky things, the things that touch our heart and stay with us."

"Tell us more about him," Jenny gently presses.

Maggie looks to the sun, now a shimmering sliver flattened upon the horizon. "I have few bad memories of my him," she says at length. "Almost none. I suppose I'm fortunate in that. I was a baby when he was off fighting the war, and still too young to understand the struggles upon his return . . . but I remember the night he died. Lord help me, I remember."

Jenny exhales sharply, as if gut-punched, instinctively reaching for Maggie as a shadow passes over the old woman's face.

Silence entombs them.

It's as if the world holds its breath . . . waiting . . .

Darius and Spider exchange a glance and then Darius finds himself asking the impossible, the inappropriate: "Will you tell us?"

When Maggie doesn't immediately respond, he reaches into his pocket—as if he has no control over his hand— and finds a nickel. Placing it on the table between them, he slides it across slowly with his index finger, the nickel hissing and scraping as it goes. Already his face is bent in sadness, his eyes unable to find Maggie's, or perhaps just unwilling, yet the nickel advances.

When it finally rests before her, Maggie doesn't pick it up, nor does she place it in her small brown coin purse. She doesn't even look up at the giver, who waits for her at the edge of his seat. Her eyes appear to take in the coin, but, in truth, her thoughts are far away, her inner eye looking on images long since relegated to the deepest burrows of her memory. She left such visions behind out of necessity, out of survival. To view them once again is painful, but she persists.

"Have you ever had a premonition?" she asks at last.

Darius glances at Jenny and then Spider. "A premonition?"

Maggie nods slowly. "I'm not talking about a dream or a thought that you later match up to some random event. I'm talking about the type of premonition that you *know* with absolute certainty has meaning. You know it the instant you have it, as sure as water is wet."

None of them speak.

"Some would say it's nonsense, I know," she says briskly, "but my father had a few of them in his time. The last was in the summer of 1973, just months before he died."

"He told you that?" Jenny asks.

"He did, and then laughed about it like it was all a big joke." She looks down, rubbing the curled knuckles of her right hand as if they held a stain that just wouldn't come out. "It was a dream, you see. He was standing among the wheat in a great field, the grain blowing lightly in the wind and stretching on as far as one could see. As he watched, a wall of flames rushed toward him, engulfed him, and then moved on. When it had passed, he was gone. All that remained was the endless field of grain with not a shaft scorched or a kernel dislodged, as if completely untouched by the cataclysm."

She shakes her head and dabs at her eye. "I don't know if he took it as a premonition of his death or a harbinger of other things, but I know it affected him. I'm ashamed to say that I ignored it, thinking it another nightmare carried forward from the war, like so many before."

Her knuckles are now red, and she pulls her hands apart and sits on them to control the obsessive rubbing. "How did he die?" she says softly, repeating the question. At first, it seems she might provide an answer, but then she does the unexpected.

Picking up the nickel, she holds it out between her thumb and finger, as if placing it on display. "I'll give you your answer, Mr. Alexander," she says, "but not until tomorrow morning."

"Tomorrow?" Jenny says, unable to hide her disappointment.

"Yes, there's something I want you to see, something you need to see. It'll be worth the wait, I assure you, and wholly appropriate to the story."

Darius gives Jenny a patient nod and then glances at Spider before turning back to the old woman and the nickel she holds so reverently.

"Okay," he says.

They sit on the patio enjoying one another's company until dusk slips by and the night settles upon them. Jenny eventually yawns, quickly covering her mouth with her hand. "I'd better be going," she says. "I've got a long drive ahead of me."

"You're welcome to stay here tonight," Maggie offers, but Jenny doesn't want to impose.

Standing, Darius says, "We'd better get going, too. Spider needs his beauty rest, otherwise, he gets clumsy. The last thing we need is for him to fall off the roof tomorrow."

"You truly think you'll be done tomorrow?" Maggie asks, now looking at Spider.

"We will," he replies, a touch of sadness in the words.

"Hmm. Pity."

Passing through the house to the front door, Maggie lingers in the hall a moment and writes something on a slip of paper. Folding it twice, she places it in Darius's palm. Before he can say anything, she tips her head at the note and says, "Tomorrow morning at nine." Her tone is firm and leaves no room for questions.

She says goodnight to them at the porch, watching as their shadows mingle with the night. And as they near their vehicles she sighs ever so softly and steps back inside, closing the door behind her.

Darius doesn't look at the note, he just keeps it curled up in his fist until they reach the driveway. When Maggie disappears into the house, Jenny and Spider practically pounce. Spider already has his pocket flashlight in hand and temporarily blinds Darius as he waves it around. Unfolding the flaps of paper, Darius reads the sparse words in a voice just loud enough for the others to hear.

As he finishes, a chill runs down his spine . . . though the night is warm.

Chapter 18

Sunday, August 21

Greenacres Cemetery is a pristine garden.

The grounds are flat and well-tended with all the grave markers set flush against the carpet of grass. Without the usual turbulence of raised headstones to break the illusion, the place has the look of a park or a vast lawn. In the northeast corner is an oasis of trees where pathways and footbridges move this way and that, sitting benches abound, and a waterfall adds a charming woodland feel. It's in this tranquil corner where cremated remains are marked and remembered.

Evan Atwood's gravesite is as humble as the man himself: a simple marker and a rectangle of green earth under a great oak tree. To the right of his burial site rests his aunt and uncle, and to the left is an unfilled plot.

"He was just fifty-two-years old," Maggie begins after they'd gathered around. "Hard to believe I've outlived him by two decades." She sighs and falls silent for a long moment, just staring at the marker. At length, she speaks again, though what she asks seems most peculiar considering their surroundings. "Have any of you seen *American Graffiti?*"

The silence that follows lasts only a moment before Spider, who can always be counted on in such situations, asks, "What's it about?"

"Seriously, Spider," Darius exclaims, "you're a cultural basket case. You've never heard of *American Graffiti?*"

"I've *heard* of it," Spider corrects, "I've just never *seen* it."

"Me either," Jenny says quickly, ducking behind the words.

Maggie nods her understanding. "I didn't expect so," she says. "It was just a hope. The movie was well before your time and seems long forgotten, more's the shame. Still, I hope you'll consider watching it at some point. My father loved it so. Now that you're restoring the Bumblebee Jacket, I think it would help you understand what she once meant."

She's about to say something else but stops herself.

Closing her eyes, she stands in the shade of the oak, quietly measuring her breaths by counts of four as she reigns in her emotions. They wait for her but a moment, yet in those precious seconds the sounds, smells, and sensations around them become strong. Far above, the sun and blue sky warm the morning air, baking the aromas of summer from the earth. The call of songbirds carries over the grounds and they hear the low rumble of a lawnmower starting up on the other side of the cemetery.

Everything is suddenly more real; every sensation has a sharp edge.

When Maggie opens her eyes it's with a sigh. "*American Graffiti* came out in the movie theaters in August of 1973," she says in a faraway voice, "and my father, who wasn't exactly the movie-going sort, saw it on opening day."

"I'm not much of the movie-going sort, either" Spider chimes in.

"Yes, but it was different in 1973, my dear," Maggie replies. "Our entertainment options were much more limited. There was no internet, or DVDs, or home computers, and there were only two channels on television. Sometimes you could pick up a Canadian station out of Vancouver, depending on how fancy your antenna was, but even under the best of conditions, the picture was fuzzy and transient. So, my father wasn't a movie-going person at a time when almost everyone went to the movies, and often.

"Something about American Graffiti struck a chord with him—and I don't think it was just the cars. He saw it a second time the very next weekend, and the weekend after that I was supposed to go with him, but I ended up going out with friends instead." She begins to rub her fingers, massaging a pain deeper than bone. "He ended up taking one of his lady friends instead."

Seeing the expression of Jenny's face, she quickly adds, "Oh, yes, he had several lady friends. Strictly plutonic, he'd tell me, but they seemed terribly smitten with him for something so innocent. He was always a gentleman, of course, so that may account for some of it. Still, he never let a woman get close after my mother. I suppose some wounds never really heal."

She falls silent again and begins searching through her purse. Finding what she's after, she extracts it and places it in Jenny's hand. "My father's favorite truck," Maggie explains as Jenny holds the faded picture out so that Darius and Spider can get a look.

"It's the truck he died in."

The words seem to slap Jenny. She fumbles and then drops the photo.

Scrambling to pick it up, she tries to hand it back, but Maggie pushes it away. "I thought you'd want that for your research," she explains. "I don't have a scanner, but I imagine the museum does. You can give it back once you've had time to copy it. I'm in no hurry."

Jenny just nods, cradling the picture in both hands now.

"Looks like a mid-50s Chevy," Darius says reverently, peering over Jenny's shoulder.

"Indeed, a 1956 Chevy 3100, to be precise. It was chopped and lowered, of course, and though the picture no longer does it justice, the paint was candy apple red." She smiles. "I remember it had a lacquer finish that was so thick it looked as if you could reach right down into it and pull out a dollop of red paint on the tip of your finger. It was gorgeous."

She sighs. "It's gone now, the truck, my father, as if they died together, which I suppose they did. He'd just dropped off his lady friend, Alice, after seeing *American Graffiti* for the third time. Alice lived on Smith Road, which is outside the city a short stretch, and he was coming back to town on the Guide Meridian." She suddenly turns to Jenny. "Darius and Spider are no doubt familiar with the local roads, having grown up here, but I wonder about you, dear?"

Jenny shakes her head. "If I'm going somewhere, I just plug the address into my GPS and follow directions. Most of the time I barely look at the names of the roads."

"Then you don't know the Guide Meridian?"

"I don't. I may have driven on it when I was up here a few years ago doing research, but I really couldn't tell you."

Maggie seems satisfied with this.

"In that case, some explanation is warranted, for it's a road with many names and a long history. Originally it was called the Guide Meridian, named so because it followed an *actual* guide meridian, a longitude line, between Bellingham and Lynden.

"To the locals, it's just *the Guide*, and to the state, it's route 539. Once you get within the Bellingham city limits, the name changes to Meridian Street, I suppose because cities have their own sense of conformity. You wouldn't know it to look at the Guide today, but it began as a plank road."

"A plank road?" Jenny says.

"Yes, made of ten-inch-thick timbers—planks—laid side by side. It was built in the 1890s if I'm remembering my history correctly, the first road to connect Bellingham and Lynden."

"A road made of wood?" Spider says skeptically. "That doesn't make much sense; wouldn't you have to rebuild it every few years as the timbers rotted?"

"We didn't always have pristine asphalt and plentiful quantities of crushed gravel just lying about, now did we, Stephen?" she says reproachfully. He winces at the use of his given name and she quickly amends it. "I mean Spider."

Her eyes find his, conveying an unspoken apology, and then she continues. "Plank roads were fairly common in those days. Of course, they're not suitable for modern cars, but they worked quite well for horse-drawn carriages, and even the early Model T, or Tin Lizzie, as they called it."

"Imagine *driving* on it," Darius says.

"Indeed; a jarring experience. The Guide of 1973 was positively modern by comparison. Still, when night settled and the moon was hidden, parts of it were truly dark and primal. The spot where the accident"—she lets out an involuntary *hmmph* and swallows the sudden rush of emotion that swells in her throat. After a pause, and in a steadier voice, she continues. "The spot where the accident happened was just such a place. Without moon or stars, it was dark as pitch; trees looming over each side. It's all gone now, of course. A Walmart is sitting there now, but I still remember that black patch of night." She lingers silently over the words.

"It was a drunk driver . . . right?" Jenny ventures.

Maggie just nods. "Some damn fool in a station wagon. Things were different in 1973. People didn't wear seatbelts and driving drunk wasn't an overly serious offense, at least until you killed someone." She begins to worry her fingers again.

"His name was Roderick Hamilton Parker, an overly elegant name for a man whose only contribution to humanity was a small mountain of empty liquor bottles. He survived the accident, of course; barely a scratch on him. I've cursed his name too many times to ever forget it. I've consigned him to hell almost as often, and I've even forgiven him on a few occasions.

"He died long ago, of course, as happens to drunks. If the alcohol doesn't destroy their body, their intoxicated actions surely do. In his case, he tripped and fell headfirst into a fifty-five-gallon drum of rainwater. A sober man would have been able to extricate himself, but Roderick was not such a person." She sighs as if to say *oh well*, and then adds, "They found him the next morning with his bare backside pointed at the sky."

"Bare?" Jenny's fingers are perched on her upper lip.

"He kicked his pants off trying to get out, must have been quite the struggle. And if he owned a pair of underwear, he certainly wasn't wearing them that day, or so I was told."

"You said you forgave him," Darius says. "Why?"

"It wasn't for his sake—though I did have moments when I pitied the fool. No. Forgiveness is about healing. I forgave him so that *I* could move on; because if I didn't forgive him, I'd be stuck in a state of self-pity, despair, and, ultimately, anger for the rest of my life. I didn't want to live like that, even though I'd lost so much."

She hesitates a moment. "When someone close to you dies suddenly and unexpectedly, you begin to live life at the edge of your seat, waiting for the next shoe to drop. These days I suppose they'd call it PTSD."

Her eyes drift to the marker at her feet.

"The state trooper who investigated the accident told me the only skid marks he found were from my father. Roderick had managed to drift into the southbound lane, and by the time my father realized he was coming head-on, he had nowhere to go.

"I sometimes imagine there must have been a moment of hesitation on his part, a moment before he jerked the wheel toward the ditch and the certain destruction that waited. Perhaps if he loved that truck less, he might have reacted more quickly. As it was, the wagon clipped the truck bed and sent it spinning out of control at sixty miles an hour. It landed on its roof. There was a fire." She stifles a cry and Jenny puts an arm around her, pulling her tight.

"I knew how bad the accident was when they towed it to the shop the next day," she continues, her voice distant. "It was a burned-out hulk; I wouldn't have even recognized it if they hadn't told me. As for my father, I never saw him again—closed casket. One day he was there, then *poof*, gone. All that remained to prove he ever existed were his paintings."

"And you," Jenny adds.

"Yes—*me*."

"That's a *good* thing," Jenny says quickly and forcefully, sensing the disdain in Maggie's words.

"I suppose,' the old woman replies, her words wrapped in a cloak of sadness, as if haunted. "I sometimes wonder, though, if the meaning of life isn't simply that some must trudge on after others have fallen." She turns her face to the sky and in a weary voice says, "I've been trudging so long."

They stand silently for a long while under the great oak.

Time, it seems, is a good substitute for consoling words.

Chapter 19

Sunday, August 21

The cemetery is a momentary distraction.

By ten o'clock they're back on the roof—Jenny included—rolling out tar paper and nailing shingles. Their mood is somber when they begin, but the warm weather soon lifts them from their melancholy.

Around ten-thirty, Maggie emerges from the house dressed in a long lavender skirt with a matching jacket. Her hair is impeccable, and what little makeup she wears is flawless, giving the impression of a sophisticated woman on important business. For a moment, Darius is sure he catches a whiff of perfume in the light breeze.

Spider lets out a low whistle.

"What, another hot date?" he teases. "All dressed up and looking elegant." He glances at Darius and thoughtfully wags his finger. "Didn't she bail on us last Sunday, too? And right about this time? Hmm, curious."

"Nothing gets by you, does it, Spider?" Maggie replies mischievously, looking up from the walkway. "I suppose I should confess; spill the beans about my torrid affair. I would, you know, but I take such divine pleasure in your speculation."

Spider grins, forcing Maggie to do the same.

"House is open; help yourselves," she calls out over her shoulder as she saunters down the walkway toward her car. Before she reaches the driveway, she throws them an airy wave, as if she were Princess Grace saying goodbye to a crowd of well-wishers.

They watch her until she pulls onto Eldridge Drive, and then turn back to their work. Spider is just bending for a shingle when his mouth suddenly drops open with realization. He smacks Darius with the back of his hand. "Church!" When Darius just stares at him, he says it again, "Church, church, church!"

"Please, Spider," his friend replies with forced patience, "I can't take the slang; not today."

"No, D—*church!*" Spider says emphatically, "the real kind of church, with angels, and vampires, and creepy crypts. That's where Maggie's going all dappered out. It's Sunday morning and she's got her churchy clothes on. It's gotta be church, right?"

"Okay, first off, there are no vampires at church . . . or creepy crypts"—he pauses, stumbling with the futility of it, and then simply nods at Spider, saying, "Church."

They take a break at eleven, descending the ladder and fetching tall glasses of iced tea from the fridge before slipping into the cool shade of the back porch. They make small talk and share their plans for the coming week. It's Spider who asks the first awkward question.

"Kind of sad this morning, huh?"

"The gravesite?" Jenny asks.

"Yeah, I'm not much for cemeteries." He shivers involuntarily. "One of the pluses of coming from a crappy family is you don't have to go to as many weddings and funerals. It was kind of hard watching Maggie, though. It's been forty-some years and you can still see how it affects her."

"It's her father, what do you expect?"

"Yeah, I know. But if it was my father"—he looks at Darius and clarifies—"my *biological* father, I don't think it would affect me one bit. Is that bad?"

"No," Darius says firmly. "There's a hundred-and-eighty-degree difference between your father and Maggie's. She misses him because he's *worth* missing. He was a good man from everything she's said. Your dad . . ." He shakes his head and leaves the words hanging.

"I know," Spider says quietly. Jenny places a hand on his shoulder and he instinctively stiffens, but then relaxes as she gently rubs his back in a consoling manner.

"Maggie has her secrets," Darius continues, "but her father isn't one of them, at least not to us, not anymore."

"What secrets?" Jenny says, suddenly curious.

Darius and Spider exchange a glance.

"Please!" she huffs. "Going to church isn't a secret."

"No, it's not that," Darius says. "It's just some little things . . ."

"Like . . .?"

He shrugs. "Has she ever taken you upstairs?"

"Well . . . no, but that doesn't mean anything. She likes her privacy; we all know that."

"Right, but when Spider and I wanted to check for water damage, she wouldn't allow it; made excuses that didn't make sense. It's not the only time she steered us away."

Jenny thinks. "I offered to help her carry some stuff upstairs last week. She told me not to worry myself, that she could handle it, and then made three trips when she and I could have done it in one. Because she's so fiercely independent I just assumed it was Maggie being Maggie." Jenny's suddenly skeptical again. "What could she possibly have upstairs that she doesn't want us to see?"

"A body," Spider says in a sinister voice.

"Shut up!" Jenny laughs, practically pushing him out of his chair.

"It's just a little odd," Darius continues.

"We could go take a peek," Spider offers.

Both Jenny and Darius look horrified.

"No!" Jenny says firmly. "We can't just go snooping about because of overactive imaginations. It would be a complete betrayal of trust. This is Maggie we're talking about."

"I'll do it," Spider says. "She already knows I'm a snoop."

When Jenny looks at him in confusion, Darius leans in and says, "The jukebox."

She nods and then looks Spider directly in the eye. "No."

"But"—

"No!"

It tickles Darius that Jenny can put Spider so easily in his place; Spider, who peed on their electric fence three times before learning his lesson and ate raw rhubarb because he was told not to.

"That's not the only thing," Darius says, hoping to deflect Spider's attention away from the second floor. "Maggie has other secrets. What about the picture in the family room?"

"The one in the silver frame?" Jenny asks.

"That's the one."

"What about it?" The words are framed as a question, but Jenny's tone and the look on her face suggest that she's already given the picture considerable thought. Whatever conclusion she's drawn she keeps to herself, waiting instead to hear what thoughts have been bouncing around inside Darius's head, ideas which may, perhaps, validate her own.

"The guy's a second lieutenant, but not from World War II, so it's not her father"—

"Who was just a private," Jenny interrupts.

"Meaning it has to be someone else close to her. The uniform is more recent, too, so it's not one of E.E. Atwood's wartime buddies."

"You're thinking husband?"

"Maybe," Darius says with a shrug. "She got the last name Lipscomb somehow, and when I asked her about the picture last week, she just brushed the question away."

"She did the same with me," Jenny says. "Twice."

The speculation continues for another ten minutes but there are no magical insights into the secret world of Margaret Lipscomb, no great reveal that unmasks her past and present. As they talk, the identity of the unknown soldier begins to take on new significance, even replacing speculation about the second floor and its unseen realm. Without realizing it, they convince themselves that the soldier, and the soldier alone, holds the key to every secret Maggie keeps.

They couldn't be more mistaken.

As they talk and sip their tea on the back patio, there's absolutely nothing stopping them from rising and walking to the end of the hall where the stairs rise incrementally to this great unknown. If they were so inclined, and their honor allowed it, nothing is stopping them from taking those stairs to the broad hallway above, with its dark oak flooring running the length of the house from north to south. At first glance, it would look to them more like a foyer than a hall. There are no doors on the rooms to the left and the right, and the hallway spills into them unhindered, revealing by steps and paces what Maggie has kept secret these long years.

It's a secret worthy of the nomenclature.

Sometimes that's the way it is with secrets: they're just up a stair and through a door.

Chapter 20

Sunday, August 21

When Maggie returns at 12:10 P.M. she has no idea what she's walking into.

As she steps from her car, her churchy clothes still looking Sunday-pressed, all work on the roof pauses. It's as if a great steam whistle has suddenly blown, calling for a fifteen-minute break or a shift change.

Darius, Jenny, and Spider gather at the lowest edge of the roof, near the ladder. As soon as she's close, all three of them pelt the poor woman with good-natured questions, as if she were discovered visiting a brothel rather than a church.

Yes, Maggie tells Darius, she was at church.

No, she tells Jenny, she doesn't have a boyfriend at the church.

Finally, in all seriousness, she tells Spider, *only during leap years*, when he asks if they dance naked in the forest during the summer solstice.

"Cool," he says.

After Darius explains how they discovered her mysterious destination, she turns her gaze toward Spider and says, "Church? Really?" Her eyes shimmer with mirth. "On a Sunday morning, no less? How did you ever come to such an astonishing conclusion, Stephen?"

Spider grimaces at the use of his given name, but his discontent lasts barely a heartbeat before he grins broadly and gives Maggie an *aw-shucks* wave of his hand.

When Darius and Jenny begin to cut into Spider, Maggie swiftly points out that neither of them figured it out. Before they have a chance to formulate a clever response, she announces, "Lunch in ten minutes."

Winking at Spider, she makes for the front door.

Maggie may claim to be a poor cook, but when it comes to the diligent use of spices, she's a master. Her chicken noodle soup is out of the can, as would be expected, and begins as the 'heart-healthy' low sodium variety. For some reason, few people think to add spices to canned soup. They just accept what pours out and call it good, even when it isn't.

Preferring a little more flavor than your standard low sodium canned soup offers, Maggie adds several shakes of turmeric, ginger, black pepper, and garlic to the broth, transforming the bland and uninspiring into a gourmet soup with extra bite.

"Turmeric has tremendous anti-inflammatory properties," she says as she ladles the broth into four bowls. "The pepper helps it metabolize properly." Next, she extolls the virtues of ginger and garlic as she places the bowls on the table beside four plates loaded up with tuna fish sandwiches and chips.

Taking their seats, they pounce on the food with ravenous hunger, the type of appetite brought on by hard work in the outdoors. The first few minutes are quiet, save for the clanking of spoons and the crunch of chips, but silence never lasts, especially among the young.

"So . . . you believe that stuff?" Darius says to Maggie halfway through the meal.

"What *stuff* would that be?"

"You know—God, life after death, heaven, hell."

"I do."

"Hmm," Darius muses, perhaps more intensely than intended.

"*Hmm*-what, Mr. Alexander?" Maggie retorts.

Darius shakes his head, vigorously at first, hoping to drive away the question, but when this doesn't work, he takes a different tack. "It's just— to be perfectly honest—you don't strike me as the . . . you know . . . religious type; hallelujah and all that."

"For Pete's sake, Darius, you make it sound as if I have the bubonic plague or something." Her eyebrows arch fiercely as if they were birds preparing to take flight. "If you must know, I'm not so much a *religious* person as I am a person of faith. There is a difference."

"Okay, you might have to explain that to me."

"Perhaps I will."

Spider grins and shakes his head at Maggie.

"What?"

"Nothing," he replies quickly, throwing his hands up in defense. "It's just I was hoping for something a little more tantalizing than church; maybe a boyfriend half your age or an addiction to slot machines."

"Perhaps AA meetings?" she suggests.

"Exactly!"

"Well, my dear boy, I'm sorry I can't *regale* you with tales of my exploits as an aging cougar. If it's any consolation, my church does have a rock band." Her voice drops to a conspiratorial whisper. "With drums *and* electric guitars." Wicked glee dances in her eyes as she adds, "It's scandalous; we'll all burn in hell for sure."

Spider grins. "See, that's better. Next thing I know you'll be getting a tattoo."

"Got one," Maggie shoots back.

Darius, Spider, and Jenny all stop and stare.

"Where?" Jenny asks.

Maggie revels in the breathless and palpable anticipation of the twentysomethings as they perch on the edges of their seats. She turns her head slowly, deliberately, her eyes taking in each of them individually. And then she smiles like the devil himself and takes a big bite of her sandwich.

Wicked.

Spider throws a hand up in protest. "You claimed it, girl! You gotta show it!"

She doesn't, and no amount of pestering through the remainder of lunch convinces her otherwise. It seems the more they plead and cry foul, the more she enjoys it. She's practically beaming as she begins to clear the dishes from the table. Eventually, they give up and start shuffling back to the hot roof and the stacks of shingles still waiting to be placed.

As the front door closes behind them, Spider shakes his head and grins. "That's one crazy old lady," he says.

"Yeah," Darius replies, slipping on his gloves. "I like her, too."

Snap. Snap. Snap.

The steady beat of the nail gun fills the afternoon as one row of shingles overlaps the one below, climbing slowly to the inevitable peak of the roof. It's a summit that seems at times as insurmountable as Mt. Everest, but they take it in parts and their accomplishments are soon visible at every turn.

August in the Pacific Northwest can be both glorious and brutal.

Today it's both.

A steady supply of semi-cool water is all that stands between them and heatstroke, so when they find their thermoses empty less than an hour after lunch, Darius volunteers to fill them while Spider and Jenny find some temporary shade.

As the front door closes behind him, Darius hears the loud thump of something heavy landing on the hardwood floor upstairs. Pausing at the base of the stairs, he listens for a moment. "Maggie?" he calls out, his left foot resting on the first step.

There's a delay, and then a voice replies, "Down in a moment."

"Do you need help with something?" He rises and places his right foot on the second step.

"No, no. I'll just be a minute."

"Are you sure? It's no trouble."

"I was coming down for some tea anyway," Maggie replies, and a moment later she's at the top of the stairs. "Just tidying up a bit," she explains, looking slightly ruffled. Breezing down the stairs, she doesn't wait for Darius, but skirts around him and hustles off to the kitchen. "Bring those thermoses," she calls over her shoulder.

Darius remains a moment on the stairs, his eyes fixed on the emptiness above, trying to discern something, anything, from the visible patch of wall and ceiling on the second floor, but there's nothing to see.

"Coming," he says in a barely audible voice.

Maggie insists on whipping up a batch of fresh lemonade. "It'll quench your thirst better than water, and it's not a diuretic like tea," she explains, taking the thermoses from Darius and setting them on the kitchen counter. "Won't do my roof much good if you all come down with heatstroke," she adds.

"That's touching," Darius replies.

Maggie shrugs.

Opening the freezer, she sifts through the contents and finds a tube of frozen concentrated pink lemonade. She sets it on the counter and reaches back in for two trays of ice cubes.

"Give me three minutes," she tells Darius as she pries off the lid to the lemonade container.

Darius excuses himself and wanders down the hallway to the bathroom, leaving the door ajar as he splashes water on his face and washes away the salty residue of sweat. The cool water feels good on his cheeks and forehead, and when he finishes, he lets it run over his wrists for a long moment, cooling the blood as it passes. It's a trick he'd learned as a teenager while bucking hay bales for Mac Johnston, whose farm was just down the road from his parents' place.

Farmers know how to keep cool.

Maggie is still puttering around in the kitchen, so Darius wanders into the family room and begins absently scanning the various trinkets and knickknacks on the shelves, the sketches, the paintings, the remnants of life. At length, he finds himself staring purposefully at the small silver picture frame with the vintage image of—*who*? Perhaps the soldier was just an old friend or classmate, maybe a cousin.

But Darius knows better.

Unlike the second floor he's seen every corner, nook, and wall of the downstairs, and in the entire space, there is just this one photograph on display. No pictures of Maggie. No pictures of her father. No pictures of youthful adventures, graduations, weddings, or births, just a single photo of a solitary soldier with a proud but playful smile upon his face.

Darius picks up the silver frame and holds it in both hands. The man is handsome—a second lieutenant, judging by the bars on his collar. He's so absorbed by the image and by speculation as to the soldier's identity that he doesn't notice the quiet that comes over the kitchen, the cessation of the steady *tink-tink-tink* of the stirring spoon against the side of the glass pitcher. Nor does he hear the chug of liquid filling thermoses, or the quiet steps of an old woman walking toward the family room.

When Darius looks up, Maggie is watching him, the three thermoses pressed together between her hands. Her eyes fall to the picture frame, linger momentarily, and then rise back up to meet Darius's steady gaze. She holds out the thermoses to him without a word, but he makes no move to take them. Instead, he turns the picture toward her and lets her stare at it a moment.

A full minute passes in utter silence as they stare each other down.

Most people don't truly appreciate the length of a minute until they count it off by seconds. An ocean of thought is capable during such a span, the mind churning and calculating and imagining infinite possibilities. One might say that a minute is an epoch unto itself: eternity in a small package.

"Looks like we have ourselves a standoff," Maggie finally says. She sets the thermoses on the coffee table and then places her hands on her hips. "I don't suppose I can convince you to hand that over?"

"I'm not holding it hostage," Darius replies innocently. He wobbles the frame back and forth in one hand. "He's your husband, isn't he? Lieutenant Lipscomb, I'm guessing." When Maggie doesn't answer, he extends the frame to her, slowly, holding it with just a thumb and two fingers.

She takes it without meeting his gaze and cradles it in her upturned palms, holding it the way one might an open book, or perhaps a bible, for her touch is reverent. Darius gives her a moment and then sticks his hand in his pocket. He looks for a moment as if he means to turn and go, but then his hand comes out of the pocket and he places a single nickel on the coffee table. With an extended index finger, he pushes it toward her slowly.

She finally meets his gaze, and the look on her face is filled with such conflict that he wishes in an instant that he could take it all back, put the nickel in his pocket, replace the frame to its rightful place, and slink out of the house.

"Lieutenant is just a title, a job description," she finally says in a quiet voice. "That's not who Jerry was." She sets the frame down on the coffee table and turns it slightly so that it's exactly as Darius found it. "You might want to have Spider and Jenny come down off the roof. I only want to tell this story once."

"Maggie . . . I . . ."

She grasps his forearm firmly and then releases, patting it gently. "It's fine. You deserve to know. I think the three of you have earned that much."

Fetching Jenny and Spider from the roof is a simple enough task but takes a good ten minutes to fully accomplish because none of them would *dare* sit on Maggie's antique furniture without first cleaning up in the hall bathroom. Spider is in and out in a minute; Jenny takes considerably longer and smells of Red Door perfume when she takes her seat in the family room.

"His name was Gerald Anthony Lipscomb," Maggie begins, "and yes, he was my husband. He was a year ahead of me at Bellingham High School when we started dating during my junior year—though, of course, we'd known each other considerably longer. He lassoed my foot when I was in second grade. I landed on the concrete sidewalk on my hands and knees, and my books flew out in front of me like bad milk tossed to the swine. I could tell from the shocked look on his face that it was unintentional, and he hurried over and helped me to my feet and then gathered up my books.

"Still, I had a rip in my skirt and a nasty gash on my right knee that wanted to bleed forever, so I didn't mind so much that he got two swats from the principal's paddle. I was standing outside the office when they administered the punishment, and though I heard the board land forcefully both times, I never heard Jerry cry out. Then he thanked the principal—if you can believe that—and I scurried away down the hall before he came out and saw me."

"Harsh," Spider says. "They wouldn't *think* of paddling a kid these days."

"Yes," Maggie says dryly, "and that's worked so well." She takes a drink of her lemonade and wipes the perspiration from the glass with her index finger before continuing. "We continued to date while Jerry was away at college, difficult as that was, and when he graduated in 1965 with a degree in mechanical engineering we quickly married—against the wishes of his parents, mind you . . . which explains the *quickly* part."

Jenny presses her eyebrows into a frown. "They didn't like you?"

"They loathed me with a capital *L* . . . or I suppose it's more accurate to say they loathed my pedigree. I was the daughter of a lowly body man after all, and they were, shall we say, well-to-do. Jerry's mother had visions of him marrying into good stock, someone who was well-connected and would help him rise through the ranks of either business or politics. She wasn't particularly picky as to which, as long as it bestowed power and prestige."

"But she grew to like you?" Jenny says, her tone hopeful.

Maggie snorts like a body man's daughter: "Not even close."

Rising, she crosses the family room to a small bookshelf against the opposite wall. Kneeling, she thumbs through the collection and then pulls a stapled paperback from the bottom shelf. Returning, she presents the book without comment.

"*The Successful Man's Wife*," Jenny reads.

"My Christmas present from Jerry's mother the year we were married," Maggie says. "I guess she figured if she couldn't have the daughter-in-law she wanted, she'd have to make do with the one she had. Lemonade from lemons, that sort of thing."

Jenny flips through the book and starts reading off chapter headings. The one titled HE'S THE MAN particularly inflames her, and she hands the book back in disgust. "Why'd you keep it?"

"Just a reminder," Maggie replies. "There are some things you don't want to forget." She returns the book to its place on the shelf and then takes a seat. "Besides, it didn't matter. Jerry joined the Army in 1966 and I didn't see his parents much after that, or Jerry, for that matter. He was sent to Engineer Officer Candidate School at Fort Belvoir, Virginia, and then commissioned as a second lieutenant with the US Army Corps of Engineers."

She grows quiet, her eyes now on the picture frame, though she can't see the image of Second Lieutenant Lipscomb from where she sits.

"Everyone was being shipped to Vietnam in those days," she continues, "and though I expected it, I was inconsolable when his orders finally came." Her face turns dark, brooding. "He was stationed at Camp Frenzell-Jones, just northeast of Saigon. During the early morning hours of January 31, 1968, the Vietcong launched a major offensive across the region, a little episode we call the Tet Offensive."

Picking up the silver-framed picture from the coffee table, Maggie turns it over and twists the four clips holding the cardboard backing in place. Setting it aside, she extracts an aged piece of paper from underneath. Unfolding it carefully, she lays it on the table before them. No one reaches for it. No one moves. When Maggie pushes back in her chair, the room remains silent.

It's Darius who eventually leans forward and picks up the Western Union telegram. He reads it through to the end in silence, and then a second time aloud.

"The Secretary of the Army has asked me to express his deep regret that your husband, Second Lieutenant Gerald Lipscomb, died in Vietnam on January 31, 1968, from wounds received during a mortar attack. Please accept my deepest sympathy. This confirms personal notification made by a representative of the Secretary of the Army." His voice trails off, and he drops the paper back onto the coffee table as if bitten.

It lays there for a long moment, and then Maggie leans forward, folds the paper twice along its original seams, and secures it back in the frame.

"I never remarried," she says at length. "And though we had time and opportunity, we never had children. Jerry didn't want to miss out by not being here, so we decided to wait until he returned." Her voice breaks. "I've regretted that decision ever since."

Jenny reaches over and takes her hand.

Maggie gives her a grateful smile and places her other hand over top. "I kept his name because it was all I had left." She casts her eyes about the family room and down the hall. "In time I bought this house, the house Jerry grew up in."

She smiles softly at their surprise.

"His parents sold it and moved to Gig Harbor shortly before Jerry transferred to Vietnam," she explains. "I always supposed they moved away to make Jerry choose between us, but the truth was they had a new business venture in Tacoma. I was never privy to such information, of course, and only learned of it years later during a chance encounter with Jerry's cousin."

"So . . . *they* sold you the house?" Spider says, slightly confused.

"Heaven's no! I couldn't afford it at the time, and even if I could his mother wouldn't have tolerated such a thing. I heard that a professor from the university bought it, and I know it changed hands at least once more after that. Karma has a way of rewarding the patient, though, and I was ten years into my career as a residential agent with Sound Real Estate when it came on the market in the early eighties. Honestly, I didn't give it much thought at first, but when the listing agent hosted a home preview just for other agents, I decided to have a look."

She sighs. "As soon as I walked through the front door the memories came flooding back, one upon the other, like waves of nostalgia. Just the good ones, mind you: the old tire swing in back, sunsets on the patio when his parents were out of town, his bedroom upstairs . . ." She blushes and Jenny smiles. Neither Spider nor Darius seem to notice.

"There were bad memories too, mostly involving Jerry's mother, but time has a way of piling such weighty baggage in a dark corner. It's always there, of course, but it's in a place more easily forgotten." Freeing her hand, she takes a long drink of lemonade.

"In any case, I knew I was going to buy the house before I finished walking through the first floor. I was a successful real estate agent by that time and owned several small rental properties, but even at that, the house was almost more than I could afford. I pursued it, of course; how could I not?"

"And you succeeded," Jenny observes.

"Indeed. The house went on the market in early April and I moved in by mid-July. Jerry and I were at last reunited." Jenny gives her an odd expression and she just smiles, dips her head to the side briefly, and adds, "In a manner of speaking."

"Didn't it ever bother you?" Darius asks. "Living here, I mean—after his parents treated you so poorly."

"No," Maggie replies dismissively. "This is where Jerry grew up. It's not the house's fault who lived here. Besides, his mother had a massive rose garden on the north side of the house that she loved more than her husband. It was a haven of color and fragrance, so, naturally, the first thing I did was tear it up." She gives them a wicked smile. "Right down to the last plant." Amused by their stunned silence, she shrugs and waves dismissively. "I was more spiteful in those days."

Chapter 21

Sunday, August 21

They spend part of that hot August afternoon in the air-conditioned comfort of the family room as Maggie recounts stories of her brief but sweet marriage to Jerry Lipscomb, her final falling out with his parents, and the drought of dates and relationships since.

When asked why she never remarried, Maggie pauses, contemplating her words. "I could give you the easy answer and say that I couldn't imagine myself with anyone else." She shifts in her seat. "The deeper truth is that I was damaged, shattered into a thousand pieces, a bit like Humpty Dumpty, I should say. Only my tumble came in two parts: the first crack was Jerry's death, and the final break was the loss of my father."

She sighs. "I was *so young* when Jerry died. I still had that wonderful sense of immortality that the young are blessed with. They never think death will find them until one day he's peering through the window, there to steal a part of their joy, a part of their innocence. Only in my case, he didn't just peer through the window, he kicked open the front door."

She shakes her head. "That *damn* telegram—that wretched piece of paper. I'm still staggered by the sheer ugliness of it, that death can so easily be dispensed . . . just a few words on paper. At least when my father died a state trooper delivered the news in person."

She stiffens her back and inhales deeply. "So, yes, I was broken."

"But you put yourself back together," Darius says.

"Did I?" She ponders the question.

After a moment, she shifts in her seat and nods, almost hesitantly. "People are born every day. Sometimes they come from the womb, sometimes they rise from their knees. In both cases, it's a new beginning. So, it was for me. The two things I know about time is that it's a steady force, unrelenting and unstoppable, despite the barriers one might throw in its path. It's also a great healer. So, when enough time had passed, I suppose I stopped feeling sorry for myself and got up off my knees."

"But you had every right to feel sorry for yourself," Jenny replies.

"Of course, I did. I'd lost my world." Maggie smiles at her. "Next time you go to the mall, or a football game, or any place where a lot of people gather, pause and look around. Every person you see, every person who lives in this city, every person who walked this earth since before recorded history has suffered, some immensely. If you were to gather every tear ever shed in misery, you'd have an ocean. It's part of being human. The only thing we can do is trudge on and try to shed just as many tears of joy and laughter. So yes, I had a right to feel sorry for myself, but I also had an obligation to move on."

She turns to Darius and studies him in silence for a moment. "Earlier, you asked me about my faith, whether I honestly believe. The answer is . . . I do. I wasn't raised around religion, but God still found me. When I was broken and, on my knees, he was the glue that put me back together. So, when you wonder at my supposed resilience, my lack of self-pity, it's not me, it's the glue."

It's well after four when they once again climb the ladder to the unfinished roof, back to the tar paper and shingles and nail gun. They work in silence, each in their own mental place, apart from the others, but contemplating the same things.

Maggie offers to make dinner at six, but Darius wants to push through until they lose the light. They'd lost valuable time that afternoon; well spent but lost, nonetheless. It may not have mattered the previous Sunday, but they're getting close to the end of the roofing job, and Darius is determined to get back on track and finish on schedule. He's not sure what *finished* means, however, and finds himself conflicted. The end of the job means the end of their association with Maggie.

No, it doesn't, he tells himself for the hundredth time as the nail gun snaps in his hand, one nail after another, one shingle after another. The roofing job is just that: a job. Their relationship with Maggie had grown beyond the bounds of the roof and mere shingles. She's now . . . what? A friend? Maybe even a mentor, with all her quirky habits and insights?

Perhaps . . . family?

The nail gun freezes above the shingle as the realization hits him between the eyes. That was it. That was the feeling he'd been experiencing all weekend, a gut-bomb of dread and delight; dread because the job was ending; delight because he was coming to know Maggie.

She *was* family.

In that instant, he realizes that Spider had called her grandma on more than one occasion—and Maggie never flinched. She never even protested, not really. The first time he did it, she cast one of her most cantankerous looks his way, but by then they'd learned that these were just makeup to hide the smile underneath.

Without any of them realizing it, a bond had been struck between the four of them. A bond not of goods and services, of roofs and cars, but something more lasting, something deeper.

"Huh!" Darius mutters as the full realization strikes him.

When the sun begins its final descent just after eight o'clock, Maggie is puttering around below them, adorning the patio table with plates, silverware, and cups for a late but welcome supper. With the light beginning to fail, Jenny, Darius, and Spider begin securing the tools and supplies for the night. Darius is just bending over to pick up a loose shingle when Jenny suddenly gasps. Without explanation, she hurries to the peak of the roof and plants her feet.

"Look at the sunset," she exclaims, her face rapt with awe.

Their work had so absorbed them that they hadn't noticed the sky turning pink and lavender. Now, as the sun settles behind the distant islands, the already magnificent colors intensify. The pinks sink into a firestorm of red and the lavenders take on the deeper hues of purple. Together, they cast long ribbons across the sky, pushing down the yellows and blues of day and replacing them with the darker shades of night.

"Maggie, look at the sunset!" Jenny calls out.

"Oh, my!" they hear a moment later.

For a full seven minutes, they watch the dying of the light. No words are spoken and the only sounds that invade their thoughts are those of a distant lawnmower and the low murmur of Bellingham preparing for night.

When the fading halo of light finally slips beyond the horizon, they utter a collective sigh and turn their thoughts back to earthly matters. For five thousand years poets have struggled to frame the sunset and yet it escapes them. Perhaps because the greatest of things are meant to be experienced not explained. Among these are love, God, and sunsets.

With dinner put to belly, they gather the plates and forks and remnants of the meal and carry them into the kitchen. Rinsing them off and placing them in the dishwasher, they turn their attention to the used pans on the stove. These take a little more scrubbing but are soon ready for the dishwasher. And when every utensil, cup, plate, and pan has been accounted for, Spider pours some detergent and starts the cleaning cycle.

With the dishes done, they turn to find Maggie leaning against the doorframe watching them. A warm smile is spread across her face and there's a glint of something in her eyes that Darius can't place. How long she'd been standing there watching they don't know but there's something wonderful about the way she looks at them.

"I have a proposition," she says, "though I won't be offended if the answer is no. It's been a long day after all, and I know you must all be tired."

"What is it?" Jenny asks.

"I happen to have several boxes of popcorn stashed away in the pantry. While it's not homemade, which I prefer, it's tasty nonetheless."

"Orville Redenbacher," Spider says with a knowing nod.

"I believe it's Pop Secret," Maggie corrects. "And what good is popcorn without a movie?" Turning her gaze to Darius, she tips her head accusingly at Spider and Jenny and says, "It's almost unseemly, don't you think, restoring a car like the Bumblebee Jacket when these two haven't seen *American Graffiti*?"

Darius grins. "It's almost criminal." He suddenly looks refreshed, as if the labors of the long day had just sloughed off his shoulders like water off oiled leather.

"Popcorn and a movie," Jenny says with a quirky smile. "What more could a girl ask for?"

"This *American Graffiti* sounds like some rite of passage"—Spider begins.

"It is," Darius interrupts.

"For car geeks," Spider finishes.

They laugh and trade barbs for a minute and then follow Maggie down the hall, past the family room, and into the living room off to the right. The much larger room has a fifty-inch television mounted on the wall above a shelf holding a DVD player, a Blu-ray player, and a cable box. Below are three shelves filled side to side with DVDs.

"*American Graffiti* takes place in 1962, and represented everything my father loved about our country," Maggie says as she scans the shelves for the disk, "the cars, the music, cruising Main Street, that sense of a bright future just beyond the horizon." She shakes her head, remembering. "It came out in theaters in August of 1973, and by September my father had seen it three times. Three times! That in itself was a miracle if you knew my father. I think I mentioned that he wasn't exactly the movie-going type."

Turning, she gives them a whimsical glance. "Drive-in theaters were always my favorite."

She turns her attention back to the shelf and almost immediately proclaims, "Here it is!" as she plucks the movie from its place.

"Yeah, drive-ins," Spider says wistfully. "I kind of wish they still had those."

"You haven't seen a movie until you've seen it at a drive-in theater," Maggie assures him. "It's not so much about the movie as the experience." She places the DVD on the disk tray and then pushes a button. "After my father gave me the Bumblebee Jacket, I was always the designated driver. Mostly because I could comfortably fit three in the front seat, three in the back, and two or three in the trunk."

Darius raises an eyebrow. "In the trunk? So . . . you snuck people in?"

"Of course. That was half the fun."

Spider laughs. "You juvenile delinquent you!"

"Well," she replies, "birds of a feather, and all that." She gives him a wink.

It's late when the movie ends, well past the shadows of dusk and long into the umbra of night. After long reflection on the movie, discussing favorite scenes and trying to sing favorite songs, they grudgingly rise and prepare to leave. No one wants to go—to end this perfect night—so they drag their feet and make every excuse to linger.

When delay is no longer possible, they say their goodbyes at the front door. Jenny gives Maggie a quick hug and then chases after Darius, bursting into a less-than-perfect rendition of *Only You* by The Platters. Darius takes up the tune and they roughhouse like brother and sister as they make their way to the cars.

Spider lingers on the porch.

"What is it, dear?" Maggie says, puzzled by his demeanor.

"There's something I need to ask," he says in an uncharacteristically subdued voice.

They talk for a moment, Spider's lips moving rapidly, eyes shifting, while the expression on Maggie's face never changes. The conversation lasts long enough to draw the attention of Darius and Jenny, who watch the inaudible back-and-forth as they lean against Darius's Honda, quite taken by the clandestine exchange.

Whatever words are said, Spider seems satisfied with the outcome and gives Maggie a big hug. Not a gruff bear hug that sweeps her off her feet, but a gentle wrapping of arms around her small shoulders, the way one might hug a grandmother.

When he sees them waiting, he hurries down the walkway, throws a final wave at Maggie, and makes for his scooter.

"What was that?" Darius asks, closing on Spider as Jenny comes around the other side, sandwiching him between them.

"Nothing."

"Didn't look like nothing."

"It's a secret." His head swivels to Jenny, then back to Darius. "You'll see."

"Now *you're* keeping secrets, too?"

Spider suddenly grins at the realization. "I guess so."

He winks at Darius and then puts his helmet on. "It's a good one, too," he adds, enjoying the tortured look on his friend's face. Without waiting, he starts the Vespa and putters up the driveway. Jenny and Darius watch him go, arms crossed, standing side by side.

"He can't keep a secret," Darius says confidently. "He'll tell us."

"I give it a day," Jenny adds. "Text me when you find out?"

"I will."

Chapter 22

Spider keeps his secret all through the next day and into the evening. When Darius is sure that he's on the verge of bursting, that he's ready to spill it all out in one long projectile exclamation . . . he doesn't. He just tucks it away inside a conspiratorial smile and says nothing.

Not even a hint.

Darius doesn't see much of Spider on Tuesday and Wednesday, so by Thursday he's sure the secret is ripe and ready for picking, but once more Spider remains closed-lipped. There's a spark in his eyes that Darius doesn't recall seeing before and he realizes that Spider is enjoying the intrigue.

When Darius gets off work at five o'clock on Friday afternoon, he feels a pang of regret that he's not going to Maggie's house, that he's not going to see her, and—perhaps more sharply felt—that he's not going to see Jenny until the next day.

Regrets and absences aside, time stands still for no one.

There's plenty of work to be done on the Bumblebee Jacket, and Darius means to make every minute count. A complete vehicle restoration is no small matter. It's not something you knock out in a couple of weekends. The task before him has barely begun, and though this summer yet breathes, he's already looking to next summer, to car shows and long drives under perfect skies.

Plus, there's Maggie.

She asked for a ride in the car when it's finished. It was one of her few conditions when she sold it to Darius. Of all the promises he'd made and kept in his life, this one had somehow taken on supreme importance, as if the very ownership of the car rested on the completion of that vow. It was no longer just seven thousand six hundred and twenty-three dollars and forty-seven cents, plus a roofing job. It was seven thousand six hundred and twenty-three dollars and forty-seven cents, a roofing job, and a ride in the Bumblebee Jacket. The thought is so instilled in Darius's brain that it may as well be etched on the car's frame, a contract in rust, permanent and fixed.

Whether Maggie views her offhand request for a ride in the same way, Darius can't say. It doesn't matter. He's already pictured the ride in his mind a dozen times.

In that vision, he imagines the Bumblebee Jacket glowing in a crisp, fresh coat of bright yellow paint, the white top down, the sun planted in the sky above. Maggie is in the front passenger seat while Spider and Jenny share the back seat. Since Sunday, he'd added a new element to the vision: The soundtrack from *American Graffiti* would be playing on the stereo.

As to their route, that was easy.

In the short time they'd known her, Maggie had mentioned several times that her favorite thing to do after her father gave her the Bumblebee Jacket was to take a ride along Chuckanut Drive, a picturesque road that winds along the Puget Sound, affording spectacular views of the rolling water, the rocky coast, and the scattered islands beyond. Along the way are several pullouts where one can enjoy the view, and Larrabee State Park has walking trails and picnic tables where they can pause for lunch.

After that, he imagines heading south to Route 20, and then west to Anacortes, Deception Pass, and Oak Harbor. They'd make a day of it, just the five of them: an old woman, three twentysomethings, and a throaty old Plymouth with fresh makeup; the most unlikely of families.

It's just after six when the sputter of Spider's Vespa can be heard echoing off the south wall of Road Runner Restoration. A second later, Spider pulls the black scooter through the only open roll-up door and kills the engine.

"Sorry I'm late," he says loudly as he removes his helmet and places it on the Vespa's vinyl seat. "I got tied up with something."

Whatever that *something* was he doesn't elaborate, but quickly throws on a pair of coveralls and joins Darius. The plan for tonight is to attach a rotisserie to the main body of the old Plymouth. It's not a one-man job, and though Uncle John offered to stay and help Darius assured him that he and Spider could handle it.

He's now having second thoughts.

The automotive version of the rotisserie operates in the same way as a chicken rotisserie. It's like placing a car on a roasting spit, which allows one to turn the car on its side or even upside down with nothing more than a gentle tug or push. It's the best way to work on the undercarriage of a vehicle and is ideal for applying paint, repairing rust, or any of dozens of other tasks that would normally require a lot of shuffling around on the shop floor. The rotisserie Darius is using will remain a part of the car until the body is painted and ready to be reattached to the reconditioned frame.

"What's first?" Spider asks.

It's no small task to attach a rotisserie to a car body and lift it off its frame, but two hours later the Bumblebee Jacket's tired body is suspended in the air. After numerous adjustments, Spider grabs the empty windshield frame and—with a single hand—turns the perfectly balanced car a hundred and eight degrees so that it rests upside down, suspended in the air. With another pull, he rights the car.

"It's like a pig roast," he says with a grin, "only with a giant bumblebee."

Darius chuckles at the thought.

Chapter 23

Saturday, August 27

"Hello?"

"We're back here," a voice calls out.

Walking down the hall, past the kitchen, and out the back door, Darius finds Maggie, Jenny, and Spider seated around the patio table, drinking coffee, and eating cream cheese Danishes. Darius falls into the chair opposite Jenny. She takes one look at him and—without asking—pours him a cup of coffee from the pot. Setting it on the table, she pushes it over to him, followed by the cream and sugar. She then picks a fat and nearly perfect Danish from the box and places it on a white napkin before him.

"Thanks," Darius says, eyeing the Danish hungrily. "Sorry I'm late."

"Nonsense," Maggie says. "It's not even ten. Spider tells me you two were up till almost midnight working on the car." She studies him a moment. "I'm worried that you're working yourself too hard."

Darius shrugs it off and takes a bite of the Danish.

"Oh yes, it's all fine and good," Maggie scoffs, slightly piqued by his lack of response. "You have the unstoppable inertia of youth, I suppose. I'm not so old that I don't remember what that was like, but I won't have you exhausting yourself and making yourself ill on my behalf."

"I'm fine, Maggie"

She glares at him.

"I'll go to bed early tonight," he offers. "All I need is a good rest."

She watches him a moment longer and then gives a slight nod. "I'll hear about it if you don't." Her eyes dart to Spider, perhaps unintentionally identifying him as her source, as if there could be any other source for such lofty intelligence as Darius's sleeping habits.

Jenny watches the exchange with a smile on her face and when Darius and Maggie have come to terms, she mixes it up a bit more. "You *must* be tired," she says. "You didn't even notice Maggie's new piece of furniture." She lifts her chin toward a spot over Darius's right shoulder and he turns to look.

There, covered by a blue cotton blanket from Maggie's closet, stands an indistinguishable mound about five feet tall, almost three feet wide, and a couple of feet thick. At first, Darius suspects it's a barbeque or an outdoor fireplace, but Maggie already has both. It could be a sofa turned on its side or an oddly shaped stack of chairs.

"What is it?"

Spider rises to his feet. "Just a little thing I got going on," he says as he takes up position to the right of the mound. "Remember that little secret you've been pestering me about all week? Well—"

He begins to lift the blanket inch by inch.

As it's a large blanket, he manages to gather a good foot of it in his hands before the bottom finally lifts off the ground. Here he pauses, letting the material hang loose around the base of the so-called furniture. The blanket looks for all the world like the well-hemmed leg of a giant pair of pants.

"Are you sure you want to see it?" Spider taunts, shaking the blanket as if he's about to drop it back in place.

Darius starts to say *just lift it*, but then his face takes on an odd look: a mix of sudden realization and spontaneous mischief. No one seems to notice. Hesitating just a heartbeat, he replies, "Nah, cover it back up," and turns his back on Spider.

In the time it takes Spider to close his gaping mouth and compose himself, Darius takes two soothing sips from his coffee cup, another bite from the Danish, and says, "How's *your* day?" to Jenny.

"*It's the secret*," Spider says, exasperated.

"How can it be?" Darius replies. "It's right here in front of us." He casts a half-hearted glance over his shoulder before turning his attention back to the Danish.

"Seriously, D?" Spider moans dejectedly. "I've been working on this all week."

Darius shakes his head. "You should have camouflaged it better. Putting a cardboard box over the top isn't going to fool anyone."

"Fooled me," Jenny says.

"Fooled her," Spider echoes.

Sighing long and loud, as if accepting a great burden, Darius sets his Danish on the napkin, gives Maggie and Jenny a submissive smile, and then turns his chair so that he's fully facing his flustered friend. "In that case, carry on."

Proceeding, this time without much ado, Spider lifts the blanket completely off and sets it in a crumpled heap on a nearby chair. As Darius correctly deduced, there's a cardboard box covering the top of the big surprise, which Spider also removes and sets aside. His finger makes some stabbing motions at the mound, which has by this time morphed into something entirely different.

A clicking and humming ensue, followed by the grainy sound of a record.

Spider steps to the side as Buddy Holly's *That'll Be the Day* bursts from the large speaker at the front of the Wurlitzer, sounding just as wonderful and alive as the first time it was ever played.

Jenny squeals with delight and claps her hands.

"Well done!" she shouts to Spider over the music.

Maggie's reaction is more sobering. Her hand rises and covers her mouth, and then joyful tears form, threatening to stream down her cheeks in a torrent. In her eyes, you can almost see the memories parading past as if a great film were playing in her head and her eyes were the screen.

When the song ends, Maggie looks across at Spider and smiles.

"More, please," she says.

As the next song plays, and then the next, Spider goes into great detail explaining his week and how he'd come over every day to work on the jukebox. Most of the repair details went over their heads and included words like vacuum tubes, actuating arm, and brake band—whatever that is. Spider also says he had to rewire most of the electronics because the old wiring was in such poor shape that it presented a fire hazard.

He also flocked the turntable.

Darius has no idea what flocking is, but—apparently—it's the fuzzy stuff on top of the turntable that the record sits on so it won't get scratched.

"How'd you learn all this?" Darius finally asks.

"I told you: YouTube. You can learn how to build or repair anything, like that lady who built her entire house by watching videos. You can probably learn how to build a nuclear bomb on YouTube."

"Yeah, let's not do that," Jenny says quickly.

Spider grins and you almost have to wonder if he's already looked that up. "I've been researching since the day we picked up the car," Spider confesses. "I think that's the only reason Maggie let me give it a try. I told her what I thought might be wrong and how to fix it, and I guess she realized how serious I was."

He glances at her and gives a slight nod.

"Anyway, I had it running by Wednesday and spent Thursday and Friday cleaning up all the individual pieces and putting it back together. Fine-tuning was a bit of a problem, but I finally figured that out too. The only thing left to do is the bubble tubes."

"Bubble tubes?" Jenny says.

"Yeah, right here," Spider says, pointing out a clear half-inch tube on the front of the jukebox that runs up one side, arches over the top, and then down the other side. "This model Wurlitzer is called the bubbler because there's a stream of bubbles flowing through these tubes." He shrugs. "When it's working."

"So, it uses an air pump?" Darius guesses.

"Methylene dichloride."

"What?"

"Yeah, I know. The stuff's toxic, but I don't think they gave it that much thought in the forties."

"I don't understand," Jenny says. "How does metha—"

"Methylene dichloride," Spider repeats.

"How does it make bubbles?"

"It's got a real low boil point, like a hundred and three degrees, so all it takes is a small ceramic resistor to heat it. After that, it's bubble city."

"So, when do we get to see *that*?"

"Soon," Spider promises.

The question of *when* they complete the roofing job is up for debate.

Spider pronounces it done just before five-thirty when the last piece of shingle is nailed into place. This might have been the case if they were to walk away leaving scraps and nail guns and tubes of tar caulking lying about, not to mention the tarps around the base of the house and other elements of cleanup still needing attention.

As it turns out, victory is declared at five-thirty, but the war doesn't officially end until seven when the last tarp surrenders and is marched off to the trunk of Darius's car. Then, with Maggie at their side, they stand for a long moment on the front lawn admiring the roof.

The job had been difficult.

At first blush, the old roof had been solid but weathered and should have lasted a good many years. Maggie's discovery of leaks, however, raised the first concern and suggested that something else was going on, something hidden.

Had Maggie waited another year or two, the roof's underlying condition may have become dire. Worse still, the leaks that would have sprung from the deteriorating barrier would have been calamitous. Roofs, after all, are shields. They protect against wind and rain and the destruction that comes with both.

In Maggie's case, the roof protects the house, but it's the second floor she's most concerned about. Now, as she stands on the lawn beside these three people who have come to mean so much to her in such a short time, she, alone among them, is aware of the disaster that has been averted. A stirring in her chest and gut presses for disclosure. With all her heart she longs to tell Darius and Jenny and Spider of their *true* accomplishment. She wants to tell them that it's not just a new roof.

But Maggie is a woman of secrets.

Old habits are hard to break.

"So, what's the deal with the Wurlitzer?" Darius asks Maggie as they gather around the patio table and settle in for a game of cards. "Everything around here has a story," he adds, "so I'm guessing there's a pretty good one for the jukebox. Am I right?"

"Of course, there's a story," Maggie replies, but before she can continue, something causes her to pause, to reconsider. "Hmm," she hums with deliberation. "That, my boy, is a question about my father, and I believe we have a twenty-question pact in play. You might want to check with Jenny before using one of her questions."

"Really?"

"*Yes*," Maggie replies in mock exasperation.

"It's okay," Jenny says with a snicker of delight. "I want to hear this too."

Still, Maggie waits . . . expectantly. Then, with a slight huff, she extracts the small brown vintage coin purse from her pocket and lays it on the table before her.

He forgot about the nickel.

Fishing in his pocket, Darius pulls out a quarter, three pennies, a gum wrapper, and a gas station receipt and dumps them onto the table. Checking his other pocket, he finds a pair of dimes and—finally—a single nickel. Wiping it on his shirt he hands it across the table.

Maggie takes the coin with a nod and a maddening smile and plops it into the purse, where it clinks against the others. Snapping the top shut, she returns it to her pocket.

Glancing over at the Wurlitzer, as if remembering, she says, "That old box must have been about ten years old when it shows up at our door. That would have been around 1954 or '55, I don't recall exactly, because I wasn't much older than the Wurlitzer. The year before, he had done some side work on a car that belonged to a friend of his, Mr. Peetoom, who owned a diner along what was then Pacific Highway, the predecessor to I-5.

"Now, as sometimes happens, Mr. Peetoom found himself in some unexpected financial difficulties, which just so happened to coincide with the completion of the custom work my father was doing for him. Without cash and hoping to preserve the friendship he held with my father, he offered up the Wurlitzer in trade—plucked it right out of his diner one Saturday afternoon, loaded it into the back of his truck, and delivered it to our house."

Maggie pauses to take a drink and notes with satisfaction that all eyes are upon her, following her every move as if she were perched on some sketchy embankment ready to tumble over. If they blinked, they'd miss it, so they don't blink.

"Now, when my father saw Mr. Peetoom untying the Wurlitzer from the truck bed, he came out of the house like a shot, not because he wanted the jukebox so badly, but because he'd have none of it. 'Howie,' he called—that was Mr. Peetoom's name, Howie; short for Howard—'Howie,' he said, 'take that right back. You know as well as I do that if you don't have music your customers will go elsewhere.'

"Mr. Peetoom insisted, of course, and my father insisted right back. I didn't hear the whole conversation because I was up on the porch, but as Mr. Peetoom tried convincing my dad to take it, he seemed to suddenly fold in on himself. His shoulders sagged, his head dropped, and his whole body seemed to wither. I saw his shoulders moving up and down and realized he was crying."

"How sad," Jenny murmurs.

"Indeed," Maggie replied. "Mr. Peetoom was honest and hardworking, but hard times come to all at one time or another. The good news is he quickly recovered from his troubles. My father agreed to take the jukebox in trade on one condition: Mr. Peetoom had to leave it in the diner until he could afford to replace it.

"A year later, a new jukebox showed up at the diner. That very afternoon, Mr. Peetoom showed up at our house again, once more with the old bubbler in the bed of his truck. This time, though, he was beaming from ear to ear, as if he were receiving rather than giving. He had a surprise for my father. After they set up the jukebox in his studio, Mr. Peetoom hauled in three money bags from the front floorboard of his truck, each bag filled to bursting with nickels."

"Nickels!" Darius blurts, perhaps thinking—*again with the nickels.*

Maggie nods. "Every nickel plugged into that jukebox in the year since he first tried to deliver it. My father refused the bags, of course, but this time Mr. Peetoom was more convincing, arguing that the machine was his, and so too the nickels."

Jenny is tickled by the whole story. "And he put it in his studio?"

"Yes. And by studio, I mean guest bedroom."

Jenny laughs.

"Oh, you would have loved it," Maggie hums, leaning forward and finding Jenny's hand. "The wallpaper consisted mostly of pages torn from magazines: pictures of cars, landscapes, buildings—anything that inspired his imagination or provided the details he needed. Everywhere you looked, on all four walls, were magazine pages and pictures. Sometimes a poster would get tossed in the mix, or an actual photograph he took on one of our outings, but mostly it was magazine pages. And always, the jukebox was playing, as if the room itself required it; as if that was the price of admission."

She chuckles in reflection.

"When he'd finish a painting, those magazine pages became suddenly obsolete and had to come down. That quickly became my job, and I did it with gusto. He'd laugh from his belly as I plucked them from the wall, hand-over-fist, and tossed them into the air so that they came down like giant snowflakes. Sometimes it looked like a regular blizzard in there." She laughs this time and then falls silent.

"When the fun was done, and the walls stood bare I'd sweep the spent pages into a dustbin. Within the next day or two, the first new images would appear, the beginning of a whole new family of pages hanging from the wall."

"Ready for a new painting," Jenny says.

"Ready for a new painting," Maggie confirms.

"Did he always listen to music when he painted?" Spider asks but then remembers what Maggie said about the jukebox always playing. "I mean before he got the Wurlitzer."

"Always, always, *always*," Maggie says emphatically, stretching out the last word. "Or at least as long as I can remember. He had an old Phillips radio for the longest time, but the Wurlitzer had better sound and he could listen to whatever he wanted."

She gives them a pensive glance. "I think the music took him to a different place. Today, psychologists would probably call it a sort of therapy, a way to deal with what he experienced in the war, but I don't think that's what it was. My father just loved life, and music is a part of life." She shrugs. "Sometimes the simplest answer is the best."

They sit and listen to the Wurlitzer as it continues its mechanical waltz, choosing each new record as if it were a dance partner. With an embracing metal arm, it would lead each partner in turn to the flocked, spinning dance floor to make beautiful music together.

While Maggie listens and remembers, Darius, Spider, and Jenny make new memories. They tuck away the sounds, smells, voices, and emotions that fill them and surround them so that someday, long from now, they can sit and recall a little bit of what made this night so special.

After a long quiet, Spider's voice breaks the silence between records. He thumbs toward the jukebox and asks, "How'd it end up in the garage?"

An innocent enough question, but it gives Maggie pause. "It just stopped working one day," she says, the words coming from her as if they were boots stuck in mud, unwilling to release.

"When was that?"

She sighs. "The day after my father died."

When all three of them turn and look at her in spooked silence, she waves their unspoken thoughts away. "Just a coincidence," she says, her words hollow and unconvincing. "Things break. Music stops."

As she says the last words, it occurs to Jenny that Maggie's not talking about the jukebox anymore, but about herself, as if it was her that stopped functioning that day in 1973. As if it were her who was placed against the wall in a garage and forgotten for four decades.

Things break.

Music stops.

But life goes on, Jenny wants to say.

When the sun sets at 8:02 P.M., Maggie rises and turns on the string of cantina lights above and around the patio, and they continue their game of cards to the yellow glow of the incandescent bulbs.

"Rummy," Maggie announces a minute later.

"Oh—my—gosh!" Spider declares. "How do you do that?

"I'm old," Maggie replies. "You know what they say about age and treachery . . ."

"You're not old," Jenny says as if wishing it so.

Maggie laughs. "I gave up pretending I was middle-aged when I hit seventy, dear. There are some battles it's best to just walk away from, that way you keep some of your dignity and don't look quite the fool. Besides," she adds, "getting old isn't all that bad. Every extra day, month, or year brings the possibility of new adventures, new friends"—she tips her head their way— "and new insights. Some never have that opportunity, so those of us who do should cherish it." In a softer voice, she says, "I squandered so many years . . ."

Silence settles over the table, broken only by the soothing vocals of Patsy Cline issuing from the jukebox. At length, Spider raises his glass slowly into the air. "To never squandering a moment," he says.

"Here, here," Maggie says quietly, clinking his glass.

"To never squandering a moment," Darius and Jenny say together, their eyes locking briefly as their glasses touch . . . and continue to touch, as if gravity has suddenly shifted and drawn the two vessels together. The pull is fleeting and then gone, and Darius finds himself clinking Spider's glass, and then Maggie's.

As *Walkin' After Midnight* fades from the Wurlitzer, the old record is removed, and a new disk is brought to place. With the first notes of Buddy

Holly's *Maybe Baby*, Jenny lights up and her hand shoots across the table, folding around Darius's arm. "Dance with me," she says.

"I don't—"

Before he can say *dance*, she comes around the table and helps him to his feet. Pulling him to the center of the patio they begin moving as one to the beat and the lyrics, much to the delight of their audience.

Standing, Spider offers his hand to Maggie. "May I?" he says.

She would later protest and claim that it wasn't so, that an old woman was incapable of blushing, but in that instant, the color bloomed brilliantly in her cheeks. Between the music, the lights, and the company, she feels for the briefest of moments as if she were sixteen again. As if all the world and the life it offered were still before her and a car called the Bumblebee Jacket waited at the curb outside.

"I'd love to," she replies with a tip of her head.

And dance she does, putting the rest of them to shame as she starts with the twist and then transitions to the watusi. Jenny catches on quickly, mimicking both dances along with her and forcing Darius and Spider to follow suit.

When *Maybe Baby* finishes all too quickly, they wait expectantly to see what the Bubbler serves up next, hoping for something fast and fun like *Heart and Soul* by the Cleftones, or *Chantilly Lace* by the Big Bopper. When the slow and heartbreaking words of *Since I Don't Have You* by the Skyliners begins to play, Maggie and Spider immediately head for their seats. Darius makes to follow but Jenny pulls him back gently . . . and then pulls him close.

Reminiscent of some sock hop from half a century before, she lays her head on his shoulder and they dance slowly around the patio, the cantina lights shimmering while the marbled evening sky hovers above. Maggie and Spider just watch in contented silence as if everything in the world were suddenly right and just and meant to last forever.

When the evening is utterly spent, Maggie walks them out to the driveway. With the roofing job done, this is the parting they've all been dreading. Jenny has plenty of reason to continue seeing Maggie, but not so much for Darius and Spider.

"We were noticing that this old place could use some paint," Spider finally ventures as they linger at the edge of goodbye. "The inside is so-so, but the outside is *way* past its prime. I mean, if this thing was iron, it'd be a rust bucket."

"Don't forget the siding," Darius prods with a shake of his head.

Spider throws his hands in the air as if suddenly viewing a calamity. "The siding is awful!" he practically shouts. Then, thinking he may have overdone this point, he clarifies. "Not all of it, of course, but there's a big section on the north wall that's on a downhill road to Crapville, and there's *no* amount of duct tape that's gonna fix it. The siding needs replacing, and now. You're one good storm away from some serious water damage."

"One storm," Darius echoes, holding up an index finger.

Maggie contemplates the duo for a moment and then elbows Jenny. "See how this hustle works?" she says as if preparing to expose a clever con artist. "It's like the mechanic who changes your oil and then wants you to get a transmission flush, a tune-up, and a brake job. Five hundred dollars later you're walking out wondering what just happened." Turning a scrutinizing eye on Spider, she says, "I suppose you'll want lunches and dinners included?"

"Certainly; I think the job demands it."

Darius plays his part to the hilt. Tapping his friend on the shoulder, he whispers conspiratorially in his ear, as if distilling the negotiations into its base parts. With dinners and lunches so quickly settled upon, they're ready to make their power move. Any respectable contractor in such a position would demand the moon, the stars, and the rings of Saturn.

Maggie waits for it, expecting brilliance; demanding it.

Spider gives her a slight nod as if the whole negotiation might hinge on his next words. "I think some . . . *iced tea* would be in order."

He says the words *iced tea* as if he were Dr. Evil demanding one *million* dollars. He then throws down an additional clause: "Sweetened. With lemons."

"With lemons!" Maggie huffs as if that single point had gone too far. "Would you like the fillings from my teeth as well? Or perhaps there's gold in the dirt under my fingernails." She peers at the tips of her fingers as if it might be so, then scoffs and says, "Lemons," once more. Jenny, meanwhile, is covering her mouth so well that only her eyes can laugh.

"Fine," Maggie barks. "I'll agree to this extortion on one condition: you agree that I'll be providing the paint, the siding, and any other materials necessary." She throws a dismissive hand their way. "There it is; take it or leave it."

Darius and Spider consult in whispers, pausing after a moment to cast suspicious eyes at Maggie and then returning to their huddle. Jenny bursts into laughter—real laughter this time, her eyes no longer able to contain it.

"Agreed," Spider says, dragging the word out.

Pretending to spit into his hand, he extends it to Maggie, who doesn't pretend at all but spits a wet one into her palm and slaps it into Spider's before he can recoil. "Deal," she says.

Jenny claps and they all have a good laugh.

They talk a few more minutes commending one another on the negotiations, and just as they've said their goodnights and turned to their respective vehicles, Maggie pulls them back around.

"One more thing," she says. The three words come out hesitantly, as if one part of her means to say the words and another is fighting against them, an internal tug-of-war. "I was hoping you'd all come to dinner tomorrow night. There's something"—and for a moment the *fighting-against* part of her mental struggle almost wins out, but she continues—"there's something I need to show you."

Chapter 24

Sunday, August 28

Maggie rises with the sun and shuffles to the kitchen to brew a single cup of coffee, which she laces with generous portions of cream and sugar. She tends to avoid the devil's cup, preferring her teas instead, but some mornings require the extra caffeine, and some days require the slap in the face that only coffee can provide.

After a few sips, she finds it too bitter and adds more cream and sugar.

As there is no morning paper to read—the subscription was canceled years ago—she shuffles toward the front of the house. Pausing at the bottom of the stairs, she glances up to the second floor. There's nothing to see, of course; leastwise not from the bottom step. Still, her mind's-eye plays witness to a parade of images—visions of things great and small. As if the insights of a thousand years were suddenly captured and placed before her.

Change is coming.

She knows this because she knows the secret of the second floor, a secret she's kept for the better part of her adult life. It was always possible, even likely, that the secret would get out by accident, and for more than forty years that moment of discovery seemed forever imminent as if always approaching but never arriving.

To her credit or condemnation, Maggie never told a soul, not even her best friend, the gregarious Beryl Dawson. Now, with the revelation of the secret finally at her doorstep, nervous tension plays with her stomach and bowels and sets her limbs to shaking ever so slightly. She imagines that if her blood were a martini it would be two parts fear, one part relief, and an olive pit of reluctance—shaken, not stirred.

Some would say that secrets come in two varieties: those meant to be kept forever, and those meant to be temporary. Maggie's was always meant to be the latter, made unavoidable by the sheer nature of the secret. But, what is temporary, anyway? The word defies firm definition because it's subject to its use and environment.

For Maggie's part, she'd always imagined it meant *upon her death*. And why not? Many secrets expire with their owners. Why should hers be any different?

Ah, but she hadn't counted on Jenny.

Though she'd seen this day approaching with the steadfast determination of a glacier, she hadn't imagined Darius and Spider, either. That's the real surprise of it all. Of course, she always imagined that someone would get wise once she sold the Bumblebee Jacket, she just hadn't counted on them coming to it so quickly. She was supposed to be gone by then, crossed over to that place where secrets no longer matter.

Everything will change tonight; she thinks with a sigh.

She knows as well as anyone that the death of a secret often brings change; whether that change is for good or ill, only time will tell. Still, there's no more hiding it. She's tipped her hand and there's no going back.

For a moment, she wonders why she hid it in the first place, what drove her to such secrecy and intrigue? Perhaps it was just a silly impulse . . . or perhaps it was because the insights of a thousand years were hers and hers alone. Hers to decipher, regard, or disregard as she saw fit, without the world as judge and jury. Perhaps that was it.

In any case, she thinks, *it ends tonight*.

Moving past the stairs, she turns into the living room and takes a seat in front of the television. Flipping through channels, she watches several minutes of three different news channels and, finding only nonsense, turns to a home and garden channel and watches absently as an old home is slowly renovated. It strikes her as very similar to what she's seen around her own home over the previous weeks, and after a few minutes, she flips to another channel with penguins.

You can't go wrong with penguins.

When her coffee is gone, Maggie contemplates a rare second cup but decides against it. Rinsing the mug in the kitchen sink, she deposits it in the empty dishwasher and then returns to her bedroom. Five minutes later she emerges in a pair of old jeans and a much newer black t-shirt. She lingers at the bottom of the stairs only a moment before starting the slow climb, already weary from the day ahead.

A secret joins them for dinner tonight, and there's much to be done.

Speculation is a time-consuming endeavor.

It's a warren of rabbit tunnels leading this way and that, and often right back to where you began. There's no rhyme or reason to it, yet it's speculation that has occupied the hours of Darius, Spider, and Jenny since leaving Maggie the night before.

The three of them met at IHOP for breakfast and talked of nothing else by what lay at the top of Maggie's stairs, speculating that *this* is what Maggie wants to show them. From their tone and hushed conversation, one would half-expect she had a few corpses stuffed into old trunks.

When they'd eaten their bacon, eggs, and pancakes and paid the bill, Darius decides to leave his Honda in the IHOP parking lot, and he and Spider ride with Jenny—just so they can speculate some more. He and Spider could have speculated together, but it's so much more interesting with Jenny.

When they arrive on Eldridge Avenue and gather in the living room, it's with much anticipation and a dollop of fear.

"Well," Maggie finally says, kneading her fingers together. "there's something I need to show you upstairs. It's something I should have shown you before now, but . . . well, there it is." She holds her hands out, palms up as if she'd just explained everything with perfect clarity and they could make of it what they would.

With a wave that looks more like a command, she leads them from the room and into the hall where she places her right foot resolutely on the lowest step—and stops. Frozen. She seems to struggle a moment, her leg trembling, but then her left foot breaks the spell, and she takes the second step. Just like that, they're following her up to the second floor—step by step—as if they'd done it a hundred times before.

The top step empties into the middle of an elegant hallway fully eight feet wide. It runs the length of the house from north to south and has three doorways on each side but no doors. A pair of long wooden benches rest against opposite walls and Maggie takes a seat on one of these, waving them on.

"Have a look," she says as if inviting them to examine a set of old spoons.

They glance around, but the hall gives nothing away.

It's only when Jenny turns and glances through the open doorcase behind her and to the left that she realizes what this is. Her body seizes up and she stands rooted to the hardwood floors as if she'd sprung up from them, a part of them. After a moment, she sways on her heels, beginning to swoon. So shaken is she that Darius takes her arm to steady her, somewhat alarmed.

She only points . . . and then Darius needs some steadying of his own. "Is that . . .?"

"Yes," Jenny says in a whisper.

Spider, upon seeing the amazing and impossible through the slant of the doorcase, turns to Maggie and studies her quietly for a moment. "All this time?" he asks, his voice low, filled with awe and admiration. He walks over and kneels before her, taking her hand in his own. "Wow!" is all he can manage.

Maggie smiles and shrugs. "Wow!" she repeats and then bursts into tears.

Taking the seat next to her, Spider puts his arm around her and pulls her close. He realizes with some alarm how frail she suddenly seems, this fierce woman who so recently taunted him and compared his ears to those of the Maasai in Kenya.

How quickly life changes.

How quickly relationships change.

He doesn't stir from his resting spot for some time, just sits on the bench next to this woman he had come to love, the woman who has become, to him, like the grandmother he never had. When at last he rises, his hand lingers on Maggie's shoulder a moment, and then he steps through the nearest doorway into rooms filled with wonder.

Chapter 25

Sunday, August 28

Oh, yes! Maggie has a secret on the second floor, but it's not bodies in trunks or stolen Nazi gold brought home by her father. It's not even a reclusive lover.

Maggie's secret is much more profound, both to her and the world.

As Spider steps through the doorway, he finds that the entire west side of the house has been converted into one large room running north to south, just like the hallway outside. Columns hold up support beams in two locations, essentially dividing the room into thirds, but without the necessity for walls.

Down the center of this space are moveable partitions, each about six feet tall and perhaps eight feet long. The vertical sides and narrow tops of these panels are covered in soft, earthy fabric, while the ends are fitted with elaborately carved mahogany, maybe five inches wide, a couple of inches deep, and only slightly taller than the panel itself. These meticulous pieces are finished in a rich coffee stain that turns the dark wood almost black.

Almost.

A deep coat of polyurethane clear coat makes the pieces glow.

There must be twenty such panels running two-deep down the length of the room. Spider will soon find a similar setup on the east side of the house.

The entire second floor is magnificent from floor to ceiling and as different from the rest of the house as night is from day or fire from ice. Someone who went to sleep on the first floor and woke up on the second would not believe they were in the same house; such is the disparity.

It's as if one part of the house resembles a tired old woman, as Darius inferred after his first visit, and the other part is that same woman fifty years earlier.

Perhaps the house is both.

Perhaps it is Maggie—or at least it reflects her.

What stuns the three young visitors, however, is not the Janus nature of the house, conjuring images of the Roman god with two faces, one looking to the future and another looking to the past. No. It's what resides on the walls and elaborate panels of the rooms in the here and now.

The place is an art gallery.

Paintings large and small announce themselves at every turn, and not just any paintings, these are Atwood originals: watercolors, oils, pastels, charcoal etchings, even some tempera, that ancient predecessor to oil painting whereby egg yolk was commonly used as a binding medium.

They lose themselves in the rooms.

Jenny, who by this time has spent a good deal of her adult life in art museums, is perhaps most at home in the environment, though her demeanor presents a contradiction. She's perpetually excited as if each new painting on the walls or hanging from the partitions is some lost Rembrandt or Van Gogh, yet little sound comes from her.

She wants to speak—you can see it on her face, shouts of joy inflating like balloons in her chest, exclamations of awe and disbelief elbowing each other to get out yet with each opening of her mouth silence spills forth, nothing more. It's as if her words have been stolen, her voice box paralyzed, or perhaps her mind is just too overwhelmed to remember *how* to form words. After all, words can be tricky things.

Darius and Spider are equally quiet, and this imperious silence gives the place the air of a library overseen by some strict matron with a whacking stick.

The old floor creaks on occasion.

That is all.

A full hour passes before they stumble back into the hall, excited, dumbfounded, and overwhelmed—if one person can be all three at once. Maggie rises from her bench slowly, her face also a mix of emotion, but one dominated by uncertainty.

This trepidation is no doubt born of the utter silence that has echoed from her secret museum for the past hour, its nothingness vibrating off the walls like distant war drums—or perhaps it's just the beating of her own heart in her ears, heartbeats and war drums having so much in common.

Regardless, the utter quiet took her by surprise.

Standing expectantly, hands clutched before her, she says, "Well?"

"How many?" Darius asks after they'd settled into chairs on the back patio. Generous portions of chocolate chip cookies, lemon bars, and raspberry strudel are laid out on a platter before them, a pitcher of iced tea standing off to the side.

"Counting the paintings downstairs," Maggie replies, "I have four hundred and eighty-three. Of those, I inherited a hundred and thirty-two from my father and collected an additional three hundred and fifty-one in the decades that followed. Most were from flea markets, second-hand stores, and yard sales between here and Seattle, back when they were cheap.

"I found seven of them in the homes of clients and prospective clients if you can believe that. I never let on that the artist was my father, of course, and because the paintings were of little consequence, the clients were more than happy to let them go for a reasonable price."

She winks. "One less thing to pack, I always reminded them."

Jenny has said little since descending from the second floor. A certain shell-shocked delirium seems to have settled upon her and Darius catches her mouthing words unspoken, nodding, or shaking her head at questions unasked.

It's a bit mental—in a cute sort of way.

Darius knows her well enough by now to guess that she's processing a whole truckload of reality, things she didn't know and wouldn't have imagined an hour ago. Her expertise in all things E.E. Atwood just got turned on its head. It's almost like starting over from scratch.

When Maggie goes to the kitchen for more iced tea and Spider gets up to select some songs on the jukebox, Darius leans in close to Jenny and whispers, "Are you okay?"

She smiles and then shakes her head briskly as if to knock the cobwebs loose. "Just . . . a little overwhelmed," she confesses. "This is like finding the Holy Grail, the Ark of the Covenant, and Atlantis in the course of the same morning."

Darius grins. "Pretty cool, huh?"

"Oh my god, yes!" Jenny gushes, taking his hand without realizing it. "I—I never even imagined. I mean, so few Atwoods have ever been found, I just assumed there weren't that many to begin with."

"Guess they're not as rare as everyone thought. I imagine this is going to water down the auction prices—and the value of the Bumblebee Jacket," he adds with sudden realization.

"Hardly!"

"But the discovery of four hundred paintings—"

Jenny cuts him off. "You said they remind you of Norman Rockwell, right?"

"Yeah."

"Well, Rockwell painted *ten times* as many. A couple of years ago, Sotheby's sold three of the paintings he did for the cover of *The Saturday Evening Post*. How much do you think they sold for?"

Darius is in way over his head.

"I don't know—a million dollars."

"Close. Try sixty million."

Darius's eyes go wide, and he looks like someone just popped him in the chin.

"Granted," Jenny continues, "that's Norman Rockwell, a magnificent painter who captured life in small-town America." She pauses, and then emphatically says, "Atwood is just as good, and his subject matter is similar."

She squeezes his hand.

"This discovery is only going to enhance the value of his paintings—especially when people find out about the car. The art world is going to explode with the news. They'll talk of little else for weeks. Months, even."

Concern crosses Darius's face.

"We need to protect Maggie's interests," he says, "shield her from some of this if we can. At the least, we need to keep it quiet until she's ready to reveal it. How do you feel about holding back information from your bosses at the museum, at least for now?"

Jenny nods vigorously as if there's no doubt.

"Maggie first."

Chapter 26

Time never holds its breath, despite our best wishes.

It's the eternal metronome, the ever-dripping water.

As the flea is to the elephant, so is the second to the year. A single flea poses no threat to the elephant and is neither seen nor felt, but fleas, like seconds, tend to congregate. If enough of them come together, even the mighty elephant is doomed.

So, it is with time.

Seconds gather in steady increments, congregating into minutes and then hours until the insignificant second is no longer so insignificant. It has the strength of numbers and is unstoppable as it marches ever forward to the beat of its steady drum.

August fades and September blooms, and we are reminded that time is not only the great destroyer but also the father of hope, for all hope looks to the future. Some may look to the past and wish they could change this or undo that, but the past is set and there's no expectation in such sentiment, just regret.

The future is where promise lies, and time takes us there.

By the middle of the month, classes start at Western Washington University and both Darius and Spider find that their work, classes, and social schedules now demand more hours from each day, so adjustments are made.

The only day that both are free is Friday, so that day is reserved for the Bumblebee Jacket. Monday through Thursday Spider spends his waking hours either in class or doing homework, while Darius, whose class load is lighter, juggles between working for Uncle John, class, and homework. There's no time for anything else.

Saturdays and Sundays are still for Maggie . . . and Jenny.

So, when Darius and Spider roll into the driveway at Eldridge Avenue at eleven on Sunday morning, Jenny greets them on the porch and teasingly chides them for their late arrival.

"We put in a few hours on the Bumblebee Jacket yesterday," Darius replies.

"Fifteen hours," Spider grumbles. "That's what he considers *a few*. The Egyptian task-masters who built the pyramids demanded less."

"Yeah, well they had workers who were more skilled than you."

Spider gives him a light push.

"Where's Maggie?" Darius asks.

"Church," Spider suggests, but then Darius points at her car, still parked in the driveway.

Jenny's smile turns to a frown. "She wasn't feeling well this morning. She's lying down."

Darius nods, a flash of concern in his eyes. "Are you doing your thing?" he asks, lifting his chin toward the second floor.

"Yes." She fidgets with her hands. "At some point, we're going to have to bring in a *proper* photographer, but I guess I'll have to do in the meantime. Maggie's been going through the pieces with me. She remembers a lot of the names Atwood gave to the paintings, like *Bonnie Buick* and *Hard Right Turn*, and others have the name written on the canvas frame." She suddenly beams. "Written in Atwood's handwriting. These are probably the ones he kept; the ones Maggie inherited."

Darius nods. "Well, if you need help with anything . . . you know." He shrugs. "Spider and I are going to work on the siding some more." He glances up at the blue sky. "Can't imagine we'll have too many more days like this before fall and winter take over."

"Probably not," Jenny agrees. "How about I make some lunch in about an hour?"

That gets Spider's attention. "Oh, yes please."

In the last couple of weeks, Jenny had taken to cooking meals whenever they were at the house, often with Maggie's help. Her skill with even the most basic of ingredients is astonishing, and Darius, though he's never met her father, frequently comments on what a masterful chef he must be, based on nothing more than his daughter's skill.

The previous Saturday, he'd mentioned that he'd like to meet her father, an innocent enough comment that was immediately misconstrued by Spider as the old time-to-meet-the-parents part of a relationship.

First, they weren't in a relationship.

Both Darius and Jenny said so—vociferously.

Second, Darius insisted he wasn't even looking for a relationship—in the least. What with work, school, the house, and other responsibilities, he simply didn't have time.

Jenny couldn't agree more.

For her, the find of the century was squirreled away on Maggie's second floor—the existence of which her bosses remained oblivious to—and she had to catalog them, photograph them, and prepare write-ups for each. The planned size of her book, *Steel on Canvas: The Legacy of Evan Elmore Atwood*, had just quadrupled in size. The last thing she needed right now, she assured them, was the complications of a relationship. The mere thought made her smile and cringe at the same time, the way one does after the telling of an off-color joke that is funny, nonetheless.

Darius couldn't have agreed more. "I can have friends that are girls *without* them being my girlfriend," he insisted.

"Of course," Jenny had said. "Friends are friends. Why complicate things."

Spider called them both liars.

The siding on the north side of the house had proven more of a challenge than first imagined. They ended up replacing more than half of it, and now, after considerable prep work, are finally ready to put a fresh coat of white paint over the entire wall.

Painting a house with a professional air-driven sprayer is something that both Spider and Darius have experienced but in a limited manner. If experience were measured on a scale with years of increasing expertise on one end and a single moment in time at the other—like, for example, the moment you roll your mom's new car end-over-end on the same day you get your learner's permit—than Spider and Darius are on the crushed-car end of the scale.

The thing is, if you're painting a house, you're going to get paint on you. It'll run down your arm while you're reaching up to finish off a piece of trim, or splash on your leg while you're mixing, or your idiot partner will accidentally spray a foot-wide swath across your back when he turns to tell you something and forgets to let go of the trigger.

Mm-hmm.

The point is that your clothes are going to get ruined.

By the time Spider and Darius finish the north wall they look like a pair of rare piebald humans. They dare not enter Maggie's house until they're sure all the paint on their splattered clothing, hair, and skin is dry. Nor can they risk sitting on the patio furniture. Instead, they park themselves on the front lawn as they refresh with iced tea and some shrimp-salad sandwiches that Jenny whipped up. There's also some potato dish that's neither scallops nor mashed but something in between.

It's delicious.

Like dancing-pink-elephants delicious.

Maggie and Jenny join them—Maggie insisting that she feels much better. Unlike the boys, they decide against simply parking themselves on the grass and instead unfold a pair of comfortable blue lawn chairs, resting their glasses of iced tea in the built-in cup holders on each arm.

"Jenny," Spider mutters appreciatively between mouthfuls as if her name were a benediction.

Darius couldn't agree more and indicates so with small sounds and half-closed eyes.

"Oh, yeah," Jenny says with a shrug. "I also clean, and sometimes dabble with art."

"Marry me!" Spider says without looking up from his plate and busy fork.

Amidst all that clatter and revelry, Maggie leans suddenly forward and scrutinizes Spider with a heavy brow. Well, not Spider per se but his earlobes, one of which is freckled with paint.

"Spider," she says, "where are your gauge-things." She makes a pulling motion with her two hands. "Your earlobe stretchers."

Spider blushes—a true rarity—as his eyes dart away to the expansive green lawn and his right foot paws at the left like a four-year-old caught with his hand in the proverbial cookie jar. "I guess I decided that I don't want to look like the Maasai," he manages.

Maggie takes that in quietly. "But how will you be hip?"

Spider looks at her, expecting a grin or smirk, but finds her mouth in a rigid, horizontal pose—perfectly serious.

In a tone almost as serious, he says, "I was thinking of growing a beard and wearing flannel."

"Mmm," Maggie intonates. "I rather prefer the earrings."

Their eyes meet, and Maggie's unwavering mouth finally begins to bend, ending in a smile that almost shows teeth.

Almost.

Chapter 27

Once Spider and Darius are fed and content, sprawled upon the lawn like a couple of sunbathing seals, Jenny and Maggie head back upstairs to the space they now refer to as the West Wing, the side of the house overlooking the Puget Sound.

Jenny muscles a gliding rocking chair up the stairs one step at a time and situates it at the south end of the room, insisting that Maggie needs a more comfortable place to sit if they're going to catalog almost five hundred paintings. Maggie, for her part, seems embarrassed by the effort but takes a seat, nonetheless, gliding back and forth and announcing how much better she feels after her little nap.

Jenny only partially believes her.

"That's *Lost Dreams*," Maggie says as Jenny retrieves a large landscape from one of the many storage racks and places it gently on an easel before her. "I'd forgotten how lovely it was," she says, leaning forward and running a finger along the outer edge of the frame, a gesture of remembrance.

The painting, which is four feet across and three high, pictures a futuristic-looking burgundy sedan parked next to the curb outside an ice cream shop. A young couple admires the car in passing and an old man with a cane stands in front of it taking in every line as if he'd never seen such a thing.

"*Lost Dreams*," Jenny replies as if a mystery had been solved. "I looked all over the back and couldn't find a mention. I was going to add it to the list of those you still need to name."

"Oh, not this one. I know it well."

"Was it one of his favorites—your dad's, I mean?"

"It most certainly was. He painted it in 1956. I remember because he was almost finished with it on my twelfth birthday." She points to the painting, to the message board on the sidewalk outside the parlor advertising a special on Black Cows—a drink, Jenny would learn, made from Root Beer, chocolate syrup, vanilla ice cream, and whipping cream.

Tethered to the sign is a single yellow balloon.

"He added the balloon for my birthday. A real balloon, he said, would last a few days, but this one would last for years, even decades. At the time, I never thought I'd still be looking at it when I was in my seventies." She makes a swallowed *humph* sound as if suddenly recognizing all the years that had passed and disapproving of their speed.

Jenny scribbles furiously as Maggie continues, explaining that the ice cream parlor was based loosely on one they would visit on occasion in Seattle.

"What about the car?" she asks. "I don't recognize it."

"That's because there were only fifty-one ever built. It's a Tucker 48—the 48 serving as both the model number and the year it was built."

"Tucker?"

"Named for its creator, Preston Tucker. He had this vision of a futuristic car that was safer and better than anything coming out of Detroit." She points again, this time at the front of the vehicle. "Don't see many cars with a third headlight, do you? This one was even more impressive because it turned with the steering wheel, lighting the way even when cornering.

"The windshield was made of shatterproof glass and was designed to pop out during a collision. This at a time when other windshields would break into large chunks of razor-sharp glass so that if the crash didn't kill you the glass certainly would."

Maggie leans back in her glider and shakes her head.

"My father was a big fan of Tucker and his car and swore that political corruption and the big three automakers in Detroit were responsible for its failure. Whether or not that's true, it's also true that Mr. Tucker, while a great promoter, was not a very good businessman."

"Well, he knew how to make a pretty car," Jenny remarks.

"He certainly did."

"Did your father ever see one—in person?"

"Oh, sure. But that was years after he painted it. I don't recall the man's name, but there was this fairground owner in Florida who, starting in the early 1950s, bought as many as ten of the cars, along with parts, photos, and documents. He created a traveling display of the collection, called it *The Fabulous Tuckers.*

"When the exhibit was as close to Bellingham as my father thought it ever would be, we packed our bags and made a road trip of it. That was probably 1958 or 1959. I still have some pictures from the trip—oh, but you'd have to search through my photo albums to find them."

"Yes, please!" Jenny says brightly, and Maggie laughs gently.

"I'll dig them out for you," she says, "but not today."

They sit together in silence a moment, staring at the picture, each lost in their thoughts. At length, Jenny sighs and says, "I can't stop looking at it. Your father sure knew how to draw you in, to capture your imagination."

"He did," Maggie replies. "He most certainly did."

Her time with Maggie on the second floor had become special to Jenny, something she looked forward to all week, even more than seeing Darius—though she'd never admit the latter, especially to herself.

It wasn't just being surrounded by the precious Atwood paintings or even the fact that Maggie was Atwood's daughter. She and Maggie—well, they fit. The woman may as well be her mother or grandmother, for they share the same fierce independence, the same love of beauty, the same pragmatism—albeit tempered with a dash of the theoretical.

By their second week together cataloging, photographing, and naming the horde of paintings, they found themselves finishing one another's sentences the way long-married couples sometimes do. When Maggie was feeling under the weather, which had happened more than a couple of times in the last month, Jenny watched over her like a momma bear, hushing Darius and Spider if they came traipsing through the house too loudly or launching their loud voices or laughter recklessly.

Jenny no longer checks into a local motel on the weekends but stays in the guest bedroom across from the family room. When they're not engaged in the extensive work required by the priceless treasure on the second floor, they watch TV together, talk around the kitchen table, or, on occasion, go for a walk in Boulevard Park.

Jenny was never close to her grandparents.

Her mother's parents live in Florida and she'd seen them a total of eleven times in her entire life. Her father's parents live closer, down in Portland, but Grandma Morgan died when she was six and Grandpa Morgan is a bit of a hermit. They'd see him on holidays but even that was hit or miss.

Maggie is fast becoming the grandmother Jenny wanted and never had. It's the same with Spider. Perhaps more so.

Shortly after revealing her secret weeks earlier, Maggie explained that the museum-like air and appearance of the second floor was due to one unsurprising fact: She wanted to turn the house into a museum. Even before her father's paintings became well known, this visionary seed had planted itself in her mind. It was a persistent kernel that never left her and over the years she told herself that someday, surely, she'd open the Atwood Museum

"But *someday* never seemed to arrive," she had confessed. "And here I am, an old woman."

Spider was quick to speak up, assuring her that seventy was the new fifty.

It didn't come off quite the way he hoped.

In the weeks since that exchange, Jenny had her own seed of inspiration, only she wasn't sure how Maggie would take to the idea. She was going to bring it up last week, but there never seemed to be a good time.

Now, as they work their way carefully through the collection of paintings, Jenny decides she's just going to ask. The worst she can imagine is that Maggie will say no, in which case they've lost nothing.

"You know, Maggie, there still might be a way of turning this place into a museum."

Maggie looks up.

"I was just thinking that when we announce the discovery of *four hundred* new Atwoods, not to mention the Bumblebee Jacket, the art world is going to be knocked on its heels. You'll have people who were never much into art who suddenly want to see these paintings. Auto enthusiasts will want to see them because of the cars, history buffs because of their depictions."

She throws a hand into the air.

"You'll have car collectors standing shoulder to shoulder with art collectors and Americana collectors. Some will come to look at the past; others, to remember it."

"I sense you're building up to something," Maggie says, smiling.

Jenny blushes. "I've known you long enough to suspect you won't like it."

"Well, chewing on it longer won't change the flavor," Maggie says. "Just spit it out."

Jenny shifts uncomfortably. "I was thinking that there's an agency that might be able to help with the funding"—she glances at Maggie quickly, and then back down. "The National Endowment for the Arts has grant programs—

Maggie laughs. Then, slapping her knee, the laughter booms through the room. Who knew that such a diminished woman could utter such a cacophony? Her lungs must have tripled in size for all the bellow they produce.

When the uproar subsides, she pats Jenny's arm. "My father would *roll over* in his grave," she says as if that's all the explanation necessary.

"Why?"

Maggie hesitates. "I was raised to believe that you don't talk politics or religion unless you're in company that won't take offense. Since we live in a society that takes offense at everything, I have to ask: Are you sure you want me to answer that?"

"Yes," Jenny replies emphatically. "I don't offend easily."

"Very well but remember that you asked." She settles deeper into her seat and thinks how best to begin, how to describe the man that, in today's world, would be an anachronism.

"My father believed . . . well, let's just say he was opposed to government handouts, and that's what he considered *most* of government spending to be—handouts. He didn't believe in spending taxpayer money on anything other than basic government operations, national defense, and the few other functions specified to the federal government in the constitution."

"What about schools?"

"No. Schools, in his mind, were the responsibility of the state or local community."

"Roads? Libraries?"

"No and no."

"Social Security?"

"You mean that program that's going bankrupt? Definitely not."

"What about welfare programs, public housing, things like that?"

Maggie shakes her head. "It's not that he didn't believe in helping those in need, he just didn't believe it was the federal government's"—she hesitates and then says, "Responsibility is the wrong word, I suppose. He believed they had no right; no right to set up big government programs at the taxpayer's expense. He swore that nothing good would come of it.

"As for the needy, there were charities for them, and if the need was too great, the states had every right under the constitution to form their own welfare, housing, or food programs."

"Wait! It was wrong for the federal government but fine for the states?"

"Of course. When the constitution was crafted, it reserved such powers to the states, because the people of the state would be closer to the problem and have a better understanding of it. If they wanted to vote a percentage of their tax to such programs, they could do it. The founders trusted the population of each state to make the decisions that were best for each state.

"If, for example, California was to set up a government health care program completely funded by taxpayers, they would be free to do so if the people of that state voted that way. The other states, of course, would watch this little experiment in public health, and if in twenty years the system was broken and the state bankrupt, well, they'd know not to try it at home. This way the different states could try and fail or try and succeed and everyone would learn what works and what doesn't without taking down the whole country. More importantly, the citizens of that state would be in control."

"So, when the federal government does it," Jenny says, "you don't know if it works or doesn't until it's too late, and by then it affects every person in every state."

"That's right. There's no place to escape it. The founders believed that if, for example, Maryland was running things in a manner that some found too intrusive, you could move to Nebraska, and take your tax dollars and business with you. That, in itself, is a form of voting, I suppose.

"And while this is all well and good, the main reason the founders crafted the constitution the way they did was to make sure this new centralized government they were creating didn't get too big for its britches. They viewed the president as a sort of glorified diplomat or office manager. Yet they knew the nature of governments and men and put safeguards in place to limit the ambition of both."

"I didn't learn *that* in school," Jenny says.

"No?"

Jenny shakes her head.

This seems to bother Maggie, but she says no more on the subject, suspecting that she may have divulged too much. "Regarding grants," she says a moment later, "I wouldn't be opposed to the idea if they came from private foundations and organizations."

"Those are okay?"

"Of course."

'Why? Because they come from donations?"

Maggie smiles. "Exactly. When taxes become optional, and you can check off a box as to where you want your money to go, I'll reconsider the grant from the National Endowment. Until then, I'd rather let my father rest in peace."

Jenny smiles and says, "Deal."

Studying the young woman intently, Maggie says, "I want to show you something."

Rising from her seat, she turns toward the east wall and takes two abbreviated steps before stopping abruptly—as if confused.

"Jenny?" Her voice is small. "I'm . . . I'm . . ." Her head wobbles on her shoulders but she's not scanning the wall. Only then does Jenny see her waver.

Leaping to her feet, she lunges toward Maggie, trying to get to her before the awful happens—before the inevitable conclusion of what has already begun.

She's too late.

With one hand stretched out before her, as if looking for support, Maggie goes down. She doesn't fall over as much as drops—straight to the floor. As if someone took her off at the knees and let gravity do the rest.

The sound she makes when she hits the hardwood flooring is disturbing. There's no calamitous tree-falling crash, a sound speaking of terrible trauma. Instead, she hits with all the cacophony of bedsheets tossed aside for the laundry: A fabric whisper.

Jenny screams.

The world turns upside down.

Chapter 28

As Jenny reaches Maggie and rolls her onto her back, the front door crashes open and thunder rises up the stairs. A moment later Spider and Darius are at her side, panicked and confused. They cast a thousand questions at Jenny but get no answers other than the obvious.

Maggie fainted.

No, she doesn't know why.

"Call an ambulance!" Darius tells Spider, but his friend is one step ahead of him.

"Maggie?" Jenny says gently, brushing the hair from the fallen woman's face. With alarm, she notes that Maggie's eyes are rolling in her head. Her eyelids flutter and a trickle of blood oozes from her nose.

Before Darius is off the phone with 911, Maggie regains consciousness and is immediately embarrassed to find herself crumpled on the floor, her head and shoulders cradled in Jenny's lap.

"Oh, my. What—what happened? Why am I on the floor?"

"You fainted," Jenny replies softly, still holding her.

"That's ridiculous. I don't faint."

"You fainted," Darius says as if his words will add weight to Jenny's.

"I. Don't. Faint."

"Stubborn old grandma," Spider mutters, shaking his head. "Of course, you didn't faint. You died. We captured your spirit with Jenny's camera and stuffed it back into your body. Welcome back . . . and don't go swimming for at least"—he glances at Darius.

"A half-hour."

—"a half-hour," Spider finishes.

Maggie tries to look cross with him but fails. She lays in Jenny's lap,

182

a puzzled look now on her face. Eventually, she shakes her head from side to side and, in a somewhat incredulous voice, says, "I'll be damned. I fainted."

Then she hears the approaching siren.

"That's not for me, is it?"

"I hope so," Spider says, "otherwise I have to throw you over the seat of my Vespa and drive you to the hospital myself."

"Thank you, but I don't need a hospital. I just . . . fainted."

"People don't faint for no reason," Jenny insists.

"Of course, they do. People far healthier than you or I have fainted because they haven't eaten, or they were dehydrated, or . . . well, I'm sure there are plenty of other perfectly valid reasons."

So vociferous is Maggie's insistence that she's not going to the hospital that they almost call the ambulance off, but by this time its steady drone is on Eldridge Avenue. A moment later the siren cuts off completely as the aid car pulls into the driveway.

While Darius rushes downstairs to usher the male and female EMTs into the house, another siren replaces the now-silent ambulance. This one—from the sound of it—is probably a full-on fire truck with ladders and hoses to go with its loud siren and tooth-jarring horn.

It's still distant but heading their way.

"Oh, dear lord, another one!" Maggie exclaims, her voice showing no sign of weakness. She has a few additional words to say about both her predicament and the approaching fire truck, and they include utterances she hasn't spoken in perhaps decades, back in the days when she wasn't above a few crass words.

Spider looks pale when he rushes down the stairs.

Reaching Darius as he comes through the front door with the EMTs in tow, Spider fires off words at the Fire personnel like a gunslinger throws bullets: "You gotta turn the truck around. She's fit to be tied. I'm waiting for her head to spin around and split-pea soup to fly out of her mouth."

The EMTs stare at him in confusion.

"Can you call off the truck?" Darius asks though it's more of a demand.

The female half of the team, still unsure of what's going on, keys her mic and advises the fire truck that they've got things covered and they can return to the station. A moment later, the siren dies as the responding fire unit turns around and heads to the nearest coffee shop.

"Oh, dear. Oh, dear," they hear Jenny muttering from above as the bustle and shuffle of feet begins to move in their direction. Then she's at the top of the stairs, still uttering the mantra *oh dear*, as she clutches Maggie's arm.

It's hard to tell who's lending support to whom because the old woman charges forward like a bulldog, bellowing, "I'm okay. No need to make a fuss." Down the stairs she comes, dragging Jenny with her as if she were a small trailer. Taking the steps one at a time with the assurance of one who's never fainted, nor been brought back from the dead by three twentysomethings, she makes it to the bottom of the stairs with such speed that one might think she was fleeing something on the second floor.

Which, in a sense, she is.

"I'll rest better in my chair," Maggie suggests, giving Darius and Spider a telling look as she bustles past and turns right into the living room. Plopping down in her La-Z-Boy, she elevates her feet and then waves everyone in, as if she'd invited them all over to watch a show.

"Well, you look healthy to me," the female EMT says, approaching with a reassuring smile. Her name is Tawnee and she winks at Maggie as she takes her wrist to check her vitals. After a moment, she declares, "I've had thirty-year-old athletes with less of a pulse."

"It's the vitamins," Maggie replies.

They poke and prod her, shine a light in her eyes, listen to her heart, and ask a series of questions: Are you staying hydrated? When was the last time you ate? How are you sleeping? That sort of thing.

Maggie should have been a used car salesman instead of a realtor.

With the ease of a shyster, she convinces the EMTs that all is well and there's no need to transport her to the hospital. There's nothing broken; no permanent damage. Whatever the "episode" was—and she uses air quotes when making this point—it had passed. What was the point in seeing an overpriced doctor when a pair of perfectly capable and qualified EMTs had already rendered aid?

If you're an EMT, how do you argue with such logic?

In the end, she convinces the pair that all is well. On their insistence, she assured them that she'll see her doctor, and will certainly call if she feels the least bit faint.

Then they're gone.

The ambulance turns around in the driveway and pulls onto Eldridge Avenue. Someplace nearby, a coffee shop waits.

Jenny's beside herself.

"You can't just rush them off like that, Maggie! You fainted."

"Yes, I fainted. What of it?"

The three glance at one another, and then at the stubborn woman in the La-Z-Boy.

"Maggie," Darius implores, "what if it's something serious?"

"At my age, dear, everything is serious." She laughs at her own joke, but the humor dies away when no one else joins in. "Fuddy-duddies," she mutters.

Jenny's not about to let it go. "And what about insisting on rushing down the stairs like that? You could barely stand, and you rush off and do something stupid like that. What if you'd fallen and broken your neck?"

"Well, I suppose the ambulance would have proven handy after all," Maggie replies.

Jenny huffs and puts her hands on her hips.

Maggie softens a bit. "How else was I supposed to keep them from charging upstairs?" she asks resignedly. "What if they'd seen the collection? It's still a secret, remember?"

"It's not worth your life," Jenny says firmly.

"Maybe not the secret but the collection certainly is," Maggie replies just as firmly. "It *is* my life. It's *been* my life. It's all I have left of him."

The room fills with a cemetery's quiet.

Taking a step forward, Spider takes Maggie's hand and kisses it as Jenny reaches out and rubs her shoulder the way a young woman dotes on a loved grandmother. Crouching at her side, Darius looks into Maggie's tired face, her eyes seemingly on the verge of tears, and he smiles at her, holding her other hand between his own.

The scene is worthy of Da Vinci or Michelangelo.

It ends too soon.

Chapter 29

Friday, October 28

Maggie has no more fainting spells through September and October, and though still not quite a hundred percent, she insists on proceeding as if she were. This causes Jenny no end of anxiety and she takes to spending Friday, Saturday, *and* Sunday night at the old house. She rises early Monday morning for the two-hour drive back to Seattle and her small office at the museum, though without the same enthusiasm she once mustered.

On Saturdays, she'd taken to preparing a week's worth of meals for Maggie—mostly lunches and dinners. Some went into the freezer for later in the week, while others were fine in the fridge. This task might have been simpler if she didn't have to make extra for Spider and Darius, but she didn't seem to mind.

By this time, a considerable amount of work has been completed on both the house and the Bumblebee Jacket, yet much remains. With the wet fall fully upon them, they had decided that they'd pushed their luck too far on the exterior of the house and turn their attention to the interior. The previous weekend they'd even managed to refinish the hardwood floors in the living room without destroying them.

At Jenny's insistence, Darius or Spider had managed to come up with a steady stream of excuses to swing by the house, putting in a visit at least once a day. *Oh, I need to get the paint code from the last can we used,* they'd say, or *How's the new floor finish holding up?*

If Maggie caught on—and how could she not—she never said a thing.

After being content with her solitary existence for so many years, she suddenly finds the house too quiet in their absence, the evenings too long. As each new Friday rolls around she can't wait to see Jenny rushing up the walkway and the boys coming for a prolonged stay.

Each weekend is a holiday.

The drive from Seattle proves particularly brutal on this particular Friday.

Usually, the going is pretty easy once you get north of Everett, but Jenny seems to run into one slowdown after another. First, it was the shredded remains of not one, but two tractor-trailer tires scattered across three lanes of the interstate. The semi that had shed them had managed to limp to the side of the road but the debris in its wake was enough to cause a full-on traffic meltdown.

An unfortunate green Mini Cooper with a British flag painted onto its roof was parked on the median shoulder as she passed, its hazard lights blinking hypnotically. Other than the semi, it seemed to be the only casualty, having struck a large chunk of tire that did untold damage to the undercarriage.

After getting through that logjam there was an unexplained slowdown near Burlington, and then slow traffic through the hills around Lake Samish.

An ugly drive.

It's close to seven when the dark gray Camaro ZL1 rumbles into the parking lot at Road Runner Restoration and shuts down as if exhausted. The suddenly idle engine *tick-tick-ticks* as things begin to cool.

The second overhead door on the south side of Road Runner Restorations is half-open when Jenny ducks underneath and strolls into the shop, hands shoved into the pockets of her pants as if she was just another body man come to have a look-see.

"You're just in time," Darius says, smiling at her and letting his eyes linger a heartbeat longer than intended—on account of eyes sometimes having a mind of their own.

"In time for what?"

"We're installing the motor and tranny."

Jenny looks down at the naked, aged frame. The axels, wheels, tires, and steering box are still in place, but everything else has been stripped from the car. The body itself is still mounted on the specially built rotisserie cart nearby, looking even worse than when it came off the frame, if that's possible. The dusty dandelion paint is still visible in spots, but most of it is now covered in primer and a hundred spots of body putty where chips and scratches once gathered.

Still, it's better than the frame.

"Shouldn't you paint it first or at least clean it up?" Jenny asks as her eyes walk over more than six decades of grime, rust, and road wear that hang on the frame like old clothes.

"Yeah, that's what I said," Spider chimes in. "It won't matter how pretty she is when you're done if someone happens to peek underneath. A bit like looking up an Irishman's kilt. And that's a whole lot of ugly I don't want to think about."

"That comes later," Darius says with a chuckle. "First we need to make sure all our modifications work together. See this?" He points at a thick chunk of metal freshly welded to the frame. "And these," he adds, pointing to another, and then another. "They're the new mounts for the engine and transmission. The Cranbrook came out of the factory with a scrawny ninety-seven-horse flathead six. Someone, I'm guessing Atwood, replaced it with a much larger motor, but, of course, that's long gone too."

He steps over to a large lump nestled against the wall. It's covered by the stained sheet off a twin-size bed and uses every inch of it. "That leaves us with this."

Peeling back the threadbare sheet fold by fold, Darius reveals a pristine engine dressed in canary yellow and chrome. He smiles with satisfaction as Jenny draws in a sharp breath, and then keeps unfolding until an equally beautiful automatic transmission is uncovered. Setting the sheet aside, he stands next to the masterpiece with his hands in his pockets and turns toward them, the softest of smiles on his face.

"It's . . . it's gorgeous," Jenny sputters.

Spider just shakes his head. "You had this all along?"

"Yeah, I was going to mention it . . ."

"Butt."

"But what?"

"No. *You're* a butt. How could you keep something like this from me?"

"I wanted it to be a surprise." He grins at Spider. "Pretty sweet, though, huh?"

"When did you get it?" Jenny asks.

Darius looks a bit sheepish. "About two years ago."

"Two years!" Spider exclaims.

"The paint is new," Darius continues, trying to ignore his friend. "I stripped it down a couple of days after I got the Bee and painted it to match the hotrod yellow." He places a hand on one of the chrome valve covers—it's almost a caress.

"This is a 426 Hemi Gen 2, also known in muscle car circles as the Elephant. It came out of a wrecked 1966 Dodge Coronet that Uncle John bought three decades ago intending to fix but never got around to. Anyway, he was nice enough to let me have the engine for my hotrod project and I've been rebuilding it ever since, buying parts a little at a time.

"It's blueprinted and balanced, has a high-performance COMP camshaft, K1 Tech crankshaft, forged pistons—I upped the compression ratio just a hair," he grins, holding up his index finger and thumb as a measure, "and it's got pretty much the best of everything, or at least the best I could afford."

Jenny is shaking her head slowly with a big smile on her face. "I didn't understand half of what you said but I like the way it sounds."

"Yeah, what she said," Spider chimes in. "Except for the part about *liking* the way it sounds. If that means what I think it means you two should get a room."

"Shut up, Spider," Darius and Jenny say in unison.

Pulling an imaginary zipper across his mouth, Spider locks it with an equally nonexistent key and then tries to talk through the zipper. After about twenty seconds of this, Jenny reaches over and rips the imaginary zipper off his face, leaving him momentarily speechless.

"You were saying?" Jenny chides as she tosses the invisible zipper over her shoulder.

"Harsh!" he mutters, rubbing his mouth the way one does after ripping a particularly sticky bandage from hairy skin. "I'm just searching for some clarification here," he says when Jenny raises an eyebrow at him.

Turning to Darius, he gestures toward the Hemi. "You're saying we're going to move that big-ass engine onto the frame over here, bolt it all down to make sure it fits properly, only to take it off again and stick it back in the corner? Am I understanding this correctly?"

"Trust me," Darius says, patting Spider on the shoulder.

"Oh, I trust you. It just sounds like a whole lot of work for nothing." When Darius gives him a look, he sighs. "Yeah, yeah—trust you. I got it."

He tries to zip his mouth again but then remembers that Jenny ripped it from his face. When she smiles at him, he gives her a condemning look, shakes his head, and says, "Harsh!"

The next hour is chewed up by heavy engine hoists, chains, bolts, ratchets, grunts, and the occasional curse. At last, they step back and admire the engine and transmission in all their glory. A pair of worn-out headers are temporarily attached to an equally pathetic exhaust system, while the brand-new gas tank and fuel pump have been pulled from their cardboard boxes and clamped to a roll-around cart, which now sits to the side of the frame. A clear fuel line runs from the tank, through a fuel filter, and into the Edelbrock 750 four-barrel carburetor.

"You all might want to step back a bit," Darius cautions as he finishes connecting the battery. When Jenny and Spider stare at him he shrugs. "Just in case."

Holding the jerry-rigged ignition in his left hand, he turns the key to 'ON' and listens as the fuel pump goes to work filling the clear plastic tubing with the amber hue of gasoline. "Here we go," Darius says, pausing for just the briefest of moments before twisting the key to the start position.

The crank turns over three times before the pistons and plugs take over and the engine roars to life. Darius and Spider exchange huge grins while Jenny hops into the air a few inches and claps with delight—then she covers her ears. "Is it supposed to be that loud? I thought bumblebees were supposed to hum, not roar."

"It's the exhaust," Darius shouts over the engine. "It's all I could find. It's mostly useless, but it would be worse without it, trust me. When we're done, she'll be loud when we want her to be, and quiet the rest of the time . . . well, mostly quiet."

"Kind of like a low growl," Spider offers, trying to help.

"Yeah, a low growl . . . deep in the chest."

"She should," Spider adds with sudden realization, "this bumblebee is part lion."

They open the overhead door all the way and let the engine run for another five minutes, listening to the symphony of steel, gas, fire, and air with satisfaction that only comes from perspiration, hard work, and determined hands. Mankind, after all, was made to build, to create, to imagine. It's in our DNA. It doesn't matter if it's a painting on the wall, a colossal dam, a poem, or a yellow street rod.

Building, creating, imagining—that's life.

There's nothing so sweet.

Everything else is just existence.

An hour later the Elephant is back on its rack and they're just putting away the last of the tools when Jenny, hands in her pockets and looking every bit the girl next door, sidles up to Darius.

"So . . . have any plans for Monday night?" she asks.

"What's Monday night?"

"Halloween."

"Oh." He grins. "Why, did you want to go trick-or-treating together?"

"I was thinking more on the lines of going to a party."

Darius cringes. "I'm . . . not a party kind of guy."

Spider is just returning from the front office and manages to hear this exchange. Shaking his head briskly at Jenny, he cups a hand to the side of his mouth, as if for privacy, and in a not-so-private voice says, "Wallflower," across the empty space between them.

Jenny snickers and then covers her mouth, but her eyes do the laughing for her. "So, you're a—what? Stand in the corner kind of guy?"

"Corner, hallway, driveway. Whatever works."

Jenny leans closer and he can smell her perfume. "Please?" she says coyly. "It'll be fun, and I don't want to go alone." Turning, she adds, "You too, Spider. I've told Chelsea all about you guys and she dying to meet the both of you."

"Chelsea?" Spider says, perking up.

"My assistant."

He seems to chew on this a moment. "No offense to Maggie, but from what I've seen of your assistants, they tend to be on the old side."

Jenny chuckles. "She's twenty-two."

"Well, in that case, we'll be there." When Darius hammers him with his eyes, Spider shrugs. "What? It'll be fun, just like Jenny says."

"And you'll wear costumes, right?"

They both turn and look at her.

Chapter 30

Monday, October 31

A monolith of manmade stone rises before Darius and Spider.

It heaves upward from the sidewalk like some western mesa but one hewn from great slabs of concrete. It stands as if it had ever been there and ever would. The towering structure gives the building an air of impregnability and solemnity as if it were a cross between a modern castle and an equally modern cathedral.

Its imposing presence imparts a sense of smallness, almost irrelevance.

Near the top of the edifice, SEATTLE ART MUSEUM is embossed into the walls in letters that must be fifteen feet high. This display begins at the rounded corner of the building on 1st Avenue and continues the length of the wall that runs parallel to University Street. Above the giant letters is an equally impressive layer of windows.

If the glass were removed and the clock turned back eight hundred years, it would be from these openings that arrows would fly and burning oil would fall.

Glass and concrete.

Immense letters.

Massive proportions.

Yet it's not these impressive features that impart smallness. Rather, it's the forty-eight-foot kinetic sculpture called *Hammering Man* which stands sentinel outside the entrance slowly wielding its hammer, unbothered by the scurrying humans below. A titan going about his business.

Crafted by Jonathan Barofsky, the looming sculpture is three-dimensional, but only barely. Its black silhouette nearly disappearing when viewed from the side.

It's here that Darius and Spider stand, next to the legs of the giant.

Somewhere inside the museum, a Halloween party is getting ready to kick off. Whether it's due to these impending festivities—which run contrary to both of their introverted personalities—or the fact that neither of them has ever stepped foot in an *actual* art museum, they find the prospect of walking through the front entrance rather daunting.

It'll be fine, they tell each other.

It's just a building.

Sure, there're some paintings on the walls, and art geeks are running around, but maybe some of them will be as cool as Jenny.

Or maybe not.

It's here, five minutes later, that Jenny finds them, still rooted to their spot under the Hammering Man. They look relieved to see her and make no effort to hide it.

"What are you guys doing standing out in the rain?"

Darius squints up at the brooding sky. "It's not really rain, more of a slow-falling mist."

"A weak drizzle at best," Spider assures her.

"Okay, so why are you standing out in a *weak drizzle*?" She frames the last words in air quotes. Then, feigning shock, she blurts, "You're not afraid of museums, are you? A couple of tough guys like you."

"Careful who you're calling tough," Spider cautions as if taking offense.

Darius shakes his head and flails a hand toward the building, saying, "It's just . . . you know, people."

"People," Spider echoes. "We don't do people."

Jenny laughs and then takes Darius by the hand and pulls him toward the entrance. Spider, momentarily conflicted, decides it's best to follow along, strength in numbers and all that.

"Where are your costumes?" Jenny asks as they reach the glass doors.

Darius holds up a large plastic bag while Spider twists and shrugs his right shoulder forward, indicating his backpack.

"Well, before you change, I have a few people I want you to meet." Leading them through the doors and into the museum's grand foyer, she scans the room quickly and then clamps onto Darius's hand once again and pulls him toward a cluster of four people standing next to a two-story column.

The small group is already dressed in their costumes and each holds a red Solo cup filled with something called witch's brew. Two of the four are dressed as Raggedy Ann and Andy, though in this case the male, Don-something, is dressed as Raggedy Ann, while the female, Tabitha, is decked out in a glorious Andy costume.

It's immediately obvious which of the two put the most effort into their outfit, as Tabitha is fussing with Don's makeup even as introductions are being made.

"This is the museum director, Lorraine Brooke," Jenny says, indicating an older woman wearing a meticulously detailed outfit that Darius immediately recognizes as Professor McGonagall from the Harry Potter movies.

Well, from the books too, he supposed.

"You may call me Professor, young Mr. Potter," she says, perfectly in character. "And you, *Mr. Weasley*," she says, turning a bewitching eye on Spider, as if appraising the *actual* Ron Weasley in one of his threadbare sweaters. Then she smiles warmly and extends a hand in greeting.

The fourth person in the group, and the one Jenny is most looking forward to introducing, is a young woman in her early twenties. She stands slightly behind the Raggedy twins and, in the rush of introductions, had gone largely unnoticed.

Until now.

"An angel," Spider murmurs when his eyes find her.

It's not just a metaphorical statement, either. The woman is costumed as a pristine white angel—an impossibly white angel—complete with upturned wings that must span six feet.

How they missed her is a mystery.

"Spider, Darius, this is Chelsea Hart," Jenny says. "Strictly speaking, she's my assistant, but the truth is she's more like my partner."

Chelsea beams at this and steps forward to shake hands somewhat awkwardly. Darius recognizes a fellow introvert when he sees one and suddenly feels more at ease as he takes her hand and greets her.

Spider, meanwhile, pulls the same ridiculous stunt he pulled when he first met Jenny. Bowing slightly, he takes Chelsea's hand in his own and kisses her knuckles as if they were spun from gossamer and might break with the slightest neglect.

"Enchanté," he says.

"Oh, my!" Chelsea exclaims, and catches her breath.

Before Spider can take things to the next ridiculous level, Darius holds up his costume bag and asks, "Is there someplace we can change?" Jenny leads them to the public restrooms nearby. With the museum officially closed, they have the place to themselves.

To anyone that knows them, it would come as little surprise that Darius and Spider waited until the absolute last minute before venturing out to find costumes for the party. Earlier in the afternoon, they'd paid a visit to the temporary Halloween store near the mall. By that time, of course, all the best costumes were gone.

As beggars can't be choosers, Darius managed to piece together a respectable pirate outfit, even managing to find a tricorn hat that hadn't been completely mauled in the holiday rush. The rest of the outfit consisted of a red sash that looked like it belonged in a bordello, a ruffled white shirt, black and red breeches, and a nifty plastic cutlass that Spider kept stabbing him with.

As for Spider, he couldn't find a single thing he liked.

Fortunately for him—that's the actual word he used, "fortunately"—his classmate, Antonio, owed him a favor due to some timely tutoring that helped him pass a final. As it turns out, Antonio's parents own a Mexican restaurant in downtown Bellingham and the struggling student earns extra money by providing advertising services for the business.

In this case, *advertising services* means wearing a giant taco costume on the sidewalk outside the restaurant and waving a sign that announces the daily specials—ninety-nine cent tacos, two chalupas for the price of one, that sort of thing.

Antonio was more than happy to loan the outfit to Spider for the evening.

When they finally emerge from the men's restroom, the giant taco walking boldly alongside the swaggering pirate, Jenny is waiting for them, though now she's dressed as Cleopatra in a shimmering gold outfit that redefines the term form-fitting. Her makeup is flawless and looks just as one might expect an Egyptian queen to appear. A circlet of dangling crystals rests on her head.

Beside her and slightly to the front, Chelsea is applying the last touches of makeup to Jenny's eyes, being careful not to smudge her angelic gown.

Other creatures and villains and comic book characters begin to emerge in the lobby, creeping out from offices and hallways and perhaps an employee changing room. Darius casts about the room, making note of a vampire, two politicians, a steampunk pilot, Marilyn Monroe, Elvis, a hobbit—it could have been a short hobo with hairy feet, hard to tell—a scandalous French maid, a cowgirl, Elvira, and at least two dozen other colorful characters, some of which are barely recognizable as their intended subjects, while others are impressively accurate.

The room continues to fill.

Jenny points out Marlinda Thomas, whispering, "She's been asking a lot of questions about *A Girl and Her Car* and *Stepping Out*."

Darius's gaze follows her subtle gesture. "The witch or Charlie Chaplin?"

"The witch."

Chelsea snorts. "She always comes as a witch."

"It compliments her features," Jenny says caustically, and then catches herself. "Sorry. That was rude. But you have to admit that her long black hair and angular face have a sort of . . ."

"Witchy look?" Spider offers.

"Exactly. Witchy. She's a total witch. I mean . . . well . . ." and then she lets it go, fussing with a piece of gold sequin on her outfit.

"So, is it unusual for her to ask about the paintings?" Darius asks. "I mean, I thought you art geeks lived for that kind of stuff?"

Jenny looks up from the errant sequin and gives him a crooked smile. "This is different. She never had any interest in Atwood before. Now, suddenly, she won't leave it alone. Plus, she overheard me talking with Chelsea about going to Maggie's, and now she's wondering what I'm up to. Two weeks ago, she even asked me if I went to Bellingham for the weekend. Nosey little thing."

"Meee-ow!" Spider says in a low voice, clawing at the air.

When Jenny gives him a withering look, he swallows and mutters, "Did I say that? I'm a taco. Tacos don't speak."

"I wouldn't worry about her," Darius begins, ignoring his friend. Then he's struck by a thought, a concerning one. "Your photographer friend didn't see any of the other paintings, did he?"

"Kermit? No. Of course not. We were downstairs the whole time."

Darius shrugs, satisfied. "She's probably just curious then."

"That's what worries me. Right now, Chelsea and I are the only ones at the museum who know about the car and the other paintings. We need to keep it that way, at least until Maggie's ready to let the world know."

"Or until security becomes a problem," Chelsea says in her high, angelic voice.

"Or that," Jenny agrees.

For the next half hour, they move as a pod of four, mingling with other groups while Darius and Spider are introduced to people whose names, they have little chance of remembering. Even if the partygoers *weren't* wearing costumes, there are just too many of them to keep straight.

Some are employees, but the bulk of the gathering consists of family and friends, with a few valued patrons added to the mix, a little something extra to thank them for their generous patronage.

The clock has yet to strike six and already Darius and Spider are done peopling for the day. Sensing this, Jenny suggests a tour of the museum. They spend the next hour slowly walking past paintings and sculptures and pottery and even some photographs.

When they find themselves nearing the party once more, Darius stops abruptly and turns to Chelsea. "Have you ever been up the Space Needle?"

The question catches her by surprise, and she shakes her head. "No. Never."

"Are you afraid of heights?"

"No. I just never got around to it."

He glances at Spider and says, "I know you've never been up," and turns to Jenny. An unspoken question seems to pass between them. "What do you say?" he asks after a pause. "The drizzle has stopped; maybe we can see the stars."

"What about our costumes?"

"It's Halloween. Everyone's in costume. Besides, it's Seattle. You could wear that any day of the week and no one's going to give you a second glance."

Spider has his hand partially raised, like some timid schoolboy.

"How high did you say it is?"

"I didn't."

"Well, how high would you guess?"

"Six or seven hundred feet." When his friend winces painfully, Darius shakes his head and says, "You're not afraid of heights, Spider. You just spent a month on a high roof walking around like you owned the place, so don't even start."

"Heights, no. Super heights, yes."

Unprompted, Chelsea moves up beside him and slips her arm around his. "I'll make sure you don't get too close to the edge," she assures him.

This seems to embolden Spider. "I didn't say I wasn't going; I just have a preference for *survivable* heights when given the choice."

"Of course," Darius replies as if that makes perfect sense.

A glass-walled elevator as futuristic as the Needle itself launches the foursome skyward at ten miles an hour. Spider braces himself against a support bar and refuses to look. At Chelsea's urging he finally relents and casts his eyes out over the city, but by than thirty seconds of the forty-one-second ride have passed and almost as soon as he takes in the view it's blocked as the elevator docks.

When the doors whisk open, they half expect to see a company of stormtroopers.

Giggling like a schoolgirl, Chelsea grabs Spider by the hand and drags him off to the western side of the observation platform. More slowly but with equal resolve, Jenny slips her hand into Darius's and, as if of one mind, they turn the opposite direction.

The view is spectacular, and Jenny gasps with wonder.

A wash of twinkling lights lays below as if a tide had washed over the city and carried with it millions of glowing starfish of every size. To the east, Mt. Rainier looms upon the horizon like a gray ghost, all color and definition stripped away by the deep twilight, leaving the mountain a pale reflection of itself as it slumbers under a blanket of snow.

They stand in silence for a thousand years, content in the moment, lost in time.

At last, Jenny turns to Darius and folds herself into him, delighting in his smell, his feel. She lifts her face toward his, eyes filled with mischief and magic, and waits for a kiss. Darius, ever the unassuming gentleman, is content to stare into her eyes.

"Darius Alexander," she says, shaking a smile onto her face.

Her lips find his, pressing into them like a warm caress. A perfect, loving caress.

The night melts around them.

Chapter 31

The original Murphy's Law proposed that if there are two or more ways of doing something, one of which will result in catastrophe, then someone will always choose the cataclysmic. The adage has generally morphed to mean that if something *can* go wrong, it will.

Other universal truths include Hanlon's Razor, which advises one to never attribute to malice that which can be adequately explained by stupidity, and Sturgeon's Law which proposes that ninety percent of everything is crap.

Darius's Law is much simpler: Distractions arrive when you can least afford them.

This basic yet uncodified law of nature is as valid as Murphy's Law and may as well be enshrined as an unwritten law of the cosmos. Some would argue that it *is* a law of the cosmos, solid and established, and only slightly lesser known than the theory of relativity or the now-debunked idea that only one idiot can occupy a village.

If there *had been* an opportune time for a distraction on this Friday of Fridays, that moment came and went at 7:37 a.m. when Darius unlocked the office door to Road Runner Restoration and turned on the overhead fluorescent lights. This fleeting opportunity would have lasted exactly forty-two seconds: thirty-nine seconds of which was used to find the shop key on his ring and unlock the door to the teardown area. The last three seconds were spent scowling at Spider, who was checking the coin return on the soda machine for any loose change that might have been left behind.

Once they walked through the shop door, distractions were no longer welcome.

Uncle John and the cosmos must not have gotten that memo, because five hours later, at twelve-thirty, the calm and noncommittal owner of Road Runner Restoration walks into the teardown area with a hundred-and-eighty-pound trailer in tow. The trailer is wearing work jeans, cowboy boots, and an Aussie hat with one flap up and one flap down. The man's thinning hair and weathered face make him look mid-seventies, but he moves like a forty-year-old.

"Darius," Uncle John says as he draws near, "I want you to meet someone." Motioning toward the trailer, he says, "This is Ward Keller. I think I've mentioned him a time or two."

Taking Ward's outstretched hand, Darius sizes him up at the same time he tries to recall any old friends Uncle John may have mentioned. Both tasks take a fraction of a second. Shaking with newfound vigor, he says, "Yeah, you were Uncle John's mentor, right?"

Ward grins. "I don't know about that, but I was his boss once. A long time ago."

"My first and only boss," Uncle John clarifies. "I started with him my sophomore year of high school and stuck around another eight years before going out on my own."

A low laugh issues from deep in the chest of the old mentor. "By *going out on his own*," Ward says, "he means he rented a rundown four-car garage just outside the city limit. I think they tore it down after he finally moved out ten years later." Ward glances around the sprawling shop. "It was nothing like this, that's for sure. I don't think he had a proper paint booth until he built this place."

"Didn't need one," Uncle John replies. "Back then we did our painting in the same spot we did our bodywork. It was a different world."

"That it was," Ward agrees, "but then or now, people take notice when you do good work, even if you're operating out of a rundown garage. It's always been that way; we just sometimes forget. Hell, I think *I* even sent some work your way."

"You know perfectly well you sent work my way," Uncle John growls, "a lot of it . . . and mostly, I think, because I gave you the friends-and-family rate."

"He did," Ward says, smiling as if he'd just got caught pulling a fast one. Then, looking past Darius, his eyes find the Bumblebee Jacket. "So, this is the Cranbrook . . ." He leaves the words hanging as he puts a hand on Darius's shoulder and then moves past him for a closer look.

Unsure what to say, Darius remains quiet, but exchanges a puzzled and somewhat troubled glance with Spider. With the prickling numbness of a limb as it goes to sleep, he feels a sense of dread settling over him. Is their secret out? Does Ward know the history and significance of the old Plymouth? He sure *acts* as if he recognizes it.

Even now, Ward's hands run over the rear of the car where E. E. Atwood cut out four inches from the length of the trunk. It's as if his fingers recognize the slow curve of the metal, the now invisible seams where it was welded back together and then smoothed with melted lead.

"He always did amazing work," Ward says in a hushed voice and to no one in particular.

"Who?" Darius asks, a little sharper than he intends.

"Evan."

"Evan Atwood?" He hears himself say, while his mind screams, *That's a secret*! *How does he know*? *How could he know*?

For a moment it seems as if all they had so carefully hidden is teetering precariously on the edge of the bluff behind Maggie's house. One puff of wind or even the trundling of the trains on the tracks below would be enough to send it toppling toward calamity.

It's a secret—a secret!

Ward straightens and looks sideways at Darius, scanning him slowly from head to toe as if there's something to discern from his hair, his coveralls, his shoes. "How do you know that name?"

Darius suddenly finds himself in a hard spot, a place he wasn't prepared to defend. His hands go clammy and he shoves them quickly into his pockets. Two questions now stand sentinel in his mind: *Who is this guy*? and *How much does he know*?

If he had the answer to either or both he'd be in a better position to choose his next words, but Ward Keller is a mystery, a six-foot conundrum who walked in off the street not five minutes ago and somehow knows E.E. Atwood. The fact that he was Uncle John's boss a lifetime ago makes no difference; he's dangerous.

Secrets are dangerous.

In the end, it's Spider who comes to the rescue. Having spent half his life answering impossible questions from impossible parents, he's practiced when it came to massaging the truth and applying acupuncture to the lie.

"We did some research after Darius bought the car," he says in a clipped voice. "It was parked in a garage for a long time—decades," he adds as if to distill the point. "We kind of figured it might have spent its whole life in this area, which means someone local would have done all the sick modifications. We were right."

"Wish I'd heard about this sooner. I could have saved you the trouble."

Darius steps closer to Ward and crosses his arms. Recognizing almost immediately that this is a defensive posture, he uncrosses his arms and tugs on his right ear instead. "How-how do you know this car?"

"I did some of the lead work," Ward replies, pointing to the invisible seams on the trunk. The words are warm but cloistered as if meant for his own edification or perhaps directed at a much younger version of himself in the form of this Darius fellow. Straightening to his full height, Ward stares off into the middle distance, as if the 1950s were just beyond his reach, resting just past the body shop's roll-up doors and paved parking lot, a prize to be admired but not touched.

"If I was your uncle's mentor," Ward says, "then it's fair to say that Evan was mine." Stepping away from the Bumblebee Jacket, he clears his throat and gives a dismissive wave of his hand. "We worked in the same body shop but at complete opposite ends of the talent scale. Meaning I was pushing a broom and he was doing custom work like you've never"— he's about to say *seen*, but then turns his gaze back on the Plymouth in realization.

"Well, like this, I suppose." He says with a flourish of his hands. "I'd been at the shop for less than three months when he first brought this old girl around." He shakes his head and laughs. "A Cranbrook!" he says. "What kind of idiot builds a street rod out of a Cranbrook?" He looks at them for confirmation, but they don't get it.

"It was 1959 for Pete's sake. It was the era of Corvettes, Bel Airs, Impalas, and Thunderbirds, and here comes Evan rolling up in a 1951 Plymouth Cranbrook. Everyone at the shop laughed at him, myself included, but he just smiled and took it in stride. That was Evan, nothing got under his skin." He runs a hand along the stubble on his chin.

"I guess I don't have to tell you that two months later we weren't laughing. That was a learning experience for me," he adds, pointing his index finger for emphasis. "See, the thing about Evan was he just didn't look at *anything* the way you or I would. He was able to do that because the man didn't have a bias or belligerent bone in his body, and that applied to cars as well as people."

His eyes find Darius and linger a moment. "You would have liked him. Remember that as you put this old girl back together."

"I will," Darius replies, swallowing the words.

Glancing at his watch, as if remembering something, Ward says, "I gotta meet some fellas for lunch, but I want to thank you for letting me intrude." He shakes Darius's hand, then Spider's. "It does me good to see this old car again. If you run into any problems and need some old-school help, your uncle knows how to get hold of me." With a nod of his head, he walks with Uncle John toward the front office and pauses at the door for another look, another glance into the past, another wisp of memory plucked from the shop floor.

Then he's gone.

Spider watches the door as if half expecting the old man to return. When he doesn't, he scratches his temple and then shuffles his feet as he slowly turns to face Darius. There's a thoughtful look on his face as if constructing a story or diagram in his head or piecing together a dozen parts plucked from the brief conversation.

"Do you consider Uncle John your mentor?" he asks. "When it comes to cars, I mean."

"Sure. He taught me everything I know."

"And Uncle John's mentor was Ward, who then says that his mentor was"—

"Atwood," Darius finishes for him.

Spider's head nods in a slow, exaggerated fashion as if he's thrusting it forward and down rather than nodding. "Freaky," he says with a knowing glance. "And I mean full-on in your face freaky-deaky."

Darius raises an eyebrow.

"I'm just saying it's like some kind of weird karma thing. Four generations of car dudes all linked together. That's some Twilight Zone shizzle, right?"

"It's a small county."

"Not that small."

They work through the rest of the day ceaselessly—some might say relentlessly—striving to get the Bumblebee Jacket ready for her date with the paint booth.

That was the plan: prep and paint.

They'd been working toward this all-important day for the past two months, always balancing workload against class-load against Maggie-load and somehow finding ten or twelve spare hours each week for the Bumblebee Jacket.

The shop is quiet as evening sets in, save for the quiet drone from an oldies radio station and the whisper of sandpaper as it makes one final sweep over the car.

By ten o'clock, the Bumblebee is in the paint booth, its various parts scattered about it as if caught and frozen amid some great explosion. The main body is still on the rotisserie, of course, but the one-piece front clip, the doors, the trunk, and the hood appear suspended and frozen in mid-air. Only upon closer inspection does one see that they're attached to nearly invisible wires that hang from the ceiling.

As Darius begins to slip on a disposable microporous paint suit, Spider asks, "What about me?"

"I've got it."

"What if you need help with something?"

"It's kind of a one-man job."

"Yeah, but something might . . . come up."

Darius pauses as he's about to wiggle his right shoulder into the suit. "If you want to watch, Spider, all you have to do is ask."

"I want to watch," his friend replies quickly, almost cutting him off.

Darius grins and motions toward a cabinet with his head. "Fresh suits are in there. Grab a respirator while you're at it. You can't be in the booth without it, not if you value your lungs. Besides, the overspray will stick to your nasal hairs and you'll be blowing yellow for a week."

Once they're both suited up, Darius leads Spider to a bench just outside the paint booth and shows him how to strain and mix the paint, diluting it with a catalyst. The paint job is going to be pretty basic since he wants to stay true to the original 1960 design.

"Does the color change once it dries?" Spider asks, looking a bit puzzled.

"No, this is just the undercoat. It's *supposed* to be gray. We'll spray it first, and then we can start with the yellow enamel."

"Sounds easy enough."

"It is. Mostly it's just time-consuming. I'll show you how to use the paint gun and you can have a go at it if you want."

"Cool! Can I do the hood?"

Darius cringes. "Why don't we start on the undercarriage and see how you do. As I said, it's easy, but it takes practice to get the rhythm and flow down. It's not just maintaining a consistent distance from the surface, or keeping the nozzle pointed correctly. There's an art to the way you sweep the paint gun past the surface, release the trigger, and then sweep the other way. If you're too slow you get runs; if you're too fast you could end up with orange peel. Too much paint in one area can also cause orange peel—or even cracking. About the only thing we won't have to worry about is fish eyes."

"Fish eyes?"

"Yeah, little dimples in the paint caused by dust or other contaminants. If we don't do anything to stir up dust, we should be fine."

"When you say we, you mean me, right?"

Darius grins broadly.

Accounting for drying time between coats and the actual application of paint, the whole process takes about three hours. The shop clock reads just after one a.m., but neither of them is tired. Their bodies are exhausted, but their minds are fresh and excited. Even in pieces, the Bumblebee Jacket looks like a completely different car.

Aside from the spot of original paint in the trunk, the only other item that required masking was the back of the glove box door, the pretty spot of yellow adorned with the lion's head, the symbol of the 106th Infantry Division.

When the clear coat is tacky to the touch, they gently unmask these areas and are pleasantly surprised at how well the paint matches. They'll have to do some very gentle blending before sealing these areas with a coat of clear, but even now you can barely distinguish the old from the new.

"We need to get Maggie down here to see this," Spider says, letting out a low whistle.

"She may want to wait until it's all done," Darius suggests.

"Nah, she's got to see this. I'm ready to cry and I wasn't even there when the car was first built. I mean, I've seen the cars you and your uncle work on, but this is different . . . somehow. I don't know, I can't explain it."

"It's all right. I know what you mean."

Leaving is a slow process.

Spider walks around and through the hanging parts and the main body on its rotisserie, marveling at the yellow and the fact that the rusty undercarriage he'd worked on so diligently is now pretty enough to eat off. No, it's *too* pretty to eat off.

Finally, reluctantly, they turn off the paint booth light and slowly close the door. A sense of renewal and excitement follows them through the teardown area and into the front office, where Darius flips off the breaker for the air compressor and shuts down the rest of the lights. At last, they step outside and Darius locks the front door of Road Runner Restoration with all the wonder and solemnity of one reading the last sentence of the last paragraph of an astonishing book.

The stars are beautiful in the winter sky.

Or maybe that's just the effect of art. Perhaps the act of creation and recreation makes all things beautiful in their own way. As if one suddenly sees with different eyes, eyes that behold what was, what is, and what can be.

"Beautiful," Spider murmurs as he takes in the sky.

Chapter 32

The new day proves dreary and damp, pitiful even by Pacific Northwest standards.

Exhausted from their ordeal the night before, Darius and Spider don't arrive at Maggie's until early afternoon, finding the old keeper of secrets and her young apprentice meticulously cataloging the paintings on the second floor.

After some small talk, mostly about how strung out they look, Darius asks Maggie, "Do you know some guy named Ward Keller?"

"Ward Keller," the old woman says with a girlish smile. "Now that's a name I haven't heard in a long time."

"That's a Star Wars reference," Spider whispers to Darius. "When they find Obi-Wan and he says *Now that's a name*—" Darius covers his friend's mouth with a cupped hand.

"Ward worked with my father for a few years," Maggie explains. "I had a terrible crush on him; you should have seen me. It was pathetic. I was about sixteen and I think he was twenty or twenty-one when Dad first introduced us. After that, well, I found every reason on earth to come around the shop when he was working but only spoke to him occasionally. Every time he'd try to strike up a conversation, I'd answer in two or three words and scurry away, no doubt blushing like the schoolgirl I was. He must have thought me terribly snobbish. After I got the Bumblebee Jacket, I'd see him on the cruise route, and sometimes we'd talk."

"Cruise route?" Jenny asks.

Maggie smiles. "It was right out of *American Graffiti*, right here in our little Bellingham. Everyone thinks that California had all the cruise routes and cool cars, but I beg to differ. Maybe ours was only a few miles long, but there were drive-ins along the way and other places you could pull over and just kill a night hanging out with friends. Mostly we just drove around and listened to music.

"My favorite spot was Mastin's, a drive-in on Samish Way. There must have been room for thirty or forty cars, and when it was lit up at night it looked like a dream."

"Samish Way?" Spider replies skeptically. "That's kind of ground zero for prostitutes and dope fiends, isn't it?"

When all three of them turn to stare at him, he blushes and shrugs. "Not like I'd know from personal experience, I've just heard . . . stuff."

"It may be that way now, Steven," Maggie replies, intentionally using his given name, "but back in my day, it was a piece of Americana. It was like our own version of Route 66, only shorter and without the giant blue whale, the wigwam motel, and the other quaint but odd attractions."

Maggie sighs. "Sometimes I remember it all as if it were yesterday: the smell of a soda fountain, the whir and click of roller skates as carhops moved from car to car taking and delivering orders, the touch of felt on my skin from a homemade poodle skirt."

Her eyes shine with brilliance as they dance aimlessly around the room, settling here and there before moving on, as if seeing things long past, things near and dear and yet so far away. None of them have the heart to interrupt her quiet remembrances and Jenny smiles to herself as she watches the memories drift across Maggie's face.

The old woman soon realizes that the young ones—these twentysomethings—are staring at her and so she clears her throat and brushes imaginary wrinkles from her shirt as if just noticing them.

"It was all simply lovely," she says wistfully.

That evening, as Darius and Spider do the dishes and Jenny sits in the living room listening to old songs on the old Wurlitzer jukebox, she leans into Maggie and in a playful tone says, "Sooo . . . you never dated Ward?"

"Oh, heaven's no," Maggie replies quickly, wondering if she can still blush.

"Why not? Was he a troglodyte or something?"

Maggie laughs, despite herself. "No, nothing like that. I suppose I just moved on, girlish crushes being what they are." She looks thoughtful for a moment. "I heard that he married one of my classmates a couple of years later—well, not a true classmate, I suppose. She was a year ahead of me.

I didn't know her except by name, but everyone said she was the sweetest thing. Anyway, I heard they had two little boys and a girl together before, well . . ."

"Before what?"

Maggie looks up at Jenny and a shadow clouds her face.

"She died."

Jenny covers her mouth.

"She was pregnant, eight months along. I guess there was a blood clot; nothing they could do. That was 1969; things were different back then." She shakes her head. "I remember being dreadfully sad for her two little boys and that little girl." She sucks in a big breath. "Anyway, it wasn't that big of a county back in the day and I saw Ward in town a few times in the seventies and eighties, though I probably wouldn't recognize him today." She snorts. "And I *know* he wouldn't recognize me. I barely recognize myself. Perils of age, I suppose."

She glances across the room at the mirror on the wall.

"Perils of age."

Chapter 33

Sunday, November 13

Grace Margaret Lipscomb grew up around cars and the men who fix them. She spent her early teens sweeping the shop floor where her father worked and even became a fair hand at masking and sanding, this at a time when such a thing was unheard of.

By the time she turned fifteen, all that ended.

She was a girl, after all, and it was 1959.

Still, the essence of a body shop was ingrained in her DNA. The sound of a body hammer straightening bent steel against a handheld dolly or a grinder worrying away at a spot of rust were as familiar as bobby pins and nylons. As was the caustic taint of burnt metal that lingered in one's nose, or the smell of primer and putty. These were as much a part of her childhood as the hula hoop and soda fountain.

Sometimes it's the most familiar that we walk away from.

The last time Maggie stepped foot in a body shop was on September 4, 1973, the day after her father died. Gas was just thirty-five cents a gallon, Richard Nixon had just told the world, *I am not a crook!* and the just-completed World Trade Center was the tallest building in the world.

It's with some trepidation that she now stands with her hands folded together in front of her as Darius unlocks Road Runner Restoration.

Swinging the door open, he finds the light switch and the low hum of the fluorescent bulbs breaks the silence of the front office. Waving everyone forward, he closes the door behind them and then takes Maggie gently by the shoulder, leading her to the corner of the office where he points to the poster on the wall. Despite the clutter of the busy wall, she sees it immediately. Her eyes light up, delighted at the discovery.

"My word," she says softly, making a *tsk*ing sound with her tongue.

210

"Did you track one of those down for my benefit or has it been here all this time?"

"It's been hanging in that spot since I was a kid," Darius says with a pleased smile. "One of those things you look at a thousand times never guessing its significance."

Admiring the poster of three men playing cards on the hood of a 1937 Ford pickup, Maggie sighs. "That's my father," she says, pointing to the man facing away with his foot on the bumper. "He sometimes drew himself into his paintings, usually just as an unrecognizable distant figure. This one was different, though. He pictured himself just like that: a hardworking man who was good with his hands and not afraid to get dirty. He found honor in creating things and making them better, whether that was cars or paintings of cars."

"What about the cowboy boots?" Spider asks.

"What about them?"

"Well . . . was that just for the painting or did he really wear them?"

"He really wore them, of course. If was the 1950s; cowboys were all the rage. He didn't wear them to work, mind you, but if he got dressed up, which usually amounted to clean jeans and a white t-shirt, he'd always have his boots on."

She closes her eyes. "I can still smell his aftershave."

As Darius opens the door into the teardown area, Spider insists on covering Maggie's eyes with his hands. This at first seems like a terrible idea, as the floor is cluttered with debris not only from the Bumblebee Jacket but from five or six other vehicles.

Spider assures Maggie—and Jenny—that he'll guide her around all the obstacles safely, and even crosses his heart and hopes to die, which probably doesn't help his case any. Seeing that she has little choice, she relents. Promising she won't peak, she closes her eyes and lets Spider guide her by the shoulders, which he does by combining his gentle maneuvers with verbal guidance: Comments such as *There's a hammer lying on the floor two feet to your left*, or *It's a little tight through here*, or *Torpedo, dead ahead*.

It's still unclear what the last one meant.

In any case, they finally arrive at their destination and Maggie keeps her eyes pinched tight. She can feel Darius, Spider, and Jenny moving into position around her, their excitement seeming to engulf her like cool flames.

"Okay, Maggie," Darius says in a gentle voice. "You can look."

She does—and gasps, quickly covering her mouth with her hand.

Taking slow steps as if treading on black ice, she approaches the body of the car and lets her hand brush lightly over the dandelion paint, visibly trembling at the touch.

"Oh, Darius," she says, her voice on the edge of tears, "she's wonderful, just wonderful."

Jenny moves up and puts her arm around Maggie, perhaps to steady her, perhaps just to be close to her. The two share a contented look, the look a mother and daughter might share.

"Can you believe it?" Jenny says her voice not much more than a whisper. Then, reaching out like Maggie, she strokes the rear quarter panel.

"I sanded that part," Spider says proudly, pointing at the panel. Then, to Maggie's obvious wonder, he reaches out and turns the car on its side in the rotisserie.

With her hand on her chest, Maggie scrutinizes the just-revealed rotisserie, bending in for a closer look. "Isn't that clever," she mutters.

Next, they show her the graphics in the trunk, the original hand-painted moniker on the inner fender, and the signature of her father, faithfully preserved under two fresh coats of clear.

Maggie cries at the sight.

Any reserve of stoic dignity she still holds slips from her grasp and she covers her mouth with both hands as the tears trail down her cheeks and gather joyfully near her chin.

"It's beautiful," she sobs.

Reaching out, she rests her fingertips on the slightly raised letters of her father's name and holds them there, as if to do is to touch him. When she speaks again, the words are choked, barely intelligible: "Why'd you have to go?" she asks as if speaking to the name.

Now it's Jenny's turn to lose it.

Pulling her friend close, she lets out a heavy sob. They stand together for a long while, a time between seasons, sharing the loss, the dream, the renewal. Spider and Darius remain an arm's-length behind them, unsure what to do.

Guys being guys.

Before leaving the shop, Darius leads Maggie to the forgotten corner behind the Bumblebee Jacket and, with agonizingly slow folds, reveals the monster underneath. Only when the tarp is fully removed does one fully appreciate the impressive size of the Mopar 426 Hemi Gen 2—the Elephant—that Darius had salvaged from Uncle John's wrecked Dodge Coronet. The rebuilt engine positively glows yellow, black, and chrome as Darius runs through a list of all the upgrades and machine work done to the old engine in his quest to make it new. "Better than new," he corrects himself.

"I imagine she'll be quite a bit faster than when I drove her," Maggie muses.

"A bit," Darius replies with a grin. "That's about seven hundred horses sitting there."

She looks up in surprise. "How much was the original engine?"

"About 97 . . . give or take."

"Well, well," Maggie says, and then she says no more.

Chapter 34

Sunday, November 20

The next week is a busy one.

With the holidays approaching, shopping to be done, work, school, and a host of other nuisances that crop up unexpectedly, the four of them don't see much of one another, leastwise not with all of them together at the same time in the same place.

This proves disheartening to all, but most of all to Maggie.

Though the words have yet to be spoken, they've come to think of themselves as an unexpected family, a cobbled-together-through-shingles-and-fenders-and-paintings-and-love type of family, but a family, nonetheless.

Despite his busy schedule, Spider still manages to see Maggie several times during the week for dinner. On Thursday, she teaches him how to make shortbread cookies—"The only thing I ever learned to bake well," she tells him.

Jenny, for her part, is heartbroken that she can't be with Maggie . . . or Darius. Sensing this in her voice during their nightly calls, Darius surprises her on Wednesday with a batch of flowers delivered to her office and an invitation to meet for dinner at a cozy little spot on the water in the quaint little town of La Conner. It's roughly two-thirds of the way between Seattle and Bellingham, but Jenny said she didn't mind driving the longer portion, telling Darius that she could drive her Camaro ZL1 to the restaurant in the same time it would take him to travel half the distance in his Honda.

He left work early just to prove her wrong and still arrived after her.

Over dessert, they Skyped Maggie.

Not that she knew what Skype was or how to use it, but Spider was there to walk her through it, and for a moment they were a gathered family once more, even if it was only through the miracle of programs and bandwidth.

When Sunday finally rolls around, their first day together in a week, the house on Eldridge Avenue is raucous with voices and laughter.

They'd agreed the previous weekend that this would be an early Thanksgiving for them, and Jenny, armed with some special tips from her father, insists on doing a majority of the cooking. Darius is determined to help however he can and washes and dries the dishes as fast as she can dirty them.

Soon, the smell of turkey and homemade pumpkin pie and eggnog begins to fill the house, and by four, a cornucopia of new smells joins the mix, turning the entire downstairs into a gourmand's delight.

Maggie says a prayer over the food and even Spider—the avowed atheist—says a hearty *Amen!* The table before them is unbelievable and they almost don't know where to start. Maggie gets things going by saying, "Pass to the left," and in this manner, every dish makes its way slowly around the table.

The carved twenty-two-pound turkey fills a giant Thanksgiving-themed platter and leads the way, followed by a massive bowl of mashed potatoes, homemade gravy that Spider claims is the best he's ever tasted, cranberries, a tray with pickles and black olives, stuffing as light as cotton and as rich as butter, candied yams, cornbread, honey-glazed carrots, and roasted asparagus drizzled with olive oil and spices.

They eat like ravenous orphans out of *Oliver Twist* . . . and then they eat some more.

They feast like kings and queens of old, yet the food never seems to diminish, as if every morsel is served in a magic dish that renews itself as quickly as it's emptied.

They eat until even Jenny has to unabashedly unhitch the top button of her trousers. When they finally push their plates and cups away, unable to eat another crumb or drink another drop, they retire to the living room and flop down like a herd of elephant seals after a fish feed.

For an hour, most of their energy is spent on digestion. They talk, yes, but their minds seem addled by too many carbohydrates. At one point, Spider swears he's going into a diabetic coma. This might have been concerning if he was diabetic, but as it was Spider everyone just laughed and went back to digesting.

As evening settles in, the living room begins to show new life.

After all, there's still a pumpkin pie, an apple pie, and two types of ice cream that need to be dealt with. Darius does the honors, taking orders for this pie or that—or both—and determining which ice cream goes atop which slice.

When everyone has a dessert, Maggie rises and lights a dozen candles scattered around the living room. Dousing the lights and plunging the room into a quiet twilight, she walks over and fumbles around in front of an old record player for a moment before returning to her seat.

A low hiss and crackle issues from the two large speakers opposite one another on the north wall, and then the vinyl sound of the Moody Blues fills the room, albeit low and enchanting. *Nights in White Satin*, a song that was surely written for shadows and moonlight, wraps around them and draws them into the melancholic clutches of the aptly named English rock band.

It's the second time they've listened to the song together.

When it ends, Jenny resets the needle and falls back into her chair, her eyes glassy in the candlelight, as if moved by great joy or sadness. Perhaps both. There's something bittersweet about melancholy.

Tuesday Afternoon plays next, followed by a few songs they're either unfamiliar with or only vaguely recall. A length, the music becomes background, as all good music should, and conversation makes its inevitable return.

"Can I ask you a question?" Jenny says to Maggie in the darkness.

"You just did," the old woman says with a smile. Then, playfully, she says. "What do you want to know, dear?

"I was just wondering about the car . . . why you sold it, I mean. You have more than four hundred original paintings upstairs and just the one car—a car that means more to you, I'm guessing, than all the paintings combined."

"It does indeed," Maggie replies with a nod.

"Then why? If you wanted to keep your secret, you could have sold one of the paintings through an auction house and gotten twenty times what you charged Darius for the Bee."

By this point, Darius and Spider are listening intently and just as eager as Jenny for an answer.

"All that is true, but who would have fixed my roof?"

Jenny smirks at her. "I'm serious."

Maggie beams at her, but then her smile dips, and her eyes grow pensive. "Promise you won't laugh?"

"Why would I—"

Maggie clasps Jenny's hand suddenly and squeezes it. "Promise?"

"Of course."

"And you two?" Maggie says, turning dubiously on the boys.

Darius and Spider fall over themselves with a mountain of promises. Spider even plunges an imaginary needle into his eye not once but three times.

"I suppose that'll do," Maggie mutters. Looking at the ceiling, she searches for the right words. "I best way I can describe it is that I was led to it."

"Led to it?" Jenny says.

"Yes, and I know how it sounds." Maggie studies the young woman as if seeing her reflection in the girl's face and eyes. "Haven't you ever had a feeling come over you, a sense that you were supposed to go to a certain place or call someone or do something . . . something specific?"

Jenny doesn't answer right away but eventually nods her head.

"And what did you do when that feeling came? Did you listen, or did you brush it off?"

"I usually brushed it off, I suppose."

"Why?"

"Because it was just a feeling." She looks at Maggie. "We all have them, right? It's just our brain processing information and trying to make sense of the world."

"Hmm," Maggie replies with a knowing nod.

"What?"

"Nothing, dear. I used to think the same way, neurons, and impulses and all that. Thirty-some years ago, however, I was walking through Whatcom Falls Park and passed a young woman sitting on a bench staring into her cupped hands. She didn't look up as I passed, and I had walked another twenty feet or so when the most powerful urge came over me. I didn't hear a voice telling me to go speak to the woman, nothing like that, but I may as well have, so intense was the feeling."

Darius, Jenny, and Spider gaze at her, fully attentive.

"I'd had similar feelings before, things in my gut telling me to do this or that, most of which I ignored, but this was different. Turning, I watched the woman a moment. It was August and the temperature was in the eighties, yet she was trembling. I suppose that's when I knew something was wrong."

She leans forward to put her pie plate on the coffee table but can't quite reach. Jenny takes it from her—almost dropping the fork—and urges her to continue.

"Well, I sat down next to her," Maggie says, looking from face to face. "What else was I supposed to do? These feelings aren't exactly forthcoming with details: go here, do this, enjoy the rest of your life, that sort of thing. It's rather annoying."

Jenny snorts with amusement.

"In any case, the young woman didn't want to talk, and so I rose to leave . . . but then felt myself sitting back down. I didn't say anything for a minute but then began to talk. I never asked anything of her, no questions or anything requiring a response or reaction, I just talked. I told her about my dad and Jerry. I talked about my upcoming trip to Kenya and my fear of flying. I guess I just talked to fill the void between us."

Spider gives a knowing nod, and says, "Voids," as if the word was ominous.

Maggie raises a curious eyebrow at him but continues. "I felt rather silly about the whole thing, but it worked, and she eventually opened up to me. Turns out the poor girl had been in a rough spot for a long time, long enough that she didn't think she could take it anymore. Cupped in her hands was a full prescription bottle, enough Valium to last her a month, and she'd come to the park intent on disappearing into the woods and downing the whole bottle."

Jenny covers her mouth but says nothing.

"If I hadn't taken that feeling seriously . . ." Her voice cracks on the last word and she lowers her head briefly, unwilling to share what's in her eyes.

"What happened to her?" Darius asks quietly.

When Maggie looks up again, a gentle smile graces her lips.

"I suppose I became a big sister to her," she replies. "Sometimes that's all we need, isn't it? Just that one non-destructive person in our life that can turn it all around." She pretends not to notice when Spider glances meaningfully at Darius.

"It wasn't too long before she was doing much better," Maggie says. "In time, she met and married a nice young man from Beryl's church and his job eventually took them to California. They have two adult children, a boy and a girl, who I suppose are about your age now." She wipes absently at the inner corner of her eye. "I get a card from her on my birthday and at Christmas, and sometimes we talk on the phone."

Silence falls between them, and then Jenny says, "All because you listened to a hunch, an inner voice."

Maggie shifts position in her chair so that she's leaning on her left elbow. "Which is why I started to listen to those little voices, those nudges, in the years that followed. The more you listen, the better you get at detecting them and understanding them."

She casts an eye toward Darius.

"During a rainstorm this last spring, as I was standing upstairs staring at the stain on my ceiling and listening to the steady drip of water falling into a plastic pail beneath, I had this sudden urge to sell the Bumblebee Jacket. The same words kept running through my mind: *Sell the Bumblebee Jacket. See what happens.* I'd never even entertained the thought before, so when it came it was a bit of a surprise and I immediately told myself no, absolutely not!

"In the days that followed, as the rain continued to collect in the bucket, that quiet urging kept coming: *Sell the Bumblebee Jacket. See what happens.*" She huffs as if the whole thing is ridiculous. "Well, I ignored it and continued to ignore it until the beginning of July. By that time, the thought had taken root and I suppose I had to try to sell it just to . . . well, see what would happen.

"Ohhhh, dear lord," she drones, "the first three who showed up on my doorstep were just awful, and I nearly gave up the whole ridiculous idea. They were greedy men more interested in the ultimate value of the car. There was admiration, I suppose—an appreciation for the craftsmanship. I just didn't like what I saw in their eyes or their hearts."

Her head slowly swivels to the chair on her left and she spends a moment appraising Darius, much the way she'd done on that day of their first meeting.

"Then this one showed up on my porch." She sighs. "I knew right away that he was the one, so powerful was the feeling that came over me, but I still didn't want to sell the car."

Darius smirks. "So, you interrogated me."

"Yes, I interrogated you. I tried to find fault with this ridiculous urging by finding fault in you, something that would allow me to keep the car and put the whole affair behind me." She shakes her head slowly. "I tried so hard to dislike you."

She stares at Darius a long moment, much the way a proud grandmother might look upon an honorable grandson. Then, shifting again, she slaps the arm of the chair, saying, "And so I sold the car, and this happened." She gestures at the three faces gathered around her. "What are steel and paint compared to this? Besides, I'm an old woman. At some point, the Bumblebee was going to have to find another home. I preferred having some say in that."

She reaches out and clenches Darius's forearm.

As Jenny rises to change songs on the record player, Spider has something on his mind, something that manifests itself as an exaggerated look of perplexity on his face, a look that brings to mind one stricken by severe constipation.

"So, just to clarify," he says, "do you talk *back* to these voices, or is it a monologue?" He tries to sound serious, even concerned, but the hitch in the corner of his mouth gives him away.

"Why, of course I talk back to them, Stephen. They're my best friends." A touch of humor rocks her stoic lips, and she leans close to him, whispering, "They want me to kill you, but I'm trying to talk them out of it."

Spider roars with laugher and scrambles away from her as she makes a pawing motion in his direction.

Chapter 35

Wednesday, December 7

Darius arrives at Maggie's in the early afternoon, after his last class, and lugs a two-foot by two-foot cardboard box of Christmas lights through the front door, setting it in the foyer at the bottom of the stairs.

"Maggie," he calls up the stairs. "I've got the lights. I'm going to unstring them in the living room if you don't mind. They're a bit of a mess."

No reply drifts down from above.

"Maggie, are you up there?"

Again, no reply.

Opening the front door, he glances at the driveway. Her car is parked in its usual spot and there's still a touch of frost on the hood where the sun hasn't touched.

"Maggie?" Darius calls again, louder this time.

Taking the stairs two at a time he goes immediately into the west wing where Maggie's glider sits empty. A home magazine carefully opened to an article about simple Christmas crafts and how to make them rests on the seat cushion with almost a dozen pages dog-eared for future reference.

Darius does a sweep of the entire upstairs.

Nothing.

He feels a bit of panic rise in his chest but assures himself it's nothing. She might be on the back patio enjoying the brisk but sunny weather. Or out in the garage trying to figure out what to do with all the clutter.

After thoroughly checking the living room, family room, spare bedroom, laundry room, bathroom, and kitchen, Darius finds himself standing outside Maggie's bedroom. The door is cracked open two inches and the interior is dark.

Giving it a slight push, the old hinges give off a woeful moan. Something is unnerving about the sound, even foreboding.

"Maggie?" Darius says again, in a normal voice this time. The slightest rustle greets him, the sound of wind coming through an open window and disturbing curtains, but there is no wind. The day is still, the window closed, and the curtains hang slack from their rods.

Darius has never been in Maggie's room and as he gropes for a light switch, first to the left of the door where one would expect it, and then to the right, he grows impatient and walks to the window, throwing open the curtains and welcoming the afternoon light.

Maggie lies motionless on the bed.

For a moment it seems Darius's heart stops in his chest, like some great clock that gives a final tick and freezes forever.

"Maggie!" Darius breathes—and then he rushes to her.

Her forehead is damp with perspiration and her hair is matted to her scalp. The bedsheets are also wet, and her breathing is dangerously shallow. Scary shallow. With each exhaled breath, Darius waits on the balls of his feet for her to take in the next lungful of air—just one more he begs the universe. When she takes that next shallow breath, holds it a moment, and lets it out, the release comes like a rush, as if it's her last.

Just one more, Darius would beg again.

He doesn't remember calling 911.

He doesn't remember greeting the ambulance and hurrying them inside.

He *does* remember the EMTs using the word pneumonia, and the dire looks they gave one another as they trundled her out of the house on a gurney. Then it was lights and sirens and the incalculable seconds it takes to drive two and a half miles to the hospital.

It's the longest ride of his life.

Chapter 36

Saturday, December 10

There's a certain noise to hospitals: a murmur of voices, a hum of activity as staff and visitors go this way and that, a mechanical whirring and beeping that underscores the whole, as if the machines were really in charge and setting the beat for everything else, which perhaps is true to some extent.

Darius wonders how anyone ever recovers in such a place.

Between the nurses who wake you every hour or two to measure, poke, and prod, and the constant noise and shuffle—not to mention the food—it's surprising *anyone* pulls through. He supposes that's probably not a fair assessment, but he's not sedated like most of the patients.

Beginning with Maggie's arrival in room 317 on Wednesday afternoon, he, Spider, and Jenny had taken turns standing the Maggie-watch as they called it. The shifts varied: usually four to eight hours at a shot, depending on work and classes. Suffice it to say that little time went by where Maggie didn't have at least one of them at her elbow to call a nurse, talk to her, or, in Jenny's case, read to her from the copious notes she'd compiled on the magnificent Evan Elmore Atwood.

It was Thursday morning when Maggie first spoke.

She asked for her hourglass, the one next to her husband's picture in the family room. When Spider—who was positively doting over her— offered to run and get it, Maggie replied, "Try driving. It's faster."

That's when they knew she was going to be fine.

All was well.

She'd turned the corner.

By Saturday afternoon, Maggie's regimen of antibiotics had done wonders.

It would still be days before the doctors even considered allowing her to go home, pneumonia being so much harder on those her age, but she was talking without having to catch her breath, and a good deal of her strength had returned.

She was also eating well, which was a good sign.

They spent some time—the four of them—playing Scrabble that afternoon. Maggie cleaned their clocks, winning three out of four matches. She used words they swore were made up, words such as ginchiest, brabble, and lunting. Yet, when they checked online, they found she was right every time.

Spider tried passing off some odd words as well, but his really were made up.

At six, Darius and Spider make a run to Taco Bell for a dozen tacos and a chicken quesadilla. Maggie's probably not supposed to have fast food in her condition, but they figure if they don't ask the nurses can't say no.

Besides, life is too short for hospital food.

When they get back a half-hour later, the door to Maggie's room is pulled almost closed, with just a two-inch gap slivered from top to bottom. When they push through, they find Jenny at Maggie's side, tears in her eyes.

"What's wrong?" Darius asks apprehensively, unsure if the tears are the result of girl-talk or something more serious. Maggie gestures for him to close the door and he does.

"There's something I need to tell you boys," Maggie says when they gather around.

Darius notes that Jenny won't make eye-contact with him, but instead worries her fingers and knuckles in much the same way that Maggie does when she's upset about something.

Spider takes a seat on the bed next to Maggie. "What is it?" he asks, his voice intentionally calm. *Too* calm for Spider, even on a good day.

"Well . . . I'm not exactly sure how to tell you." She sucks in a gulp of air, something to stifle the wail and woe that threatens to burst from her chest. "Pneumonia didn't just happen," she finally says. "It's a symptom of a much bigger problem. Something I've been fighting for a while now."

The room goes quiet, a solemnity broken only by a soft sniffle that escapes Jenny.

Sometimes life gives you rainbows and picnics, other times it gut-punches you and leaves you gasping for breath and wondering what just happened. This time it's the latter.

"What is it?" Darius asks in a broken voice. "Cancer?"

Maggie shakes her head. "No. Not the dreaded *C* word, but something just as bad. Worse maybe, and a bit rare. It's—well, it doesn't matter what it is, and I've never been able to pronounce it correctly anyway. The point is I'm running out of options."

Wh—what's that mean?" Spider asks in an unsteady voice.

"Well, it means there's one or two more things they can try." She smiles at them and then a tear rolls down her cheek.

That's when Jenny loses it.

Moving to her side, Darius sweeps her into his arms as Jenny buries her face in his chest and just sobs in great heaving shudders. At the same moment, Spider rises and then backs away until he finds the wall and can go no further. Slumping to the carpeted floor, he glances around the room as if not seeing, as if a dark veil had been pulled down. His eyes have a watery sheen which he does not attempt to hide. His soul is scraped bare and written all over his face.

Maggie, unable to help any of them, looks at her hands instead. She absently notices the age in her skin, as if for the first time. They were once the hands of a young woman with her whole life before her, but that was fifty years ago . . . or yesterday. Funny how it all seems the same right now.

"I was hoping I'd never have to tell you," Maggie eventually says in a voice that's almost a whisper. "I thought it might resolve itself and I could go on another twenty years." She shrugs. "Maybe I still can. That's life, I suppose. You just never know." She manages to smile. "I keep thinking about that road trip we discussed, taking the Bumblebee down the Pacific Coast and stopping at some of the places I visited when I was young."

As she says this, Spider seems to return from the desperate, desolate place to which his mind had slipped. He remains on the floor, but his tortured face now turns her way, and she can see that he's trying to compose himself—for her sake, she supposes.

Of the three, it's Spider that Maggie worries about the most, the boy who had no parents worthy of the name and no grandparents to speak of. A young man who by all measures should have been a ward of the state, an institutionalized criminal, a plague on society. Instead, the young genius refused to be molded by his environment. He chose his own way, a better way.

Even geniuses are subject to the mental traumas of a broken childhood.

It's no secret to Maggie that she's come to represent the grandmother that Spider never had. She knew this after their first month together. Darius's parents and grandparents treated him like their own, of course, but with Maggie, he had once again made his own choice, taken his own path.

She is his: the grandmother who scolds him, teases him, always has treats, and tells the type of stories that grandmothers tell. The type of stories and moments that Spider had longed for his entire life. As for Maggie, who gave up the hope of children or grandchildren long ago, Spider is the answer to the empty spot in her soul. Jenny and Darius are part of that as well, but there is something special about Spider, as if he's a puzzle piece that completes the whole.

She is his and he is hers.

Isn't life full of surprises.

Chapter 37

The minutes and hours march on, carrying the evening with them.

Spider, Darius, Jenny, and Maggie talk of many things, past, present, and future, and eventually, when enough time has passed, they find smiles again and the occasional notes of humor, but it is a far different room than the one of early afternoon.

Maggie talks of death, confronting it as if it were a temporary annoyance.

"I'm not afraid to die," she says as the hour draws late. "The longer you live the more death feels like a homecoming rather than a departure. Most of my family and friends are on the other side—present company excluded," she adds briskly.

"It's one thing to speak of death when you're young and immortal," she continues, "when it's still a far, distant land. As you get older, however, that place becomes the next exit on the right and you begin to give it more thought, to form some opinions on the subject."

"Like what?" Darius asks tepidly.

Maggie smiles. "Nothing profound if that's what you're looking for. There is some comfort, don't you think, in knowing that billions have gone before you? When you look at it that way it seems the most natural thing in the world as if it's just one more box on life's check-off sheet. You know: Be born, learn the basics, try new things, discover love, learn more, discover sorrow, and then exit the stage, trying to leave the world a better place than you found it. I always imagined it was a bit like stepping through a door and pausing there just long enough to wave the next one through."

"Sounds great when you put it that way," Jenny says, not meaning a word of it.

Turning to her, Maggie says, "You have to change the things you can, dear, and accept those you can't." She fiddles with her hands and sighs. "I learned that all too late, of course. I was a beast to my father after Jerry died, an absolute beast. I didn't want to hear about his faith, or how Jerry was in a better place, especially since his *place* was with me."

Her eyes are haunted. "It was harsh, I know, but I was angry. My world had been shattered and the only thing I could do was challenge the very same faith that had kept him sane throughout his captivity, the faith that gave him hope and kept him alive."

"Still, I imagine he had an answer to all that," Jenny whispers.

Maggie huffs and crosses her arms. "Of course, he did; he always had an answer.

"What did he say?"

"He quoted Thomas Jefferson."

"Jefferson?"

Maggie nods. "I don't remember the quote word for word, but Jefferson once wrote that we should question with boldness even the existence of God; because if there is a god, he'd rather we believe in him because of reason rather than blindfolded fear . . . or some such nonsense," she adds with a smirk as if the words mean nothing.

"I think my father regretted choosing that particular quote at that particular time. Just because he was my father and I loved him doesn't mean we didn't bump heads. I always said that if hardheadedness paid in gold, that man would have died richer than Midas."

"Hardheaded," Spider says with a weak smile. "That explains a lot."

It takes a moment for his words to find meaning, and then the room fills with soft laughter and they nod at Maggie, each in turn, taking away any objections she might offer.

"I'm nowhere near as stubborn as I used to be," she says in her defense, and Spider leans over her and hugs her. She wraps her hand around his arm as he holds her, closing her eyes against the tears that suddenly push through.

Long they stay that way, the moment growing into itself until even Darius feels a lump growing in his chest and rising in his throat. Here is love. In this room. At this moment. Love that is overpowering and all-controlling. Love that says all will be well, for how can the universe shatter a bond such as this?

At this moment, if asked, Darius would have difficulty putting words to his feelings, for all seem so inadequate, so trite and superficial. When emotion transcends chemicals and neurons, it transcends its earthy bounds and becomes something beyond mortal measure.

It's love, plucked from the ether of the cosmos.

Eternal.

As it happens, Maggie's not the only hardheaded person in the room.

"It's the same with me and my dad," Jenny says after they'd composed themselves and returned to their positions in the stark hospital room.

"When I was in high school, we argued all the time, usually because I'm as bullheaded as he is and refused to accept that he might be right. After these little rows, he'd bake a batch of white chocolate macadamia cookies—my favorite—and then wait for me to show myself. It kind of became our thing: a mutual ceasefire."

"Girls and their dads," Maggie says wistfully. "You and I are fortunate."

Jenny nods. "Fortunate I didn't gain three hundred pounds from those cookies."

After a silence, Maggie tells them, "My father found God in Stalag 4B. He found faith and hope in a land devoid of hope, devoid of even the *hope* of hope. In a climate of fear, surrounded by evil men and evil deeds, he found the one think that kept him going—even after Jimmy Boggs died. He found faith.

"Years later, with my husband dead in a different war, it was *this* that my father called on and held to, while I went another direction. A darker direction. I may have been raised with my father's faith, but Jerry's death sent me reeling and I left it behind. It wasn't until decades later that I realized what a mistake this was. By then, my father was dead and my life was a hollow existence. I drank too much and spent too much and lived recklessly as I tried to fill this big empty hole that once held my soul. I marched for causes I later came to despise and spoke out for things I didn't care about. Nothing filled the emptiness. Eventually, I quit trying."

She takes a moment to look them each in the face. "Those are my lost years."

"Lost years?" Darius asks.

Maggie nods. "Make no mistake, everyone leaves this life with lost years. Some lose it to drugs or alcohol, others to self-pity, laziness, or apathy. Mostly it's a combination of things. Too many people spend their entire life waiting for something to happen and never bother to rise from their chair to see that it does."

The room is pin-drop quiet, a reflective moment.

"So, how did you get your faith back?" Darius finally asks.

Maggie smiles. "One day I got up from my chair and went looking for hope. I found faith instead if you can imagine that. It was the faith of my father. I'd come full-circle."

Maggie grows quiet again, and the room with her. As the minutes pass, her face takes on a tortured look, as if wracked by pain or the anticipation of pain. When she speaks again, the words are haunted and distant.

"He remembered every detail of the war, you know. Every friend who was killed and how, every hungry night in the POW camp, every fear, as if it was happening at that very moment."

She runs a hand across the top of her hospital gown. "It's no wonder he painted and listened to music. He never escaped the POW camp *during* the war, but he certainly found ways to escape its memory, fleeting as those escapes were."

Her eyes stare off at some distant spot through the window, as if to a different place and time, as if finally coming to terms with something she has struggled with for far too long.

"My father had a lot to say about good and evil, most of it learned by hard experience. I just wish I'd paid more attention when I had the chance."

"That's the way it is between parents and their children," Jenny consoles.

"I suppose," Maggie replies, though she doesn't sound convinced.

When visiting hours end, Jenny wants to stay the night at the hospital. The staff already thinks she's Maggie's granddaughter and she's slept on the couch near Maggie's bed for three nights running. Maggie won't hear of it, though, and insists she go to the house and get a proper night's rest.

Grudgingly, the three of them make their way to the elevator and then through the lobby to the parking lot beyond. Away from Maggie, they're finally able to voice their worst fears and sorrows, and Jenny is once more on the point of tears but somehow manages to control it. This is a good thing, because Spider is also standing at the precipice of tears, and if one of them goes, both go.

Darius is beyond tears.

He shed his fair share in the hospital room, and though utterly devastated at Maggie's news, he now has something more purposeful fixed in his mind. He can't heal this woman who has become so dear to him, but there is something he *can* do. Perhaps something more important to Maggie than anything else he might venture.

"I need your help," he says quietly, eyes cast to the ground.

Jenny looks at him, both worried and curious, but says nothing.

Spider does his best to look and sound like his typical self and almost pulls it off. "Anything you need, D. Just give the word." He throws the comment out almost recklessly, but Darius knows it carries the weight of his entire being.

"I think we need to move up the timeline." He looks up. "I think we need to get the Bumblebee done as soon as possible . . . just in case."

They're silent a moment and then Spider nods. "Just in case."

"How much is left?" Jenny asks.

Darius sighs heavily. "At least a year's worth of work if I keep at it the way we've been going. Obviously, that won't do. Plus, there are parts I need that I don't have the money for." He shakes his head at the impossibility of it all. "I'll figure it out."

"I have some money saved—" Jenny begins, but Darius won't hear of it.

"I'm going to head over to the Road Runner," he says. "See what I can get done."

"Dude, it's almost eleven. That means it's *almost-almost* midnight."

"I know," Darius says resignedly. "Not like I'm going to be able to sleep, though. I was thinking I can wheel the frame into the sandblasting booth and get it cleaned up. If I can get a couple of coats of primer on it tonight, maybe I can paint it tomorrow. That's one step closer."

"Well, I'm coming with you," Spider says grudgingly, already missing the sleep he's giving up. "I know I'm still new to all this, but I've gotten pretty good at taking things apart, and I imagine you'll need some of that."

"You have no idea," Darius says with a sad smile.

"What about me?" Jenny asks. "What can I do?"

Darius thinks a moment: "How are you with wiring?"

Chapter 38

Tuesday, December 13

When Maggie is finally released from the hospital, it's Jenny who drives her home.

Spider and Darius insisted on being there as well, but they have finals. This didn't seem to matter to either of them, and they were prepared to ditch class, but Jenny insisted they go. Why they listened to her is a bit of a mystery, but they'd be the first to admit that she had a way with people.

As soon as class ends, the brothers in all but blood walk briskly across campus, ducking their heads against the wind and the slanting rain. At the car, Darius fumbles through his pockets but can't seem to find his keys. Spider is quick to point out that they're in his other hand, and, feeling foolish, Darius unlocks the doors with two taps on the fob. Piling into the car, they shake off the rain and shiver against the northwest cold.

"Can't believe I did that," Darius mutters once his teeth stop chattering.

Spider chuckles unsteadily and gives a big shiver. "You got a lot on your mind."

Darius just nods and cranks the heat up as he lets the engine warm and the fog dissipate from the windshield.

"Yesterday," he says, "I pulled up to an intersection out in the county and sat there for about five minutes waiting for the stop sign to turn green."

"Did it?" Spider asks.

"Nope. It just sat there on its pole, all red and octagonal."

Spider grins and shakes his head. "I think I got you beat. On Sunday morning, I was heading to the hospital on my friggin' Vespa—cold and soaked to the bone—and I pulled up to this crosswalk and stopped because this little kid in a red rain slicker was waiting to cross. He had a white hat on and I wasn't paying much attention—you know, thinking about Maggie and all that. After a minute or two, a car behind me honked and then drove around. Well, I yelled at him and pointed to the kid . . . and that's when I realized it was a fire hydrant. A red fire hydrant with a white cap."

It's Darius's turn to chuckle. "Aren't we a pair of fools?"

"Yeah. Fools," Spider agrees quietly. Then, in a broken voice suddenly filled with pain, he adds, "The end of the world will do that to a guy, I suppose."

"That's a bit dramatic," Darius tells his friend, even as he chokes on the words.

"I know." Spider's quiet a moment as he struggles to contain the hopeless sorrow. "How can things just go on, as if nothing is happening?" he finally asks.

"I don't know. I suppose that's just life."

"Yeah? Well, it sucks."

"Maggie might tell you otherwise."

"Of course, she would," Spider scoffs. He gives the dash a light punch with his closed fist—followed quickly by a second blow that's considerably more forceful as if the dash were Death himself and by beating him in a round of fisticuffs, he might win Maggie's immortality, or at least buy her a few more years.

It's a fantasy, of course.

If the eternal ledger were so easy to change, Death would be one bruised up son-of-a-bitch. Everyone on the planet would want a piece of him and his medieval robes.

"Maybe Atwood was right," Darius suggests.

"About what?"

"About the body being like a car and the soul is the driver."

Spider groans and gives him a look that only a scientist can muster.

Darius shrugs. "Maybe there *is* a higher mind that survives and carries on. You don't know. Nobody knows. I mean, the brain is just an organ, like the liver, the kidneys, and the lungs, right? They may be able to regulate our blood flow, keep us breathing while we sleep, and send chemical and electric messages that affect our . . . well, our basic programming, to put it in computer terms. But it's the intangible mind that determines who we are, right?"

"The brain *is* the mind," Spider replies, not buying into the argument.

"Who says?"

"Science."

234 · SPENCER KOPE

"The same science that once said the earth was flat and stood at the center of the solar system, or that you could cure someone by applying leeches to them, or that light was transmitted through the universe by a mysterious substance known as luminiferous ether?"

"It's not that simple."

"Isn't it?" Darius studies his friend a moment. "We think that because we live in the twenty-first century that we have the answers to everything, that we're so smart. I would have thought that you, of all people, would have realized by now that questions are like rabbits: The more you have, the more you get."

"That doesn't make sense."

"It kind of does."

Spider says nothing and appears intent on the wind and rain beyond the windshield.

"When Copernicus formulated his model of the universe," Darius presses, "did that end every question we had about the universe, or create centuries of ever more detailed questions and answers? Newton discovered gravity over three hundred years ago, and we're still not sure exactly what causes it.

"So, what are you saying?"

"I'm saying that if God exists then this *vaunted* intellect and understanding of the universe that we seem to think we have is like an ant trying to understand a lawnmower." He glances over at his friend. "You know I've never been the religious type, but I've been thinking about it a lot since we met Maggie."

"Church," Spider mutters.

"I mean, it's not just about where we came from and where we're going, it's about finding purpose in life. Don't you find it a little depressing to think that we just cease to exist when we die, as if we were no more important than a dead leaf from a wintering tree? We rot away and nothing is left. In time, no one even remembers you existed, and eventually, even the earth is wiped away as the sun goes supernova, or the universe collapses back into a black hole as if nothing matters."

"You're asking me to consider things I simply can't believe—"

"What about this idea of ten dimensions?" Darius presses.

"Eleven dimensions," Spider corrects. "What about it?"

"When you were at Stanford getting your degree in applied physics, you talked about worlds within worlds, parallel universes, and other things I could barely wrap my head around. Stuff that sounded . . . well, pretty fanciful."

"It's called the many-worlds interpretation, and it comes from quantum mechanics."

"Whatever. The point is, you said that many in the scientific community think it has real merit, even though it supposes that there are an infinite number of universes that account for every possible outcome of our lives. In one world I might be a rock star or a classical pianist, in another I'm struggling to survive after a coronal mass ejection from the sun destroys all electronics and ninety percent of the country's population dies of disease, starvation, and social unrest."

"On a billion other worlds, Maggie isn't dying," Spider says quietly.

Darius sighs. "On a billion other worlds, we never meet her. Which is worse?"

"For us or her?"

The words force Darius to pause a moment, and he's suddenly aware—*acutely* aware—of the increased tempo of the wind and rain as the torrent whips and lashes the car; he feels the wind's force as it gently rocks the Honda with each gust.

When he finally finds his words, it's against this tempestuous backdrop, as if the subject of god and faith are forever meant to be juxtaposed against a storm: A tempest of differing opinions, thoughts, and viewpoints, sometimes violent and earthshaking.

"You can believe in these infinite worlds and other strange dimensions," Darius finally says, "but you won't even consider something as simple as a soul. You realize that if God exists, he might be from one of these other dimensions you talk about. Maybe a twelfth dimension, something we call heaven. A place we return to after we're done here."

Spider glances over at him, the scientific scorn momentarily absent from his eyes.

"When you ask why we can't see god or departed souls, someone might ask *you* a similar question, like *why can't we see into these other dimensions?* Or better yet, how do we know these other dimensions exist if we can't see them?"

"It's just a theory," Spider replies a bit defensively, "but it's based on basic principles and observable phenomena in quantum physics."

236 · SPENCER KOPE

"Theory? Is that the scientific community's word for faith?"

Spider issues an exasperated noise that's somewhere between a huff and a snort.

They sit in silence for a long while, listening to the wind. At last, Darius punches Spider lightly on the shoulder, as if they were boys again and he'd just lost a round of *Flinch* or *Jinx*.

"You know you're my brother," he says, "and I don't mean to antagonize you or challenge your scientific beliefs, but since we first met Maggie, I've started to realize that maybe a little faith isn't so bad. I mean, in your version of things, we just cease to exist when we die. So . . . what's the point? What's the point of anything?"

Darius lets that sink in a moment.

"Besides," he continues, "if God *does* exist, wouldn't he be the greatest scientist of all?" He glances at Spider, as if appraising him. "Probably some super-nerd like you, only with cosmic powers."

Spider gives a rueful snort and shakes his head.

The wind howls on.

When they reach Maggie's place, Jenny intercepts them at the door. She's upset and flustered about something but assures them that Maggie is fine.

"What is it?" Darius presses.

"I think someone accessed my work computer," she blurts in a hushed voice.

They stare at her, confused.

"I have pictures and descriptions of the paintings," she hisses, pointing to the second floor. "That, and all my notes, plus the hundreds of pictures I've taken of the Bumblebee Jacket during the restoration."

"Oh," Darius says, looking a bit floored.

"That's not good," Spider says as if it's both a question and a statement.

Jenny looks like she's going to cry. "I've been careful to lock my computer screen when I leave the office, but I must have forgotten yesterday. I was only gone fifteen minutes and wasn't overly concerned when I returned to find the screen open. Then," she shakes her head, "I realized the screensaver hadn't come on. I have it on a ten-minute delay," she explains.

"Anyway, I started poking around and found the Atwood file open." Turning to Darius, she insists, "I'm certain I closed it."

The three of them fall silent, weighing the implications.

"Didn't you say one of your coworkers, Madelaine or something, was asking a lot of questions about the two paintings you had photographed?" Spider asks.

"Marlinda!" Jenny groans.

"Any chance she was snooping around?"

"I don't know that she's that brave. Still, she's the busybody type, always prying." A thought suddenly occurs to her and she lets out a long sigh. "She *did* ask me last month if I was coming back up here for more research, referencing a picture of Chuckanut Drive that I posted on Facebook. I was vague, of course, but I think she came to her own conclusions. She told me to let her know if I needed help with anything."

"Have you noticed anything else odd or out of place?" Darius asks.

Jenny hesitates. "Once or twice," she admits. "Nothing big, though. I just assumed I was being paranoid. You know, freaking myself out about the information getting out prematurely." She crosses her arms indignantly. "I hate secrets."

"Anyone else you can think of that might have taken an interest in your work?"

Jenny thinks about it but then shakes her head.

"What about that Stu guy?"

She snorts. "Maybe if the paintings were filled with breasts."

Darius chuckles.

Normally, Spider would be right there, chuckling along with him, but he seems taken by a thought. A moment later, he nods to himself, as if settling an internal debate.

"Can I borrow your keys?" he asks Darius. "Just for an hour or two?"

"What do you need my keys for?"

"Well, the car doesn't run without them." He gives Darius a dubious look. "I thought you were supposed to be smart?"

Darius doesn't press the issue, he just hands over the keys.

Without a word, Spider ducks out the door and races through the wind and rain to the waiting Honda. He manages to grind the starter getting the engine to run, and then does a seven-point turn in the ample parking area.

"Lights," Darius says to the window, watching the car-shaped shadow disappear in the murk.

Just before reaching the end of the driveway, the Honda's headlights miraculously come on and a sigh of relief is heard in Maggie's foyer.

"What's he up to?" Jenny mutters.

"I can't even guess."

True to his word, Spider returns in just shy of two hours.

As he shakes off the cold and rain, he produces a plastic bag from under his coat. Walking to the kitchen he sets it on the table and drapes his storm-blown coat over the back of a chair.

"What's this?" Jenny asks.

"Oh, just something I pieced together," Spider replies as he begins to peel back the plastic. Reaching into the bag he extracts a black lump which quickly manifests as a . . . well, a coffee cup.

"Really?" Jenny says, obviously disappointed.

Darius, however, remains silent. He knows his friend too well to think that he disappeared for almost two hours—braving wind and rain—for something as mundane as a coffee mug.

"Trust me, this is going to solve all your problems," Spider continues. Sticking his finger into the cup momentarily, he holds it out for Jenny's inspection. Emblazoned on the front in bold white letters, the mug reads CTRL ALT DEL.

"Control, alt, delete?"

Spider grins. "Yeah, you know—reboot. Like when your computer freezes." He seems to think it's pretty funny. Tipping the cup forward so that the top opening is facing her, he points inside. "This is the important part."

Leaning forward, Jenny sees a small black lump, perhaps the size of a bottlecap, attached to the inside wall of the cup. A section of black wire extends from the mass, ending in a USB plug. Below all this is what appears to be four AA batteries bound together with electrical tape and glued to the inside bottom, along with a second black rectangle that is unidentifiable.

"What is it?"

"A mug cam."

"A what?"

"A mug cam. You know, like a nanny cam, but with a coffee mug. It's my own design." Turning the mug so the slogan on the front is again visible, he points to the blacked-out area in the loop of the *R* in CTRL. "This is a pinhole camera."

He hands the mug to Jenny.

Tipping it over and studying it from every angle, she says, "I'm guessing I shouldn't use this for my morning tea?"

"Yes. Please let's not do that," Spider says briskly. "The mug is easy enough to replace but the camera is high-end."

She looks at him, as if just now realizing the truth.

"Did you *build* this?"

"Of course, I did."

"When?"

"Just now. That's what took so long."

"Took so . . ." Jenny begins, but then she just shakes her head.

Pleased with himself, Spider taps the opening. "I'd suggest putting some pens in it, or something like that. It'll keep anyone from looking down inside or using it for *actual* coffee. Just put it at the back of your desk facing your chair, that way anyone sitting down will be visible."

He takes a moment to show her how to connect it to her computer when she's ready to download any images, so she can view and delete anything captured by the stealth camera.

"It's motion-activated and will take one frame per second when tripped." His face suddenly scrunches up, as if just thinking of something. "You might want to turn it to face the wall when you're at your desk, otherwise you're going to get a lot of pictures you don't want."

Darius watches as Spider and Jenny discuss the hidden camera—feeling a hint of pride for his brilliant, eccentric friend. What started as a gross intrusion that might jeopardize the entire Atwood collection had somehow turned into a rather enjoyable covert mission.

They're going to catch Marlinda—or whoever—in the act. Red-handed, as they say.

Darius's intrigued eyes suddenly narrow as something occurs to him.

"What about a key logger?" he asks Spider.

His friend nods his understanding. "If the screen was locked, that would explain how she was able to access it."

"Key logger?" Jenny questions.

"It's a small device that plugs into the end of the cable from your keyboard to the USB slot at the back of your tower." He hesitates. "That's assuming you're not using a wireless keyboard . . ."

Jenny shakes her head.

"Or a laptop?"

Again, she shakes her head.

"Good," Darius continues. "When you get to work tomorrow, trace your keyboard cable to the back of your computer. If it plugs directly into a USB slot your fine, but if it plugs into something that looks like a thumb drive, which in turn plugs into the USB, then someone has attached a key logger to your system. It records every keystroke on the keyboard: that means notes, passwords, websites, you name it."

"But, how could someone do that and not get caught?"

"It takes like three seconds," Spider explains. "And since no one looks at the back of their computer unless they're moving it or plugging something in, the chances of it being found are minimal."

Jenny looks a bit creeped out.

"I hope your both wrong."

"We probably are," Spider assures her. "Most people have never heard of a key logger." When Jenny looks down at the mug cam still in her hands, Spider shoots Darius a concerned look.

The unspoken words between them are accepted with a subtle nod. Whatever this is and whoever is behind it, they're going to have to let things play out.

For now.

Chapter 39

Wednesday, December 14

It's just after eight a.m. when Darius's phone rings. The caller ID displays Jenny's number, so he answers on the second ring, barely getting out a *Hello* before she hisses in his ear.

"I found it. What now?"

"Found what?"

"The logger thing."

"The key logger? You're sure?"

"I traced it out from the keyboard," Jenny replies in a low, conspiratorial tone. "It's just like you said. I even pulled up a picture online and found the exact model."

"Is it still in place?"

"Yeah, I didn't touch it."

"Good, leave it there."

"What?"

"Leave it there," Darius repeats. "Spider and I talked about it last night, and if you remove it whoever placed it there is going to know. Any chance you have of identifying them after that is gone."

"But I have the mug-cam."

"Pointed at your chair," Darius reminds her. "What if whoever did this comes in as soon as you step out and retrieves the logger without being caught on camera? You want her to come back and reinstall it after she downloads."

Jenny tosses this around, obviously unhappy at the idea of leaving the key logger attached to her computer any longer than necessary. "Do you realize how much information I have on this computer? The Atwood file that was accessed has maybe five percent of the total. If she finds the rest of it, we'll be completely exposed. The paintings, the car, all of it will be at risk."

241

"What if you move the files onto a thumb drive, including those in the Atwood files. Something portable that you can take with you."

"Or lose."

"Okay, make two copies: a working thumb drive and a backup. We have a small safe at the shop and I'm sure Uncle John won't mind if I throw a thumb drive in there for safekeeping."

There's a long pause, the cusp of a decision.

"All right," Jenny replies quietly.

The words leave her mouth with something attached, like a ship's anchor dragging across her tongue. Whether it's apprehension or relief is hard to tell, for it carries the flavor of both. One moment it's there, the next it's gone.

Such are choices.

Whether good or bad, we live with the consequences.

Chapter 40

Christmas Eve arrives faster than any of them could have imagined, and with it comes a large woman with a booming voice and a decidedly cockney accent. Beryl Dawson, Maggie's tea-pushing British friend, had landed at Seattle-Tacoma International Airport the previous afternoon, and right from the start, it seemed as if she'd brought the spirit of Christmas with her, perhaps tucked in her luggage. Indeed, if she had a beard and a red suit one might mistake her for an equally jolly fellow with a sleigh who tends to be popular this time of year. A hearty *Ho, ho, ho*! issuing from her lips would surprise no one.

It's this booming, wonderfully rich voice that Darius first hears as he steps onto Maggie's front porch. He listens for a moment and smiles before turning the knob and shuffling through. Once inside, he glances down the hall with a cautious eye and then covertly slips a large package wrapped in craft paper behind the front door. Quickly hanging his winter jacket on the coat rack mounted above, he adjusts it in a feeble attempt to better obscure the mystery bundle.

Satisfied—or perhaps just convinced there's nothing more to be done—he saunters down the hall, rubbing the cold from his fingers. Beryl's thundering voice washes over him as she describes in colorful detail how she met her husband, Harold.

"Mind you, I didn't disapprove of the view," she booms, but he was a wee thing back then. Arms like sticks and a stomach no bigger around than my leg, or at least no bigger around than this one." She slaps her substantial right thigh. Leaning forward suddenly, her voice low and conspiratorial, she adds, "Back in them days I was right fetching, a willow of a thing."

She waves the past away with a dismissive backhand. "In any case,

Harold finally grew into his bones when he was seventeen or eighteen . . . and he's still growing to this day." She booms out the last part as if it were the most ridiculous thing ever.

When the laughter subsides, it's Jenny who spots Darius leaning into the doorframe, watching the gathering with a quiet smile. Rising, she closes the gap between them and kisses him softly on the lips as her arms find their way around him.

They'd only met Beryl the night before but already she was as much a part of them as Maggie. Jenny had left work a little early the prior afternoon and picked her up at the airport. By the time the two of them reached Bellingham, they were old chums.

Beryl was simply one of those people you couldn't hate.

Even if you tried, she'd soon win you over.

Dinner promises to be a sumptuous feast, even by Christmas Eve standards.

Jenny spent the better part of the day in the kitchen, testing the limits of the expansive culinary knowledge her father had instilled in her over many years. Spider helped her as he could, leaving Beryl and Maggie to catch up, drink tea, and play cribbage.

While two-thirds of what Jenny and Spider prepare is for the evening meal, the rest will remain in the fridge or on the counter for an even *more* magnificent Christmas Day feast tomorrow. This includes a fantastically tempting Tunis cake for Beryl's benefit. Spider learned that this unique sponge cake, which is topped with thick chocolate and marzipan fruits, is a favorite holiday treat in England. He never verified this, of course, but Beryl's *ooh*'s and *aah*'s seem to confirm the rumor.

At last, they sit, and dish after dish makes its way around the table. Soon, a gentle cacophony of silverware, plates, serving bowls, and cups settles over them. They eat until they can eat no more, Spider outdoing the lot of them.

The best conversations are those found around a table amongst the remnants of a ravaged meal. Here, one tends to talk unguardedly due to the satisfaction in their belly. Being able to steadily pick at the olive tray or take a little more mince wine is simply a bonus.

So, it is this night.

They talk and laugh, mostly at Beryl's outrageous stories. For a blessed, holy night, they forget their troubles, forget their sorrows, and live in the moment, as if all of life is a postcard—a single moment captured in time and meant to be lived forever.

"You don't *cruise* in England, dear," Beryl chortles in reply to a question from Spider. "Mostly we crawl." She elbows Darius. "Generally, from one pub to the next."

They have a good laugh, and then Jenny turns to Maggie. "I bet you have loads of stories about cruising Bellingham, don't you?"

The old woman gives a half-hearted nod. "Oh, a few. These days they seem to all blur together into an idealized period of happiness when the rest of the world didn't matter."

"Tell us one," Spider urges.

Maggie waves it away. "I've told you enough."

This was true to an extent. In the proceeding months, Maggie had told them perhaps a dozen stories about the old cruise strip, yet they were always begging for more. She'd told them about the various car clubs, each with their unique jacket or identifying plate, and the dances they'd organize.

She told them how Mick Dolan's girlfriend spilled a strawberry shake on him when they hit a monster pothole on Holly Street. Everyone knew about the pothole and avoided it, but as Mick's girlfriend was practically in his lap at the time, it's understandable how he missed it. The cold of the shake had an instant effect on him, and he planted his feet into the floorboard as he lifted himself out of the frigid slurry that was now pooling on the leather seat beneath him.

"When I say he planted his feet on the floorboards," Maggie had clarified, "I mean he *thought* he planted them on the floorboard. Instead, his right foot hit the gas and the old Dodge sedan jumped the curb and drove halfway through the front door of the brand-new record store."

It was stories like these that whetted their appetite, but Maggie was sparing with them as if they were small chocolate treasures she didn't want to share. This, of course, made them want them all the more.

"Come on, Maggie," Darius says, just short of begging.

Jenny smiles at her. "Just one." She holds up a single index finger as if it were a contract or a solemn oath. "It's been weeks since you've shared."

Maggie looks from face to face, finally landing on Beryl's annoyingly broad grin. The old Brit seems amused that a bunch of twentysomethings hold such sway over her perennially hard-headed friend. Or perhaps she too has noticed that Jenny, Darius, and Spider are more like grandchildren than friends. Perhaps that's why she grins.

"*One* story," Maggie says in defeat. She holds up a single index finger—just like Jenny—as if to seal the deal. Tipping her eyes toward the ceiling, she thinks for a moment, and then an amused look crosses her face. "All right. I'll tell you why Patsy Woolman stopped wearing pantyhose."

"Ooooh!" Beryl purrs salaciously.

"Who's Patsy Woolman?" Spider asks.

"It doesn't matter. A classmate."

Repositioning herself in her seat, Maggie hesitates for only a moment, as if recalling the incident and placing it in the proper order. "This would have been the summer of sixty-one, sometime after July 4th because people were still lighting off firecrackers and rockets, the remainders of their Independence Day celebration. As you can imagine, the Bumblebee was a recognized and popular car on the cruise route, not just for its customized look, but because I always had at least two or three other girls with me."

In a quick aside, she says, "One time, we managed to squeeze four in the back and three in the front." She crinkles her nose. "Probably could have gotten four in the front, but Henrietta was a little on the plump side."

She pushes the thought away. "In any case, we were parked at Mastin's drive-in on Samish Way. We ordered some fries and colas, and while we were waiting for them to arrive, Patsy jumps out of the car and runs over to this beautiful 1957 Studebaker Golden Hawk."

Maggie leans forward a bit. "Now, Patsy was always a bit of a flirt, the kind of girl you expected to get in trouble . . . if you know what I mean."

"Preggers," Spider says with a slow nod.

Beryl raises an eyebrow at the British slang.

"If you mean pregnant, then yes," Maggie replies. "In any case, I don't know what she saw in the driver of the Studebaker. I don't even remember his name, just that he had a certain Neanderthal protrusion to his brow and his vocabulary was on a starvation diet."

Jenny chuckles.

"But he had a nice car," Beryl says loudly, drawing out the statement. "You Americans are always up about your cars, aren't you?"

"You're American too," Maggie reminds her.

"Yes, but I'm an import, dear; a Jaguar to your Buick."

This earns her a round of smiles and grins.

"*And so*," Maggie says loudly as if to remind them that she's in the middle of a story, "Patsy is talking to Neanderthal when Bent Jorgensen—"

"Wait, wait, wait!" Spider interrupts. "Bent? That's a name?"

"Yes, it is," Maggie replies, "now *hush!*" She glances sternly all the way around, but no one else is up for a good hushing, and they remain quiet. "As I was saying, Bent Jorgensen rolls through the parking lot looking for an empty drive-in stall. He'd just finished rigging up his exhaust with some sparkplugs and had them wired to a button under his dash. The result of pushing this button was a blast of flames that would shoot out the tailpipes. He hadn't fully tested the makeshift flamethrowers, however, which proved a bit of a problem. You see, Bent thought the flames were the coolest things ever, so he hit that button a lot.

"He was just turning toward an empty stall when he figured he'd give the button one long push, something to impress the girls. Flames shot out, as usual, but when he let off the gas the car backfired and a surge of unspent fuel and air rushes through the exhaust. This just happened to coincide with the point in his turn where his exhaust was perfectly lined up with Patsy and Neanderthal."

Jenny covers her mouth.

"The blast of flame not only reached them but danced around their legs. It wasn't enough to set their clothes on fire, but it melted Patsy's nylon stockings to her legs and left her with a couple of minor burns. She never wore pantyhose again; in fact, I think she developed a phobia over them."

"Ouch," Jenny moans, wincing at the thought of melting nylon.

"Indeed."

"I didn't know they had nylons back then," Spider says as if confused.

"Oh, heavens yes," Maggie assures him. "DuPont invented nylon in 1935—it was the very first synthetic fabric, you know. It didn't take long—1940 to be precise— before nylon stockings made their appearance. Of course, the early nylon didn't stretch, so stockings had to be manufactured in a wide range of sizes, none of this one-size-fits-all stuff. It wasn't until 1964 that the first stretch nylons made their appearance."

"So, like, you remember when all that happened?" Spider asks, fascinated.

"Good grief, Spider. I'm not *that* old," Maggie says with a chuckle. "I wasn't *there* when nylon was invented—any more than I was *there* when Noah built the ark."

"Oh . . . yeah, I know. It's just that . . . well, that all seems so specific."

"I once had an interest in textiles," Maggie sighs. "I got into real estate in 1970, six years before the Carter administration and the double-digit interest rates that put the industry on hold—bad timing on my part. Like many licensees back then I started exploring alternative careers, and textiles caught my eye." She shrugs. "I couldn't tell you what the appeal was. Sometimes something just strikes your fancy.

"I thought about enrolling in Western and getting a degree in textiles, which, I suppose, is what lead me on my quest for knowledge—inquiring minds and all that. I think I was the poster child for textile curiosity. It was all so fascinating. This went on for months until one day I just stopped. Again, I couldn't tell you why. The fever just died. I put my books away and got a job at the old Sears department store off Cornwall Avenue, working in the candy shop. By the mid-eighties, real estate was starting to look good again and I picked up where I left off."

As the story trails off, the quiet of approaching night settles in. Outside the windows, the sun makes its last bow and steps behind the horizontal curtain of the far horizon. The waters of the Puget Sound take on a deep shade of mysterious blue, growing darker by the minute.

It's perfect; mesmerizing.

"So, to be clear," Spider says after a long moment, "you *weren't* there when Noah built the ark?"

He dodges the pillow as it flies past his head and then grins at Maggie so hard his cheekbones squish his eyes.

After the party, Jenny, Beryl, and Darius clean up in the kitchen. Jenny and Beryl insist on singing Christmas songs, which are encouraged by but not always participated in by Darius. The clink and clank of plates and silverware issues from the room in a low drone, lorded over by Beryl's rich and deep voice. So cheery is the sound that one might think that Mrs. Claus herself was scrubbing up after supper.

Spider joins Maggie in the living room, and she pats a seat next to her, saying, "Keep an old woman company."

"You're not old," Spider scoffs.

"Mentally, no," Maggie muses, "It's just in the body, I suppose. It's funny how you can reach my age and still be the same person inside who you were in your twenties and thirties . . . perhaps with just a touch more wisdom." She sighs. "The body though, that's another story. It's much like a suit or a dress, I suppose. Beautiful, firm, and flawless when worn for the first time, but with continued use it starts to lose its luster, eventually becoming threadbare and all gone to fray at the seams."

She rubs a hand across her bare arm and then down her cheek. "My skin is so thin now—threadbare, like the suit—and the shine of newness is a deeply buried memory."

"You look fine to me," Spider says softly, the hint of tears rising in the wells of his eyes as the trauma of recent events crawl forward from a dark place in his mind and stretch out before him.

Maggie sees it in his face.

Taking his hand, she says, "Sorry. You're right, of course. I'm like the Mona Lisa, a few cracks but otherwise just fine."

As the evening fades into night, there is yet one surprise to unveil.

"You're killing me," Spider hisses at Darius when Maggie steps from the room.

"I'm getting to it."

Spider tips his head toward the kitchen, saying, "Show her, already!"

"What on earth are you two talking about?" Jenny whispers. Beryl, too, seems keenly interested in their hushed conversation.

Without explaining, Darius holds up a finger and then scurries silently from the living room. They see him bend down next to the front door and hear the crinkling of paper and the soft hiss of material rubbing together. A moment later, he's back in the living room, a large, folded bundle in his arms. He quickly sets it out of sight behind the couch and then hops into his seat just as Maggie returns from the kitchen with two steaming cups of chamomile tea, one for her, one for Beryl.

"Are you sure I can't get anyone anything?" she asks as she draws herself into the room.

They all decline her offer simultaneously, but in a way that draws her suspicion.

"What?" she asks, drawing the word out. When her eyes land on Spider he feigns innocence a moment and then points at Darius.

Turning, Maggie says, "Young man, you know I don't like secrets."

Darius laughs. "Who are *you* kidding."

Maggie doesn't miss a beat. "I'm an old woman. I'm allowed my secrets." She waves away the observation as if it were an affront. Beryl snickers and then hiccups—no doubt from the mince wine—and caps it all off with a tremendous snort of amusement.

The snort is what sets them all to laughing.

It's a contagious type of laughter that begins with something funny but not terribly so, and then feeds on and grows with each successive laugh, snort, and belly grab. It takes a minute for the living room to return to normal, and by this time Darius has retrieved his package. He waits for Maggie to wipe an amused tear from her eye and, stepping up behind her, places the mystery package gently into her lap.

"What's this?"

"Unwrap it."

As she begins to unfold the bundle it becomes clear what she's looking at. "Oh, my!" she exclaims one moment. "It's lovely," she says the next. The phrases repeat several times, mingling with others. Jenny, who knew this was coming but had yet to see the finished product, moves behind Maggie's left shoulder, occasionally reaching out to rub her fingers over the seams and the patterns.

The custom-made upholstery for the Bumblebee Jacket is crafted from a rich ivory leather with a mixture of vertical pleats and what Dallas refers to as *dragon scales*. Two-thirds up each seatback is a magical combination of embossing, stitching, and embroidery that comes together to create an oval with a lion's head laid in. Stylish letters arch over the top, spelling out the name E.E. ATWOOD.

"We're keeping the bench seat in back unchanged," Darius explains, "but modifying the front to look like two seats with a package tray in between. Dallas is using different types of foam and padding to add some body-fitting contours."

Maggie is struggling not to cry; you can see it in her face.

Realizing this, Darius continues, hoping the others don't notice. "We'll wait until right before the seats are ready to be installed before covering them with the new upholstery. That way they won't get scratched or torn sitting around."

From a small paper bag secreted behind his back, he now produces two strips of metal. Handing them over, Maggie gasps anew. The chrome emblems contain raised letters that spell out BUMBLEBEE JACKET in the elegant script of a futuristic mid-50s automotive font.

"Normally these would go on the front fenders where the old Cranbrook emblems used to be, but with all the modifications to the front, I think they'll look better at the bottom front of each door. A little splash of chrome against a field of yellow."

He studies Maggie a moment, all jest and sarcasm gone from his face.

"What do you think?" he asks.

She doesn't answer right away but her fingers continue to caress the leather seat covers as if all her concentration is focused on maintaining control. When her words finally come, her voice is cracked and broken.

"I think it's lovely," she blurts. "Just lovely."

She gives a loud and uncontrolled laugh of pure joy and then cries with the same.

Jenny and Beryl join her.

Chapter 41

Jenny's office is locked and dark when she arrives at the museum Tuesday morning. It's earlier than her usual start time but she has a lot to do. The planned unveiling of the Bumblebee Jacket and Atwood's collection of paintings is still months off, even with the accelerated schedule, yet the list of things to do seems to grow longer with each passing day.

If she had a year it still wouldn't be enough.

Fishing the keys from her purse, she unlocks the office door, turns on the lights, and flips the switch on her Keurig, looking forward to a morning cup of tea. It still surprises her how quickly she made the transition from coffee. She blamed this on Maggie at the beginning, but after making Beryl's acquaintance she realized who the real culprit was.

She walks to her desk and listens to the sterile hum as her computer comes to life. Slipping off her coat, she hangs it in the corner, straightens her blouse, and returns to the Keurig. Unwrapping a bag of Earl Gray, she waits for the machine to announce that it's READY TO BREW and then selects the largest setting. When the last of the heated water dribbles into the cup and stops with a sputter she drops in the tea bag and lets it steep.

Taking a seat in front of her computer, she remembers to turn the mug cam toward the wall neutralizing its motion sensor. She wonders if anything was captured on surveillance over the long weekend and decides to check just as soon as she clears out her inbox.

Facing the monitor, she reaches for the mouse and gives it a wiggle to find the cursor. Nothing happens. Looking down she notices a piece of white paper resting between the mouse and the pad. Its placement suggests intent and as she pulls the paper free the writing on the underside is immediately apparent. It's a note.

Three short sentences fill the small space and Jenny reads them in seconds.

Her face may have paled for a moment, but if it did no one saw it so swift is the anger that rises in her cheeks to replace it. Springing from her seat she closes the blinds on all six windows, locks the door, and then rushed back to the computer.

Dragging the mug cam close, she extracts the USB cable from inside and connects it to the front port on her CPU. Opening the extraction program, she downloads all the still shots captured over the weekend. There are twenty-seven. Twenty-one of these show a member of the cleaning crew entering the area just in front of her monitor as he reached for her garbage can and then returned it empty a few moments later.

The other six images are less innocent.

Only half of the mouse is visible to the right of the frame, yet on Saturday at 6:17 P.M. a partial hand is seen reaching in and lifting the mouse while a second-hand slips the note onto the pad. The hand—what's visible of it—shows no rings or nail polish, just narrow fingers and Caucasian skin.

It could be half the employees at the museum.

Reading the note a second time, Jenny feels a chill run up her spine, as if even now the intruder watches her, crafting machinations and pulling unseen strings that she can only guess at.

Her stomach tightens as nausea threatens to overwhelm her.

"You said your door was locked?" Darius clarifies minutes later when Jenny calls in a panic.

"Yes, but that doesn't mean anything. There are three levels of keys for the building. I'm a level two, so my key opens almost any door, but it also means there are dozens of people who have identical keys."

"Including what's-her-name? Melissa?"

"Marlinda. Yes, including her."

"What's the note say?"

Jenny turns it over in her hand and reads aloud. *"Hope you had a good Christmas. Your secret is safe with me. Or is it?* And then there's a smiley face."

"Did you check the—"

"Mug cam?" Jenny finishes. "Yes, right before I called you. There's part of a right hand in the frame, but that's it."

"Male or female?"

"Androgynous. Maybe you can tell but I can't."

"Can you email them to me?" He passes her the email address for Road Runner Restoration and starts walking to the front office.

The images come through a minute later and he opens them in an old version of Photoshop. "Fingers are kind of thin," he mumbles to himself. "Wait! Check out the fingertip on the index finger, just below the nail."

Jenny shuffles the images and finds one with a good angle—probably the same one Darius is looking at. "Okay, what about"—she stops abruptly. "Is that a scar?"

"That's what it looks like. It's a small one but it's something."

Jenny feels a sense of triumph sweep over her as if she'd already turned the tables and demoted the hunter to the prey. "So, if I find the scar, I find the cretin who's been snooping around my office."

"Exactly."

Chapter 42

With half the museum staff out on holiday vacation, Jenny spends the rest of her week in a vain attempt to find a telltale scar. Who would have thought such a simple thing would prove so difficult? As the last day of the year comes around, she's ready to forget work and live in the moment.

Even the subject of Maggie's ailment seems taboo.

When Darius mentions the particularly miserable day she'd had on Thursday, Jenny recoils, saying. "I don't want to think about it." Her voice cracks as she adds, "Can't we pretend everything's fine, just for today?"

When Darius kisses her forehead and whispers, "Of course," she tucks into him and gets lost in his arms for a long moment, swaying together in the foyer as the light of a crisp winter day filters through the front windows.

Just before two, it begins to snow.

The flakes are sparse at first, dancing on the wind in twos and threes. By two-thirty, however, they've grown plump and plentiful. Word had gotten out to the other snowflakes because the poorly attended dance of two o'clock is rapidly replaced by a full-on royal ball—and every flake of every stature is invited.

The ground is soon covered.

While none of them have work or school on this final day of the year, Darius, Jenny, Spider, Maggie, and Beryl all feel that endearing sense of elation that comes with snow, that sense of school being canceled, of sled rides and snowball fights.

In the living room, Maggie opens all the curtains facing the road and they sit for the better part of an hour watching the gentle breeze push the flakes about. Spider digs a Bluetooth speaker out of his backpack and pulls up a list of classic Christmas songs on his phone. Soon, the pleasant drone of Perry Como, Bing Crosby, and Andy Williams fills the living room and drifts down the hall. Hot cocoa and miniatures marshmallows are standard fares during this winter exhibition, and while few words are spoken among them this only seems to add to the transient magic.

At six o'clock they enjoy the last rich meal of the holidays, once again courtesy of Jenny with assistance from Beryl and Spider. Games fill the evening, along with another viewing of *American Graffiti*, this time for Beryl's benefit.

"So, you just drive around?" she keeps asking in bewilderment, apparently having trouble with the concept of cruising.

They count down the last ten seconds to midnight and usher in the New Year with shouts and cheers, sending the old one scurrying on its way. They enjoy the moment, watching random fireworks burst overhead in blues and golds and reds as the citizens of Bellingham celebrate. They forget for the moment that the new year holds the threat of great sorrow, the kind of pain that only dissipates with time.

Yet there is hope, small though it may be.

There is also love.

Where one fails, the other may sustain.

Chapter 43

Wednesday, January 4

By noon on Wednesday, Jenny has managed to covertly check the right index finger of all but four full-time employees at the Seattle Art Museum. The scar has eluded her to this point, and now, looking at the last possible suspects, a sense of impending dread slowly creeps in. Three of the name are of no real concern but the fourth weighs heavily, like a millstone around her neck threatening to pull her into the muck.

Rather than dwelling on the name, allowing it to putrefy in her gut like bad fish, she goes on the offensive. Rising from her chair she storms out of her office like a woman on a mission. Following the hall to the end, she takes a right and then a quick left. The door is open, so she plants herself against the doorframe at a slight lean, arms crossed, a serious look on her face.

The figure behind the desk is odious, slippery, and vain—a low man held high.

When he sees her and smiles, Jenny feels her gut tighten.

"Well, well," Stu Yates says with an impish grin that might have been charming if not for the carrier. He leans back in his chair, perhaps imagining that Jenny has finally come around to his way of thinking. She anticipated this and decided not to waste the opportunity.

"Can I see your hands?" she asks pleasantly enough.

"My hands?" Stu's grin grows broader as if a game is afoot.

"Yes."

"Why do you want to see my hands." His voice is almost singsong.

Jenny shrugs, staring at her fingers. "You know what they say about a man's hands . . ." She sighs and pushes off from the doorframe. Strolling across the carpet, she exudes sensuality. It's a game she has always loathed in other women, the use of one's body as a weapon or tool, but in Stu's case, she's willing to make an exception.

Reaching his desk, she leans across so that she's resting on her forearms. If she was inclined to wear revealing tops the view and proximity might have slain Stu where he sits. As it is, he ogles her dumbfoundedly, unable to find words.

"Hands?" Jenny breathes.

Stu's hands dart toward her, exposing his slender, almost feminine fingers. It only takes a glance.

Pushing up and stepping back, Jenny's face is suddenly fierce and filled with contempt. "I should have known!"

Stu is beyond confused. "What do you mean?"

Without another word, Jenny reaches into her pocket and extracts the unsigned note she'd found under her mouse. She tosses it onto Stu's desk.

"What's that?" he pretends, shifting sideways in his seat.

"Don't deny it!" Jenny snaps. "I caught you on camera."

"Camera . . .?" Stu begins, but then decides that denial is pointless if her claim is true. "Now come on, Jenny. Just because I figured out what your little project is and left a note under your mouse doesn't mean a thing and you know it."

"It does when you're threatening to reveal a museum secret," Jenny hisses, moving in close.

"We're a museum; we shouldn't have secrets."

"Yeah, well this is different. If you knew what was going on, you'd understand why." She leaves the statement intentionally vague, a last-minute inspiration. Stu doesn't need to know she found the key logger plugged into the back of her computer. Not yet at least.

"What do you want?" she demands, crossing her arms.

"What makes you think I want something?"

"Please!" Jenny sputters.

Stu shrugs. "Why don't we talk about it over dinner?"

"Dinner?"

"Yeah, I think better when I'm full."

She doesn't answer right away but seems to think about it. The longer she delays the more confident Stu grows. "When?" she finally asks.

"How about tonight?"

"No. I have plans."

"Tomorrow, then?"

"No." Jenny snaps. Then, sighing, she uncrosses her arms. "Friday."

Stu gives her an annoyed glance. "You're going to make me wait until Friday? Something this important?" He lowers his voice and leans closer. "Something this valuable? I mean, we *are* talking about millions of dollars, right? Not to mention what it'll do for your career."

"This isn't about my career," Jenny replies sharply, "it's about my passion. Something you couldn't possibly understand."

As she turns to leave, Stu's words follow her, accompanied by a lecherous grin. "Oh, I understand passion," he says, eyes never rising above her waist.

Jenny whirls on him. "I'm not sleeping with you, Stu. Get used to the idea because it's not up for negotiation."

"Sure," he leers, nodding in a patronizing manner. Reaching up, he touches his forehead as if tipping a hat, a gesture that makes most girls think he's sophisticated. "Friday, then," he says.

Chapter 44

Le Baiser is a small but trendy restaurant in the Fremont District of Seattle, a stone's throw from Lake Union. On any given day, the masts of sailboats can be seen rising from their moorings nearby, though catching sight of the water upon which they rest is more challenging, with much of the view blocked by structures nearer the shore.

French for "The Kiss," *Le Baiser* offers an interior designed for maximum privacy. As such, the plush bench-like seats at each booth have backs that rise at least five feet, crowned with expertly carved wood accents recycled from an era long since passed. Elegant dividers are placed strategically around the room so that no booth has an obvious view of another.

The visual separation works well but does little to mute the sound, a feature Jenny notes as she takes a seat. The all-too-familiar hum of conversation, the gurgle of cups being filled, and even the gentle rubbing of stainless-steel utensils against the ubiquitous white porcelain plates fills her ears, as if directly before her and behind her. A thousand such sounds surround her and fill the background. They'd be welcome and pleasing if not for the circumstances. Still, the acoustics will make it easier to hear, a thought that makes her smile ironically.

The waiter offers her a menu and then fills her water glass.

"We won't be needing these," she says, indicating the wine glasses, and with a courteous nod, he whisks them away.

Jenny arrived early on purpose.

Stu had offered to pick her up at her apartment, of course, but she had no intention of revealing her address or home phone number to such a man. Nor was she willing to place herself in a position where she would be dependent on him for a ride home—or elsewhere, as she imagined was his plan.

She had long held Stu in low regard but her contempt for him had grown considerably in the proceeding days. It didn't take much to figure him out. On their introduction, when she joined the Seattle Art Museum, she had measured him correctly. It was the consuming smile, the overly eager laugh, the hungry eyes. It wasn't long before her suspicions were confirmed, mostly by the whispered comments of the youngest and prettiest interns and employees.

Women admired him, but only those, it seemed, who were just girls in women's bodies, much the way Stu was a boy in a man's body. Or, perhaps it would be more accurate to say that Stu Yates was the type of man that *stupid* boys aspire to, condemning themselves to always be boys in men's bodies and never real men. He puts on the pretense of wealth and sophistication the way other men put on a winter jacket, zipping it to the top so nothing is exposed.

These thoughts fill Jenny's head for the next twenty minutes as she waits for her nemesis to arrive. When he does, it's his voice that leads the way. Soothing and cool to some, it's like a rusty hinge to Jenny.

"You look fantastic," Stu fawns as he slides into the booth opposite her, his eyes already molesting every curve and hidden fold of her body. More compliments fall from his lips until Jenny shuts him down.

"I'm not one of your interns, Stu. I'm not going to suddenly realize what a catch you are and fall into your arms, so why don't we just have dinner and discuss . . . what we came to discuss."

The waitress arrives as she finishes, and she immediately orders a random salad with a name she can't pronounce and some crepes. Stu orders in French, selecting his usual: a chicken dish and a glass of red wine. Women usually melt when he utters the foreign words with practiced confidence, but Jenny just glances around the restaurant with a bored look on her face.

It vexes Stu, but he's had tougher challenges.

Their food arrives just ten minutes later, an interval that seems like hours to Jenny, who's had to endure a non-stop verbal resume detailing the many talents and achievements of Stu Yates. The guy is so comfortable in his bombastic skin that he doesn't even notice her complete silence. Or if he does, he takes it to mean she's hanging on every word.

She's not.

The food is a welcome reprieve and quiets him for a time but only until his plate begins to look a little sparse and his wine glass stands empty for the second time.

"Are you sure you don't want some," he says, rubbing a finger along the lip of the wine glass. "The Chateau La Tour Carnet is excellent."

"I'm not much for wine," Jenny lies.

"Champagne?"

"There's nothing to celebrate."

"Sure, there is," Stu replies. "I finally got you out on a date. That's worth celebrating, right?" He gives a wink. "It's been a challenge, but I knew you'd come around eventually."

Jenny drops her napkin on the table where it lands like a hammer.

"This *isn't* a date, Stu, despite how charming you think you are. I'm here to discuss the—" she glances around and lowers her voice. "I'm here to discuss the car and the paintings. I'm here to find out why you hacked into my computer and accessed confidential files."

"Confidential!" he scoffs dismissively.

"Yes, confidential!" she snaps. "You know perfectly well what's at stake, that's why you used it to blackmail me into coming on this . . . date."

When Stu doesn't respond, she presses. "What did you think you were going to do with this information? Honestly!"

"Whatever I want," he replies suddenly, forcefully.

"Like blackmailing me into sleeping with you?"

He shrugs.

"Why would I ever do that?" Jenny asks, dumbfounded. "And what kind of man does that make you if you have to extort sex from women?"

"The kind who gets laid," Stu replies with a smirk.

"Not by me." Jenny slides to the end of the booth and begins to stand, but Stu grabs her forearm.

"I guess you don't want them back," he says.

"What?"

"The files."

"You copied my files?"

Stu just sneers and raises an eyebrow. "Of course, I did. Why else would I go to all that trouble?" He stares at her a moment and then lowers his voice, trying to sound sympathetic. "Come back to my place for a drink. I'm sure we can work something out."

"You bastard!" Jenny's hand flies before she realizes what she's doing. The force of the slap rocks Stu backward, stunning him. As his eyes begin to focus, he notices Jenny standing before him—hands on her hips—and it appears as if there are four of her, but . . . no. With a sinking sense of foreboding, he realizes that three of the figures look different—very different as it turns out.

When recognition finally comes, Stu Yates feels a rare sensation: Fear.

Lorraine Brooke, the director of the Seattle Art Museum, glowers at him with a fierce maternal stare. Standing on either side of her are Darius Alexander and Steven Zalewski, the one they call Spider. He recognizes them from the images and notes he downloaded from Jenny's computer, and from the Halloween party.

Jenny has a hand on Darius's chest, restraining him. She doesn't think to do the same for Spider, however, and with a blur of motion, the underestimated genius throws a punch that connects with the middle of Stu's face. He controls the blow enough to avoid breaking the nose, but the strike is painful and bloody, nonetheless.

Jenny looks at Spider in shock.

"Eight years of Taekwondo," he mutters. "Finally had a reason to use it."

"That's assault!" Stu wails, holding a bloody napkin to his face and steadying himself against the back of the bench seat. "You're going to jail; I'm going to see to it."

Spider's fist flies again, this time breaking the nose.

Stu hits the floor with a guttural *ummah* that knocks the wind from his lungs. Gasping like a fish out of water, he tries to regain his breath as he cradles the nose.

"Spider!" Jenny gasps, both surprised and a bit pleased.

"Hey, if I'm going to jail . . ." He leaves the rest of the sentiment unspoken.

Lifting Stu from the floor, Darius and Spider place him on the seat at the edge of the booth and let him regain his breath and composure. They request a cup of ice from the kitchen and use some of the restaurant's thick napkins to fashion an ice pack.

"You broke my nose, asshole," he says to Spider, the words coming out nasally and indignant. Before he can threaten to call the cops again, Lorraine steps in front of him.

Extracting a Ziploc bag from her purse, she holds it up for his examination. Inside, the key logger is visible.

"Recognize this?" Lorraine asks. "Spider wore gloves when he removed it from the back of Jenny's computer, so your fingerprints should be well preserved." Holding it out for several more seconds in shaming silence, she sighs and then returns it to her purse.

"What are you going to do with it?" Stu asks.

"Well, I talked to the museum's attorneys and learned that computer trespass in the first degree is a class C felony, punishable by up to five years in prison and up to a ten thousand dollar fine. Plus, there's the whole bit about extortion, a class B felony. That one should get you ten years and up to twenty thousand dollars in fines."

Lorraine pauses to appraise Stu. "Did you want to call the police, or shall I?"

"No! Please," Stu says, looking as if he might burst into tears. "I was only messing with her," he practically whispers.

"Is that what we're calling it these days?"

Stu looks down, unable to meet her gaze.

Lorraine is silent for a long moment. Then, slowly, she lowers herself in front of Stu until she's resting on one knee.

"Here's what we're going to do—what I'll do for you, so you don't have to spend your best years in prison getting man-handled. Tomorrow morning when the museum opens, you'll deliver all the documents, pictures, and files you stole from Jenny's computer to the front desk. Give them to Hector, the head of security. He'll be expecting them."

Lorraine takes Stu's hand and squeezes it, forcing him to make eye contact. "This includes all copies, whether digital or hardcopy. You'll wipe any files you might have saved to your home computer, too. And from this day forward, you'll never speak about Atwood, the car, or the paintings again. I don't care if you're ninety years old and on your deathbed."

Stu is nodding his head in affirmation, but Lorraine still wants to hear it.

"Do we have an understanding?" she asks.

"Yes."

She nods. "I'll be keeping the evidence and a complete written report . . . just in case."

"I'll do it. You don't have to worry," Stu blurts. "I'll put everything in your office, that way Hector doesn't have to know."

"No," Lorraine replies. "You won't have access."

"I won't—" Stu begins, but then he understands. "I'm fired?" he asks as if the thought were completely foreign.

"Your actions are criminal, your attitude toward women is appalling, and, frankly, you're a lawsuit waiting to happen."

"So, I'm fired?" Stu repeats.

"You're fired."

Chapter 45

There's no trusting some people.

Jenny knows this perfectly well, so despite Stu's oath of secrecy on pain of prison, she and Lorraine had returned to the museum Friday night and immediately drafted a press release. The notice indicated that the museum would be making a significant announcement on Monday afternoon at two p.m. and invited the media to attend. The release didn't directly address the more than four hundred original Atwoods discovered in Bellingham, nor does it allude to the Bumblebee Jacket.

The truth is they had no idea what to reveal and what to hold back. The only thing Jenny knew for certain was that Maggie was going to have the final word. She'd see to it.

As two P.M. approaches, Jenny takes her place near Lorraine at a podium in the museum's cordoned-off main hall. Behind them is a display of the museum's meager few Atwood paintings, plus twelve that Maggie had offered on loan, including her beloved *Stepping Out* and *A Girl and Her Car*.

"Welcome, ladies and gentlemen," Lorraine begins at precisely two. "It is my great pleasure today to reveal something we don't often see in the art world: The discovery of not just a handful of lost paintings, but a trove, a treasure hidden away, in fact, for a half-century. The artist is a Washington native whose work has been compared to Norman Rockwell and J.C. Leyendecker, and for good reason, as you'll see. His name was Evan Elmore Atwood, and today you will be among the first to gaze upon a magnificent slice of Americana that was lost to the world until only recently.

"As it turns out," Lorraine continues, "the leading expert on Atwood is none other than our own Doctor Jenny Morgan, the assistant collections coordinator in our Curatorial Division. She's also the one who helped discover these Atwoods, which is a story in its own right."

She waves Jenny to the podium.

"Doctor Morgan is going to provide you with a slide presentation"— she directs their attention to a large screen set up off to the left— "after which we'll have time for questions and answers."

Whispering, "You got this, girl," Lorraine gives Jenny a wink and steps back.

Moving to the podium, she glances out at the sea of faces before her, flinching at the burst of camera flashes. In the very back, at the edge of the bustle and commotion, a lone figure stands erect and attentive. Looking smart in her Sunday best, the woman holds a small coin purse filled with nickels in her hands, as if they should bear witness to the events to come. Jenny exchanges a smile with her as their eyes meet and hold. Then drawing a deep breath, she addresses the crowd.

"Let's begin," she suggests, "with a most unlikely car . . ."

Ninety miles away in the teardown room of Road Runner Restoration, Darius stands with his hands deep in the pockets of his dirty overalls, his eyes intent on the floor as he ponders his first words. Before him are gathered the heart and soul of the body shop: Uncle John, Dallas, Skinny, Armando, and Jason. Eric would have been there too, but Uncle John finally got tired of him showing up late and doing a "piss-poor job," so he had reluctantly fired him the previous week.

Things seemed to run more smoothly in his absence.

When Darius asked his uncle and coworkers to gather around, he hadn't exactly thought through what he was going to say. Spider, who's now lingering behind him, wasn't much help.

Watching his nephew and puzzled by his hesitation, Uncle John says, "Go ahead, Darius. Whatever it is, spit it out. You've got our attention."

"We already know you're gay," Skinny says soothingly, "and we embrace all genders in this body shop." He steps forward and tries hugging Darius, much to the delight of the others.

"Stay away from him, bitch," Armando shouts. "He's mine."

The ruckus that follows only serves to delay Darius's announcement that much longer, adding to his apprehension. After another minute of lighthearted shop banter, he clears his throat, and the room grows quiet.

"First," Darius says, "I want to thank you all for the work you've done on the Bumblebee Jacket. You know how much the car means to me, and it's nice to know that the people I trust most—at least with cars," he adds, drawing some snickers— "are the ones helping out."

He pulls his hands from his pockets, glances back first at Spider then at the yellow convertible, and says, "There's a little more to the car's history that you need to know and it's a bit of a secret." He shrugs. "It's a *huge* secret."

Those gathered are now curious, Uncle John most of all.

"When I bought the car," Darius continues, "I thought it was the wickedest old lead sled I'd ever seen, even though most of what I saw at that point was my vision of what the car *could* be. It was just the kind of project I was looking for."

He pauses, glancing from face to face. "You've all seen the name in the trunk," he says, knowing it to be so, "and there's a story that goes with it—a pretty cool story."

Over the next twenty minutes, Darius and Spider tell them everything: The discovery of Atwood's identity, the name of his daughter, even the existence of the rare poster in the front office, though this turned into a bit of a boondoggle as they all decided they needed to go take a look.

When most of the story has been laid before them, Darius drops the last shoe. "The car is worth millions," he says bluntly, "and though I have no right to ask you to keep this secret, that's exactly what I'm doing. Jenny is giving a press conference right now and the media is going to want answers she can't give."

"Like *Where's the car?*" Dallas says, astute as always.

"Exactly. Online sources will lead them to Bellingham quickly enough, and if they're half as good as most of them think they are they'll spend some time checking in with the local car clubs and body shops."

He holds his open palms out to them. "I just need time to get the car done. After that, we can find someplace secure to store it." He hesitates. "Things have changed with Maggie. It seems I don't have the kind of time I thought I did." He chokes on the last words and covers his mouth with his hand.

Spider steps forward and places a hand on Darius's shoulder. "Maggie's dying," he explains, simple and to the point. "We have a couple of months at best. Darius promised her a ride when the car's done and we're going to see that she gets it."

To their credit, the shop—every man of them—swears themselves to secrecy.

Despite the newspaper articles, the magazine pieces, the broadcast news reports, and the many inquiries around town in the coming months, not a word leaks out.

Maggie's secret remains so, known but to a chosen few.

Chapter 46

The alley behind the grocery store looks like a scene straight out of some thriller, as if Tom Clancy had returned from the dead and was using actors to visualize a chapter in one of his high-tech novels. Any passerby was sure to call the police and report that something strange, something *very* strange, was taking place. They might not be able to say exactly what it was that piqued their interest, only that it was . . . strange.

As it turns out, this puzzle comes in pairs.

The first pair—and most obvious—stands near the trunk of a gray Camaro, their hands folded together in front of them as they patiently wait for something to happen. Around them are gathered various leather bags, one of which is emblazoned with the logo for *Art & Artists Magazine*. The pair would be wholly unremarkable except for the black bags over their heads.

One is a man, the other a woman; that much is clear from their attire.

Other than that, they're unrecognizable and easily mistaken for hostages plucked from some distant shore—perhaps from an embassy takeover or an airline hijacking.

Standing next to them on either side is the second pair in this puzzle: Jenny and Spider. They look casual as they stand there, Spider occasionally checking his watch, as if nothing untoward was happening and this was just the way you stand around waiting for a ride. They chat with the hooded couple, even laugh now and then.

An employee from the grocery store soon exits the back door with two thirty-gallon garbage bags, one dangling from each hand. She gets to the dumpster and is about to toss them in when she happens to glance up and catch sight of them.

Hesitating, she seems unsure whether to run or hit the ground.

"It's okay," Jenny shouts her way. "It's just a game."

The male hostage, realizing what's happening, chimes in. "Yeah, we're fine. No worries." Under his breath, he hisses, "Is it the cops?"

"Grocery store employee," Spider hisses back.

Dumping the bags quickly, the confused girl makes a hasty retreat. A minute later, the backdoor cracks open again, and the sliver of a face—a different face—peers out at them. They all wave, including the hostages.

"What took so long?" Spider demands when Darius pulls in a few minutes later.

"Fender bender," he replies. "The road was backed up for three blocks. All the lookie-loos had to slow down to get a peek."

"Lookie-loos," Spider says with a chuckle and a shake of his head.

"Yeah, don't pretend you don't slow down for a look. I've seen you."

"It's not that," Spider says, waving the thought away. "It's that word: Lookie-loo."

He's still chuckling when Darius begins escorting the hooded man and woman gently into the back of the rented work van. He takes a moment to rig a hasty divider of black fabric between the cab and cargo area and then, satisfied that no one can see out, says, "Okay, you can take off the hoods."

"Thank god," the woman replies. "It was getting claustrophobic in there."

"Sorry about all this," Jenny says, almost cringing. "I guess we're a little paranoid. Spider thought it would be a good idea if you didn't see what vehicle we're using. Something about GPS."

Spider opens his mouth to explain but Jenny shuts him down with a wave of her hand.

"Not a problem," the male says with a grin. "It was kind of fun. For a moment there, I imagined I was a war correspondent in Syria meeting up with some reclusive source. Art photographer sounds a bit bland by comparison." Stretching out a hand to Darius he grins and says, "I'm August Wheeler, photographer for *Art & Artist*."

"I'm . . . I'm Alpha," Darius replies, giving Spider a dubious look.

August positively beams at the pseudonym. "He must be Bravo," he says, thumbing at Spider.

"He's something," Darius mutters.

"Tabitha Vreen," the woman says, extending a hand. "I'm with *ARTnews*." She shakes Darius's hand briskly and then turns to Jenny with a mischievous look in her eyes. "How in the world did you meet these two?"

"A phone call," is all Jenny reveals.

Tabitha nods and turns up one corner of her mouth. "I thought maybe you hired them to parachute into Chechnya to rescue some lost masterpiece."

"That's next week," Jenny replies with a coy smile.

Darius makes sure the five-minute drive takes fifteen. He takes unnecessary roads that lead away from their final destination, drives by the railroad tracks as a train moves slowly by, and passes a large construction site on the other side of town before finally turning toward their destination.

As they near Road Runner Restoration, he asks them to put their hoods back on. Parking in front, he exits the driver's seat and comes around to the back of the van, where he opens the rear doors and swings them wide. Reaching in, he takes Tabitha's hand and guides her out, leaving her in Jenny's care as he goes back for August.

Meanwhile, Spider unlocks the office door, then the door into the teardown area. Turning on all the lights, he waits there, feeling a bit apprehensive about their guests.

Jenny brings up the rear as Darius leads the hooded photographers through the front office, around the counter, and then into the teardown area. Once situated inside, he and Spider leave Tabitha and August with Jenny while they go and retrieve the bags of photography equipment from the van.

"Okay, you can ditch the hoods," he says a minute later.

What greets August and Tabitha is probably not what they expected. Instead of a garage, storage building, or even a shop floor, they find themselves surrounded by black plastic. It cascades down from improvised walls that stand eight feet tall, creating a sort of black-clad room inside what is a much larger room.

On the floor in the center of this sectioned-off area rests a sea of yellow in the form of a 1951 Plymouth Cranbrook convertible, or what used to be a Cranbrook. The beast that sits there now is as different from its vintage origin as a lion is from a cat. Its rich yellow contrasts nicely against the black backdrop. The paint looks as if a thousand dollops of yellow had been plucked from a setting sun and laid down one by one, giving depth and dimension to the color.

The car has come a long way since it visited the paint booth in November.

The body is back on its frame, which is now fully reconditioned and painted gloss black. The interior has been painted, the doors hung, and a brand-new high-tech gauge cluster has replaced the old speedometer in the dash. Where the old instrument panel had rectangular gauges for amps and fuel to the left of the speedometer, and two more for oil and temp to the right, the new version has round, computer-driven LED displays.

The new carpet has also been installed, along with the refinished and reupholstered back seat.

Everything forward of the cowl is still missing, except for the protruding front section of the frame, of course, and the reconditioned Corvette axle and suspension attached to it. The one-piece front body section—now in glowing yellow—rests on stands nearby, and the hood hangs from a rack. Both are finished and ready for installation.

Despite the progress, it's clear that there's a lot of work left to be done.

The photography session lasts the better part of two hours, with Darius and Spider answering what questions they can and sidestepping those they can't. At times they assist August and Tabitha by moving pieces this way and that to provide the best angles and background.

The cameras never stop flashing.

At one point, Spider slips up and instead of referring to Darius as Alpha, he calls him *D*. August catches the mistake immediately and flashes a telling grin. Still, how many guys are named Darius. If anyone was going to whittle down names that start with *D* they'd focus on the most obvious: David, Daniel, Donald, Dennis, Daryl, or even Dwayne.

Not Darius.

Who names their kid after a long-dead Persian king?

As the session finally winds down, Jenny produces two thumb drives from her purse.

"Early pictures of the restoration," she explains as she hands one to August and the other to Tabitha. She doesn't explain that the shots were carefully selected so as not to reveal anything about the interior of Road Runner Restoration. To August and Tabitha, they may as well have been taken in a barn, or an airport hangar.

The return trip to the alley behind the grocery store is equally obfuscating, though Darius takes a completely different route this time. Once at their destination, Darius says his goodbyes to August and Tabitha and then leaves the two hooded photographers where he found them, safe in the company of Spider and Jenny.

They stand there for two full minutes, unmoving.

Spider half expects someone to peer out through the back door of the grocery store again, or come out, spot them, and run away while yelling for someone to call 911. When it doesn't happen, he seems a bit disappointed.

Watching the timer on her phone as the seconds tick down, Jenny finally drops her hand and says, "Okay, you can take them off."

Chapter 47

Weeks pass. The world turns. Life goes on.

So, it is and ever will be.

It's just after six on Friday evening when the rumble of Jenny's charcoal gray Camaro trumpets her arrival on Eldridge Avenue. Coasting to a stop in front of the garage, she leaps from the car and races to the front door, a fistful of magazines clutched in her hand.

"We made the front cover," she fairly shouts as she bursts through the front door, waving the magazines in the air. She finds Darius, Spider, and Maggie gathered in the kitchen, looking slightly amused at her excitement. "Front cover," she says again, handing each of them an advance copy of the March edition of *Arts & Artists Magazine*. There, sprawled across the cover, is the pristine image of *A Girl and Her Car*.

Maggie's face melts when she sees it.

"Oh my," she says, holding the magazine in her hands and running her fingers gently over the image. She finds her way to a chair and slumps down into it. "My father wouldn't believe this," she says, as if suddenly out of breath. "No sir."

Jenny comes around and places both hands on Maggie's shoulders. "They said it was the best picture for conveying the entirety of the find. It's your father, but it's also you and the Bumblebee Jacket. I think it's perfect."

"Odd, how it looks different on a magazine cover," Maggie muses, continuing to stare at the image as if trying to determine its authenticity.

Reaching around, Jenny flips the magazine open and thumbs through to page 22. The article title *E.E. Atwood: A New Legacy* graces the top, and the next six pages detail the discovery of the Atwood Treasure, along with images of seven never-before-seen paintings.

Three images of the Bumblebee Jacket appear on the fifth page, a story unto itself, complete with the wonderful tale of a father lovingly transforming a 1951 Plymouth Cranbrook into a rolling work of art, a gift for his only daughter on her sixteenth birthday.

A closeup of the cover image appears on page six, juxtaposed with one of the restoration images from Road Runner Restoration. It shows young Grace Margaret Atwood hugging the beautiful car in her yellow sundress. In years to come, this will be the image of Atwood's daughter that lasts.

Maggie would be thrilled if she knew.

"I have more news," Jenny says with unhidden glee in her eyes. Extracting a manila envelope from her folio, she lays it faceup on the table. A standard mailing label adorns the center, addressed to her attention at the Seattle Art Museum. The return address reads Smith and Clark Publishing.

"What is it?" Maggie asks.

"An offer."

Maggie smiles, having grown accustomed to Jenny's manner of teasing, which is not unlike her own. "What kind of offer would that be?" she asks.

"The kind that pays two hundred thousand dollars."

Spider nearly chokes on his tea while Darius sits straight up in his chair and gives Jenny a look as if to say *What is this?*

Maggie doesn't twitch an eye. "That's a sizeable enough amount," she muses. "I'm a little out of practice, but who do I have to kill?"

Jenny laughs. "It's for the paintings. They want to reprint them as posters and calendars, and I think they even mentioned coffee mugs. How they'll get a whole painting on a coffee cup is beyond me, but I suppose they must have figured something out."

"Reprint the paintings?" Maggie says, pondering the idea aloud.

"It's a great way to raise awareness," Jenny assures her, the excitement in her voice slipping a little.

"No doubt, no doubt. The last time my father signed a poster contract he was dead in a year and the company went out of business."

Spider presses forward in his chair, a hint of amusement on his face. "Are you superstitious, Maggie?"

"Don't be ridiculous," Maggie retorts. "Of course, I'm superstitious."

They all have a good laugh.

Before the conversation can continue, Spider holds up a finger and says, "Serious financial discussions require serious music." Before they can ask him what he means, or even wonder at the words, he slinks off down the hall and disappears into the living room. A few seconds later *The Great Pretender* by The Platters begins to spill from the room, issued forth by the old Wurlitzer which now rests in the front corner of the room.

As Spider returns, his head and hands sway with the music, pausing on occasion to grip an imaginary microphone and lip-synch the words. Taking a seat next to Maggie he throws an arm around her, pulls her over, and gives her a peck on the cheek.

"Now we're ready to talk business," he announces.

It seems an easy thing to accept a fat check for something as uncomplicated as the right to reprint some old paintings. For most, it would be a two-step process: sign the contract, cash the check. But Maggie is not like most people, especially when it comes to her father's paintings.

She worries about losing control of the images. She worries about how they might be used. She worries most of all about her father's reputation, both as an artist and a man, and wonders how this deal might affect how his work is viewed in years to come.

Her deep skepticism permeates her words and pulls at the creases of her brow.

When Jenny reminds her that Leonardo da Vinci's Vitruvian man is an iconic image that appears on T-shirts, in movies, and on scores of products, and that Norman Rockwell did some of his best work for the Saturday Evening Post, she seems to soften.

"You've talked about turning this place into a museum," Jenny says. "What if this is what it takes to make that happen?"

Maggie doesn't immediately reply but worries her fingers as they rest on the tabletop. It's an endearing habit that draws a smile or two.

"I've been a businesswoman my whole life," she finally says. "I know that two hundred thousand wouldn't be close to what it would take to open a museum, even a small one like this. Security alone would require half that amount just in the first year." She pauses and sighs. "But I suppose it's a start."

Jenny looks giddy. "So, is that a yes?"

Maggie hesitates and then smiles. "It's a yes."

When the room erupts, she quickly shouts them down. "Don't' be so happy about it. If I'm opening a museum, even if it's one of those weekend-only places, I'm going to need some help. Since you three are the only ones foolish enough to believe in this hair-brained scheme, consider yourselves drafted."

They cheer, and in the ensuing celebration Maggie manages to rustle up an unopened bottle of vintage red wine and they drink a toast to an old woman's vision and the birth of the E.E. Atwood Museum.

It's been said before but bears repeating: Roads are life.

They take us this way and that, sometimes by design, sometimes by accident. As Maggie, Jenny, Darius, and Spider steer their way toward a new adventure, a new destination, the way forward is clear. The road is a bright shiny path before them, freshly birthed and unblemished, a tribute to man's unharnessed ability to dream.

It will not remain so.

There's no way they can know for certain what's coming. Perhaps that's one of the mercies of future events, that they can't be foreseen. If they were to catch a glimpse of what's to come, would they shy away and console one another with the reassuring words that it was a beautiful vision, or would they press on, dauntless and determined?

This too is yet unknown.

Chapter 48

The waiting room is comfortable as far as waiting rooms go.

Overstuffed chairs line the walls, art draws the eye, and magazines stand in wall racks or lay scattered on end tables. Some of the gathered clients read, few make eye contact, and still fewer speak. It's a room that's aptly named, a place for waiting. A place for pondering, perhaps worrying—as if there weren't already enough things in life to worry about.

It's the type of room that people find themselves in without really knowing why.

Darius checks his phone, not because he's expecting a text, but because it's the type of thing one does in such a room, something to add motion to an otherwise still place. His eyes dart to the hall door for perhaps the hundredth time. It's the door Maggie went down a half hour ago and hadn't returned from.

Jenny normally accompanies Maggie to her appointments—even insists on it, but the media attention from the press conference is still going strong and she found that she couldn't get away this week. Darius quickly volunteered, of course, despite his dislike for such places.

As his eyes draw away from the hall door, a motion brings them back with the snapping swiftness of a mousetrap. He's disappointed to see a middle-aged man emerge and quickly pull on a coat. As he makes for the exit, a look of relief—or is it peace—seems to settle on the man. What this means, Darius can only guess.

Minutes continue to pass until a full hour has filled the clock. If it was a pitcher of milk, it would now be spilling over the top and growing into a puddle on the table, much like Darius's emotions as he continues to wait, an ever-expanding knot growing in his stomach.

It's with much relief, then, when Maggie finally exits the hall door. She pauses just inside the room and gives Darius a good, long stare as if seeing him for the first time and committing every detail to memory.

"I think I'm ready to go home," she finally says, and taking Darius by the arm, she lets him escort her from the building, lifting her face to the waiting winter sun.

After settling her into the passenger seat of his Honda Civic, Darius hurries around and hops into the driver's seat. He starts the car and cranks up the heat and the defrosters. He makes no move, however, to put the car in gear for the journey to Eldridge Avenue. Instead, he fixes his eyes on Maggie and waits. She, of course, makes no effort to meet his gaze and casts her eyes this way and that—anywhere but the driver's seat.

"Maggie . . .?" Darius finally says.

She sighs deeply, resignedly, and upon reaching the end of this long exhalation, the sigh seems to quiver ever so slightly, as if shaken by something from within.

"What is it?" Darius presses.

She tells him all of it, every word she can remember, every question she asked, every answer she received. When she finishes, Darius sits perfectly still, his white knuckles gripping the locked steering wheel as tears stream down his face.

"Come," Maggie says with a disapproving tone, "we'll have none of that." Reaching into her purse she extracts a tissue and hands it to him. A moment later she retrieves a second one for herself.

As they sit in silence, each contemplating unwelcome words bearing unwelcome news, Darius notices that Maggie is clutching something in her purse. It's the hourglass from her family room. When she notices his eyes on it, she reluctantly extracts it and cradles it in both hands on her lap.

"Good luck charm?" Darius asks. He tries to force a smile, but it fractures at the edges and fades into a pained look filled with more tears.

"It's a comfort to me at times like this," she explains and then sighs deeply. "It wasn't always so." She leaves the enigmatic words where they fall. Reaching over, she takes Darius's hand in her own and together they sit, two souls bracing for what must come.

It's a while before they speak again, and instead of delving into her grim prognosis, Maggie pats the hourglass in her hands—a convenient distraction—and says, "Jerry gave this to me the week before he went off to Vietnam. I happened to see it in a quaint little antique store in La Conner and he bought it when I wasn't looking. The next day he had it engraved."

She tips the top toward Darius until he can read REMEMBER THE HOURGLASS, which is etched into a brass oval glued to the top. He'd seen the etching before, of course, when the hourglass was sitting next to Jerry's picture in the family room.

"He said the words would remind me that his tour of duty was only a year and that he'd be back with me before I knew it." She makes a *tsk*ing sound, leaving the sad irony unstated.

With a dissatisfied *hmmph*, she turns the hourglass over and watches the grains begin to fall.

"Time is a funny thing," she muses. "Just look how fast the grains fall when you look closely as if it's an avalanche, or perhaps a waterfall of small stones. Yet it's not all that fast when you sit there and stare at it. Sometimes it seems you can see each grain as it tumbles loose and drops through the gap. When the sand runs out and you turn it over again, and again, and again, time becomes a sort of monster."

Her next words are slow and quiet.

"Jerry returned, of course, but in a box. His . . . death . . . hit me hard, and I suppose it was a form of retaliation, but I buried that hourglass at the bottom of a storage chest and didn't see it again for more than thirty years."

She shakes her head as if trying to understand the long-ago deed. "It wasn't the fault of the hourglass that he died but try explaining that to a grieving widow." She runs a hand along the length of the antique as if every part of it is now cherished. "These days I use it to remind myself that life is a gift, every hour, day, and year of it."

Sniffing away the tears, she holds the keepsake out between them. "There are enough grains of sand in this small hourglass to account for every hour of my life. That's between six and seven hundred thousand grains. Quite a shocking number when gathered all together and placed under glass."

She pushes the metal and glass timepiece into Darius's hands and insists that he take a closer look.

"In recent years," she says, "I've stared into that glass and wondered how many grains were wasted on foolish errands, petty squabbles, and ridiculous gossip. How many grudges did I hold and how long did I fume over them? How much good did I do?" She raises an eyebrow. "How much bad?"

"You're only human," Darius manages.

"I am, God help me, and despite all our differences and similarities, we humans have a knack for recognizing what's important only when it's too late, don't we? We complain incessantly about how horrible our job is; we envy our neighbor's new car and wonder why we don't have one; we ignore the love in front of us because it's just not good enough." She sighs. "We complain about our life right up to the point when we learn that it's ending."

She laughs at the revelation and shakes her head. "How pathetic." Waving away the thought, she makes a proposition. "If you don't have anywhere you urgently need to be, I'd like to ask you a favor."

"Anything," Darius replies.

Maggie smiles. "It involves a fifteen-minute drive, but I assure you the view is worth it." She gives nothing else away, just points him south and then tucks her hands in her lap.

The experience of driving along Chuckanut Drive is exhilarating in any season but there's something about winter that brings out the rugged nature of the carved byway. Perhaps it's the threatening sandstone cliffs above or the tempestuous nature of the Puget Sound below, its waters glistening under the cold morning sun like ten million diamonds cast upon a dark blanket of amethyst blue.

It might be because emerald trees rise from the water's edge and march relentlessly to the top of Blanchard Mountain, giant soldiers with a single purpose here at the one spot in the west where the Cascade Mountains touch the sea.

The 24-mile stretch of road has been likened to Big Sur, though on a smaller scale. Perhaps that is all the explanation required.

For Maggie, the road is all this and more. Some things have changed since both she and the road were young — time makes such things inevitable. Still, the rugged spirit of the frontier trail lingers on, present in every turn, invigorated by every gasp of wonder.

As the endless curves hug the mountainside, carrying Darius's Honda ever south, he imagines what it must have been like for Maggie those long years ago, cruising along in the Bumblebee Jacket with the top down and the wind blowing in her hair.

The thought leaves him hungry for nostalgia that isn't his.

Just past Larrabee State Park, Maggie directs Darius to a pull-out along the side of the road, the same pull-out, she explains, that was her favorite spot as a young woman. Darius parks the Honda near a rock barrier facing the Puget Sound and a world of water, trees, and rock suddenly fills his windshield, a breathtaking canvas that moves and shimmers in the light winter wind.

They sit for the better part of an hour, just the two of them, sometimes talking, sometimes lost in comfortable silence. Neither wants the moment to end, but such still moments never last and it's with a heavy heart that Darius finally starts the Honda and turns to the north.

The hardest part of his day still lies ahead.

Spider and Jenny are both aware of Maggie's appointment that morning, just one more in a series of appointments, or so they thought. It now falls on Darius to deliver the worst news one can get, and to the two people who deserve it the least. As hard as Spider will take it, Darius worries most about Jenny.

Heartache has a way of multiplying: First, we grieve at the news, and then we grieve at how it affects those we love. As hard as it'll be telling Spider, Darius knows that Jenny will take the news worse, heartbreakingly so.

Sorrow follows him back to Bellingham. It follows him to an old house on Eldridge Avenue. A high place on a bluff, now special beyond measure.

Chapter 49

Saturday, March 11

The next two weeks are as close to a nightmare as Darius can imagine.

After breaking the news first to Spider and then to Jenny—each of whom collapsed, Spider into a chair, Jenny to the ground—they had consoled one another through many days and nights. They hid their grief from Maggie, putting on tortured smiles and pretending nothing had changed.

Maggie couldn't stand it.

On the fourth day, she chastised them. "There's nothing as uniquely brutal as self-awareness," she told them, "but it's honest at its core. We spend our lives lying to ourselves about why we can't do this or why we won't do that. Well, I've always prided myself on being self-aware, knowing my weaknesses and strengths, as much as that sometimes bothered me. I'll not spend my last days like this, pretending that all is well."

She glares at them for good measure.

"And one more thing: I'm not going to break, so quit treating me as if I were a damn spiderweb cast from glass."

After that, things were considerably improved.

By seven A.M. on Saturday, March 11th, Jenny, Darius, Spider, and Maggie find themselves southbound on Interstate 5, riding low in Jenny's intimidating charcoal Camaro. Maggie rides shotgun and is "tickled pink" by the car's low rumble, the throb in the air when it accelerates, and the way it pushes you back in your seat when Jenny's lead foot mashes down on the gas. It reminds her of the cars she grew up around, the cars that cruised the strip with her on Friday and Saturday nights.

No Nissans or Hondas or BMWs, just straight-up American steel.

With Maggie in the car, Jenny's a bit easier on the gas pedal but you wouldn't know this based on the sounds emanating from the passenger seat. Hunkered down in the back seat, Darius and Spider chuckle at each squeal and smile at every *Oh, my!* Sometimes this draws back Maggie's hand, which flails around as she tries to swat them.

It's a good respite from the dark days that came before.

Maggie last visited her husband's grave the previous summer, an absence due to distance rather than preference. The journey takes them south through Seattle, then to Tacoma, and finally over the Tacoma Narrows Bridge to the small yet picturesque town of Gig Harbor. There, nestled alongside State Route 16, is the Haven of Rest Cemetery.

Jerry's final resting place wasn't Maggie's choice. She was given little say about *any* of his final arrangements. When Jenny asks why she simply replies, "Because I was his wife, but they were his parents." She sighs. "In truth, I was still young and impressionable. Jerry's mother had never approved of me and was rather fond of browbeating me. It drove my father mad."

"So, she told you they were going to bury him in Gig Harbor and that was it?"

"That's pretty much the way it went. They'd moved to Gig Harbor before Jerry deployed to Vietnam and had settled on the idea that they would retire here. Naturally, when Jerry died, they wanted him near."

"What about you? He was your husband."

Maggie gives a light shrug. "I was a secondary consideration." She catches herself and laughs. "Who am I kidding. I wasn't even a tenth consideration." She gives a sort-of snort from the passenger seat, as if unwilling to commit to a full snort, as if unwilling to waste the energy.

"Jerry's mother was the product of superior breeding, as they say, a winner in the DNA lottery. The problem was she knew it and reveled in that smug knowledge. Everything she had and was had come from riding on the coattails of her fine ancestral stock. In her mind, I was unworthy of her son. He was a West Point graduate, after all. What was I? The lowly daughter of a body man. No doubt she worried about the quality of any grandchildren I might give her. God forbid I should taint the family gene pool."

Maggie forces a smile, simply and beautifully, only the edge of her lips betraying any pain in her body or soul. "The old hag was probably relieved when grandchildren were no longer an option."

Jenny parks the Camaro and shuts it down but makes no move to exit.

"She was wrong about you," she eventually says, her voice quiet.

Maggie stares out the windshield. "I sometimes wonder," she eventually says.

The Haven of Rest Cemetery is breathtaking in a way that makes one momentarily forget about its slumbering residents. Sprawled upon its eastern horizon, Mount Rainer rises from the earthy haze, its snowy peaks brooding over all that lies below, and in this part of the country that's pretty much everything.

The grounds of the cemetery are park-like, the gravestones set in the turf so they're barely noticeable, and the green sweep of lawn stretches in all directions, broken here and there by trees or an outbuilding or the tranquil pond with its surface fountain.

Maggie guides them to a quiet spot with few markers.

A polished marble bench rests to the side of the grave, running parallel as if it were placed there for a final viewing rather than as part of the grave. At the base of the bench is a brass plaque dedicating the resting spot to the memory of First Lieutenant Jerry Lipscomb, son of Walter and Barbara Lipscomb.

There's no mention of a wife.

The bench is a monument in a cemetery without monuments. It's the type of display that calls out the spot, pretentiously announcing that *someone special lies here.* Darius notes that the cemetery has few other benches, and those that do exist are in scenic spots or rest areas. None of the other gravesites have been afforded such an honor. Not one.

Maggie, ever observant, even now in her waning days, watches as Darius silently sorts through this. He doesn't say anything, but when their eyes meet a few moments later, Maggie gives him a tired smile and says, "They spared no expense." When Darius nods his understanding, she adds, "We're all pathetic in our own little ways."

There's a whole world caught up in those simple words—an epic tale.

But, that's someone else's story.

Maggie spends the better part of an hour at Jerry's side, sometimes sitting on the bench, other times lying on the ground, ever talking to him, perhaps telling him that she'll be coming along shortly. When she finally rejoins Darius, Jenny, and Spider inside the chapel, there's a contented, peaceful look on her face, as if she'd come to terms with something that had long weighed on her.

"Well, that's that," she says with a sigh.

Chapter 50

Saturday, March 18

Maggie never showed it, but the trip to Gig Harbor the previous weekend had taxed her system and strength, and though she put on a good show the next day, displaying more spunk and energy than she had in weeks, the truth was that she was spent.

On Tuesday, it all came to a head.

Jenny arrived to find her unable to get out of bed. Even with Spider's help, Maggie's legs couldn't seem to find perch under her, and he ended up carrying her to the La-Z-Boy in the living room. Tended by Jenny nonstop throughout the rest of the day and week, she seemed to regain some of her vigor, but it was mostly for show. Maggie had reached a point of diminishing returns. Each setback was harder to bounce back from, each exertion of energy harder to replenish.

Time was simply running out.

As the hour pushes toward midnight and Darius works toward exhaustion, his mind is unclear and wandering, possessed of a single instinctual goal that consumes him, but which has somehow escaped him. Here and then gone. All he knows is that he *must* get the rear bumper attached. There's some significance in this, but he'll puzzle that out later.

Jenny called earlier; worried about him, as always.

They talked for a considerable time, yet he can't remember a word of their conversation. It was something about the paintings and Maggie, but everything else has slipped away. The only thing that remains crystal clear in his mind is the soft impression of her words in his ear. Her voice had always had a soothing, meditative quality as if the whole world could be burning down around you, but you know it's going to be fine.

Even the memory of it seems enough to keep him going.

Darius misses Spider.

His friend hasn't spent much time on the Bumblebee lately, perhaps because he feels his place is with Jenny and Maggie, or maybe he figures he's just slowing Darius down. Both are true, but the latter only partly so.

Spider was ever a distraction, but usually a welcome one. He generated endless stimulation in the long hours of the night, and the extra pair of hands he provided may not have been skilled, but they were enough to hold a wrench or help align a bracket.

Darius could have used those hands a few minutes ago when placing the bumper.

Most of all, Spider lessened the quiet solitude of the shop.

Darius finds the place oppressively silent without his friend. Even with the music playing in the background and the clank and rattle of tools, the job has become lonely, even tedious. When there is no one to share small victories with, those victories become meaningless. Likewise, when Darius steps back to look at a task just completed, there's no one beside him to grin and clasp him on the shoulder, no one to use odd slang terms to say how totally bitching the car looks.

Yes, Darius misses Spider.

Yet, as much as he would have him here, his friend is where he needs to be, and that's at Maggie's side. Spider and Jenny have been spending every possible moment with her these days. Without them, Maggie would be in a hospice somewhere, and as gracious and wonderful as most hospice workers are, they're not family.

Spider and Jenny *are* family.

They, along with Darius, are the family Maggie chose.

Sitting on a five-gallon bucket that once held lacquer thinner, Darius fiddles with the rear bumper, trying to attach a bolt. He fiddles and fiddles and fiddles. Exhaustion is a burden he knows well yet he doesn't seem to recognize it when it settles upon him. He has always imagined it as the weight of steel feathers on a bird, or lead shoes on a man, or the tonnage of two elephants on the back of one.

Such exhaustion never seems to pounce on you all at once but settle in your bones and muscles by increments. For most the warning signs come early and they wisely retire to a lounge chair and a good book. They still pay the price the next day, of course, a necessary invoice billed not in hours but aches and pains. Still, they're no worse for the experience.

For the driven, those like Darius, exhaustion is a different animal, a dangerous adversary. It stalks them as they go about their business, oblivious to the warning rustle in the bush or the soft pad of heavy feet. The only weapon against such a beast is rest—a hard prescription for the bull-headed and the unwilling.

Even now, the beast circles Darius.

There are things one can do to keep exhaustion at bay.

Music is usually the first choice but must be loud and lively. Barry Manilow will stuff an apple in your mouth and serve you up to exhaustion without a hint of remorse. Styx, Van Halen, Def Leppard—all good choices.

Barbara Streisand—No!

Darius usually opts for something only slightly more contemporary, groups like Nickelback, Nirvana, and Pearl Jam. Part of this may be his bias toward groups from the Pacific Northwest, but in truth, he simply likes the music.

Despite his refusal to accept what is increasingly impossible to ignore, Darius pushes on, fighting through the fatigue, pushing the beast back into the forest. If one were to ask him at this moment why he was pushing so hard, what was so important that it couldn't wait until the next day, he would just smile and mutter a nonsensical answer.

Right now, there's a bumper and bolt that need to meet.

That's all that matters.

The bumper is not original to a 1951 Plymouth Cranbrook, but rather a one-off custom design made specifically for the Bumblebee Jacket by E. E. Atwood. The backside still contains notes and markings from where it was cut and welded together. Its design is simple: It runs perfectly straight across the back of the car and curves up at the ends, where the taillights come down to join it, turning each taillight into an elongated upright almond of chrome and plastic.

It's striking in its simplicity.

With the right side of the bumper clamped to its bracket with a locking vise-grip, Darius holds the left side steady as he tries to fit a chrome bolt through the bumper hole and on through the bracket. It's a simple task that somehow eludes him.

He tries again and fails again.

Feeling the bumper grow heavy in his hand, he pulls it back from the car so as not to scratch the paint and rests it on his knee. Reaching behind him, he grabs hold of another empty five-gallon can and pulls it around, placing it under the bumper and next to the car. He lets go carefully, making sure the bumper doesn't twist or pull into the car. Satisfied that it's well-supported, he leans back on the can and wipes his brow with his right forearm.

Guns N' Roses blares from the radio. The song is legendary, yet Darius can't remember its name at the moment. He was never much good with song titles, but this is one he played over and over again in high school and it bothers him that he can't recall it.

"November Rain," a voice says behind him as if reading his mind.

Whirling, Darius loses his balance on the can and tumbles to his knees. The can tips over and rolls across the concrete floor, coming to rest against the front wheel of a 1964 Chevy Nova parked across from the yellow Plymouth convertible.

When he looks up Darius finds Jenny staring down at him, eyes wide with her hand covering her mouth. "Sorry," she says sheepishly. "I thought you heard me come in."

Rising to his feet, Darius composes himself quickly.

"No, it's good." He makes a jerky movement as if shaking off the adrenaline. "Skinny always talks about how this place is haunted and for a split second there I think I believed him."

"Skinny thinks the shop is haunted?"

"He's superstitious that way."

"Has he ever . . . seen anything?" Jenny's eyes dart around the empty shop, half expecting some shadowy form to appear in a dark corner.

"No, but he says he gets these feelings, like ghost eyes are watching him. He's not very good at explaining it, and no one else has ever seen or felt anything, so we just chalk it up to Skinny being Skinny."

Jenny doesn't seem so sure.

Regardless, she's a welcome sight in her jeans and loose white top. Her hair is pulled back into a clip revealing her entire face, which seems to glow from somewhere deep within. Darius drinks her in, memorizing

292 · SPENCER KOPE

every line of her face, the drop of her neck, and the sway of her back. In his exhausted state it takes a moment for him to realize that she's noticed his appreciating eyes. Embarrassed he looks away, but she takes him by the chin and pulls him in.

The kiss is warm and gentle, but when Jenny tries to wrap her arms around him, he pulls back. "I'm filthy," he says apologetically, gesturing at his clothes.

"That's okay, you can take a shower and get some fresh clothes at Maggie's."

"No, I've got a couple more hours in me." He looks back at the car. "I need to get the—" he waves a hand toward the long strip of chromed steel.

"Bumper?" Jenny offers.

Darius just nods, perhaps realizing just how tired he is.

"You need rest," Jenny says. "You need some decent food, a shower, and some time with your friends."

"I'm running out of time," Darius says quietly.

"We all are."

When he looks up, perhaps startled at the response, she presses further. "Maggie cares more about your company than a ride in her old car."

"I promised—"

"That was before we knew," Jenny insists. "Things have changed." She breathes in the shop air and holds it a heartbeat before letting it out in a loud rush. "If there's one thing I've learned from Maggie in our short time together it's that life is precious and unpredictable. Every grain of sand that slips through the hourglass is one that can't be recovered. You can't just crack open the glass and refill it.

Darius doesn't answer.

"I know you don't want to accept that Maggie's dying," Jenny continues, "but hiding in the shop and killing yourself trying to get the Bumblebee done isn't going to change what's coming."

"I know that," Darius replies, his words terse from fatigue.

"She loves you like a son."

"I know that too."

Jenny sighs. "I'm not saying you have to abandon your promise. It's just"—she shakes her head— "all this is going to be a moot point in a couple of weeks or months. What will be important then? The time you spent with her or the time spent here?"

"You think I'm being foolish?"

"No," Jenny replies forcefully, stepping close. "It's *noble*. Noble in a way that people have forgotten." She takes his chin in her hand again and studies his eyes; peers into his soul. "I just don't want you to regret these days."

Darius grows quiet, thinking. If he was tired before, he's exhausted now.

"Come back to Maggie's," Jenny urges softly. "Grab a shower and I'll make you something to eat. In the morning, the four of us can have breakfast together, just like we used to."

He lets her lead him away from the patient convertible, lead him away as if he'd been made invalid from the long hours and parade of days. Pausing just inside the office, Jenny turns off the lights and closes the door to the teardown area behind them. Locking the front door, she leads him toward her Camaro.

"My cars over there," Darius says.

"You're too tired to drive."

"I'm filthy dirty, Jenny. I don't want to mess up your car."

"Stop worrying."

"At least take my car; it's already dirty."

She scoffs at the idea. "A Honda! You're joking, right?" When she shoots him a grin he manages to smile back, but only barely.

He doesn't remember the ride to Maggie's.

Chapter 51

March 29

Hope is a bit like a rubber band: It expands, it contracts, it can fit many things, but if you expect too much of it something is likely to give, and that something might be you.

For some, hope becomes a rock, a pillar in the distance, a lighthouse on a storm-tossed shore. Its mere presence provides comfort and the promise of a better tomorrow. It sits in front of them, ever-present, as solid as the granite mountains that seem to have spawned it or the bricks that laid its foundation.

Every story in recorded history dating back to Homer has featured hope in one manner or another. The unmeasured number of these oral and written stories seem to rival the stars themselves. Tales of narrow escapes, impossible victories, and miraculous recoveries have been passed down to us through the ages. One of the very first stories, Homer's *Odyssey*, tells the tale of Ulysses, who, at the end of the Trojan War, struggled with gods and monsters for ten long years as he made his way home.

Hope drove him.

Humans escaped certain annihilation when Martian invaders were struck down by a virus; a boy found adventure and pirate treasure on a distant island; a hobbit and his dwarven companions were plucked from certain doom by giant eagles; astronauts patched together a broken space capsule as the world held its breath.

These are the stories of hope.

Even death was defeated in Mary Shelley's novel, *Frankenstein*, published anonymously in 1818, though this last example didn't turn out so well.

Humanity has forever longed for such stories, tales that take one right up to the cliff of despair only to clutch you back from the precipice at the last moment, leaving you gasping and filled with a sense of relief.

Hollywood was built on hope.

Stories such as The Odyssey, War of the Worlds, Treasure Island, The Hobbit, and Apollo 13 are the stories of life, both real and imagined, and they're woven into our very fabric by the threads of hope.

This is not one of those stories.

As wonderful as it would be to say that Maggie slowly regains her strength, defeats her disease, and lives another thirty years, it's simply not the case.

Even the most deserving, it seems, are sometimes denied.

Hope dies.

Such is life.

On Sunday, March 19, Maggie takes another turn and finds herself once more in the hospital. After several difficult days, she begins to regain her strength, but progress is slow, and her recovery is never quite complete. Ten days later, still weak and beaten down, the hospital releases her. As Darius wheels her from the elevator, past the reception counter, and out the front door, she vows never to return.

It's a vow she intends to keep.

Back on Eldridge Avenue, Jenny turns the living room into a glorified, oversized bedroom. At Maggie's request, she positions the painting of A Girl and Her Car in the corner of the room, just right of the television so that it's always in view. On the end table next to Maggie's chair, she sets the picture of Jerry in his fresh lieutenant's uniform. This too faces her, his striking image always in view.

The hourglass stands watch next to him.

With this reordering compete and her world set back to some semblance of normalcy, Maggie quickly drifts off to sleep. There is no clatter of hospital carts wheeling up and down the hall, no beeping machines, no distant, unintelligible chatter, just the quiet, ever-present heartbeat of an old house and the people she loves.

Home blessed home.

"I'm going to take a leave of absence," Jenny announces twenty minutes later as they huddle around the kitchen table. Her voice is low, the type of voice our ancestors might've used in a sick house. It's disquieting, a reminder of what lies ahead.

"What about the paintings?" Darius asks.

"And your book?" Spider adds.

"It'll wait," she replies. Her next words are strained as if pressed through layers of intertwined emotion that she somehow manages to contain. "I don't know how much time we have left with her." She wipes at a single tear that appears on the inside edge of her eye. "I just want to make it count."

Darius and Spider don't reply but stare at the tabletop until one begins to imagine that the varnished wood grain holds some secret that, if deciphered, might banish death, and make this all go away. A hidden truth that might return them to the happy family they once imagined themselves.

Again, this is not one of those stories.

There are no illusions as the long, final vigil begins.

Chapter 52

Wednesday, April 12

Jenny hears Beryl before she sees her.

As the passengers from Delta flight 438 exit up the passenger bridge, Beryl's rich booming voice, thick with cockney English, can be heard rising above all others, drifting over their heads as if held aloft by helium balloons sporting the Union Jack.

Loud talkers are generally annoying, but Beryl seems to be the exception. She's rather entertaining in her limitless excitement, and more than one person is smiling to themselves as they exit the tunnel. When the woman herself finally pours out and spots Jenny, no less than a half dozen people say goodbye and wish her well as she breaks off from the group.

"Quite the celebrity," Jenny says playfully as she approaches.

"Don't let 'em fool you," Beryl proclaims loudly, "it's all about the breasts." She hefts her bra up as if the world didn't exist and it was only the two of them. "Quite a bit saggier than they used to be," she adds in a quieter tone. Letting go, she grabs Jenny suddenly by the shoulders and pulls her in for a quick peck on the check and an enormous hug that threatens to engulf her.

"So good to see you, dear," she practically purrs, holding her for a long moment before letting go.

"You too," Jenny replies with a soft chuckle.

They make their way to the baggage claim and wait for the luggage carousel to begin its slow spin, talking all the while about the flight, the weather, the small alligator that keeps finding its way into Beryl's backyard, and the ridiculous price of coffee compared to tea.

When the carousel finally lurches to life it doesn't take long before Beryl's single bag drops down the chute and drifts toward them. Leave it to Beryl to have the only luggage that looks like it was stolen off a Harry Potter movie set. When Jenny retrieves it, she notices several people glancing her way and smiling.

Since when were the British so entertaining?

It's not till they've reached Jenny's car—another source of delight for Beryl—and are on the freeway heading north that the unavoidable settles down between them.

"So, how's our girl?" Beryl asks, her voice surprisingly subdued.

"It's day by day now," Jenny replies. "She's a whisper of herself—won't take any food. I've tried forcing her to eat, but I think I'd have better luck getting a giraffe to hop on one leg."

Beryl gives a long *hmmm* and fishes a tissue from her purse, expecting she'll need it. "Tough old broad, that one," she says after a moment. "I always thought she'd outlast me by a decade; I counted on it. No one wants to be the last among her fellows if you know what I mean."

"I just found her," Jenny whispers, and a single tear escapes her eye, falling as if it carries all the world's sorrow, as if every tear that came before and would come after had been condensed into this one drop, now shed for Grace Margaret Atwood.

Beryl reaches over and takes her hand, but otherwise doesn't look at her, determined that at least one of them should remain tearless at any given moment. Instead, she does her best to remain stoic, eyes ever on the road, ever on the future, searching for hope in a wasteland.

"Did our Mags ever tell you about *Pieces of Heaven*?" Beryl asks at length.

Jenny gives a stunted shake of her head. "What's that?"

"It's a short story she wrote some years after her father died, a sort of therapy I suppose. She only mentioned it to me after we'd known each other for ages, and it took me another two years before she let me read it, stubborn old hen. It was bloody brilliant, and I told her so. Tried to get her to send it off to the magazines, didn't I, but she'd have none of it."

"I didn't know that Maggie wrote?"

"That's because she doesn't, not really. Just this one story, far as I can tell."

"What's it about?"

"Oh, a young boy whose father dies in a car wreck, the same wreck that paralyzes the boy." She jerks her head up with sudden realization. "That sounds rather horrid, doesn't it? I assure you it gets much better. You see, some years later the boy is on the operating table for a new procedure that might fix his paralysis, highly experimental and all that, only he dies while under anesthesia, doesn't he?"

"I think we're back to horrid," Jenny observes.

"Yes, yes, but the rest of the story is about all the people the boy meets in the afterlife, relatives he knew and a lot more he didn't, people he might have impacted, and, of course, his father. Maggie called the story *Pieces of Heaven* because that's what we all are: pieces of someone else's heaven. The more friends and acquaintances you make, the greater your heaven. Even those who are still living can be part of someone's heaven, you just can't sit down and have a good chin wag with them—not yet leastwise."

"Chin wag?"

"Talk, dear. A good talk."

"Do Facebook friends count?" Jenny asks. "Because if they do, I'm golden."

"I'm not the almighty," Beryl says with a deep chuckle, "but I'm guessing they have to be real friends."

Taking Jenny's hand up into her own, she says, "In any case, you'll be part of Maggie's heaven now, just as she'll be part of yours someday when you make the journey." She smiles. "And part of mine." She gives the hand a good squeeze. "We can all sit around wagging our chins and having a spot of tea—on the moon if we prefer. It'll be lovely."

"Tea on the moon, that does sound lovely."

"Little dusty for my taste," Beryl replies with a haughty sniff, "but we'll make do."

They drive on in silence, past the endless cars and the people within, and Jenny begins to wonder who waits for each of *them* on the other side. She wonders if perhaps we all aren't linked together somehow, in this life or the next, soul to soul, like some celestial version of Six Degrees of Kevin Bacon.

"Pieces of Heaven," Jenny mutters against the rumble of the Camaro. Beryl smiles at the words but doesn't glance over, her eyes ever on the road ahead.

Chapter 53

Sunday, April 16

Darius is alone in the body shop, both in body and spirit.

He sits on an empty, upturned five-gallon can, head in his hands, despair in his pocket. It's not like him to accept defeat but he's starting to realize that the dream, the beautiful dream, is over. What began as a quest to build a car had turned into something so much more. It was a journey of discovery, the seed of a new, unconventional family, the revelation of truths in a world seemingly gone mad.

The Bumblebee Jacket was the mother of all these things and yet— here at the end—after all she has given him, Darius fears he has failed both the car and Maggie. He had made many promises in his life and took quiet pride in those to which he remained true, while an aching sense of shame accompanies the memory of those few where he failed.

There is nothing to describe how he feels now, however, here at the edge of failure, knowing he'll have to say goodbye to Maggie before the car is finished; before he can give her a promised ride. What makes this worse is that he's come to realize that it's not simply a ride, not to Maggie anyway.

Every step closer to the car's restoration is a sweet remembering, a step back to better days, to an innocent time—if ever there was such a thing. It's as if Darius is not only rebuilding her car but her youth along with it, all the happy memories from a time before loss and grief. A time when she was sixteen, when the world was fresh and wonderful, and she had a yellow sundress and a car to match.

Darius thinks about Atwood's vision of the soul, the idea that it has a conscious part and a subconscious part. Maggie said that her father believed the conscious part could get beat down by life, even broken, but the subconscious part was forever divine and untouchable, unassailable by anything the mortal world could throw at it.

For Maggie, it was just a casual observation during one of their discussions, an idea she handed out as if it were candy from her pocket, quickly forgotten. Yet, despite his agnosticism, this was something Darius had latched onto, something he could believe in. So strong had this vision of the immortal settled upon him that it became the true force behind his push to finish the car as if to restore the car was to wipe away all that the world had done to Maggie, to restore her to the young girl with the glowing soul who had a father who loved her without measure.

Here, at the end, that hard-sought goal teeters on the edge of failure.

Maggie's life is now measured by a scant few grains of sand— mere hours, a day or two at best. Darius's long march has turned into a hopeless fight.

The grief of it overtakes him.

He's spent, used up.

There *will* be a risen Bumblebee Jacket. He knows this, he understands it with the clarity of a monk, it just won't be in time for Maggie. By his best estimate, there are at least another two hundred hours of work needed before the car is complete, and that's skimping on the things that can be hidden or overlooked until later, like the headliner on the convertible top and the lift supports for the hood.

Two hundred hours may as well be two thousand.

Darius feels like crying.

Lost in this world of despair, Darius doesn't hear the soft intonations of the keypad outside the first roll-up door, so when the motor and pulley clank into action and the heavy door begins to lift, he springs from his seat in a startled daze. Wiping self-consciously at his eyes, he waits while the gap at the bottom of the door increases and the outside world comes rushing in.

The light is intense—a beautiful April day of which he'd been utterly oblivious.

"Well, champ, how's it going," a voice says in a calming cadence.

Uncle John.

The old body man is shocked to see the state that Darius is in. He pulls the boy into a bear hug, the way he used to when his nephew was so much younger and smaller, a time that seems like only yesterday.

"You've been hitting this too hard, son," Uncle John says. He locks eyes with Darius and studies him for a long moment before throwing a thumb over his shoulder. "I thought you could use a little help."

Only now does Darius recognize the sound of car doors closing outside and voices drawing near. The first to come around the corner and step through the opening is Dallas, followed closely by Armando and Skinny. Behind them are other faces, some familiar, others that Darius has never seen before.

Counting Uncle John there are thirteen in all, and bringing up the rear is Ward Keller, his uncle's old boss and the man who knew Evan Atwood and his daughter . . . once upon a time.

"Hey, kid," Ward says with a grin, placing a hand on Darius's shoulder as he passes.

After a quick look through the boxes of new parts and the buckets of old, the crew hovers around the old Plymouth, walking this way and that, looking under the hood and into the interior with equal curiosity and admiration.

The walkaround and inspection takes perhaps ten minutes. After that, the men seem to know instinctively what needs to be done and set about doing it, each gravitating to their specialty. Little guidance is needed from Darius, nothing more than a quick answer regarding the engine, or clarification on the weather stripping.

The men are professionals, and it shows.

There's a certain joy that comes from working with true craftsmen, and it's this joy that lends a tingle of electricity to the air inside Road Runner Restoration and turns hard work into something almost spiritual. The more the men labor the more invested they become in the endeavor as if slowly realizing that this, the last ride of Grace Margaret Atwood, is something they will carry with them the rest of their lives.

In tribute to the car, the young girl who inspired it, and the age of innocence that they both sprang from, Ward places a call to a lifelong friend who just happens to own a classic rock station in town. Soon, the uplifting voices of Buddy Holly, The Platters, Pat Boone, Dion and the Belmonts, Chuck Berry, Bill Haley, The Del-Vikings, and the Cleftones take turns filling the shop.

As the evening progresses, other singers and songs will follow, their voices carrying the crew long into the night. It's as if the music is a giant invisible pair of hands cupped beneath them, holding them up and lending them resolve. Perhaps they are the otherworldly hands of Evan Elmore Atwood, here at the end to see things through.

For the first time in weeks, Darius feels a flush of relief. An ember called hope stirs once more inside him, growing slowly to a flame of certainty.

The rest of the night is magical, bordering on mystical.

If you were to ask any of the men what they did or what was said, they would have a hard time recalling, but every last one of them would feel their soul stir at the question, as if party to a great and wonderful secret, one they dare not put to words.

Chapter 54

Monday, April 17

The men of Team Yellow—as the eclectic assortment of body men have come to call themselves—are back to work on the car before seven A.M., fueled by copious amounts of coffee from the Hilltop Restaurant just north of town, courtesy of Ward, and a trunkful of muffins and pastries from the Haggen grocery store on Woburn Street, courtesy of Uncle John.

Just after nine, a pristine red 1959 Corvette with white inserts rumbles down the driveway and parks opposite the roll-up door. It's followed moments later by a two-tone blue 1957 Ford Skyliner and a rose-gold 1958 Chevrolet Biscayne. Four men and two women emerge hesitantly from the cars, perhaps fearful of intruding on what they seem to know is a last-minute scramble to reach a tough goal.

Uncle John brakes away from the driver's side door panel he's installing and instinctively wipes his already clean hands on the rag in his back pocket. Strolling across the shop floor, he steps through the roll-up door and is immediately enveloped by an odd echo that seems to assail him from two sides. It only takes him a moment to understand the source: The three new arrivals are all tuned to the same radio station that's blaring from the shop, which is currently cranking out *Mr. Sandman*, by The Chordettes.

Uncle John can't help but smile.

"Morning folks," he says by way of greeting. "What can I help you with?"

A tall, stocky man in his mid-seventies with a thick head of white hair takes the outstretched hand and says his name is Pete. He introduces the others and says they're members of the original Twilighters, one of the many car clubs popular when last the Bumblebee Jacket ran circuits on the cruise route.

"Heard you have a special car you're trying to finish," Pete says.

"Heard that, did you?"

Pete shrugs. "Word spreads. One car guy tells another"—the woman beside him clears her throat, and Pete corrects himself. "Car *person*." The woman, his wife as it turns out, gives him an approving smile. "You know how it is," Pete tells Uncle John. "The vintage car community is small."

"What else did you hear?"

"That the original owner was a woman who graduated Bellingham High, Class of '62, someone who used to cruise town like the rest of us motorheads."

Uncle John smiles. "She did, indeed."

Glancing toward the open roll-up door, Pete's wife, Carol, asks, "Do you mind if we take a look? We don't want to get underfoot, just, maybe stand at the door . . .?"

Uncle John hesitates. With plenty of work and little time ahead of them, his first impulse is to turn them down, but something in his gut pulls him in another direction. "I suppose it can't hurt," he finally says.

Pete starts to say something but stops.

"What is it?"

He seems apologetic. "There are others . . ."

Uncle John gives a guttural laugh and drags his eyes across the sky before resting them once more on Pete. "What the hell," he says in resignation. "Bring 'em."

By others, of course, Pete means close to two hundred vintage cars and their drivers from a dozen car clubs. By nine-thirty, they start arriving by twos and threes, and the sound of that lone FM radio station begins to take on the theatrical quality of a Greek amphitheater, projecting the music with stunning clarity.

Around ten, a lowered, chopped 1957 Chevy pickup rolls in. It's not unlike the one once owned by Evan Elmore Atwood, though instead of Candy Apple Red, this one is a mesmerizing silver. From the bed of the truck, the driver carefully unloads a large propane-powered griddle. As he lights it and lets it warm up, his wife extracts four large Tupperware containers from a cooler and sets them on the tailgate. Soon, the smell of bacon and eggs and buckwheat pancakes fills the air.

The feast is not for the other club members, but the men inside the shop.

When the food is ready and Pete breaks the news to Team Yellow, the men are both humbled and surprised. With broad grins, they line up, plates in hand, and devour everything in sight, down to the last crumb of bacon.

The gesture is well received.

After that, it doesn't matter how many vintage cars show up. As far as Team Yellow is concerned, they're all on the same mission. Of course, by this time enough cars are lining the streets and nearby parking lots that passersby begin to gather for a look, perhaps thinking it a car show, which it may as well be.

As the men thank the club and start back to work, Pete pulls Uncle John aside.

"Would it be inappropriate if we asked to come along when you go to give this lady a ride?" he asks. The look on his face suggests that he's afraid of insulting Uncle John.

"Not for me to say," the old body man replies. He thumbs at Darius. "This is his show."

Seeing his uncle gesturing his way, Darius wanders over.

"Pete, this is my nephew, Darius Alexander," Uncle John says. This time, he points the thumb in Pete's direction, saying, "He has a question for you." Without clarification, he turns and starts back toward the open shop door. *The Great Pretender*, by The Platters, begins to issue from a hundred different car radios.

Darius just looks at Pete, waiting.

"This woman you promised the ride to . . ."

"Maggie," Darius says.

"Maggie," Pete says as if committing it to memory. "We were wondering if you might like a vintage car escort when you take Maggie on her ride?" When he sees the look on Darius's face, he quickly adds, "We can follow behind and we'll stay out of the way." He waits in silence, and then, in a smaller voice, adds, "It's been a while since we've done anything more important than car shows."

Glancing toward the open roll-up door, he studies the splash of yellow in the back, taking a moment to choose his next words. "Back in the day," he continues, "a lot of the clubs would go out of their way to help people. If you saw someone with a flat tire you'd pull over and fix it. We had these little cards—like business cards—that we'd hand out to anyone we helped, just so they'd know it was the Twilighters that changed their tire or fetched some gas." He pauses again. "I suppose those were different times."

"Not so different," Darius says softly. He studies the man for a moment as if sizing him up. "You won't get in the way?" he asks.

"We'll follow behind. A proper entourage; a proper send-off."

The words *send-off* jar Darius, reminding him of what he'd put out of mind, but he nods his head, nonetheless. "I think Maggie would like that."

Pete exhales and grins, but then remembers the purpose of the ride. "What time do you think you'll be ready?"

"Maybe one or two this afternoon. We're getting close."

"We have some people here who know how to polish a car like no one else," Pete suggests. "When you're done putting her together, we'd be honored to clean her up and get her ready if you're willing. We know how to do it properly, no belt buckles dragging over fresh paint or anything like that."

Darius nods. "That would be a big help. Most of us are running on empty . . . or maybe that's just me." He gives a tired smile as Pete clasps his upper arm and then releases, giving him a fatherly pat.

"We'll be waiting," the Twilighter says, and for a moment it's not the old man that Darius sees before him, but a nineteen-year-old kid with motor oil for blood and teeth that flash like chrome.

Time changes everything.

Time changes nothing.

Chapter 55

Miracles often come quietly . . . but not this one.

On a bright Monday afternoon in mid-April, a delicious yellow 1951 Plymouth convertible called the Bumblebee Jacket rolls out of Road Runner Restoration to the thunderous applause of hundreds. What was impossible only yesterday has somehow become reality, and as he makes his way to Broadway Avenue and turns right onto Eldridge, Darius says a silent prayer of thanks to a God he's not sure he believes in.

The Bumblebee's engine, the massive 426 Hemi, also known as the elephant, rumbles under the hood as it sucks in air and gas and turns it to fire. A more appropriate name for the engine might have been the dragon, for her roar is as pronounced, and but for her extensive exhaust work, she may well breathe fire. The very air shakes in its presence, warning off lesser rivals.

In the wake of this magnificent car and its barely tamed engine is an entourage unlike any other. There are two hundred cars if there are ten, each a masterpiece of American design and engineering, crafted from raw steel in the days when Detroit was still king, and Honda was a motorcycle company.

The parade of vehicles includes mostly cars and trucks from the 1930s to the early 1970s. Among them are the legends of American steel, names like Camaro, Mustang, Barracuda, Corvette, Impala, Malibu, Nova, Fairlane, Bel Aire, Thunderbird, and GTO. In lesser supply are cars like the Hudson Hornet, the Mercury Monterey, and the DeSoto Sportsman, the forgotten jewels of American ingenuity.

Some are original, some have been upgraded with better engines, custom paint jobs, or modified bodies. Others are in progress, only hinting at future glory. The uncoupled train of steel and rubber stretches for miles as they follow behind the yellow 1951 Plymouth convertible. They don't stop when Darius pulls the Bumblebee into Maggie's driveway but continue to a point just north where they turn around and begin to form up for the escort.

All but one, that is.

A midnight blue 1969 Dodge Dart Swinger follows the Bumblebee Jacket down the driveway and parks off to the side. A lanky man in his seventies or eighties exits and stands near his front fender, waiting.

Not to milk-toast the subject, but death generally comes in one of two ways: The first is suddenly and unexpectedly. This surreal departure tends to leave loved ones in a state of shock, often eliciting a deeper form of grief. Those affected by such a death often find themselves living at the edge of their seat, wondering when the next proverbial shoe will fall.

The second kind of death is one of duration, like Maggie's. The days, weeks, or months provided by this death allow one to have final conversations, to mend old wounds, and to say what too often goes unsaid. The price of this slower death is often discomfort and pain, a price many gladly pay for a last word, a last kiss, a final embrace.

The other drawback to a slow death is that your loved ones must watch you wither as your body slowly starts shutting down. It's a bit like locking the doors and closing the windows on the way out.

This is the way of it for Maggie.

"Careful now, lads," Beryl cautions, "she's a bit wonky."

"The only thing wonky about me are the Brits I associate with," Maggie manages, trying to laugh but failing.

"Right. Your legs were always made of rubber, then?" Beryl replies.

"We'll be careful," Darius assures both Beryl and Maggie as he and Spider simultaneously place a hand under each arm and another along Maggie's back. Gently, they lift her to her feet—which promptly crumble beneath her.

"Rubber legs," Beryl notes. "Mm-hmm."

"Set her back down," Jenny says, dismayed at the sight of Maggie's knees bending under her as her body sags toward the floor.

"We'll have to carry her," Darius says.

He feels the old woman's frail hand on his forearm. It's not the same hand that tended the landscaping last fall or shoveled a bit of snow from the walkway in December.

"I'm sorry, son," she tells Darius. "I just don't seem to have the strength left."

"That's because it's all in your heart," Spider says, kneeling next to her and grasping her other hand. "And here," he says, touching her forehead. "It's where you've always been strongest."

Maggie manages a weak smile and then nods her head, bracing up the way one might before tackling a summit or jumping from a high board. "Take me to my car, boys," she says slowly. "Drag me if you must."

"There you go. That's the bloody spirit!" Beryl rumbles . . . and then discreetly turns away and rubs a tissue under each eye. The outburst brings a type of watery smile to the faces of the others, both heartwarming and heart-wrenching to behold.

"Well, if you're going to drag her," Beryl says through a sniffle, "I'll certainly help."

This time Maggie manages a robust laugh, one that echoes from healthier days and happier times. "Oh, my dear brit," she says.

"My lovely, stubborn broad," Beryl replies, taking Maggie's outstretched hand.

Spider insists on carrying Maggie to the car.

In recent days he's taken to calling her old mum, mostly due to Beryl's influence but also because it's closer to mother or grandmother, and, in his mind, more appropriate than calling her Maggie, especially now, at the end.

Darius opens the passenger door and helps first Beryl and then Jenny into the back seat. Quickly moving over to the driver's seat, he crawls in with his knees on the seat and helps as Spider slowly lowers Maggie into the front passenger seat.

"Good?" he asks Maggie. She nods as her eyes walk across the dashboard and then to the leather seats and new carpet, growing misty as she takes it all in.

Spider hands the seatbelt across and Darius clicks it into place.

"It's so beautiful," Maggie manages to say. Taking Spider's hand, she kisses the back of it. Her lips may as well be butterfly wings for all the impression they make. Next, she takes Darius's hand and does the same, holding it to her cheek a moment before letting go.

As Spider hurries around the back of the car to get in on Darius's side, a figure appears at Maggie's door. Without a word, the man places a hand on the old woman's shoulder and then leans down and kisses the top of her head.

"Ward," Maggie says through building tears.

"Mags," the old body man replies. Leaning closer, so that their heads touch, he lingers a moment and then whispers, "I'll be right behind you."

Maggie could tell you all about Chuckanut Drive.

She could tell you that Chuckanut was native for "long beach far from a narrow entrance" and that the road was first carved from the Chuckanut Mountains in 1895—little more than a farm road. She could tell you of the Sunday drives her father would take her on, winding their way along the cliffside path, past the hairpin turn near Oyster Bay, and then down into the fertile flatlands of Skagit County.

Most of all, Maggie could tell you that Chuckanut Drive was God's finished canvas, that greener trees had never been seen, nor had water looked so deep and mysterious. She has said these things and more, has said them time and again, but today there will be no retelling.

Maggie clings to what energy she has, saving it for the end.

Pulling into the turnoff south of Larrabee State Park, Darius parks the Bumblebee with her nose facing the sound. The April rains have spared them so far, so he leaves the top down and wraps Maggie in a blanket from the trunk. It takes a full twenty minutes for the vintage motorcade to make its way past, their radios still tuned to the same station, creating an interesting effect as the cars stream past one by one.

None of them stop or honk or so much as rev an engine as they continue their way, but all eyes look for Maggie as if to see her is to prove the pilgrimage was real and worthy and that the day was well spent. Even as withered and frail as she is, Maggie's head still manages to rise prominently above the front passenger seat's backrest. Her gaze is cast upon the Puget Sound, whose deep waters—unlike all else—have remained unchanged throughout her eventful life.

As the extended column of vintage vehicles tappers out, a single vehicle brings up the utter rear, as if posted there to catch up stragglers. It's the midnight blue 1969 Dodge Dart Swinger: Ward Keller's car. He slows as he passes, slows but doesn't stop. His eyes find Maggie and he watches her, perhaps thinking of those long-ago days when she'd show up at the shop as her father mentored him. He watches until the Dodge coasts beyond view and the tears cloud his vision, and then he watches no more.

There are endless merciful things in life, but time is not always one of them. It marches on, despite pleas and prayers, despite all efforts.

The sun begins to recline in the western sky, and still they sit.

Darius offered to drive Maggie back to her house an hour ago, but she'd have none of it, saying only, "A little more time. Give it a little more time," as if waiting for a late bus or a tardy friend.

She's quiet for a great while, sometimes with her eyes open, sometimes with them closed. On more than one occasion, Darius, or Jenny, or Spider lean in close to console themselves that she's still breathing, that life still lingers.

When at last she stirs, it seems to come with clarity. Her mind is strong but the body that carries it has drawn back into a shadow of its former self. Turning to look at Darius, and then straining but failing to look back at Spider, Jenny, and Beryl, she says, "Remember the hourglass."

It's an admonition, a charge.

"I've spent my sand," she whispers, "down to my last grain . . . and it was *good*." She puts all her energy into the last word, and it takes her a moment to recover. "Thank you . . . all of you." She reaches out a hand and lays it on Darius's face. "Don't waste your sand."

The coughing fit that follows is violent.

Darius cradles her until the attack subsides, feeling the last of her strength ebb with each spasm. When it's over, she's utterly spent, pale and breathing in shallow spurts. "It's time . . . for me . . . to get out . . . of my car." Darius reaches for his door handle to come around and lift her out, but her hand catches his arm.

She pats her chest and says, "*This* . . . car."

Laying back, she sighs as she's once again cradled in Darius's arms. The radio grows silent, and then, softly at first, the melancholic strains of Ben E. King's *Stand by Me* begin to issue from the speakers. Darius watches as her eyes flutter and become more alert, and then a small, contented smile forms on her lips

"Perfect," she whispers.

And then Grace Margaret Atwood, wife of Gerald Lipscomb and beloved daughter of Evan Elmore Atwood, closes her eyes for the last time and breathes out her last grain of sand. As the breath pushes from her body, it carries her soul with it.

The sun is deep in the western sky and hidden by clouds, yet at that moment it bursts from its shroud in a radiant display of pure light that bathes the golden car in still more gold. An uncanny display—beautiful and startling.

In the weeks, months, and years to come, Spider will question what he sees in the light, a vision hidden from the others as if meant for him and him alone. He'll believe it, and doubt it, and dismiss it, and embrace it, but he won't be able to shake it.

As the sun fills his eyes at Maggie's last breath, he sees a young girl in the sky before him. She's wearing a simple floral sundress with various hues of yellow and she looks back for only a moment, smiles, and then turns away and races across the empty sky with her arms outstretched, running toward the light—running toward the man who kneels there with his arms spread wide. And as she falls into her father's embrace the vision passes, ending as quickly as it began.

The sun slips once more behind the clouds and all that remains is the soft rustle of weeping from the car and the dulcet though heart-wrenching words of Ben E. King as *Stand by Me* draws to an end.

An hourglass stands empty.

Epilogue

Twenty-three months later . . .

The hardest things in life are beginnings and endings, albeit for different reasons. Birth, death, marriage, divorce, a new job, the loss of a job. All pivotal moments rest at a fork in the road, a place of choices. It's here at such a fork that our story might have ended but for two small truths. First, Grace Margaret Atwood was a remarkable woman of secrets and surprises, and second . . . well, beginnings are so much better than endings.

Within days of her passing, Jenny, Darius, Spider and Beryl were summoned to a law office on Dupont Street where it was revealed that Maggie had left them something in her will. In this case, *something* proves to be an enormous understatement.

With no children of her own and no family to speak of, she had left them *everything*: The house, the paintings, all of it. There were only two items held back: The first was the Wurlitzer jukebox that had entertained them on so many occasions, which she bequeathed to Spider and Spider alone. The second was a teapot, cup, and saucer collection which went to Beryl. It was the very same set that Beryl had given Maggie for Christmas the first year of their friendship.

Unbeknownst to them all, Maggie also owned seven rental properties in and around Bellingham, three of which were paid for, and four with meager mortgages that were a fraction of their monthly income. In a city of exorbitant home prices, the seven single-family rentals are worth a small fortune.

Maggie left no instructions on what was to become of her house or paintings, nor on how they should spend the money. The will simply said that it should be divided evenly among the four of them, to be used as they saw fit.

As to that, the inheritors seemed to have immediate ideas on just what that might entail, and within five minutes of being told—and with the attorney staring on in fascination—they sketched out the beginnings of a plan on the law office's expensive stationery.

Almost two years from the date, on March 15, the birthday of Evan Elmore Atwood, a museum named in his honor and featuring a significant body of his work, opens on Eldridge Avenue. In addition to the collection of nearly five hundred paintings, only a portion of which can be displayed at any given time, the museum has set aside space for various artifacts and images from Atwood's life.

Maggie's old house has had a bit of a renaissance.

After a complete renovation, it's no longer a home but a gallery. The downstairs was entirely gutted and turned into a museum space that perfectly matches the second floor. An extensive construction project against the north wall created a vast, open wing running east to west. This elegant space provides more than three thousand square feet of display area, along with room for a small office, a workshop—mostly for conservation and framing—and ample public restrooms.

A small gift shop near the entrance to the home-turned-museum offers a wide variety of posters, limited edition lithographs, coffee cups, and coasters, all courtesy of Smith and Clark Publishing. A few art books are available near the register, most notably the New York Times bestseller *Steel on Canvas: The Legacy of Evan Elmore Atwood*, by Dr. Jenny Morgan.

In a glass and mahogany showcase positioned in the center of what used to be Maggie's living room is displayed a simple mohair coin purse, likely from the 50s or 60s. Its clasp is open, and a small horde of nickels spills out, eighteen in all. The story of the twenty questions for twenty nickels is told on a printed museum plaque next to the purse, and if someone were to count the nickels and come up with eighteen, they might wonder at the discrepancy.

It's a puzzle, yes, but one soon to be resolved.

The case is large enough to host two additional items and an accompanying museum plaque. The first of these is Maggie's hourglass with its engraved admonition. Beside it, still in its original silver frame, is the uniformed picture of Jerry Lipscomb.

The biggest change to the house is unquestionably the garage.

The entire front wall has been removed and replaced with glass, allowing for a sturdy two-piece slider in the very center of the wall that can be pulled open wide enough to allow a car to pass. The old, worn concrete floor had been ground, polished, and acid-stained into a brilliant display of colors and patterns, designed by Jenny and then polished to a deep luster. It's a piece of art unto itself, though considerably more modern than anything Atwood might have painted.

Maggie's old Wurlitzer sits against the south wall.

On permanent loan to the museum from Spider, the jukebox can often be heard playing as patrons listen with delight while they stroll about the large space, absorbing all that the garage has to offer.

Maggie once alluded to some photo albums.

Nothing had come of the casual comment because, at first, it seemed they had all the time in the world for such things, certainly enough time to page through an album or two and comment on the photos. What time they *thought* they had turned out not to be the case, and the mysterious albums were all but forgotten.

As they emptied the house in preparation for the upcoming demo work, it was Spider who found the two boxes at the back of Maggie's large closet. Pulling the tops open, he found not one or two albums, but dozens, all of them filled to bursting with old black and white photos.

Every image was meticulously labeled by Maggie, and as the museum came close to completion, Jenny selected dozens of the most telling images and created a collection of enlarged canvas prints, some measuring as much as four feet across. These now adorn the walls of the garage: Pictures of Atwood at his easel, or behind the wheel of his truck, or relaxing in a hammock. There's even one of him in his uniform, taken just before he shipped off to Europe.

Some images are of Maggie, including one taken on her sixteenth birthday, a young girl in a sundress hugging a car. It's the very photo Atwood later uses to paint *A Girl and Her Car*. The original yellow sundress hangs next to the image. They found it tucked away inside Maggie's closet, still inside a dry-cleaning bag with a tag marked 1966.

The centerpiece of the garage, and indeed the entire Atwood collection, is, of course, the Bumblebee Jacket. In the many months leading up to the museum's completion, the car had become legend, and not just in the art world. With her top down and a line of velvet ropes positioned around her to keep admirers at a safe distance, she sits in the center of the polished garage floor, an irreplaceable work of art that was sweated into existence by the most remarkable of artists, an expression of his love for his daughter.

The old car with the heart of an elephant still gets to stretch her legs from time to time, roaring up and down the road, or perhaps taking a subdued drive out to an overlook on Chuckanut Drive, a place with special meaning. It's usually Darius, Spider, Jenny, and her assistant Chelsea on these drives. Spider and Chelsea sit in the back, enjoying the sound of the wind as it slips overhead.

On occasion, they've been seen holding holds.

Now that the museum is officially open, these road trips will be fewer, perhaps only a couple of times a year. This is not only because of the difficulty in extracting the car from the garage but—more importantly—because the insurance company valued the Bumblebee at eleven and a half million dollars.

They're not fond of it moving.

A second vehicle occupies the garage with the old Plymouth.

It's a 1956 Chevy 3100 pickup in candy apple red, and though it's not Atwood's original truck, it looks the part. Jenny commissioned Uncle John to build it using dozens of photos from Maggie's albums. It seems Atwood's daughter may have loved the old truck as much as he did, for she saved every image she could find.

The build is remarkably true to the original.

The roof is chopped the same, the posture of the truck is the same, and even the wheels are meticulously identical to those in the many pictures. Indeed, Evan Atwood himself might have a hard time telling it from his own.

On this day of days, the opening of the Evan Elmore Atwood Museum, Darius spreads the word to both patrons and friends to gather in the garage at three for a special event. The crowd grows so large that they pull open the glass sliders and allow the gathering to spill out onto the lawn.

Stepping behind the velvet rope and standing next to the Bumblebee Jacket, Darius motions for Jenny and Spider to join him. Perplexed, they do as they're asked, though neither has a clue what Darius is up to.

After greeting the crowd and thanking them for coming, he introduces Spider and Jenny and then relays the story of the twenty nickels for anyone who hadn't yet read the plaque. As he finishes, he looks at Spider and Jenny and says, "I took some liberties with Maggie's nickels. I hope you don't mind." Reaching into his pocket, he extracts two small items that he conceals in his hand.

"I have a friend who's a gifted metalworker," Darius explains. "He can take a coin—a nickel, for example, and turn it into something else without losing the stamped detail. In this case, he drilled a hole through the center and folded the metal over so that the outer side of the band shows parts of Jefferson's face, and the inside of the band shows bits of Monticello."

To clarify his words, he opens his hand. Resting in his palm are two wedding bands, one slightly larger than the other, each crafted from a single nickel.

With Spider beside him and hundreds of witnesses before him, Darius Alexander drops to one knee and raises a polished nickel band to Jenny.

"I've loved you since the day we met," he says. "Marry me."

Here, at last, at the end and the beginning, we must finally part. And if you're wondering if Jenny says yes, dear friend, then I encourage you to remember the opening line of our story. That being that roads are a special kind of magic: Sometimes they take us exactly where we belong.

About the Author

Spencer Kope grew up just outside Bellingham, Washington, and spent his teenage years working in his father's body shop. A former Cold War-era Russian linguist and graduate of the Naval War College, he spent seventeen years working for various intelligence organizations, most notably the Office of Naval Intelligence. In 2004, he joined the Whatcom County Sheriff's Office and has served as their crime analyst since. He started writing when he was eighteen.

CPSIA information can be obtained
at www.ICGtesting.com
Printed in the USA
FS?W011300200921
84 6FS